STALKED BY TERROR

Andrea moved briskly along the road, forcing herself to be calm. She had walked another ten yards when the noise came again. She stopped in her tracks. In the trees to her right, a branch cracked. Leaves rustled loudly, as if something huge walked upon them.

Something was following her. She made herself continue walking. Something crashed in the woods. She did not stop this time, but looked back as she began to run. In the darkness between the thick tree trunks, a patch of whiteness moved with stealthy grace. She caught a glimpse of two red sparks in the gloom.

Suddenly she knew with horrible certainty that whatever stalked her did so at the bequest of the townfolk of Marissa. What unspeakable monstrosity had they set on her heels?

Trees rushed by. Darkness opened to swallow her, a long tunnel leading to madness. She rushed headlong into it while the thing came ever closer.

Then she heard the click and scrabble of movement on the road. Whatever it was, it had left the cover of the trees . . .

TERROR LIVES!

THE SHADOW MAN   (1946, $3.95)
by Stephen Gresham
The Shadow Man could hide anywhere—under the bed, in the closet, behind the mirror . . . even in the sophisticated circuitry of little Joey's computer. And the Shadow Man could make Joey do things that no little boy should ever do!

SIGHT UNSEEN   (2038, $3.95)
by Andrew Neiderman
David was always right. Always. But now that he was growing up, his gift was turning into a power. The power to know things—terrible things—that he didn't want to know. Like who would live . . . and who would die!

MIDNIGHT BOY   (2065, $3.95)
by Stephen Gresham
Something horrible is stalking the town's children. For one of its most trusted citizens possesses the twisted need and cunning of a psychopathic killer. Now Town Creek's only hope lies in the horrific, blood-soaked visions of the MIDNIGHT BOY!

TEACHER'S PET   (1927, $3.95)
by Andrew Neiderman
All the children loved their teacher Mr. Lucy. It was astonishing to see how they all seemed to begin to resemble Mr. Lucy. And act like Mr. Lucy. And kill like Mr. Lucy!

DARK REUNION

STEPHEN R. GEORGE

ZEBRA BOOKS
KENSINGTON PUBLISHING CORP.

Also by Stephen R. George:
 Brain Child
 Beasts
 Dark Miracle

ZEBRA BOOKS

are published by

Kensington Publishing Corp.
475 Park Avenue South
New York, NY 10016

First printing: April, 1990

Printed in the United States of America

To Val,
for getting me through it,
and tying it all together

ACKNOWLEDGMENT

Thanks to Chester D. Cuthbert
for proofreading the manuscript,
for offering invaluable criticism,
and, of course, for the books!

PROLOGUE

December 1965

The sky over McAllen, Texas, was clear. By mid-morning, the temperature was warm enough for T-shirt and shorts. Mary stood at the kitchen window and looked into the backyard. The little girl in the sandbox giggled as she played, then turned to look at the window as if she had sensed her mother watching.

Mary waved. The girl waved back.

She returned to the table, spread the documents out before her, and studied each carefully. Her fingers trembled as she lifted the new pieces of identification. Lawrence had found an expert to do the work, and the money they had paid had been well spent. Her social security card looked perfect, as did her driver's license. The name on both was Mary Olsen.

Olsen.

She formed her lips around the name, speaking it slowly. "Olsen. Hello, nice to meet you. My name is Mary Olsen."

She giggled softly at the sound. It felt strange coming from her mouth. It would take time, she thought, before the new identity fit her, before it became second nature.

She drew a deep breath, sighed it out, and for a moment allowed herself to feel sad. Sad for all that was lost.

It had been six months since she and Lawrence and

7

three-year-old Gillian had fled Marissa. Six months of running, changing jobs, changing towns. She had wondered, at first, if the running was really, absolutely necessary. Lawrence was adamant.

"If we want to be free of Marissa forever, then we have to keep moving. Not for much longer, I promise."

And now Gillian was four. *My God, where does the time go?*

She gently spread the final sheet of paper between her fingers. It was a birth certificate. This had been the hardest of the new identification to obtain, and it had cost them a lot. She stared down at the expertly crafted paper, and felt tears fill her eyes.

The birthdate was correct, as were the statistics for weight and length. But the name was wrong.

Wrong. Wrong. Wrong.

Andrea Theresa Olsen.

A tear fell from her cheek and spattered the paper. She wiped it off immediately with her sleeve. So much money, and she would ruin it with tears.

Lawrence was right. Changing Gillian's name was the most important step of all. The child was the reason, after all, that they had fled from Marissa. Themselves, and three other families. Thankfully, nobody had deduced the full extent of Gillian's craft talent.

She wondered, for a moment, how the others were faring. Would they, too, have gone to these lengths to protect themselves? Where were they right now? What were they doing? Really, it didn't matter. Anything was better than the dark circle rising in Marissa.

She carefully folded the birth certificate and pushed it into the envelope with the rest of the papers.

She rose to pour herself a fresh cup of coffee when she heard the delighted squealing from outside. Curious, she moved to the kitchen window to see what it was about. Gillian . . . no, it was *Andrea* now . . . Andrea, was sitting at the edge of the sandbox, arms raised in delight. Around her, three of her dolls danced as if they were puppets.

Mary felt a stab of icy fear. Her breath caught in her

throat. She ran to the back door, flung it open, then ran into the yard.

"Gillian!"

The little girl, laughing joyously, turned to face her grinning.

"Mommy! It's the dark horsey! It found me! It wants to play!"

Mary halted a yard away, staring in horror at her daughter. The child's body bucked and swayed as if she were riding on the back of a wild animal. Her laughs were loud and cheerful.

"Gillian, stop it!"

"But Mommy, it found me!"

Mary lunged forward and tugged the child violently by her shoulders. "Stop it! Do you hear me? Stop it now!"

Gillian toppled backward to the grass, landing solidly on her rump. The dolls stopped dancing and fell inert to the sand. The look of pleasure on Gillian's face turned to one of shock and fear.

"It wasn't my fault, Mommy. The dark horsey found me. It wanted to play. It wasn't my fault."

Mary kneeled beside the girl and stroked her dark hair. Her fear had turned into a tightly clenched fist in her stomach.

"Gillian, you must never play with the dark horsey again. Never, ever, ever again. Do you understand me?"

The girl swallowed hard. Tears filled her eyes. "It wasn't my fault."

"Gillian," Mary said, more gently now, "the horsey doesn't come unless you call it. I know it's hard, sweetie, but you must never think about it. Not even in your dreams. The dark horsey is bad. It's evil, sweetie. It wants to hurt you."

The girl did not look convinced. In a hushed voice, Mary said, "And it will hurt me and your daddy too, sweetie. You don't want that, do you?"

Gillian shook her head emphatically.

"Then don't ever think about it. Will you do that for me, sweetie?"

9

Gillian nodded.

"That's a good girl." She hugged the girl tightly.

Gillian pulled away and looked up at her with questioning eyes.

"Are we ever going back to Missa, Mommy?"

Mary stiffened. Gillian had never learned to pronounce "Marissa," but the childlike rendition sent a spear of terror into her. She held the girl's shoulders tightly.

"No, darling, we'll never go back there. Never again. It's an evil place. A bad place."

Again, the girl did not look convinced. Mary drew a shuddering breath. "Promise me, sweetie, promise me you'll never talk of that place again, never think about it."

"Is it like the dark horsey?"

"Just like it. Bad. Evil. Do you promise?"

"I promise."

"That's a girl."

"But what if the dark horsey comes to me? What if it finds me again?"

"It won't."

"But—"

"It won't, but if it does, just ignore it. Don't play with it."

Gillian nodded. Mary felt herself calm down, felt the fear in her stomach soften.

"I want you to come inside now," Mary said softly. "There's something I want to tell you. Something very special."

"What?" The child's eyes gleamed in delight.

"It's about your name. A secret."

Gillian jumped to her feet and tugged at her mother's hand, eager for the secret to be shared. Mary followed the girl up to the house. A terrible sadness settled on her. In time, the child would forget. Forget about Marissa, forget about the dark horsey, forget that her name had been stolen from her.

For now, she tried to think of a way to tell her daughter that she would have to give up the only thing that had ever, truly, belonged to her.

PART I

Arrival

Twenty-five years later . . .

CHAPTER ONE

May

At the mouth of the alley, Matthew drew his revolver. He heard the shuffle of leather as Bryce did the same. Behind them, like a nightmare, the Metro Liquor Depot parking lot throbbed with emergency lights.

"I don't like it, Matt. It's too dark."

"I'll take the point. You use your flash."

He heard Bryce fumble with the straps of his belt, then light lanced out ahead of him. His own shadow leaped into the alley and climbed the dirty walls. He held his revolver loosely, finger resting comfortably on the trigger, and stepped forward. As Bryce followed, the shadows hopped and jumped.

"Keep it steady, damn it," Matthew muttered.

Bryce grumbled. He played the beam across the width of the alley. There was garbage everywhere, large boxes piled by loading doors, chunks of Styrofoam spread across the ground. The sheddings of industry. Matthew kicked a large piece of Styrofoam and it lifted into the air, spun, and fell with a dull thud. Something squealed in the darkness. A rat darted from one pile of trash to another.

"Jesus, Matt, cut that out!"

"Sorry."

A hundred yards away the alley opened onto brightly lit Washington Avenue. The sounds of the city impinged only faintly. Reflected light from the parking lot caused the walls to throb, as if they were alive. Matthew's skin crawled.

"Looks like our boy got away," Bryce said hopefully.

"Guess so," Matthew said, almost eager to accept the possibility.

"Let's get out of here, Matt. I don't like this."

"Another minute. Let's just—"

"What the hell is that?"

"Where?"

Bryce played the beam wildly between the narrow walls. Shadows careened and swooped like drunken giants. In a moment, when his hand steadied, the circle of light fell upon a swirling pool of mist less than fifteen yards ahead.

"Where the fuck did that come from?"

"It's just mist, Bryce. Calm down." Matthew stepped closer.

"It wasn't there a second ago."

"Sure it was."

"Look." Again, Bryce swung the flashlight beam. This time, it speared into a wall of mist that rose to obscure Washington's lights. "It's grown, Matt."

Matthew drew a deep breath. His heart suddenly pounded. His palm slicked with sweat around the butt of his revolver. He swallowed hard. "Okay. Back out slowly. We'll get help."

Bryce retreated. Matthew followed, keeping his gun aimed on the swirling wall of mist. In the beam of Bryce's flashlight, it looked almost blue.

"Some sort of chemical spill, I bet," Bryce muttered.

Matthew said nothing. This mist was not a chemical spill. They would have seen it the moment they'd entered the alley. But it had appeared as they approached it, as if it had been waiting for them. It swelled and billowed as if it were breathing. He swallowed again, trying to control the fear that was quickly growing inside him.

Don't start imagining it's alive!

They were nearing the mouth of the alley when the mist parted like a veil, and the figure stepped toward them.

14

Matthew's heart leaped.

"Stop!" He raised his gun.

The figure stumbled closer, steps faltering and unsure. Bryce played the beam franticly. Shadows leaped and jumped like frightened deer. Still, the figure approached, its movements sudden and jerky, as if it struggled with something. In the mist behind it, two red points glowed brightly.

Those can't be eyes. There's no fucking way those are eyes!

"I said hold it! Stop! I'll shoot!" His voice reverberated inside the narrow walls, sounding panicked to his own ears.

"Matt, he's got a gun!"

Matthew dropped to his knees. For a second, no longer, Bryce managed to focus the beam directly on their assailant. Matthew steadied his aim and squeezed off three shots. Thunder echoed down the alley. The smell of cordite surrounded them.

Bryce again lost control of the flashlight, playing it wildly between the two towering walls. "I think you got him, Matt!"

Matthew stood slowly. With his gun held out at the ready, he walked toward the fallen gunman. Bryce came carefully to the rear, turning the light down. It took Matthew a second to realize what he was looking at, and then the air rushed out of his lungs in a sob. He fell to his knees and dropped his gun to the alley floor.

Footsteps sounded behind them as Young and Whitten responded to the shots.

"Shit, Willson, you're in deep trouble here."

"He must have found the gun in the alley, Matt. It isn't your fault."

"It's j-just a k-kid."

Matthew blocked out the voices. Bile rose in his throat. He choked it down.

The gunman was a boy. Maybe thirteen years old, probably younger. In the harsh light of Bryce's flashlight, he looked a lot like Matthew's own son. If not for the color

15

of his skin, it might have been Peter's twin. The slugs had caught him in the upper chest and neck. His lips hung slightly open, revealing the whites of his teeth. His brown eyes were blank, lifeless pools of liquid.

"Oh, hell, it's just a kid," Bryce said in disgust, as if the fact needed repeating.

Matthew covered his eyes with his hands, trying desperately not to see. When he opened them again, Bryce was shining his flashlight into the alley. Matthew tried to slow the rapid pounding of his heart.

The mist was gone.

July

When she heard the door open downstairs, Andrea Willson stiffened. She turned to Peter. His dark eyes were narrowed with concern. He stood and stepped past the television to the window, then peered outside. Beyond him, she could see the halos of the street lamps dappled by trees. Just another perfect summer night in the mid-to-upscale suburb of Rosedale.

"He left his car lights on," Peter said softly.

"I'll go tell him."

She led him to the door, then opened it quietly. Downstairs, a chair rattled. A door slammed. A voice rose in anger.

"Aren't you frightened?"

She pushed him toward his bedroom. "I'm frightened for him, that's all."

The boy turned to her, stared at her a moment until she waved him away, then closed his bedroom door softly. Andrea drew a deep breath and held it.

Please, Matthew, don't be drunk.

But she knew that he *was* drunk. It had become his natural state since the shooting of the boy. In the short space of two months she had watched the man she loved turn from a quiet, thoughtful father and husband into a red face, bleary eyed, violent drunkard. She paused at the

16

top of the stairs and listened. A glass smashed in the kitchen. Matthew's voice rose in anger again. A cupboard door opened and slammed shut.

She moved slowly down the stairs, gripping the banister tightly.

Matthew erupted from the kitchen as she reached the bottom of the stairs. His face was sweaty, his eyes wild. His once tidy crop of black hair jutted at odd angles from his scalp.

"Where's the bottle I put in cupboard above the sink?"

"I threw it out, Matt."

He drew a deep breath and raised himself up, supporting his stature with a hand on the kitchen doorknob. "You threw it out?" His voice sounded like a plaintive child's.

"You promised me there'd be no more liquor in the house."

He shook his head. His eyes unfocused, wandered a moment, then snapped back to her. "You threw out *my* fucking bottle."

She said nothing. He wobbled on his feet. His eyes filled with a dark rage and pinned her like an insect.

"You cunt," he said softly.

She could not help it. She gasped, and stared wide-eyed at him. Even drunk, that was not like him.

"Matthew, please."

"You fucking cunt."

It's not Matthew speaking, it's not him, it's not the same man.

She backed away, now frightened by the anger in his eyes, the hatred in his voice. But even drunk, he was faster than she, and stronger. He lunged at the bottom of the stairs and got a grip on her leg, pulling her roughly down. Her behind thudded on the steps and she yelped.

"Matthew!"

He pressed his face close to hers. She gagged at the liquor on his breath.

"Next time you think about throwing out something of mine, think twice."

17

He punched her squarely in the left eye. It was a carefully aimed, premeditated strike, and it snapped her head backward and sent her to the floor. Stars danced behind her eyes, and darkness seeped in. She heard an upstairs door opening, heard the feet stamping on the carpeted steps.

"Leave her alone!" Peter's voice was high with indignation.

"You told her where I hid it, didn't you?"

"Get away from her."

"You little bastard."

"Dad!"

The sound of a fist hitting flesh drew Andrea away from the abyss of darkness that was reaching for her. She scrambled to remain conscious. Shook her head to clear it. Her face throbbed.

Matthew was gone. Peter was lying next to her on the steps. He was sobbing. Blood spilled in strings and globs from his mouth to his T-shirt.

She touched his shoulder.

"Peter, are you okay?"

He looked up, bleary eyed, and nodded slowly. She helped him to his feet. "Go upstairs. I'll deal with him."

"Are you okay?"

She stroked his cheek with her hand. "Go upstairs. Everything will be fine."

He stared at her a moment, then nodded, and slowly climbed back upstairs. When she heard his bedroom door shut, she went through to the kitchen.

Matthew was sitting at the table. He was weeping copiously, his face buried in his hands. His service revolver was laid out in front of him. He looked up when she came in.

She stepped toward him, but he held up his hand to stop her.

"I can't go on like this," he said. His hand curled around the butt of the revolver and lifted it slowly. He placed the barrel in his mouth and clasped his lips around it.

18

"Put it down, Matt."

His eyes were squeezed shut. His finger tensed on the trigger.

"Put it down, Matthew."

She stepped toward him again. When she was next to him, she reached out, placed her hand gently over his, and loosened his grip on the gun. She pulled it from his mouth. His hand relinquished its hold. When she had it clear of him, she carried it to the counter and laid it down carefully. Matthew started weeping again.

She returned to him and lay her arm across his shoulder. He would not look at her. She helped him to his feet and led him, stumbling, through to the living room. She made him lie down on the sofa, his head propped on a cushion. He continued to weep.

"Sleep, Matthew."

He obeyed.

It was nearly two hours later when he woke. Sitting in the kitchen, newspaper spread out before her, she heard his first movements, his groans. She had made a full pot of coffee, and now she poured a mug, black. She folded the newspaper and carried it and the coffee with her through to the living room.

Matthew was sitting up. He held his head with both hands and groaned.

"How do you feel?"

"Terrible," he said slowly. "I dreamed I beat the shit out of you and Peter."

"Matthew."

He looked up. His eyes widened. His face turned white. "Oh, Christ."

She handed him the mug of coffee. "Drink this."

He accepted gingerly and sipped it, wincing at the taste.

"Just drink it."

He took another sip. He looked up at her again. Her eye, she knew, looked bad. His face was not capable of looking any guiltier.

"Matthew, I've got something to say."

He locked eyes with her, looking solemn.

"Listening?"

"Yes."

"Okay. In the past two months you've changed. You've turned into a drunkard, and now a violent one. It wasn't only me that you hit."

She had not thought it possible, but his face turned even paler.

"I know you've been through a lot. I know it wasn't your fault you shot that boy. And I know it's not your fault they crucified you for it. But that's all water under the bridge. You can't change any of it."

He sipped the coffee, saying nothing.

"I can't handle it anymore, Matt. Not the drinking. Not the depression. None of it. You and Peter are all I have left in the world. I don't want to lose you. But I can't stay with you like this."

He blinked slowly. Her words seemed to have cut into him like knives.

"If you drink again, I'm gone. For good. And I think Peter will come with me."

"Andrea . . ."

"No discussion, Matt. I'm laying it out for you. You touch another drink, and that's it."

She let her words sink in, then stepped toward him with the newspaper. He took it from her and stared at it stupidly.

"I've circled a job in there that looks good. You need to get away from Minneapolis. This one looks right up your line."

He ran his eyes down the column of classified ads, finally coming to the one she had circled. She remembered the wording clearly. She had read the ad perhaps fifty times, attracted to something in the words, a strange feeling of déjà vu, as if she had dreamed them previously. It was the only one she had circled.

WANTED: Experienced peace officer to work in

two-man rural force. Home provided. Excellent benefits. Experienced only, please. Address queries to: Marissa Township Council, General Delivery, Marissa, MN.

He read the ad, looked up at her quizzically, read it again, then smiled.

"What's so funny?"

"Marissa," he said. "Didn't you know?"

"Know what?"

"I was born there. My parents moved away in the early sixties. I was just a kid."

The coincidence made her pause for a moment. "If you're from there," she said at last, "then you should have a foot in the door."

"What about your job?"

"I can sell real estate just as easily there as here."

He read the ad again, nodded, folded the paper, and placed it on the coffee table.

"There's more coffee in the kitchen," she said. "Drink all you can handle. I'm going to bed. Tell me your decision tomorrow."

Before he could answer, she turned, walked from the living room, and went upstairs.

CHAPTER TWO

October

Andrea was lost. The feeling had started the moment she left Minneapolis. At first it was merely a reaction to leaving the Twin Cities for the first time in fifteen years. But now, driving along State 210, the entire world a mosaic of reds and golds and browns with the sudden shift into autumn, the feeling was much more than spiritual. She was really, without a doubt, map in hand, lost.

When the red, white, and blue Mobil sign appeared ahead, she sighed with relief. *Thank God!* Here, at last, was a sign of civilization. It meant that somewhere in the area there were cars. Cars driven by people.

She slowed the Pontiac and turned into the station. The attendant was a teenager dressed in oil-stained overalls. His hands were black, nails blacker. He leaned down to peer in the driver's window, and his blue eyes widened appreciatively. Self-conscious, Andrea squeezed her thighs together. The denim of her jeans whispered softly.

"Fill her up?"

"Actually, I'm lost."

His face brightened, eager to be of help. "Where you headed?"

She lifted Matthew's letter from the seat and showed him the crude map. "Marissa. There's supposed to be a turnoff. Isn't there?"

He studied the crumpled piece of paper, leaving a smudged thumbprint in one corner. His eyes narrowed, then he regarded her carefully. His look was guarded. "Why would you want to go there?"

Her first instinct was to tell him it was none of his business, but she held her tongue. "I'm meeting my family," she said at last.

He looked away. Without bending down again, he pointed back along the blacktop toward Fergus Falls. "You missed the road. It's about three miles back. There's a sign."

"A sign?"

"Might be hidden by trees."

"Oh." She felt ridiculous, stupid, a flat-footed city dweller.

"You want some gas?"

The gauge read nearly three-quarters full but she nodded anyway, still embarrassed. "Okay. Top it up."

When he finished, he came back to the window, shaking his head. "Three sixty-five," he said.

Andrea blushed, pulled out her wallet, and gave him a five. "Keep the change."

Once she was on the road again, she felt a little better, though still embarrassed at her own stupidity. How had she missed the sign? Five minutes later, when she found it, she understood how. As the boy had said, it was hidden in the trees at the side of the road. Even the road, alarmingly narrow, was hard to see.

She slowed to a halt and studied it curiously.

MARISSA 10 MILES
HUNTING FISHING CAMPING GASOLINE
RESTAURANT

The background was green, the lettering faded white, almost illegible. How much summer tourism would Marissa attract with a derelict sign like that?

We're going to be living there.

Angry, not knowing who to direct it at, she slammed her

foot on the accelerator, threw a cloud of gravel dust into the air, and turned onto the road.

Turning onto County Road 16 was like passing into another world. Trees and shrubs and hillsides, comfortably distant only ten minutes ago, now pressed in at arm's length. She was a blood cell coursing through a massive artery, and the orange patchwork world around her was the body of some gigantic creature she would never, ever, in her whole life, see or understand.

The feeling of enclosure intensified as she drove north. The surrounding forest, climbing steep grades on either side of the road, appeared to be mostly oak and elm. Although widely spaced, their numbers were so great as to appear like a solid mass. Trunk merged into trunk, branch into branch, leaf into leaf.

Sometime, long ago, the road had been divided with yellow lines. Now, all that remained were flaking remnants. The route ahead curved crazily, never affording a view of more than a few hundred yards. She drove for nearly fifteen minutes, keeping her foot steady on the accelerator, the trees on either side of her a blur.

The town appeared slowly, like a movie fade-in. She barely caught a glimpse of the first house before she was past, and craned her neck to see better. A mailbox flashed by on her right, the opening of a narrow drive covered in leaves, and between the trees, as if hiding, a ramshackle collection of leaning walls and windows.

Choking back her disappointment, she drove on. Soon, the houses began to appear regularly on both sides of the road. Some, as the first, were small, almost decrepit. Others, she was relieved to see, were quite modern and attractive. All stood well back from the road, accessed by curving driveways. In one or two she saw cars parked, and felt a deep pang of relief. Cars meant people.

Downtown Marissa opened up before her around the next bend in the road, and she caught her breath in surprise. Matthew's letter had told her the place was "quaint" and "rustic" and "attractive," and yet still she was not prepared.

The road forked, forming a circle around a small central island of grass. A single tree reached up into the suddenly wide sky, a million branches twined and intertwined in a black tangle. Around the tree four or five benches sat smothered in brown leaves. There might have been fifteen or twenty store fronts facing into the circle, and she picked out a pharmacy, a grocery, a hardware store. A few pedestrians strolled the sidewalks, and some glanced over at the Pontiac as she moved slowly around the perimeter. Although there were cars parked in the street, none were moving but her own.

She released an involuntary giggle. "Oh, Matthew, this is great," she said to the car.

She drove slowly around the circle, looking in the store windows, sometimes glancing up at the towering oak. Almost directly opposite the road she had come in by, she found the sign she was looking for.

LAKE DRIVE

Again, the trees pressed in. Marissa was almost invisible within its surrounding forest, as if the trees themselves had given permission for this human habitation, but would not countenance being upstaged.

She came upon the driveway less than a minute after leaving the town circle. "You can't miss it," Matthew had written. "We've got the only house on that stretch of road."

Unlike the other homes she had seen, this one was not hidden by trees. Its sharp angles and high roof seemed to push the trees back, as if it had made this room for itself and wasn't giving back an inch. She liked the *obviousness* of the place immediately. It was neither the grandest nor the most decrepit of the homes she had seen so far.

She hardly had room to get her own car off the road before she came up against the bumper of Matthew's yellow Volkswagen. Just seeing the car sent a thrill of anticipation through her. She grinned and honked the horn twice.

The front door opened, and Matthew peered out. His face brightened when he saw her, and he bounded down the limestone path to her car. She hardly managed to get the door open before he reached in and pulled her out. His large hands lifted her, supported her, and finally crushed her close. She felt his lips on her cheek, then on her eyes, then finally on her mouth.

When he pulled away, she was breathless. "And a hello to you too," she said softly.

"You found the place okay?" He gripped her hand and pulled her up toward the house.

"Yes, I—"

He spun, not letting her finish, and kissed her again. "You're going to love it here, Andrea. It's fantastic. It's perfect for us."

She looked up at his narrow face and smiled. The tension that had made him look old and weary was gone. She looked into the blue eyes of the man she had married, and felt something catch in her throat.

This place is working for him, she realized. *It's restoring him.*

"I love it already," she said softly, kissing him. It was not entirely a lie.

He grinned and again pulled her toward the house. They were halfway up the path when the door opened. Peter was dressed in a plaid shirt and faded Levi's. At thirteen he was tall, gangly, and bent with the loose lankiness of a boy aching to fill his own boots. Almost a slouch. Yet in his face, she saw Matthew. *His father's boy.*

He walked easily down the path and stood in front of her, nearly as tall as she. He smiled. "Hello, Andrea."

She smiled back. "Hello, Peter." Then she reached for him, opened her arms, and hugged him. On the trip up she had feared that the advances they had made in their relationship might have been lost through the three-week separation, but his arms squeezed her tightly and she knew her fears had been unfounded.

"Come and see the house," Peter said once they had disengaged. "You'll love it. You and Dad have the best room in the place."

Andrea nodded. Around her, the trees rustled, sounding like a sigh, as a gentle breeze sent airy fingers through the forest. A barrage of red and gold leaves tumbled to the ground.

We're going to be okay, she thought as Matthew took one of her arms and Peter took the other.

As if the forest had read her thoughts, as if Marissa itself had been awaiting her arrival, another rush of wind, sounding like a long satisfied sigh, breathed through the trees.

With one of her men on each of her arms, she walked up to the house.

CHAPTER THREE

"Matthew, it's beautiful!"

Matthew moved past her, then turned to her smiling. "Courtesy of Marissa Township."

She moved into the living room, heels clicking on the hardwood until she stepped onto the carpet. Afternoon light, flooding through bay windows hung with sheer curtains, filled the room with the colors of autumn. At the back of the room, supporting a vase of fresh red roses, sat a dining table. A china cabinet rested in one corner, its shelves bare and hungry. Two sofas and an easy chair formed a friendly circle around a glass coffee table in the living room, all facing an open hearth.

"Come and see the kitchen, Andrea," Peter said from the hallway.

Holding Matthew's hand, she followed the boy. Again, she was astounded by extravagance. An abundance of natural wood cabinets and counters provided warmth for the room. The built-in appliances left plenty of counter space. A mixture of stainless steel and copper pots hung from a rack above a central work station. Glass sliding doors led outside to an extensive deck, where a number of patio chairs were placed in a rough circle. She turned to Matthew, her mouth open.

"It's just wonderful, but how can we afford it?"

He placed a finger on his lips for silence.

She ignored him. "Your salary could hardly pay for this,

and it will take time for me to become established. It's crazy . . ."

Matthew was grinning now. "I told you, this is part of the job."

She frowned. "But the picture they sent you showed a little cabin."

"That's where we were supposed to end up." He leaned on a counter, regarding her affectionately. "After Chief Cunningham retired, Murray Carlyle assumed his position. Murray was supposed to move in here. This is the chief's house. We were supposed to get Murray's old place. But Murray didn't want to move. Said this place was too big for a single man."

"Oh, Matthew." It was all she could say. Compared to their home in Rosedale, this place was a mansion. It was a mansion in any sense of the word.

"Gift horses don't take kindly to having their mouths probed," Matthew said. "Don't fight it."

"We could get accustomed to this," she said.

"Nothing wrong with that. We're going to be here for a while."

Andrea said nothing. She turned to Peter, who was leaning against the sliding doors. "You miss the city, Peter?"

He shrugged, then shook his head. "Nope."

He certainly *looked* happy, she had to admit. Just as Matthew looked more relaxed. She sighed again. Beyond Peter, in the backyard, the trees pushed close, and she spotted the opening of a pathway. A lot of exploring to be done. Perfect for a thirteen-year-old boy.

She heard Matthew moving behind her, but the sounds did not register. When she turned, his hand was raised to touch her neck. The action was purely affectionate, one that any lover might make. Yet it caught her off-guard. Before she could stop herself she recoiled from him, breath emitting from her throat in a gasp.

Matthew froze. The hand, poised to caress her neck, lowered slowly to his side. A faint light glimmering in his eye extinguished itself. The hurt that blossomed on his

29

features he quickly brought under control.

"Oh, Matthew, I'm sorry," she said, horrified at her reaction. She stepped close to him, pressed her face to his chest, and hugged him tightly. "It will take time, but everything will be perfect. I know it."

She felt his chin nodding against her hair, and then he disengaged himself. The hurt was gone completely now, relegated to some inner corner. "Listen. Tonight we'll hang around here. Pete and I will whip up some dinner, and you can get comfortable in the house. Tomorrow we'll take you on a tour of the town, maybe even visit Aunt Clarissa. Right, Pete?"

When Pete didn't answer, Andrea turned around. The boy had entered the garden and was walking toward the path in the trees. As she watched, he moved into the forest until she could not even see the blue of his shirt between the trunks.

"Where—"

"He'll be all right. He likes to walk. C'mon." He picked up her hand and led her from the kitchen.

She hardly heard Matthew's voice as he showed her the rest of the house. She kept thinking of her reflexive withdrawal from his touch.

Stupid! Everything had been fine until then.

Marissa, she thought, might help them rebuild their lives, but unless she was careful, her own thoughtlessness would certainly undermine everything.

Peter ran. The trails seemed to open up before him, as if they were leading him. He lifted his feet high off the ground to avoid tangles of roots.

As he moved deeper into the forest, he began to feel more comfortable. The trees closed in on all sides. Soon, he was able to imagine that Marissa didn't even exist. There was only the forest, stretching forever around him in all directions. He liked to imagine that. No roads, no houses, no cars. Just the trees. Just him.

He allowed his mind to wander as he ran. He stopped

30

paying attention to the branches in the trail. It wouldn't matter if he did. No matter which fork he took, he always ended up at the same place. His secret place.

Instead, he thought about Andrea.

Although he could not understand it fully, it really had been nice to see his stepmother again. Over the past few days, Dad had grown restless, edgy. This morning, an aura of excitement had enveloped the house like a lightning storm. Today was the day! Andrea was arriving!

Back in Minneapolis, she had worked hard to get close to him. At first, he had resisted. She wasn't his mother. She was Dad's wife. There was a big difference. But Andrea had been smart. She hadn't tried to take the place of Mom. She had stated it plainly, dropping the ball right in his court to deal with.

"I'm not your mother, Peter. I never will be. That's not what I want. But I love your father, and he loves me. I'm going to be living with you guys. There's no getting around it, and there's no getting away from it. I don't even care if we're friends. I just want us to get along. It will make it easier for all of us. What do you say?"

How could he argue with logic like that? Besides, he did like Andrea. She was okay. And although he had never admitted it, there were times when he thought of her as Mom. Once he had even called her that, and she had looked at him steadily for a long time.

"You don't have to call me that if you don't want to, Peter," she had said.

But at that moment, he had wanted to. It had slipped out.

Now, thinking about her, he was glad she was here. The family seemed whole again. Maybe, if they worked at it, they could make things like the way they were in Minneapolis. Maybe even like the way they were before Dad . . .

He blocked the thought from his mind before it could intrude.

Don't think about it. That only makes it worse.

The sudden concentration snapped him from his

reverie. He slowed his pace, trying to ascertain exactly where he was. The look of the trail was familiar. A fallen tree branch blocked the way ahead, but he hopped deftly over it. The trail began to curve to the right. He followed, unthinking. In moments it opened into a small clearing, perhaps twenty yards across.

Here it was. His secret place.

He entered the clearing slowly, almost reverently, breathing hushed. As always, his skin tingled.

He stepped through the high grass and moved toward the dead tree to his right. It had fallen over, probably years ago, and now formed a perfect bench. Empty Pepsi bottles, a couple of candy wrappers, marked his previous visits. He seated himself on the rough bark and scanned the clearing. Although autumn had changed the landscape into a golden tapestry of decay and transition, here flowers bloomed. A small stream rushed noisily over smooth rocks.

He closed his eyes, breathed deeply, and calmed himself.

"I'm here," he said aloud.

He kept his eyes closed, listening carefully. Within moments, the sounds of birds and small animals ceased. Silence pressed down upon the clearing. The temperature had been comfortable, perfect for walking, but now a sudden chill gripped him.

He shivered and opened his eyes.

Blue mist crept through the grass, swirled around the ends of the dead tree, and moved in toward his feet. He grinned.

A pillar of mist rose before him. The blue vapors swirled. The outline of a standing figure appeared in the mist, delineated only by swirls of blue vapor. Where the head should have been, two red points sprang to life.

"Hello, Longshadow," he said softly.

"Hello, Peter." The voice was barely a whisper, like wind through grass.

"My . . . my mom got here today."

A ripple of movement passed through the mist, sudden, unexpected, like a pebble dropped in a perfectly still pond.

I surprised him. He didn't know.
"Thank you for telling me."
"Okay."
"Are you ready?"
Peter grinned, nodded. "Sure."
The mist reached forward to envelop him.

That first night in Marissa, Andrea had great difficulty falling asleep. The insomnia seemed to be caused by a great many factors, a plethora of unfamiliarities. Unfamiliar bed, unfamiliar house, unfamiliar night sounds. Primarily, however, there was the excitement of being reunited with her family. Three weeks ago Matthew and Peter had made the trip to Marissa to prepare things, while she had remained in Minneapolis to clear up their affairs. The first week had been a relief. She had forgotten how nice it could be to live on one's own. No bathroom to fight for, no dishes to clear up, no unexplained noises in the middle of the night. By the second week she had begun to realize how much Matthew and Peter were part of her life, how empty she felt without their presence. It was silly, she knew. She would drive up to Marissa herself soon. Yet she could not rid herself of the feeling that somehow, irrevocably, her family had been split asunder.

By that third week alone, her expectation of the coming trip had sharpened, and every day seemed to drag on forever. The chore of transferring all their bank funds, finalizing the sale on the house, last-minute packing, had taken much of her attention. Not enough, however, to dampen her excitement. The trip up from Minneapolis yesterday should have been the climax to the previous weeks, yet upon nearing her destination the reality of the situation had settled heavily on her. She had split off from her old life. Completely. With frightening finality. And this strange place with its brooding trees and blanket of leaves was her new home.

Lying in bed that night, with Matthew beside her, ghostly groping fingers of their old life set their grip upon

33

her and would not let her sleep. Matthew next to her, breathing heavily in sleep, jostled with her emotions to regain his place in her life. The yawning unknown of what lay ahead pitched in to keep her tossing and turning.

It was many hours past midnight when she finally succumbed to the darkness, more from exhaustion than anything else. Outside, a gentle breeze sent leaves scrabbling in the backyard. Trees rustled, and she imagined she heard leaves toppling through the air. To her exhausted mind the sound was like laughter, pleased and self-congratulatory. For one last time her eyes slowly opened, and she focused on the frame of the bedroom window. She could see nothing but darkness outside, thick and impenetrable. Then her breathing deepened, and she slid into a deep and dreamless sleep.

CHAPTER FOUR

When Andrea woke the next morning, Matthew was already up and about. She dressed without showering, not yet ready to invade a strange bathroom, combed her short hair into a semblance of order, and graced herself with a quick inspection in the dresser mirror. At twenty-nine she had finally lost the angularity that had haunted her through her youth and early twenties, and the reflection that looked back at her was that of an attractive young woman, trim, dark-haired, and darker-eyed.

Marrying Matthew changed you, she thought. *He turned a girl into a woman.*

Matthew and Peter were sitting at the kitchen table, both sipping from tall glasses of orange juice, when she came downstairs. Both looked up, grinning.

"I didn't wake you," Matthew said. "If your first night was as restless as mine, you needed the extra hour."

"I'll get used to it, I guess."

"Tonight will be different. I promise. What will you have for breakfast?"

"I'll wait until lunch."

"Good. We can get this day rolling."

Matthew lifted his glass and drained the juice. Peter did likewise. For a moment she was struck by the similarity between father and son. The same Roman nose, the same sharp jaw. *There's none of my blood in Peter,* she thought wistfully, for the thousandth time. *I can never be a real mother to him.*

They both lowered their glasses at the same time, and Peter smiled at her as if he had read her thoughts. It took a moment to convince herself that there was no malice in the turn of his mouth. He was simply glad to see her.

"I thought you two were going to show me the town," she said too quickly, trying to hide the inadequacy she suddenly felt.

Matthew rose to his feet. "Better grab a light coat," he said. "It's a bit crisp outside."

Even in her coat the cold had sharp teeth. The sky seemed darker than yesterday's, Andrea thought, and a northwesterly breeze pushed the low cloud cover into roiling, ponderous motion. Leaves skittered nervously at their feet along the pothole-ridden road. Matthew held her right hand, while Peter walked a few yards ahead, hands stuffed into his pockets, kicking a pebble. Once they had walked twenty yards away from the house, toward the town circle, it was easy to imagine that civilization was something distant and intangible. The ochre forest loomed menacingly on either side of them, ripe with a pleasant earthy odor, a mixture of decaying leaves and near stagnant water.

They passed a road on the right, marked with a sign that read WEST DRIVE. She glimpsed closely spaced cabins amid the trees, the metallic colors of parked cars. "Where does that lead?"

"Loops back to the town circle," Matthew said. "I guess you could call it a residential area."

Andrea chuckled. After a few more minutes of walking, the trees thinned and the road turned sharply, opening into the town circle. Matthew guided her up onto the sidewalk.

"Isn't this amazing?" he said. "You couldn't design a better-looking place if you started from scratch."

Andrea had to agree. Like yesterday, the only cars on the street were parked. A few pedestrians walked slowly on the

36

sidewalks. She could almost believe they had been doing so all through the night, as if the town were some sort of clockwork mechanism. In the curiously revealing light of midmorning the buildings facing into the circle looked old, almost ancient. Matthew led her counterclockwise around the circle. He pointed out the grocery store and post office, a small hardware store, a clothing store, a craft and gift shop, a quaint little café that looked packed, the village pub.

"Everything we need, right here," he said. "I suppose we could run into Fergus Falls to do serious grocery shopping, but they'll give us credit here."

Andrea nodded, captivated by the quiet beauty of the town. She could almost imagine that barter might still go on in Marissa, that money might have no place in the town's economy at all. Beyond the glass of the store-fronts pale faces peered out at them curiously, and after a few minutes she began to feel they were staring only at her. Matthew, too, noticed, and squeezed her hand.

"Don't worry about them," he said softly, leaning close. "It's a very small town. You're new. They're curious, that's all."

At one point, two boys and a girl, all around seven years old she guessed, erupted from an opening between two buildings. almost crashing headfirst into her. Startled, she pressed into Matthew. The three children stopped in their tracks, staring up at her. Their faces were smudged with dirt, eyes glittering like jewels. A smile turned the lips of the girl, but one of the boys gripped her hand and pulled her along. As they ran, they peered back, eyes fixing on Andrea, as if she were some sort of rare animal in a zoo. Again, Matthew squeezed her hand reassuringly, and she offered him a thankful smile.

Peter had paused ahead, and now he pointed at the oak tree in the center of the town circle. "Guess how old that tree is, Andrea."

She craned her neck to peer up at the massive tangle of branches above. A few leaves dropped and twirled to the ground as she looked. "I don't know. A hundred years?"

"Two hundred and fifty," Peter said.

She studied the tree again, honestly impressed by its antiquity. *Such a tree belongs in a town like this,* she thought. Or had the town intentionally been built around the tree? She imagined Marissa's early settlers gathering around the gnarled oak, planning the development of their town. Somehow the idea was frightening. *Or had the oak been the one doing the planning?*

She was about to turn away when she noticed something gleaming amid the dark branches and darkening leaves. She looked again, carefully, and discovered many such gleams. "Are those decorations hanging from the branches, Matthew?"

"Yeah, I think so. They use it as a Christmas tree. Probably never take the decorations down."

"An oak tree?"

Matthew shrugged. "It's big. It probably looks great." Before she could respond, he pulled her along. "Let's go visit Aunt Clarissa. She's dying to meet you. You'll love her."

They left the town circle, entering a narrow road marked EAST DRIVE. Unlike the glimpse she had of West Drive, the cabins here were widely spaced, set well back from the road, the forest climbing steeply behind them. They had walked perhaps a hundred yards when the chill gripped her.

She paused in her tracks, shivering. The breeze had died to nothing. The trees were silent. Yet fingers of ice gripped the bottom of her spine.

"Are you okay?" Matthew said.

The feeling of coldness suddenly intensified. She began to shiver violently.

"You look like you just saw a ghost," Matthew said, gripping her arm tightly.

"No, it's . . ." She could not find the words.

Then Matthew was guiding her, hands supporting her gently but firmly. "You should have had breakfast," he said reproachfully.

She did not respond. Peter had stopped walking, had

38

turned to regard her curiously. There was something in his eyes that frightened her, as if he too had felt the grip of horrible cold, but was saying nothing. She forced herself to look away from him.

"I'll be okay," she said.

Matthew continued to support her. "Clarissa's place is just around the bend. We'll get something in your stomach. You'll be fine."

She nodded, following obediently. The breeze picked up again, and the branches of the trees shook. Leaves dropped, moving at their feet. Their sound was harsh, scratchy, like mice rummaging behind a wall.

I've been here before. The thought popped unbidden to her mind, and she shook her head angrily. *Only in your dreams, honey.* But the cold did not loosen its grip.

Aunt Clarissa's house was set back from the road. A dark green Dodge Dart, at least twenty years old but still in showroom condition, sat in the driveway, hood up to reveal an immaculate engine. The front lawn, if the grassy spaces between the evenly spaced oak trees could be called such, was miraculously clear of leaves. *Somebody loves raking*, Andrea thought as both Matthew and Peter supported her, leading her up the path.

The front door opened as they reached the steps, and a small, redheaded woman wearing a green dress and spattered apron stepped out. Her round face lit up and her brown eyes widened in pleasure.

"Matthew! Peter! And you must be Andrea!"

Andrea felt strong hands gripping her forearm, pulling her away from Matthew and Peter, as if she were some sort of package being passed along a line. Clarissa pulled her through the doorway, directly into a small living room so jammed with furniture and plants and bric-a-brac that there was hardly room to stand. The small woman seemed to be a bundle of energy, and spoke continuously.

"I've waited so long to meet you, Andrea. Matthew sent pictures, but it's not the same as seeing a person in the

39

flesh. You're not what I expected. So young and pretty. When Maureen, bless her heart, died so suddenly, we were *so* worried, King and I, and that Matthew and Peter would be alone. A man needs a wife. A boy needs a mother. Such responsibility for a girl so young! Do you feel capable, my dear? Life can become such a drudge when one is pressed into duties one is not quite ready to assume. But you *are* pretty, and a man can be swayed. Matthew must be pleased. Come, come, step into the light, let me see you better."

As if she were a tiny fish caught in a powerful current, Andrea allowed herself to be pushed in front of the living room window. Aunt Clarissa stood before her, hands resting on her shoulders. The older woman came up to Andrea's chin, and her brown eyes gleamed.

"So pretty! But what did I expect? Matthew was always attracted to beauty, even as a boy. Maureen, now there was a beautiful girl. Did you know Maureen? You two are so unalike. She was very tall, you know, statuesque, almost Scandinavian. Blonde as snow, fair-skinned. When Matthew married her we were worried at first, because she was not local. But Maureen was a wonderful girl. Just wonderful."

Matthew, who had stepped into the living room as Peter closed the front door, placed a hand on his Aunt's arm. "Clarissa," he said carefully, "no more talk of Maureen."

Clarissa blinked, as if she'd been suddenly woken. Her red cheeks blanched. "Oh! I'm so sorry! How thoughtless of me!"

Andrea blushed, shook her head. "No, it's all right."

Clarissa peered up into her face. "My dear, you look positively weak kneed! Are you all right? You look ready to faint! Sit, sit, don't keep standing there! How thoughtless of me."

Clarissa steered her to a plush easy chair by the fireplace and lowered her gently into it. The moment Andrea was seated, the dizziness that she had managed to keep controlled suddenly surged and engulfed her. She swayed precariously, gripping the arms of the chair to keep her balance.

"She felt a bit faint on the road," Matthew explained. "Empty stomach, probably."

Clarissa bent down and peered into her face. "Oh, my poor dear. It's probably the fresh air. Would you like some tea? I make wonderful tea. It will fix you right up."

Andrea nodded gratefully. Tea sounded perfect. "That would be nice."

Clarissa smiled and stood. "King! King! Come and meet our guests."

The moment the words were spoken, an old springer spaniel stepped slowly around the corner of the kitchen door. Its movements were stiff, careful, almost as if it were in pain. The once brown parts of its fur were fading, the white parts turning yellow, as if it had lain too close to a hot fire. As it approached Peter near the front door, its stubby brown tail began to wag. The boy reached down and scratched it behind the ears. Next it moved to Matthew, paused for a brief petting, then waddled over to Andrea. Its floppy ears were thick with burrs, its eyes sagging and red-rimmed. Yet in those liquid brown eyes she detected a glimmer of what the dog had once been, a remnant of its youthful playfulness. The warm muzzle rested in her lap, the eyes peered soulfully up at her, and the tail began to wag. After passing judgment, King lowered his rump, leaned against her legs, and turned to face the room.

"King likes you, dear," Clarissa said, smiling brightly. "That's a good sign, isn't it, King?"

At hearing his name, King's tail began to wag, thumping against the leg of the chair. Clarissa marched through to the kitchen and began to make tea. Matthew pulled up a straight-backed wooden chair and sat down next to her, squeezing her hand.

"Sorry about Clarissa. She doesn't mean anything by it."

Andrea sighed, smiled, and squeezed back. "I know.

41

Don't worry."

"She likes you. I know she does."

She smiled. "It's fine, Matthew, really."

He opened his mouth to say something, thought better of it, smiled, and nodded. Peter moved into the living room, looking uncomfortable with his hands stuffed into his jeans. He leaned against the door frame. "How long are we staying?" he said softly.

Matthew shrugged. "Long enough to say hello."

Peter drew a deep, resigned breath, and moved to an ornate-looking seat by the window. With hands still stuffed into his pockets, he slumped into it, turning his attention outside. Clarissa returned a few minutes later, balancing before her a tray laden with four mugs and a plate of iced pastry. She allowed Andrea first pick, then turned to Matthew and Peter, finally leaving the remaining pastry within Andrea's reach. Andrea sipped delicately from the mug of tea, worried it might be some herbal mixture. She was relieved to find it a good old-fashioned dark brew, and savored the warmth of it as it settled inside her. The sweetness of the pastry perked her up immediately, and she soon began to feel better.

Clarissa took a seat at the other side of the room, eyes darting from Peter to Matthew to Andrea, but mostly focusing on Andrea. When the older woman finished her first pastry, she slapped the arm of her chair.

"King!"

The old springer spaniel rose to its feet, wagged its tail, and moved to the pastry plate. As Andrea watched, filled with a mixture of astonishment and disgust, the dog picked up a single pastry, held it loosely in its mouth, and carried it over to Clarissa. Clarissa greeted the dog with a warm pat, removed the pastry from its mouth, and began to eat it. She tore off a corner and gave it to King, who then lay down at her feet. Seeing the look on Andrea's face, Clarissa grinned.

"He needs to feel useful, dear," Clarissa explained. She reached down to pet the dog again. King's tail wagged.

"That's gross," Peter said, cringing, echoing Andrea's feelings.

"You'll never see another dog like King," Matthew said.

I'm not sure I would want to, Andrea thought, but nodded politely.

From his new position by Clarissa's feet, King regarded her steadily. There was a gleam in his brown eyes that seemed almost intelligent, and it made her feel uneasy. She sipped her tea, looking away from the dog.

"Matthew," Clarissa said after finishing the new pastry, "would you and Peter mind taking a quick look at my car? I couldn't get it started this morning. Andrea and I shall chat."

"Sure. Come on, Pete." He squeezed Andrea's hand, then walked to the front door with Peter at his heels.

Once they were outside, Clarissa turned her attention to Andrea. *She wants to talk to me alone*, Andrea realized. *There's nothing wrong with the car.*

Clarissa leaned forward in her chair. Her eyes gleamed.

"My dear," Clarissa said carefully. "You have made a terrible mistake in coming here."

CHAPTER FIVE

Andrea drew back, surprised. "What?"

"Marissa is not the kind of place to raise a family."

"But Matthew was born here," she protested.

"And my sister took him away before Marissa could change him."

"If you didn't want him here, you should have told him not to take the job," she said angrily.

"The council acted without my permission. If I had known, I would certainly have acted to keep you away."

Andrea shook her head, surprised beyond argument.

"Besides, my dear, you yourself don't like Marissa."

Andrea blushed. Had her discomfort been that obvious? "It's not that I don't like it," she said quickly. "It's just so . . . different."

"Marissa is a unique place," Clarissa agreed.

"But Matthew likes it here," Andrea said. "He was very happy to get the job."

Clarissa smiled, as if she saw through Andrea's words to some deeper, truer meaning. "Marissa looks after her own," she said softly. "Many people here remember Matthew as a boy. He was only six when his mother, my sister, took him away." The frantic energy that had infused her words with such menace only moments ago now seemed to focus itself in her intent stare. "But you, my dear, will find Marissa boring."

"I'll be working from a real estate office in Fergus

Falls," Andrea said. "That should keep me occupied."

"Fergus Falls?"

"It's not a long drive. No worse than commuting in the city, I expect."

Something happened to Clarissa's eyes. They narrowed, became almost steely. "Marissa looks after her own," she repeated. "But you should look out for your family."

Again, Clarissa's words rang with menace, or warning. Outside, the old Dodge's engine roared to life, revved a few times, then cut out. Clarissa's eyes turned to the window. In a moment the front door opened and Matthew came inside.

He rubbed his palms on his jeans as he came into the living room. "Seems to be working now."

Clarissa smiled, hands once again moving. "Oh, my. I must have flooded it this morning."

Matthew grinned, shook his head, then turned to Andrea. "Ready to go?"

Andrea nodded, placed her teacup on the tray, and stood. Clarissa stood also, bustling over beside her to squeeze her hand.

"It was so nice to meet you, my dear. Matthew and Peter are so lucky to have you looking after them."

The echo of Clarissa's previous words sent another tremor of unease through Andrea. At the door she turned and smiled at the older woman. "Thank you for the tea and pastry."

Clarissa gripped her hand and squeezed again. "Please, you'll come and visit? Anytime you like?"

Andrea smiled, embarrassed. "Yes, of course."

King waddled up to the door and pressed against Clarissa's leg. His tail wagged softly. A low growl emerged from his throat, and he barked once, scarcely audible at all. Clarissa beamed. "You see? I told you he liked you!"

Outside, Andrea gripped Matthew's hand tightly as they walked back down the road toward town. If anything, the morning seemed slightly cooler now, and once or twice she felt drops of moisture on her face. The sky above was gray, brooding. Peter walked ahead, hands stuffed in his

45

pockets, kicking at the falling leaves. He looked as if he was deep in thought.

Matthew, on the other hand, seemed to have fallen into a good mood. He talked and chattered as they walked, alternately squeezing her hand or pressing close to her.

"I told you you'd like Clarissa. Isn't she great? You'll be able to visit her whenever you want. Even King likes you!" He laughed aloud. "That's a good sign if I ever saw one. I think you're going to love it here. I think everything is going to be great."

Andrea listened, squeezing his hand at appropriate moments so that he would know she was paying attention, but said nothing.

Clarissa leaned against the door frame and watched the three figures recede down the road. She kept watching until they had disappeared around the bend. King nudged at her leg for a better view. She reached down to stroke his neck.

"She's gone, boy, you can calm down now."

The old spaniel looked up at her with feigned innocence. She laughed and continued to stroke him. "You can't fool me, old friend."

She closed the inner door, forcing King away from his vantage point. He whined softly and padded through to the living room. Clarissa followed.

She was troubled. Deeply troubled.

When she had first discovered that the council had worked behind her back to bring Matthew back to Marissa, she had been furious. She had been loud and strident with her complaints, but to no avail. The deed had been done. The invitation tendered. Matthew and his family were coming. A year ago the council had been firm in their resolve to steer clear of that path. Somewhere along the line, Deirdre Farrell had planted seeds of dissent. And now, thinking about it, she could understand that Deirdre would have had little trouble in being persuasive. The evidence, after all, was on her side.

Look at Marissa. Decay and stagnation evident everywhere you looked. Easy prey to an offer for quick salvation.

But this road was dangerous. So very dangerous.

She lowered herself into her seat and patted her leg to attract King. He padded over and collapsed in a heap at her feet. His tail thumped softly.

A dark circle was not the way to revive Marissa. The costs of such an effort could be terrible.

Deirdre, you foolish woman, you will be the end of us all.

And yet, she had to admit, it was nice to have family around her again. It had been so long.

She shook her head, angry. *Look how easily you yourself are swayed! And it is not you who will pay the price!*

It was Peter.

Already, she could sense changes in the boy. In the three weeks he had been here, he had turned moody, introspective. He hardly seemed the same boy at all. They would not force him, of course. There was no danger of that. His participation must be willing. But a boy—especially a boy like Peter—could be so easily swayed. In his own way he exerted a raw, natural power over the things around him. That was his very attraction, of course. But he was not strong enough to resist.

She closed her eyes, allowing her fingers to continue stroking King's head.

Well, she would watch out for the boy, do what she could to help him. If that meant resisting the will of the council, then so be it. Let them punish her. What could they do? She was an old woman now, with little to lose. That decided, she smiled, breathed deeply, and relaxed.

Still, the sense of foreboding would not leave her, and she forced herself to consider what she had been trying to ignore.

Andrea. Matthew's wife. *His second wife*, she corrected herself. A true outsider, with no relation at all to Marissa.

And yet, from the moment Andrea Willson had set foot in the house, Clarissa had sensed it. There was something about the woman. Something she could not quite identify.

47

King, too, had sensed it. He had taken to her immediately, and that was the most surprising of all. She was an outsider. King should have seen that immediately.

Troubled, she shook her head.

Andrea Willson was not what she seemed. How, exactly, she would fit into the drama currently unfolding was not yet clear.

Clarissa scratched King's head.

"I think, special friend, we are headed for trouble," she said.

King whined softly.

That evening, Andrea found herself alone. Matthew had gone to the station to do a little work, and Peter, without warning, had departed after dinner on one of his solitary walks. The house was silent around her, and by seven o'clock she was drumming her fingers on the kitchen table.

I've been here twenty-four hours and I'm bored out of my mind.

On impulse, she decided to walk into town.

When she entered the town circle she saw immediately the cars parked in front of the Three-Horned Bull. Light spilled from the pub into the deepening twilight of the street, and she saw Matthew's official black and white cruiser. He had told her that he dropped in at the pub every night for a coffee. Tonight, apparently, was no different. She began to walk around the circle. At Robertson's Market she paused. If she bought some groceries, she would at least have an excuse for being here, a meager justification for visiting the pub.

For snooping, you mean.

Nonsense. She simply wanted to introduce herself to Marissa's social whirl.

With firm resolve, she pushed open the door of Robertson's Market and entered the store. An older woman, plump and red-cheeked, smiled at her as Andrea picked up a basket. Andrea smiled back. She proceeded to walk the aisles, filling the basket with things she hoped

48

they needed at home. Within five minutes she returned to the counter.

"Will that be everything for you, Mrs. Willson?"

Andrea opened her mouth to respond and slammed it shut.

The red-cheeked woman smiled apologetically. "Matthew said you might drop by sometime. I didn't think you could be anybody else."

Andrea blushed and tried to smile. *How many other people know about me?*

A large man appeared from behind the meat counter. He removed a bloody smock as he approached, and folded it neatly in large hands. He grinned at her. "You'll have to excuse my wife," he said. "She likes to think she knows everybody."

He moved in behind the checkout counter, patting the plump woman on the behind. He turned to Andrea with a wide smile. "I'm Ewan Robertson, and this is my wife Barbara."

"Hello." She could not bring herself to say anything else. Being identified, named, by people she did not know, was disconcerting.

She waited impatiently as the groceries were packed. An uncomfortable silence had settled, and appeared to be unbreakable. When Barbara Robertson finished tallying the bill, Ewan pulled a small black notebook out from under the counter.

"You'll charge that?"

Without thinking, she pulled out her wallet. "No. Cash."

She handed him the bills, and knew immediately that it had been a mistake. The offer of credit had been a way of breaching barriers of formality, and she had refused. In a small town like Marissa, she was firmly proclaiming herself a stranger. But Ewan nodded, took the money, and made her change. She took it, thanked him, and left the store as quickly as she could.

Outside, she walked a few paces, then leaned against the side of the building and breathed deeply. A simple trip to the grocery store had turned into a trial. Next time, she would accept the credit.

Stupid, stupid.

With the two bags of groceries tucked under her arms, she began to walk around the circle. As she neared the pub she heard music, then voices raised in laughter. Peering through the narrow, leaded glass windows, she glimpsed a crowd of faces, male and female, floating in a smoky haze. At the door she paused, nervous as a bride entering a church. She felt, suddenly, a surge of unreasonable terror. When she opened the door, she imagined, the music would stop. Faces would turn. She would wither under the gaze of those suspicious, probing eyes. And Matthew would not come forward to claim her. *I don't know her.* Forever establishing her an outsider. So strong was this feeling that her hand actually began to tremble as it hovered over the tarnished door handle, and seeing it she realized how juvenile she was being.

She snorted derisively at herself, shook her head, and opened the door.

Fingers of smoke reached out to pull her in. The music swelled, giving no hint of stopping. One or two faces turned, faces she did not recognize, then turned back to their conversations. Dim lighting from wall lamps seemed to exude warmth into the packed room. She glanced around, trying to find Matthew, and found that he had already spotted her. His narrow face bobbed atop a sea of shorter heads, grinning at her, swimming toward her from the other side of the room. The expression on his face was one of pleasure. His eyes looked slightly red.

Andrea felt something inside of herself shrink, and a glimmer of the terror reasserted itself. *Please, Matthew, don't be drunk, don't have been drinking at all, don't . . .*

Then he was next to her, leaning over and kissing her on the lips.

"Andrea!"

She laughed with relief. The only thing on his breath was coffee, laced with chicory. His eyes were red from the smoke in the room.

"Do you want to come in for a drink or something?"

She nodded at the groceries. "No. I just wanted to say

hello. I better get home with these."

"I was about to leave myself."

She smiled warmly at him. "Matthew, stay here if you want."

"Been here long enough. I'm starting to choke." He took one of the grocery bags and cradled it easily beneath one arm.

A round, sweaty face materialized out of the crowd behind Matthew and nodded at her. Below the face, she saw a police uniform like Matthew's. Except this man's shirt was wrinkled and stained, and unbuttoned to the middle of his chest. A belly the size of a watermelon strained against his leather belt.

"You must be Andrea! Joining us for a drink?" His voice was loud and coarse.

Andrea did not know what to say. Again, she had been surprised by being recognized. She turned to Matthew for help.

"Andrea, this is Murray Carlyle, my partner. The other half of Marissa's police force."

Matthew had mentioned already that Murray Carlyle was six years his junior, but seeing him now Andrea thought he looked much older.

"Joining us?" he repeated.

Andrea shook her head but said nothing. Matthew, she knew, liked his partner. It was a survival trait among cops, he had once told her. A cop would love the world's biggest asshole if it was his partner. She, on the other hand, was not bound by inscrutable police bonding rituals. She had formed an immediate aversion to Murray Carlyle.

He nodded as if he understood her unwillingness to stay longer. "Mondays or Tuesdays are better for getting acquainted with this place. The air should be breathable then, at least." He grinned at her, then drew on a crooked-looking cigarette and added to the smoke in the room.

"Good night, Murray," Matthew said, slapping the other man on the back.

"I'll walk you to your car."

They stepped out of the pub onto the sidewalk, and Andrea greedily sucked in a deep lungful of the fresh

51

outside air. Matthew stretched and yawned.

"It's getting dark quickly," he said.

"Wait until winter," Murray said. "You'll get up when it's dark, and you'll go home when it's dark." He closed the pub door, sealing in the music and the smoke and the raised voices. He flicked his cigarette butt into the street, where it sparked and smoked.

Andrea leaned into Matthew, allowing him to pull her close with his free arm. They were near the cruiser when the commotion began in the park at the center of the circle.

"What the hell?" Murray said.

Andrea followed his gaze, glimpsing a shadow shape flitting behind the giant oak. It was too dark to see clearly, but the impression of furtive movement was strong.

"Hey!" Murray yelled.

For a moment the shadow stopped moving. It seemed to crouch, as if placing something on the ground next to the tree. Then, hissing in the darkness, a match flared. For a moment Andrea saw something pale in the flickering light, and she held her breath. The match dropped.

A large tongue of flame leaped into the air from the ground. A high scream cut into the darkness, inhuman and filled with terrible agony. The shadow jumped, moved behind the tree, and darted into the darkness at the other side of the circle.

"Oh, Christ, he's burning an animal or something," Matthew whispered. He dropped the bag of groceries and ran toward the park, Murray hot on his heels.

The scream of the burning animal had turned into a whistle, like steam escaping from a kettle, almost inaudible. Andrea found herself walking slowly across the street, clutching her bag of groceries, as if she were in a dream. Matthew and Murray had reached the diminishing flame and were silhouetted in the flickering light. Behind her the door of the pub opened, and questioning shouts rang out.

As she came up beside Matthew the smell of gasoline surrounded her, and then, cutting through even that, the sharp tang of burned meat and hair. A makeshift wire cage

52

lay on the grass. Something black and smoking trembled within it. The thing moved slightly, shuddered, and released a whimper.

Murray Carlyle chuckled, a dry sound. "Somebody's got it in for cats," he said, then laughed.

"It's still alive," Matthew said.

As if to prove his point, the burned cat moved again and screamed piteously. Andrea felt herself begin to shudder, tasting the bile rising in her throat. "Matthew, do something."

"It's too late," Matthew said softly.

"Matthew, do something, for God's sake, it's still alive!"

The panic in her voice seemed to galvanize him. He pulled his revolver from its holster and kneeled down by the smoking cage. The hideous cat wailed again, sounding so human that Andrea almost collapsed. Then Matthew cocked the gun, pushed the dark barrel between the wires, and fired. The powder flash made her blink, but the sudden loud bark seemed to cut through the dreamlike haze surrounding her. The cat stiffened and lay still.

Something brushed Andrea's elbow, and she turned to find a group from the pub pressing close. Their faces were solemn, their voices hushed, almost reverent.

"That looks like Barbara Robertson's cat," she heard a woman say.

From across the street, toward Robertson's Food Market, another scream erupted. All heads turned, including Andrea's. Ewan Robertson was hugging his wife fiercely as she struggled to escape him, smashing at his chest ineffectually with her fists.

"Gray Eyes! Gray Eyes!" The name of the cat, warped by her grief, was a wail of sorrow.

"Better get Andrea home," she heard Murray Carlyle say.

Then Matthew was leading her away from the gathered crowd, across the street, pushing her into the car. She kept her face pressed to the glass. The night turned into a blur of darkness.

CHAPTER SIX

The lean-to shook as Willy moved, and Jack Burgess watched as his son rose to his feet, a dimly perceived orange and black shadow in the firelight.

"Where are you going?"

"I need to pee," Willy said.

"What?"

"I have to pee."

"Pee?" Jack grunted in disgust. There were some things about Willy that he could not understand. Too much of his wife's influence. "You mean piss?"

"Pee, piss, what's the difference?" There was a note of anger in the boy's voice.

"Women pee, men piss," Jack said drunkenly.

"Then I've got to piss," Willy said in a flat voice.

Jack drew a deep breath and grinned. "Keep the fire in sight. I don't want to come looking for you."

The boy grumbled his assent and stumbled away from the small camp, weaving and bobbing like a slapstick drunk, until even his outline was invisible against the trees. Jack leaned back against his open pack, raised the bottle, and poured bourbon down his throat. This was the first night of their three-night camping trip, and already he felt as if he knew his son a lot better. Of course, the booze was helping things along. It always helped.

He grinned, raised the bottle to his lips, and took another swallow. The night was cool, getting cooler, bu the liquid fire reached tendrils of warmth to all his extremities. His thoughts buzzed dully in opaque swaddling.

Sometime later, he was not sure exactly how much later, a noise from the fire startled him, and the warm glow slipped back to wherever it had come from. He leaned forward, blinking his eyes to clear them. A thin mist was groping between the trunks of the trees, sending vaporous fingers into the glowing coals of the fire. The coals hissed and sputtered, as if water had been poured on them.

"What the hell . . ."

Jack dragged his attention from the fire and looked into the trees. The mist, faintly luminous, filled the surrounding woods with delicate blue light. He could see more clearly now than an hour ago.

How long had Willy been gone? Surely the boy could have pissed three times by now?

He pushed himself into a wobbly crouch and placed the bottle of Wild Turkey carefully on the ground. The liquid sloshed noisily. His last swallow remained in his mouth as a bitter aftertaste, but the alcohol-induced blanket of comfort was gone. He blinked again and breathed deeply, suddenly intensely aware of his surroundings.

"Willy?" he said softly.

His voice was a small thing, instantly swallowed by the woods. No answer came.

The fire sputtered again, and Jack drew a sharp breath. The mist was poking into the lean-to, almost tentatively, as if searching for something. For one wild moment Jack reeled under the impression that the glowing blue fingers had a mind of their own, that some diabolical intelligence was controlling them, and he pushed back instinctively. The retreat came too late, and an eddy of the blue mist passed across his ankle.

"Jesus!"

There had been no pain at the touch, only a sensation of cold. A cold quite different from anything he had ever experienced before. He lunged to his feet and stumbled away from the lean-to. His precipitous escape sent the already fragile structure into a final collapse. Loose branches fell across the already feeble fire and extinguished it. It hissed for a moment, then its dying smoke seemed to merge with the mist. A chill stabbed into Jack' guts. The mist surrounded their camp, extending into the woods in all directions as far as he could see.

Where had it come from?

He glanced nervously down at his feet to find them obscured by the glowing blue carpet. His legs throbbed uncomfortably as tendrils of cold seemed to reach right through his boots and socks and into his bones. The mist roiled in eddies and currents, as if something moved below it, hidden from view. Jack fought down his panic and returned his thoughts to his son.

Where the hell could the boy have gone?

"Willy!" He shouted the name this time, and his voice echoed through the trees. As if in response, the mist' movements altered slightly. Jack shuddered. He cupped his mouth and shouted again. "Willy!"

After the echo died, he listened intently. A few second later, as if from far away, he heard the response.

"Dad?"

"Where are you, boy?"

Another delay as the echo died.

"I don't know! I can't see through the mist! It's—"

His son's voice was suddenly interrupted by another deeper voice. Jack could not hear the words. Only a thick whispering sound. In a moment he heard Willy again, as if talking with a friend. Jack's insides turned hollow. Who could be out in the woods at this time of night? The chill in his bones deepened.

"Willy! Walk toward my voice!"

No answer. This time, when the panic rose within him he did not fight it, but instead allowed it to jolt him into action. He dropped to his knees and began to grope through the mist. It felt as if he had plunged his arms into an icy stream. His forearm jammed into the still hot remains of the fire. He swore in pain, but kept searching. His breathing was thunder in his ears, matching the beat of his heart. When his hand hit the mist-shrouded backpack, he almost wept with relief. He rummaged through the hastily packed contents, tossing what he did not want back into the mist, until he finally came across the cold metal of the fully loaded Winchester magazine. Immediately behind the pack he found the rifle, half covered in loose branches from the fallen lean-to.

He stood with the rifle hugged to his chest, facing the direction Willy had wandered off in. Mist swirled between the trees, obscuring the ground. In the distance it seemed to rise, forming a bluish wall.

"Willy!" he shouted as loud as he could.

The only reply was a faint murmur, possibly voices, possibly not. A fear, one Jack had never before known, encompassed him. Not fear of physical harm, or fear of embarrassment, as he was accustomed to. This was something different, something stronger. It reached deep within him, as if its roots had always existed in the depths of his mind and soul. He had heard the phrase before, but had never quite grasped its true meaning:

Fear of the unknown.

Now that meaning hit home with a force that left him breathless.

"Willy! I'm going to fire a shot! Walk toward it!" He waited for the echo to diminish, then pointed the rifle at the sky and fired. The blast cracked like a whip between the trees. Even the mist seemed to recoil from it.

A voice sounded in response. "Dad! There's something . . ."

What happened next froze Jack. Willy's voice wavered, broke off, and erupted again as a scream. There was a note of high, raw panic in the sound that Jack had never heard before. The knowledge that it had come from his own son's mouth made it worse.

"Willy! I'm coming, son! Stay where you are!"

He ran in the direction of Willy's scream. The mist swirled at his passing, tiny whirlpools spinning and sinking with each step. Jack kept his eyes on the trees ahead, lifting his feet high off the ground as he ran.

Branches stung his face and whipped his neck, bringing tears to his eyes. But he did not slow down. The panic was gone, replaced by a force he did not quite understand. He knew only one thing: his boy was in trouble.

"Aaaaaaaaiiiiiiiiiiiiiiiiiiieeeeeeeeeeeeeeeeeeee!" The scream seemed to go on and on, dying for a moment, then picking up again where it had left off. It was Willy.

What could make the boy scream like that? The terror in that sound was unfathomable, and for a moment even his concern for Willy was not strong enough to face the thing that could cause it.

He slowed to a halt, stumbling over mist-covered roots. "Willy! Where are you, boy?" He gasped for breath between words.

Willy's answer was predictable.

"Aaaaaaaaaaaaaaaaaaaaiiiiiiiiiiiiiiiiii . . ."

Jack ran again, altering his direction slightly. The mist billowed in his path. Within seconds he found himself surrounded in the blue haze, completely blind. He held the rifle barrel ahead of him, swinging it like a cane. The trunks of trees, only dimly perceived shadows, passed on either side of him.

"Willy!"

The mist swallowed his voice. Willy's scream had mercifully stopped. Or had it been smothered by the thickening mist? Either way, Jack was lost. He paused, unwilling to stumble along blindly, and listened.

Nothing. Silence. Even the mist, gently swirling around him, made no sound.

He did not know how long he stood there. His breathing slowly returned to normal. He was aware only when the mist began to thin again, when the trees became visible on either side of him. Ahead, huge dark shapes began to appear, as if solidifying within the mist.

It took him a few seconds to realize what he was looking at, and a few seconds more for his terror to mount. As the mist cleared, the shape of the standing stones became more apparent, the sacred circle easily identifiable. How was this possible? Their camp had been a good six miles south

58

of the circle.

The mist took me here. As he thought it, he accepted it.

Almost unwillingly he stepped forward, toward the circle. As a boy, at ten years old, when his mother had first brought him to the Nemeton for baptism, he had remarked how much it looked like the photographs of Stonehenge he had seen.

"These are our own earthworks," his mother had said.

Now, in the eerie blue light cast by the mist, he was struck again by his boyhood impression. The ancient mystery of that distant place pervaded the atmosphere, as if this smaller circle were somehow connected to the larger, somehow shared its mystery.

He moved ahead, rifle held at the ready.

"Willy?"

No answer. No scream. Nothing.

He had just stepped inside the outer ring of stones, far enough to glimpse the altar stone in the center of the circle, when he found Willy's jacket. The green denim was shredded, as if by a knife. Or talons.

"Oh, Christ." He moved deeper into the circle, and found more of Willy's clothes. Pants, torn and covered in something that glistened black in the pale blue light. A boot, leather split as if it were paper.

Could it have been a wild cat? At this time of year?

No. Something else. Something to do with the mist.

Trepidation made his hands tremble, and he almost dropped the rifle. He hugged it against his chest and moved beyond the inner row of stones, into the sanctuary.

He found the remains on a small mound, hidden from view. They looked like a burst tomato. The stench of blood was thick. What was left of the body glistened in the darkness.

This isn't Willy. Not my boy. Not Willy.

He fell to his knees and turned his head. Violent spasms racked his body. He began to crawl, moving as far away as possible from the horror he had discovered. The earthworks echoed with his moans and cries.

He looked up a few minutes later when tendrils of cold

wrapped around his wrists. The mist was back.

This time, he felt no fear.

He pushed to his knees, then to his feet, wobbling precariously. The mist rose in a wall before him, hazy blue and inviting.

"What did you do to my boy?"

As if in answer, a shape seemed to define itself in the haze. Its outlines were visible, Jack suddenly realized, only because of the mist. Whatever it was, it was tall, and terribly thin. It moved toward him, pulling wisps of blue vapor after it like a cloak.

Jack felt his breath catch in his throat, found himself unable to speak. Something else helped define the invisible form. Strips of what looked like soggy paper hung from what might have been shoulders. It took him only a moment to realize what the strips were. Not paper. Skin.

His stomach churned violently. He slapped a hand to his mouth to silence a gag.

On one of the strips, like an old friend, he recognized a faint pattern. It was the scar on Willy's shoulder, from a fall he'd taken as a small boy. In a crazy flash of memory, he saw himself cleaning the wound, comforting his young son.

The sound that came from his mouth was not a word, simply an expression of horror. The mist swirled as the outline of a long arm raised itself. Jack found himself focusing on the misty delineation of a crooked finger, the long blade of a fingernail. Willy's skin slid across an invisible bicep, leaving a smear of red. A sound came from the thing, like a boulder being moved from the mouth of a cave.

Was it speaking to him?

The words, low and whispered in a voice hoarse from disuse, somehow intimate, rushed past his ear. *"You have something that I need."*

He flinched as the invisible arm lay gently across his shoulder. Shivering as the unspeakable cold embraced him, he followed as the thing led him into the mist.

60

CHAPTER SEVEN

Settling in was as difficult as Andrea had anticipated. After that first weekend, she spent most of her time alone. Matthew left for work every morning at dawn, and Peter caught a bus in the town circle to take him to school in Fergus Falls. It was a routine they had grown accustomed to while she had remained in Minneapolis. She busied herself by cleaning a house that did not need cleaning, until she was so familiar with her new environment she felt she had lived there for years.

Within days, the memory of the burned cat lost its horror. Matthew was adamant. It was just a prank. A sick teenager, probably from Fergus, out for a laugh. *"This kind of thing never happens in Marissa,"* he assured her. She did not say it, but she thought otherwise. *You're wrong Matthew. Dead wrong. This is exactly the kind of thing that happens in Marissa.* Although the memory of the cat faded, her conviction did not. There was something strange about Marissa. Something she couldn't quite put her finger on.

Her feelings of being an outsider, a fish out of water, were intensified by the days alone. She hardly saw Matthew at all. His normal hours finished at six every evening, but he was so intent on making a good impression, on learning everything there was to learn about Marissa and his job, that he often stayed at the station house late into the night. When she did see him, first thing in the morning and before bedtime, he would kiss her warmly, squeeze her, talk to her, and yet there seemed to be a gap growing between them. They had not made love since she had arrived in Marissa, and it had been nearly a month before that. She began to wonder if they ever would again. We're cordial strangers under the same roof, she thought.

She sensed the same thing with Peter. Away at school all day, when he returned home he isolated himself in his room, or disappeared for long, lonely walks. More and more, she found herself alone, and not liking it one bit. Instead of bringing her family closer together, as she had hoped, Marissa was pulling them apart, driving a wedge between them.

On Thursday she came to the conclusion that she was doing herself no good by sitting around the house all day long. She had planned on taking two weeks to settle in before introducing herself to the real estate office in Fergus Falls, but now she realized that she was only depressing herself by waiting so long. Matthew was fitting in, Peter was fitting in—she was the only one having trouble adjusting to life in Marissa. With that in mind, she drove into Fergus Falls on Thursday morning, stopped in at the offices of McQuage and Ronson, Realtors, and kick-started her career back to life. She had come equipped with a flattering letter of introduction from her office in Minneapolis, and was greeted warmly. Business was brisk, she was told, and experienced agents were in short supply. They were happy to have her.

She spent the remainder of the day familiarizing herself with Fergus Falls Real Estate Board areas, including outlying Otter Tail County properties, and began Friday morning with a task she had both dreaded and looked forward to at the same time: cold calling. When she returned to Marissa in the early afternoon, she was in high spirits. Going back to work had been the very thing she needed to put her in the proper frame of mind.

For the first time, as she drove north along the narrow road that led into Marissa, she viewed her surroundings with something close to pleasure. Though dark and close, the trees had somehow lost their menace. The gray sky above showed patches of blue. Marissa itself, as she drove around the town circle, seemed almost warm and welcoming. Faces on the street turned to her, some offering smiles. She could almost believe she had imagined their previous suspicious stares.

What had seemed unlikely only a few days ago now seemed possible. With work, maybe, she could make Marissa her home. If she accepted the town, then it would accept her.

The house was empty when she got home—with Matthew at work, and Peter at school—and the thought of being alone depressed her. Although she was not feeling hungry, she still felt uncomfortable with the memory of her near fainting spell a week ago, so she forced herself to eat a sandwich. Afterward, wearing a light jacket, she left the house and walked into town. The air was crisp, but comfortable. The breeze, from the northwest, was light, almost feathery. The woods whispered at its passing.

Robertson's Market was busy. It was the first time Andrea had seen other shoppers in the store, and the scene surprised her. She found herself jostling for space with sour-faced women who kept their faces down.

It became apparent after only a few moments that Ewan Robertson was running the market alone. The poor man kept shuffling between the cash register at the front and the meat counter at the rear, rubbing his hands furiously on his smock to clean them of blood and fat, his face ruddy and sweating. A gleam of panic nestled at the corner of his eyes. At one point, during a mad dash for the meat counter, he saw her, and a warm smile tugged his lips. He nodded a brief greeting, and then passed by. She had wanted only to give her condolences, but found herself picking up items she did not need in order to wait for an opening.

When, at last, it looked like Ewan was momentarily alone at the front counter, she brought her small basket of produce to him and placed it by the register.

"It's so busy, Ewan!" She tried to add a tone of levity to her voice.

His return smile was forced, almost fragile. He shrugged. "Popular place."

Andrea felt a stab of sympathy, then renewed guilt at the way she had initially rebuffed the overtures of welcome Ewan and Barbara had offered. "I'm so sorry about your cat," she said.

Ewan nodded, and his face ran through a series of emotional expressions that she could not read. "Gray Eyes was Barbara's cat," he said. He picked up the first of Andrea's items and began to punch them through the register. "Her special friend."

"It was horrible."

Ewan nodded. "It will take her time to get over it."

"If there's anything I can do, please let me know."

Ewan paused, and his sharp eyes focused on hers. For a moment a connection was established, and Andrea felt her smile matching Ewan's. "If you would like to visit her sometime . . ."

"Of course," Andrea said. "I'd love to." And she was surprised to find that she actually meant it.

Ewan Robertson paused in his handling of the groceries and regarded her speculatively, as if he were redefining his opinion of her. "Barbara would like that," he said at last, then finished ringing up the rest of the unwanted groceries.

Before he could ask her, Andrea said, "Could I have this on credit, Ewan?"

He blinked, and his smile widened another notch. "Of course." He pulled the black notebook from beneath the counter, wrote her first name at the top of a page, and scribbled a number.

When she left the market, cradling the small bag of groceries, she was feeling very good. *I've made my first friends in the new town,* she thought. Sunlight, dappled by the branches of the oak tree, warmed her face and glinted in her eyes. Two children, a boy and a girl, scampered past her in giggling pursuit, and she found herself laughing with them. Almost reluctantly she began walking toward Lake Drive, wishing she had a reason to linger in the town circle. The beauty of Marissa was finally getting through to her.

She was nearing Lake Drive when she saw Peter running across the center of the circle toward an opening between two stores, and she stopped in her tracks.

Why wasn't he in school?

She raised her hand to wave at him. He did not see her, and paused for a moment before stepping into the shadowed opening. Curious, she crossed to the center of the circle, aware as she did so that she was near the place where Gray Eyes had burned to death. She avoided the stain on the grass, and focused instead on the alley where Peter had gone.

She saw the boy again, just inside the opening. A bar of sunlight illuminated his face and half his body. He appeared to be talking to another person, but Andrea could not see anything in the shadow. Again she prepared to call his name, but hesitated. He held out his hand, and from the shadow across from him, another hand raised itself, entering momentarily into the sunlight. Andrea sucked in a harsh breath and held it tightly. The hand, appearing to be suspended in the air, was ancient and withered. Skin, thin as parchment, stretched over a knobby formation of bone. A single ring glinted in the sunlight.

Peter touched the offered hand, and accepted something from it. Andrea frowned, trying to see what had been passed to the boy. From here, it looked like a potato, but the sudden tension in the boy's arm indicated something more substantial. A stone? The boy looked down at it, then up into the shadow. He smiled, and nodded. Who was he talking to? The need to know the identity of the person hidden in shadow became almost overpowering, and it was only with great effort that she remained standing where she was. As quickly as Peter's encounter had begun, it was over, and the boy darted out onto the pavement, jogged along the street, and disappeared up Lake Drive.

Andrea released her breath with a whistle. Her skin felt cold and clammy. She found herself staring at the space between the two stores, trying to fathom the shadows. The more she stared, the deeper they became, until her mind produced swirls of movement. She shook her head and lowered her eyes. When she looked up again, something glinted in the depths of the alley.

The ring?

No. It had been too high for that.

Eyes, then.

Yes, eyes. Again, a chill gripped her, and she became certain that whoever, or whatever, cowered in that alley was at this minute studying her. She felt the power of that imagined gaze as if she were being physically handled, and in a moment she began to tremble. She felt frozen to the spot, like a rabbit caught in the headlights of a speeding car, powerless to move.

Overhead, a passing crow cawed noisily, pulling her from the trance.

It was over. Just like that. She slumped as if exhausted. Heart pounding, palms sweaty, she moved quickly across the street toward Lake Drive, and did not look back. All warmth had drained from the air. It was only as the trees surrounded her, rustling golds and browns, that she comprehended the feeling that had come over her.

She felt as if she had escaped, just barely, a terrible calamity.

Deirdre Farrell leaned against the cool alley wall. Sweat beaded her forehead and trickled down her back, between her breasts. Her heart was still pounding.

Peter had taken the stone. The boy, as usual, was eager to learn, eager to advance. He was young and inexperienced, but still he frightened her. In her whole life, she had never before encountered a male who lived within the craft. Their rarity was legend. And Peter Willson, though he did not yet know it, was powerful. Given time, he would have become a force to be reckoned with. Fortunately, his time was quickly running out.

The stone was the next step. With it, he could focus and refine his talent. That was what she had told him. It had not been a lie. What she had not told him was that Longshadow could reach him through the stone. Already the boy had performed tasks that would keep him silent. To speak would be to incriminate himself.

She smiled at the thought. The Woerloga would be pleased that the transfer had gone so smoothly. Another tie with which to bind. What he would not appreciate, however, was that the boy's mother had been a witness.

Deirdre clasped her hands tightly, squeezing her long nails into her palms. After the boy had gone, she had turned to see Andrea Willson standing under the oak tree, staring into the alley. Fear had gripped Deirdre like a huge fist, and Longshadow's warnings had clamored in her mind.

Beware the woman! She will protect the boy.

Standing there, concealed in shadow, she had felt Andrea Willson's eyes probing, searching for her. She had muttered a spell of protection, but still the woman had stared at her, as if she could see through shadow itself to find her.

Finally, the spell had worked, and Andrea Willson had fled. But she had seen! She knew now that the boy had the stone. Would she interfere?

Surely, Longshadow could stop her. Surely the Woerloga was powerful enough for that!

She remained in the alley a few minutes longer, pressed against the wall. She closed her eyes. Above, one of her crows circled lazily, cawing for her attention. She looked up at it.

"Go, special friend, tell the Woerloga."

The bird cawed and swung out of view as it moved over the forest.

Deirdre drew a deep breath. She closed her eyes again, allowing her mind to drift. She sensed the living forest around her, sensed the presence that now stalked it, sensed the terrible impatience of the creature.

The taking of Jack and Willy Burgess had given him the foothold he needed. She had worked hard to convince Doreen Burgess that the sacrifice was a necessity. Longshadow, unfortunately, had been too eager. He had taken both men. It was going to be difficult explaining that to Doreen.

She focused on an image of the blue mist, the cloak he would soon be able to shuck.

Be patient, Woerloga, be patient. The boy is progressing nicely. Soon he will be yours.

In her mind, the mist swirled and rose to form a manlike shape. She opened her eyes before she could see more. She did not need her imagination to add menace to Longshadow's presence. He could do that very nicely by himself.

She thought, again, of the boy's mother. *Interfering bitch.* She hoped the Woerloga would allow her the privilege of destroying the woman. That, she thought, would be a pleasure to savor.

Smiling, she stepped from the dark alley into the sunny circle.

By the time she reached the house, Andrea was shaking badly. She hardly managed to keep a hold on the bag of groceries. She found Peter in the kitchen, sitting at the table with a glass of milk, a sandwich, and a paperback. He looked up as she entered, smiling warmly. She placed the groceries on the counter, and hugged herself to stop her trembling. Peter frowned, his face etched with concern.

"You don't look so good, Andrea."

She swallowed hard. "Just hungry, I guess."

Peter raised his eyebrows. "You should eat," he said.

She nodded, and turned away from his dark eyes. For a moment his gaze had pinned her, making her feel as she had felt in the town circle.

I can't let this sit, she thought. *I have to bring it out in the open.*

With trembling hands she began to put away some of the groceries, and without turning to face Peter, she said, "I saw you while I was in town."

Behind her she heard Peter move. The silence was intense. "Oh, yes?" Something had happened to his voice. There was a tone of reticence, extreme caution, she had never heard before.

"No school today?"

"I wasn't feeling well this morning," he said. "Dad knows."

She forced herself to keep going. "Who were you talking to in town?"

Peter did not reply. After a few seconds Andrea made herself turn around. The boy was staring at her, his brow furrowed. He looked, she thought, as if he were struggling with a problem, or perhaps arguing with an inner demon.

At last he shrugged. "I didn't see anybody," he said. He raised the glass of milk and sipped slowly, his eyes never leaving her face.

"But I saw you. They gave you something."

He blinked, placing the glass carefully on the table. With a tone of levity that was patently false, he grinned and said, "Couldn't have been me."

The lie rose between them like something solid, something living. The dynamics of their relationship shifted suddenly, changed tracks, and Andrea felt it physically jolt her. Peter remained motionless, his eyes fastened on her. She found herself laughing lightly, hardly believing the sound. "Don't lie to me, Peter. I saw you."

Peter jumped to his feet. His knees knocked the table. Milk spilled. The glass fell and shattered, and she flinched at the sound. The boy moved toward her. Even at thirteen he was nearly her height. His shoulders hunched, and his eyes narrowed. The constriction of anger on his face made him look much older, almost like Matthew.

She pushed back against the counter, gripping the edge fiercely. Fear, sharp and eager, mounted within her.

But Peter stopped short of her, and only stared.

69

He spun on his heel and grabbed his jacket from the back of the chair. He pulled the sliding door so hard that it rattled ominously in its frame. Stunned, mouth agape, Andrea watched the boy kick a pile of leaves into furious life, then march resolutely into the paths beyond the yard. In a moment he disappeared from sight.

A gust of wind sent leaves skittering through the open door, into the kitchen. The sound of their scrabbling snapped her out of her trance, and everything hit her at once. The trembling that she had managed to control up to now suddenly intensified, and a feeling of desperation engulfed her.

She closed the sliding door, then stumbled through to the living room and collapsed onto the sofa. There, though she tried not to, she sobbed herself into sleep.

PART II

Changes

CHAPTER EIGHT

Andrea woke to find the living room window growing darker. The nap seemed to have helped. The sense of hopelessness that had gripped her in huge clumsy fingers was now gone, or at the very least had receded to a manageable distance. She marched resolutely upstairs and opened Peter's bedroom door. The boy was not yet home.

Let him stay out all night. The moment she thought it, she felt a stab of guilt. *That was unmotherly.* With lips pursed thoughtfully, she closed his door.

In the bathroom she gave herself a slow, thorough inspection. She rubbed sleep from her eyes, combed her hair, splashed cold water in her face, and brushed her teeth.

By the time Matthew got home, she had composed herself fully. She had decided not to mention the incident with Peter. It was something she had to deal with herself, between her and the boy. Otherwise they would never get back to a normal relationship.

She greeted Matthew with a long kiss.

"That's worth coming home to!"

"It's worth waiting at home for." She pulled his face to hers for another kiss.

After a few moments Matthew disengaged. "Are we alone?"

She stiffened. Had he somehow sensed what had transpired between her and Peter? She nodded too quickly,

73

but Matthew, thank goodness, didn't seem to notice. He grinned and kissed her again, this time bringing his hand between them and cupping her breast. The movement was so natural, so unexpected, that she had no time to withdraw. Her mouth opened to him, and she pressed the length of her body against him. A wave of desire rushed through her, leaving her breathless and dizzy. She managed to bring up her forearm and pried some distance between them.

"What?" he asked innocently.

"Peter might come home any minute," she said breathlessly.

"He's a big boy. He could be out for a while yet."

He reached for her again, and this time there was no denying him. His arms crushed her to him, and his mouth was on her neck, moving lower. Her desire mounted, and her legs trembled beneath her. Only Matthew's arms kept her upright.

How long has it been since we made love?

They had not spoken of their abstinence, not since before Matthew and Peter had left Minneapolis. There had been an understanding between them. *When it happens again, it happens, we won't push it.*

Well, Andrea thought giddily, it's happening now.

She was not sure how they moved from the foyer to the stairs, or how Matthew managed to maneuver them up to the second floor; she was aware only of his nearness, his hands, his mouth, the words he whispered in her ear alternately coarse and loving. When her shoulder bumped into the door frame of the bedroom, she hardly felt it. Matthew edged sideways to push her through.

Her will, her thoughts, disappeared into a glow of need and desire. At one point, as Matthew moved above her, inside her, smooth muscles rippling across his back and shoulders, she found herself focusing on a single coherent thought: *Why did we allow it to drag on so long?* The answers seemed thoroughly inadequate.

The climax banished all thought. She helplessly buried

her face in the crux of Matthew's neck.

Afterward, limbs entangled, face to face, Matthew stroked a familiar pattern on her lower back and buttocks. The cumulative effect of his touches was a feeling of security and serenity she had not experienced in a long, long time. She gazed into his eyes, and finally became disconcerted when it became obvious he was gazing right back.

"What is it?" she said at last.

His naturally stern look softened. "Just thinking about how much I need you. Trying not to think about what I'd do without you. Thinking how damned lucky I am you didn't pack up and leave me."

Although startled, she tried not to show it. Matthew did not often express his emotions. In a moment he grinned, pulled her face close and kissed her firmly on the lips, then swung his legs out of bed.

"That made me hungry."

"I'll make something."

"I'm game for spaghetti." He raised his eyebrows. "You?"

She chuckled wryly. Spaghetti was the one meal Matthew could prepare with even a small degree of proficiency. To refuse the offer would be tantamount to turning away from the only break from cooking she was ever likely to get.

"Spaghetti sounds great."

Peter came home after dinner and climbed upstairs to his room without a word. Matthew turned to watch the boy, surprised. Andrea listened for the closing of his door, and sighed with relief when she heard it.

"He must have had a bad day at school," Matthew said.

Andrea blinked. So Peter had lied about that too. Matthew did not know that the boy had missed school. She looked down at the book in her lap and said nothing.

Peter did not emerge from his room through the

remainder of the evening, and for this small blessing she gave silent thanks. She had no wish to experience the almost physical *coldness* that had grown between her and her stepson. She and Matthew waffled between reading, watching television, dozing off, and gazing into each other's eyes. She could not remember the last time they had spent such a relaxing and, to her, satisfying time together. It was nearly 11 P.M. when they turned off the downstairs lights and climbed slowly up to bed.

She was not sleepy, and neither, apparently, was Matthew. As soft moonlight angled through the east-facing window, casting faint shadows on the floor and walls, he made love to her again. This time it was slow, almost sleepy. His words were mumbled, hardly intelligible; his motions easy, liquid; her responses in kind. In contrast to the earlier roller coaster of passion, this was a leisurely ride in the country. Andrea felt herself suffused with waves of pleasure, engulfed by the sensations of Matthew on top of her, and by the sensations he excited within her, smothered by his strong presence. When, at last, the climax came, it was a slow, rising tide that seemed to go on forever. It left them both shaking and trembling in each other's arms.

"I love you, Andrea," Matthew said when they had parted.

She kissed him gently on the lips, unable to speak. She felt choked with emotion, and with relief. With Matthew, at least, her relationship was returning to normal.

As usual, trying to polish his veneer as the "sensitive modern man," he attempted to engage her in meaningless and sometimes absolutely ridiculous conversation. Against her better judgment, but feeling that the time would never be more right, she brought up the subject of Peter.

"Do you think Peter is changing, Matt?"

He drew a deep breath. "Changing how?" He snuggled into the pillow.

"I don't know. He seems to be really involved in himself

76

these days."

"He's thirteen. All thirteen-year-olds are involved in themselves. Hell, if you want to talk about physical changes, there are probably more of them at that stage of life than could be induced with megadoses of radiation."

"Thanks for the lecture on puberty. But that's not what I meant."

He blinked, suddenly more attentive. "Are you and Peter having problems?"

She stopped breathing for a moment, the temptation to tell him everything fading fast. The tone of his voice had not seemed to indicate receptiveness to such news. She pursed her lips and shook her head. "No, it's just that he takes a lot of walks by himself. He just doesn't seem like the same happy-go-lucky Pete."

Satisfied, Matthew yawned and closed his eyes. "Well, that's growing up, isn't it?"

She sighed and said nothing more. Matthew continued to chatter for a while, but soon was snoring. She felt relieved. She feared that, if she talked any longer about Peter, Matthew would really begin to suspect something was amiss with his family.

After half an hour of listening to Matthew snore, she realized that her afternoon nap had effectively ruined the night for sleeping. Reluctantly, she pushed the blankets aside and rose. In nightgown and slippers she stepped into the hallway.

She had taken three steps toward the top of the stairs when she paused. Light leaked from beneath Peter's closed door. She could not remember him ever having slept with a light on before, and she frowned as she stared at the thin slat. In a moment she realized that the light was not quite right, that it was, in fact, a luminescent mist. Cold fingers traced circles at the base of her spine, and she shuddered.

Almost involuntarily she stepped toward Peter's bedroom. The metal of the doorknob was cold to the touch, much colder than the surrounding air.

She turned the handle and pushed open the door. A thin

77

mist covered the floor. It seemed to have entered through the partially opened window. She could see the walls of trees beyond the glass, the mist caressing their trunks. The explanation, of course was simple. The day had been warmer than she had originally thought, and the night had cooled quickly. The result, quite naturally, was mist. More of a fog, really. The bluish aura was from the moon hanging over the house.

She laughed nervously. Peter lay on his back, breathing deeply, oblivious to the eerie atmosphere of his room. He had not yet developed Matthew's full-fledged snore, but that would come soon enough, she expected. His lips sputtered at each exhalation, his eyebrows twitching in a dream. Seeing him so, she was struck by his boyishness, and felt immediately guilty at her earlier unmotherly thoughts.

Just a boy, confused about puberty, and I blew up at him. Then, surprising herself: *He needs a mother to take care of him.*

As if on cue, Peter groaned, rolled over, and pushed the sheet off his shoulder. She moved toward the bed. Mist swirled around her feet. She shivered at the coldness of it. She pulled the blanket up to his neck and covered him. Peter sighed, as if even in sleep he appreciated the attention.

She gently stroked his hair. *I'm sorry about this afternoon, Peter, really I am. We can work it out, I know we can.*

He sighed agreeably. She stepped away from the bed and moved to the window, sending the carpet of mist into swirling turmoil. The view outside was beautiful, in an eerie sort of way. Mist stretched into the trees and rose to form a blue wall, as if reaching for the light of the moon.

At first she thought she had caught sight of her own reflection in the dark glass, but as the mist swirled outside, she froze. For an instant, less than a second, she was staring into a bloody, ragged face. Except the face wasn't there. Only strips of what looked like skin, bloody and moist, hanging over an invisible bust. She could see trees through

78

the outline. In the brief insanity of the moment she found herself focusing on one of the strips of skin, at a small mole bristling with hairs. Her flesh crawled, and she stumbled back, almost tripping over her nightgown. The sound that emerged from her throat was close to a scream, but quickly aborted.

Outside, mist swirled, rose, and enveloped the horrific countenance. She blinked, and it was gone, leaving only her reflection in the glass. Even as she watched, the mist seemed to withdraw, sliding back into the trees, like a genie sucked back into its bottle. Within the space of ten breaths, the yard was clear, the trees fully visible.

Behind her, Peter coughed. The sound startled her, and she spun. The boy continued to sleep, unaware of her presence, or of the presence outside.

What presence? There was nothing there. You imagined it.

She shook her head and tried to stop her trembling, realizing she was spooking herself. But the feeling would not go away.

Then, in a flash of horrible understanding: *Peter didn't leave his window open. That thing outside opened it.*

This fantastic suspicion turned to hard certainty as she entertained it, and she could not rid herself of it. The thing outside had been staring at Peter. She had surprised it.

Don't be ridiculous. This is the second floor. What was it standing on?

But logic had no sway with her. She shook her head, trying to enforce a degree of calmness upon her jittering nerves. She quietly moved from the room, closing the door behind her. The night was playing tricks, that's all it was. In the hallway, she drew a deep breath and released it in a hiss. The house, she suddenly decided, was too dark.

She moved quickly downstairs and turned on all the lights. In the kitchen, she put on a kettle of water to boil, then prepared a pot of tea. Afterward, she drank it hungrily, cradling the mug like a freezing man holding a warm coal. She burned her mouth with the deepness of her draughts, but did not care. Even after the hot liquid had cured her shivers; even after an hour of sitting in silence had begun to make her drowsy; even after she had repeated a hundred times that it had been her imagination and that she had seen nothing but swirling mist; she could not shake the feeling: she had inadvertently stumbled into something unspeakable.

CHAPTER NINE

Matthew woke before dawn. His sleep had been full of nightmares, and he was glad to be free of them. Beside him, Andrea continued to sleep. She had rolled onto her left side, as usual, and now lay with her hand curled loosely beneath her chin. Dark hair tangled on the pillow. The natural pose imbued her with an aura of childlike vulnerability; he had to resist the urge to stroke her face.

He rose quickly, showered, dressed, and ate a Spartan breakfast. Outside, he paused by the cruiser and took a deep breath of the morning air. Cool, fragrant. He opened the driver's door, prepared to slide in, then paused. His eyes had been drawn to movement behind the house, and he supported himself on the edge of the door to get a better look. Faint wisps of morning mist coiled through the grass. An eddy of vapor, like spilled silver dust spurred by the wind, drew his attention. He realized his stomach muscles had tensed sharply, and now relaxed them, released his breath in a hiss.

"You're spooked," he accused himself. It was the damned dreams he'd had last night, still clinging to him.

The mist continued to coil. Likely it would dissipate by the time the sun was fully risen. He sucked a deep breath, slid behind the wheel, and started the car. Traces of nightmare flashed across his mind, images seen in the shards of a smashed mirror. Peter's face. Andrea. Mist, mist. Blue mist. A hand dripping blood.

81

He found that he was shaking, and gripped the wheel tightly.

The mist had reminded him of his dreams, that was all. He remembered them clearly now.

Mist. Mist everywhere. And something in the mist. Something old and unseen, searching for him, seeking his family.

He stepped on the gas, calmed by the roar of the engine. Without looking back he threw the transmission into gear and depressed the accelerator. The tires spun on the dew-slicked gravel. He tried to keep his mind blank as he drove into the town circle.

The Marissa Township Police Station was a non-descript square, one-story red brick building, hunkered in the shadow of roadside trees just outside the town circle on the road to State 210. It was the only building in Marissa that looked even remotely official, and although ancient by the more refined tastes of urban architecture, it was the herald of Marissa's foot-dragging march into the future. This morning, lights beamed through the front glass door, and from the windows. Murray's car was parked poorly in its space, and Matthew was forced to park at an odd angle.

He checked his watch in disbelief. Not yet 7 A.M. During the month and a half he'd been here, this was the first time Murray had beaten him to the station. He had grown accustomed to spending the first couple of hours of every day alone, a time he had devoted to working his way through Marissa's past police records. Thinking about having to face Murray this early cast a shadow over an already disturbing morning, but he forced the sour expression from his face as he entered the building.

The reception area was empty, but a cigarette on the reception counter spilled coils of smoke into the air. He shook his head in disgust and moved to his desk. He had barely seated himself when Murray came through the door from the back room. The sound of the toilet flushing followed him like an aftershock. His wide face had a freshly scrubbed look. His hair was combed back into a wet sheen. Sporadic globs of shaving foam littered his neck and the open collar of his shirt.

"Morning, Matt. Wasn't expecting you this early." Murray fumbled with his collar button. He moved directly to the front counter and flipped the cigarette into his mouth.

Matthew forced himself to be civil. "Good morning, Murray." He refrained from pointing out that he was *always* in this early.

His lack of patience for slothful cops was a throwback to his first year as a metro-Minneapolis constable, when he'd been partnered with a veteran named Frank Vernon, who filled the bill for *Pig!* in every respect. A year with Frank had turned Matthew, on the job anyway, into a fastidious neatnick. He knew he pissed nearly everybody off at one point or another, even Andrea on odd occasions.

"I would have called you soon, anyway."

Matthew, in the process of opening up a drawer to retrieve the file he had been reading yesterday, paused and listened more carefully. Murray sounded more serious than usual.

"What's up?"

Murray drew on his cigarette, exhaled a cloud of smoke, crushed it out in the ashtray by his elbow, then fumbled for the pack in his shirt pocket for another. After lighting it he moved to his desk and sat down.

"Do you know Jack Burgess?"

Matthew paused before shaking his head. The name sounded vaguely familiar, and yet he could not place it.

Murray grinned, drew on his cigarette, and flicked ash on the floor. "You will, buddy, you will. If every town has its troublemaker, then he's ours. Him and that shitbag son of his, Willy." Murray shook his head in disgust.

"What about them?" Matthew asked.

"His wife called me this morning," Murray said. He shook his head, as if contemplating a distasteful memory. "More like last night," he amended. "Half in tears, half pissed off, just the way I'd be if I lived with Jack Burgess."

"Will you get to the point," Matthew said impatiently.

Murray regarded him speculatively, then grinned. "Matt, I can see you're itchy for some action. Small-town life too slow for you?"

Matthew sighed, but said nothing. Murray would get it out eventually. No sense pushing him.

"Anyway, she called me. Jack and Willy are missing. Went hunting last Sunday, supposed to be back yesterday. No sign of them."

Matthew blinked, his mind clicking into gear. "Hunting for what? Marissa's a restricted zone."

Murray sighed. "Hell, I know it. We'll deal with that when we find them. Point is, they wandered off into the woods, and they haven't come back yet."

Again, Matthew sensed his brain shifting gears, as if up to now he had not been fully awake. The names had sounded familiar, and now they registered. "This isn't the same Willy and Jack Burgess questioned in a hunting accident a few years back, is it?"

Murray's eyes widened. "How did you know about that? You've been reading the files." He chuckled. "Christ, you're dedicated." He shook his head, drew on his cigarette, and exhaled a plume of smoke. "Almost the same, not quite. *A few years back* was twenty-five years ago. Before my time. Jack was the son back then, William the father. Old Willy Burgess found a body in the woods, shot twice. Probably murder, but no way to prove it. Jacky corroborated his dad's story. Now Jack's got his own boy. Willy's not as bad as Jack used to be, but he's damn close if you ask me."

"Do we call in the state police?"

"Jesus, Matt! If we waited for those assholes, we'd never get anything done. We can handle this. Jack and Willy are probably holed up, shit-faced drunk. No sense wasting state time on stuff like that. We'll talk to Doreen Burgess first, take it from there."

Matthew nodded, a tingle of anticipation mounting in his guts. The strangeness of the day's beginning had receded, wiped out by this news. He hoped Jack and Willy Burgess were safe, that they were, as Murray suspected, holed up somewhere and shit-faced drunk. Still, the prospect of doing some real work was exciting, and he found himself smiling.

The interview of Doreen Burgess did not go well. The woman was distraught, hardly able to speak coherently. Her appearance was disheveled, her face swollen from crying, her hair a black tangle. Even under better circumstances, Matthew imagined she would look rather harried.

"They've been gone *too* long," she kept repeating. "There's something wrong. They're *both* gone."

Matthew was struck by a facial similarity between this woman and Andrea, something in the bones. He wondered if Andrea would end up looking like this, but could not imagine it. Andrea took good care of herself physically. Somewhere along the line, Doreen Burgess had let herself go. In the end, she was not able to tell them much more than Murray already knew.

Back in the car, Murray lit a cigarette and opened his window to release the smoke. "Poor bitch," he said to Matthew. "I wouldn't be surprised if they just ran out on her. Hell, I would."

Matthew ignored the comment. "What's next?"

Murray turned to him and grinned. "You got better shoes than that, Matt?" He nodded disdainfully at the polished black leather beat shoes Matthew had brought with him from Minneapolis.

"I've got boots in the other car," he said.

"Good. You'll need them. We're going to do a little rough walking today." He took a final deep drag from the cigarette and flicked the remainder out the window. He turned the ignition and squealed the tires as he pulled from the shoulder onto the road.

Back at the station, while Murray added a few items to an already prepared pack, Matthew laced up his hiking boots. It was obvious that Murray had planned this jaunt last night. So why hadn't he phoned? Why keep it a secret? He swallowed his resentment.

"You want to phone Andrea and let her know we'll be gone for a while?"

Matthew did not like the condescending look in Murray's eyes. "We'll be back in good time," he said.

"Probably. But she seems a bit skittish. Wouldn't want her panicking, calling in the troops or anything like that."

Matthew's hackles rose. He stared intently down at his boot laces to stop himself from snapping back. He counted to ten, then looked up at Murray. Murray was smirking, his eyes speculative. *Son of a bitch is goading me intentionally*, Matthew thought.

"Andrea's okay," he said. "It takes a while to get used to Marissa."

Apparently realizing he was treading on thin ice, Murray did not pursue the matter. He grunted and moved to the rifle rack behind his desk. He unlocked it and removed two Winchesters. He tossed one to Matthew.

Matthew caught it, then hefted it warily. "You think we'll need these?"

"Wild animals, buddy," Murray said, jacking the finger lever and inspecting the empty chamber. "Don't want to get eaten alive, do you?"

Matthew conceded silently that he did not.

They took Murray's car again and drove south on the county road toward State 210. This stretch of road, the ten miles between the town and the highway, was the loneliest Matthew had ever driven. The trees seemed to close in from both sides, a crushing mass of dying leaves. He had driven this way many times during the past six weeks, and still did not like it.

Five miles before the highway, Murray slowed the car and turned east onto a small rutted track that Matthew had not even been aware of. He slowed considerably, but kept the car at a constant speed. The road meandered crazily through the trees, rising and falling with the land. At times it turned into pure mud.

"There's a trick to driving roads like this," Murray said without looking at Matthew. "You'll get it eventually. You keep a car moving, slow but even, nothing will stop her. Nothing. Getting stuck is all in the mind. Fuck this four-wheel drive shit."

"Shouldn't we have started looking up at the lake lodge?" Matthew asked, trying to get off the subject of cars and driving.

"Only the tourists start hunting there, Matt. This is a local spot. If Jack and Willy went hunting, they went this way."

Although they traveled along the muddy road no more than a mile, perhaps a mile and a half, it seemed to take forever. When, at last, it opened into a raised clearing, Matthew heaved a sigh of relief. Parked to their left, front bumper pushed into a bank of bushes, was a blue half-ton.

"That's Jack Burgess's truck," Murray said.

He parked beside it. Both men got out. Matthew peered into the cab. The seat and floor were littered with crushed beer cans. The key was still in the ignition.

Murray bent down and raked around on the ground. He stood up a moment later, red-faced, and held something out to Matthew. It was a spent .30-.30 cartridge. The ground, Matthew saw, was littered with them.

"Our boys are out for some fun," Murray said. He walked back to the car. "Might as well get on with this."

By the time they were actually set to step out of the clearing and into the woods, it was close to 11:30 A.M., and Matthew wished he had taken the trouble to phone Andrea. He had not thought they would get started this late. To have given in to Murray's teasing was childish.

Murray activated the car radio and spoke into the mike. "You there, Fiona?"

In a few moments, Fiona Campbell's voice piped through. "What do you want, Murray?"

"Matthew and I are taking a walk down at Oddball. Looking for Jack and Willy. Might be gone for a while."

"Let me know when you get back."

Murray glanced at Matthew, his lips curled in a smile.

He picked up the mike again and held it to his mouth. "You still there, Fiona?"

"What is it, Murray?"

"Give Matthew's wife a call, will you? Let her know he might not be home for supper."

"Will do," Fiona said.

"Thanks," Matthew said sheepishly.

Murray laughed and picked up his rifle. "Come on, buddy, let's hunt."

CHAPTER TEN

Andrea woke to the ringing of the phone. She blinked and stared at the ceiling. The bedroom was bright with daylight, and for a moment she felt confusion. How long had she slept? Why hadn't Matthew wakened her? Then the memories came back. Peter's room. The mist. The face outside. She hadn't returned to bed until nearly 5:30 A.M.

The phone rang two more times before she reached across Matthew's empty side of the bed to answer it. It was Fiona Campbell, the switchboard operator, who had phoned to tell her that Matthew and Murray were searching for a couple of missing hunters in a place called Oddball Trail. Questions filled her mind, ready to burst out, but she held her tongue in check.

Don't act like a worried housewife. Not in front of these people.

After hanging up, she felt fully awake. The clock radio read 12:30, and she shook her head in disgust. Tonight would be worse than the last, she thought. If she continued in this pattern, she would never get back onto a regular sleeping-waking schedule.

She rose, showered, dressed in jeans and a comfortable sweater, and went downstairs. Peter, of course, was nowhere to be found. Today, at least, was Saturday, and she would not have to worry about him missing school. She made a pot of coffee, waited for it to brew, then sat down at the kitchen table with a mugful. Outside, leaves fell in a constant rain from the trees, piling thickly on the ground. She sipped the coffee, savoring the strong taste of the dark liquid. Against her will, she found herself examining a memory of the previous night. Even in memory, the blue mist seemed to have the power to chill her. Had she really seen something hovering at Peter's window, staring in at the boy?

Common sense proclaimed loudly and clearly that she had not. But a deeper sense, not at all common, rooted in the dark recesses of her subconscious, affirmed her suspicions. She had seen what she had seen.

The house suddenly seemed far too large, far too silent, as if the wooden beams and panes of glass were, themselves, waiting for something to happen. She finished her coffee quickly. She suddenly felt the need to get out of the house, to walk in open space and fresh air.

Although six cups remained in the pot of coffee, she turned it off, grabbed a light coat from the hall cupboard, and went out.

By the time she reached the town circle, she was feeling better, clear-headed. The cool, fresh air on her cheeks, the sun shining through gaps in the clouds, refreshed her, banishing the dark thoughts she had entertained at home.

At Robertson's Food Market she paused, but did not enter. The market was crowded. She watched through the front window as Barbara Robertson rang through a basket of groceries. Her face was a mask of passivity, but in her eyes Andrea sensed a deep sense of loss and despair. *For a cat,* she found herself thinking, almost incredulously. Her first instinct was to enter the store, to reach out to the other woman, to provide support, and on any other day, she told herself, she would willingly offer such succour. Today, however, she could not. Her own emotional state was too fragile. Within minutes both she and Barbara Robertson would be in tears. Support like that you could get from enemies!

"Andrea!"

She spun on her heel. Aunt Clarissa waved at her from across the circle. Andrea felt her smile tighten and raised her arm to wave back. *You've avoided her up to now, but you can't keep doing that.*

Clarissa darted into the street without looking, her green rain coat flapping behind her. Andrea forced the smile on her face to become more natural.

"My dear, I haven't seen you all week! I hoped you'd come and visit, but I knew you'd be busy settling in, and I didn't want to bother you, but I had *so* hoped we could get together for tea and pastries, and King, too, my dear, has been asking for you. Once he latches on to a person, he never wants to let go."

Andrea found herself smiling despite herself. There was something so forthright about Clarissa, that her usual personal defenses crumbled. Was it possible that the threat, or warning, she had heard in Clarissa's words during their first meeting had been simply the concern of a slightly eccentric great aunt?

"I've been meaning to come and visit, but it's been hectic . . ."

"Of course, of course, my dear! No need to explain to me. I know what moving is like. I've never done it, you understand, but I can imagine what it must be like. Uprooting oneself from familiar soil, then being transplanted to an alien place. Oh, yes, I can imagine it very well. And Peter has told me how difficult it has been for you, adjusting to life here in Marissa. I don't expect you feel comfortable even yet, dear. Not to worry. Such things take time."

Andrea felt the smile slide from her face and could not get it to return. "Peter has been seeing you?"

Clarissa, who had snaked her arm through Andrea's and was pulling her along the pavement, suddenly stopped, realizing she may have said something wrong. She turned to Andrea, whose brown eyes were wide and questioning.

"Why, yes, my dear, he comes to visit. He walks, you know, and it's nothing to drop by for a chat."

Andrea remembered how Peter had been the last time

they had visited Clarissa's together. *"How long do we have to stay?"* She could not imagine the boy visiting alone.

"It's just that Matthew and I hardly see Peter at all anymore," she said, and realized she had let some of her confused emotions slip into the words. She smiled to try and hide it.

But Clarissa had noticed, and her eyes narrowed speculatively. "Come, my dear. Walk with me. We shall talk."

Andrea had no will to argue. She allowed herself to be dragged along, almost glad to have somebody leading her. When Clarissa stopped outside a small storefront, Andrea, unquestioning, stopped with her.

"Would you mind if I dropped in for just a moment, dear? Then we'll walk to my house and I'll make us some tea and we shall talk. A ladies afternoon!"

Andrea glanced up at the hand-carved wooden sign.

CRAFT SHOP
GIFTS

"Should I come in with you?"

"I shall only be a moment."

She was not sure whether this was an affirmative answer or not, but she followed Clarissa into the dimly lit interior anyway. She blinked as she entered the shop, forcing her eyes to grow accustomed to the dim lighting. She closed the door behind her. A bell above the door tinkled sweetly. The air smelled of tanned leather and potted plants. Clarissa moved immediately to an inner doorway hung with a bead partition, parted the strings with her hand, and pushed through it. Andrea, left alone, glanced curiously around the shop. There were postcards, fishing plaques, all sorts of leather goods including belts, ties, and purses. All were decorated in intricate designs cut into the hide.

She moved to the counter and bent to study a display of stone broaches. Like the leather craft, the stones were inscribed with various patterns. She could hear soft voices from behind the bead partition, but could not pick out the words. She recognized Clarissa's voice. Why, she wondered, would Clarissa come to what was obviously a tourist den?

She reached out to touch one of the broaches, stroking its surface with the tip of her finger. The stone was cool, yet the inscribed pattern felt warm. A pleasant tingle moved up her arm. This disconcerting effect caused her to smile, and then to giggle softly.

"Beautiful," she whispered.

Behind her, beads rustled, and Andrea spun around, feeling guilty at her furtive poking.

"Yes, they are beautiful, aren't they?"

A shape pushed out of the beads and moved toward her, coalescing into the image of an old woman. Her narrow face was pinched into an expression that might have been pleasure, or might have been suspicion. Small eyes, black as obsidian, glittered in a roadmap face. A long, dark coat hung down to a point somewhere between knees and floor, giving her body more bulk than it deserved.

"I . . . I was just looking," Andrea said, as if she had been caught stealing.

"Yes, of course you were."

She moved closer to Andrea, and the dubious expression turned into one of definite pleasure. Andrea sighed with relief, troubled at her own reactions more than anything else.

"I've never seen broaches like these," Andrea said.

The black eyes studied her, glinting like wet steel. "They are charms, my dear, not broaches."

"Oh."

Again, she felt uncomfortable. The old woman stepped past her and reached out a wrinkled hand to touch one of the charms. "These are our pride and joy. You should really have one."

Andrea did not know what to say. The old woman turned, lifted her hand to her throat, and parted the dark coat. Against her chicken neck, Andrea saw the charm. The long fingers stroked it.

93

But Andrea's eyes were drawn to something else. To the large ring on one of the bony fingers. She felt her heart skip a beat, felt cold sweat pop on her shoulders and neck.

She had seen that ring before. For a moment she was transported back to yesterday, and was staring at Peter in the gap between two buildings. As if reliving the experience, she watched him reach out, watched the ancient hand lower and place something in his. The ring glinted in a shaft of sunlight. *This ring.*

Andrea gasped, stepped back, and raised her eyes to the other woman's face. The black eyes twinkled, as if realizing some sort of recognition had taken place.

"You really should have a charm," she said.

Her voice was soft, almost a caress. Andrea felt gripped by a chill, her knees wobbling.

Then the old woman stepped past her, toward the door. The bell tinkled at her exit, the door closed, and Andrea was once again alone.

The beads rustled, and she spun. It was only Clarissa, this time accompanied by a smaller woman who carried a plain brown bag to the cash register.

"My dear, you looked positively ill!" Clarissa's voice was sharp with concern.

"Who was that who just left?"

Clarissa blinked.

"An older woman," Andrea said, raising her hand, "wearing a ring."

"Do you know her?" Clarissa asked carefully.

"Who was it?" Andrea insisted, panic edging into her voice.

Clarissa stepped close to her, steadying her with a strong hand. "No one you need concern yourself with, dear. An old hag. She . . ."

Andrea jerked her arm free. "Who was she?"

This time there was no denying her. Clarissa sighed. "Well, if you must know, her name is Deirdre Farrell. A terrible gossip. If there's one person in this town you *don't* want to know, it's her."

Andrea turned away and stared outside into the town

94

circle. Deirdre Farrell was gone.

Behind her, the shopkeeper was speaking to Clarissa. "Will that be all?"

She heard a mumbled reply, and in a moment Clarissa was holding her elbow again, speaking softly. "Come, my dear, you need some tea."

Andrea allowed herself to be led outside, but once on the pavement she disengaged from Clarissa's helping hand.

"I'm sorry, Clarissa. I can't this afternoon. Perhaps tomorrow."

Taken aback, Clarissa stepped away. But there was no hurt in her eyes. Only concern. "My dear, if I've said anything . . ."

Andrea smiled, making an attempt to put things right. "It's not you, Clarissa. It's just . . . I can't explain. Please, we'll talk some other time. I promise."

Before Clarissa could respond, she turned away, walking quickly back toward Lake Drive, then toward home.

CHAPTER ELEVEN

Deirdre Farrell paused as she entered East Drive. She turned and peered across the town circle toward the Craft Shop. Andrea Willson was still standing on the pavement, and now Clarissa was beside her. The two women were talking quietly.

"Clarissa, you interfering bitch."

For a moment, Andrea's eyes seemed to pin her, and she stepped back into the cover of the trees by the side of the road. She felt suddenly very angry. Clarissa, the meddling fool, had introduced Andrea to the Craft Shop. An outsider!

Her hands wrung each other, and she exerted conscious effort to stop them. Across the circle, Andrea was walking quickly away from Clarissa, leaving the older woman alone on the pavement.

You are right, Woerloga. She is dangerous.

She shook her head to loosen the feeling. Across the circle, Andrea had stepped into Lake Drive and was now walking toward home.

Deirdre looked up to the sky. Far above, a cluster of small dark shapes circled lazily. She stared at them, concentrating.

Follow her. Watch her.

The sound of a caw drifted down, then one of the birds broke free and swung over the town circle, toward Lake Drive. She watched until it was out of sight, then shuffled toward home.

She walked quickly up the weed-choked path, kicking leaves aside. The front steps sagged beneath her feet and creaked ominously as she climbed them. She tugged at the front door, once, twice, three times before it unstuck itself with a groan and opened.

Her anger exploded in a curse. "You rotting heap!"

The house did not reply. She slammed the door behind her, so hard the windows in the kitchen rattled. She paused, then listened.

Somebody was here.

"Longshadow?"

The house creaked and groaned.

"Cardew Longshadow, are you here?"

She smelled him then. A sudden waft of turned meat. She breathed it deeply, allowed it to surround her, fill her, hardly able to keep the smile off her face. Mist spilled from the living room and rolled across the floor toward her feet. Its touch was cold. It made her shiver. But she did not move. She peered through the doorway. The room seemed full of mist.

"Master, I did not know you were coming."

The mist billowed. And then, without warning, the blue veil parted and he stepped toward her. She blinked, not daring to believe her eyes. The shape that now faced her was not Longshadow, but the boy, Peter Willson. She stepped back, shocked beyond words.

The boy smiled at her.

"It is me," he whispered, and she froze at the sound of his voice.

In a moment, understanding came to her. Her eyes widened. "Have you taken him already? How—"

He raised a hand to his lips for silence, his eyes narrow in anger.

"Do not speak in front of him!"

She clamped her lips. Her eyes could not leave the shape before her. She could see now that Peter Willson was not himself. Over his shoulders hung the now rotting skins of Jack and Willy Burgess. A dead hand swung against his belly. Where his eyes were, two red sparks glowed. As she watched, Peter stepped toward her. The mantle of dead flesh stepped back. The boy and the Woerloga separated.

As the separation completed, Peter's face went slack. The glow departed from his eyes. He stumbled forward, his hands held out for support. She reached out and caught him, then leaned him against the wall. He blinked. Blinked again. Then looked at her, wide-eyed.

"Wow!" His voice was full of wonder.

In the living room, the blue mist billowed. The shape of Longshadow now stood alone, invisible but for the swirling mist about him, the hanging strips of skin.

Peter turned to her, grinning. He gripped her elbow, so tightly that pain shot up through her arm. He didn't seem to notice.

"Wow! He took me places. It was great!" He turned to Longshadow, stepping toward the mist. "Can we do it again? I don't mind, really."

"Later," the Woerloga said softly.

Deirdre frowned. Longshadow had sounded weary.

Peter spun, full of energy. "It was great!"

She nodded, smiling. "Yes, I'm sure it was."

"I would never have believed it, if he hadn't shown me."

"There are many things he will show you."

"When?"

His eagerness was infectious. She found herself grinning. "Soon. Very soon. But for now, you must run home."

"But why?"

"Your stepmother may know about us. She may try to stop what is happening."

"She doesn't know anything. I never said a thing."

"Still, she may interfere."

Peter turned to face Longshadow. The mist swirled. "What should I do?"

"Do as the old woman says."

Again, she sensed a terrible fatigue in his words. Peter turned to her, expectant.

"Run home. Do not be swayed by her."

He stared at her a moment, then nodded abruptly.

After he had gone, she turned back to the Woerloga. The mist was drawing in toward him.

"I thought you had taken him. When I saw—"

He laughed then, a soft sound. "Even had I wanted it, I could not have done so. The pain of flesh. I could not bear it any longer."

She nodded, now understanding. "You must not rush things. Your time will come. You are weak now, but you will soon be strong. Remember, you have not worn flesh in two millenia."

He laughed again, and this time her skin crawled at the sound of it. "I had forgotten how much of a burden it could be."

The mist had drawn even closer around him now, as if he were sucking it in. It surrounded him like a cocoon. In a moment she could not see the cloak of dead skin. Only the two red points of his eyes.

"What about the boy's mother?"

"Watch her. We will deal with her soon. She is dangerous."

The voice seemed to come from far away. As she watched, the mist collapsed upon itself, as if sucked through a hole in the air itself. She blinked, and the house was empty.

"Be patient, master," she said to the empty room. "Be patient, and all things will be yours."

Peter, thankfully, was not home.

Andrea threw off her coat, not even bothering to hang it up. She knew, even before she stepped through the front door, what she planned to do. Still, she could hardly bring herself to follow through. Instead, she went into the kitchen and put on a kettle to boil. Outside, she watched leaves topple from the trees, hypnotized by their twirling descent. After the kettle boiled, she poured the water into the teapot and added a teabag.

Just do it. Get it over with.

She left the tea to brew and slowly climbed the stairs, as if carrying a great weight. At Peter's bedroom door she paused.

My mother used to do this, she thought. *I promised myself I never would, but this is different, this is necessary. . . .*

She forced herself to remain calm as she opened the bedroom door.

Like his father, Peter was obsessively neat. The bed was tightly drawn, the clothes in his cupboard hung up and organized. She started with his chest of drawers, moving from drawer to drawer.

Socks and underwear in the first, nothing else. She left it as neat as she had found it, and moved to the next.

T-shirts, sweats, a single sweater she had not seen him wear in months. She closed the drawer and moved to the next.

By the time she was on the last drawer, she felt ashamed. She had found nothing. Yet she could not stop. Not now. Not after going this far.

She sat on the edge of the bed. Where would he have put it?

On impulse, she kneeled down and checked beneath the bed. She found a shoebox. She pulled it out, placed it on top of the bed, and opened the top carefully.

The stone was inside. Like the charms she had seen in the Craft Shop, it was inscribed with a complex pattern. This one, however, was different. It was larger for one thing, almost the size of her hand. And for another . . .

Curious, she lifted it from the box and turned it slowly.

The charm had three distinct sides. Each side resembled a rough-hewn face. She ran her fingertips over what might have been eye sockets, a mouth. Three faces. The thing felt heavy in her hand. The pattern, like the charms in the shop, felt warm to the touch, as if each line were a vein coursing with blood.

The moment she thought it, she wished she had not. Repulsed, she moved to replace it, and that's when she

100

noticed the other things in the box. A handful of what looked like dirt. A few leaves. Twigs. A gnarled, dirty root, carrotlike in shape.

Frowning, she reached her free hand into the box to touch the root.

And that's when Peter came into the room.

She felt his presence, rather than hearing or seeing him, and before turning her head she knew that he was there. She managed to hide her shock, and immediately moved to the offensive.

She hefted the stone. "You lied to me, Peter. I *did* see you in that alley. This is what you were given."

His hands were stuffed into his pockets, and he leaned nonchalantly against the door. She could not read the expression on his face, and this frightened her. His shoes were mucky, his face slightly flushed. As if he had been running along the paths. And something else. A smell. Something rotten. Her nose wrinkled involuntarily.

She stood, still holding the charm.

"And I know who you were with," she said. Her heart hammered, and she wished she had not invaded his room.

He tensed at this last statement and stood straight. She sensed a new aggressiveness in his stance and involuntarily backed away. His eyes gleamed.

"It was Deirdre Farrell, wasn't it, Peter?"

He stepped toward her, his face impassive. She suddenly felt very frightened. For a moment she flashed back to when Matthew had hit her, and was struck, again, by the similarity between father and son.

"Why didn't you just tell me? What was the big secret? There's nothing wrong with meeting people. But you could have said something. You didn't have to deceive me."

Now he smiled, and she realized, horrified, why. She had backed up against the window frame; there was nowhere else to go.

He stepped up to her, until his face was close to hers. She could not escape his eyes. *He's going to hurt me. Just like Matthew did.*

But Peter only reached out a hand and gently removed the stone charm from her grip. He turned away, placed it carefully in the box, closed the lid, picked up the box, and slid it beneath the bed.

She moved away from the window and stepped beyond the bed toward the door.

Peter stood and came toward her again.

"Peter, I didn't mean to rake through your room. I didn't *want* to, but I was worried about you."

She was suddenly in the hallway, and Peter was standing in the doorway, staring impassively out at her. There was no anger in his face, no resentment, no love . . . nothing.

"For God's sake, say something!"

And he did.

"You're not my mother," he said, softly, almost a whisper, his eyes locked on hers.

Then he closed the door in her face.

CHAPTER TWELVE

In the woods, Matthew developed a new respect for Murray Carlyle. Behind a desk, Murray looked out of place, as if he had forced himself into his clothes. His round face, shaggy hair, and twelve-hour beard did not add up to Matthew's image of the quintessential cop. Murray's presence in the station seemed somehow preposterous, a bad joke carried too far.

But here in the woods, he discovered something else. Murray Carlyle knew what he was doing.

While Matthew picked his way along the rocky trail like a girl hopping through a swamp full of frogs and snakes, Murray moved smoothly, athletically, stepping carefully here, there, never losing purchase, never faltering. Inside an hour, Matthew was exhausted.

"Take a break, Murray," he gasped, slowing, finally leaning against the handy trunk of a crippled tree.

Murray, ten yards ahead, stopped and looked back. His face was flushed with exertion, a slight sheen of sweat on his forehead. He grinned.

"It's good you moved back here when you did, Matt. Look at you!"

Matthew refrained from swearing bitterly. He slowed his breathing, made himself relax and conserve energy.

"I'd like to see you coping with Minneapolis freeways, my friend."

Murray continued to grin, tipping his hat in acknowledgment of the scored point. He pulled the pack from his shoulders, dropped it on the leaf-covered ground, and unzipped it. He pulled out his cigarettes, stuck one in his mouth, and lit it. Somehow, the smell of cigarette smoke amid the forest was pleasant. A statement that men were here, that they were doing civilized things.

"Did you bring water?"

Murray rummaged some more, pulled out a plastic bottle, and tossed it. "Only a mouthful or two, or you'll feel sick."

To hell with sick, Matthew thought. He was *parched.* He uncapped the bottle, raised it to his lips, and sucked back four large swallows. He felt immediately better, not even minding when Murray shook his head in disgust.

He leaned back against the trunk, surveying the surrounding woods. He could see nothing but trees. The sky had turned cloudy, and for the moment the sun was obscured. He had a vague sense that they had been traveling in an easterly direction, but was not sure they were still on that track. As far as his woods sense went, they might have been ten yards from the road, or a hundred miles.

"Where are we, Murray?"

Murray removed his hat and scratched his sandy blond hair. He was sweating more profusely now that they had stopped. A dark stain marred the front of his shirt.

"We've come about three miles," he said. "Jack and Willy didn't exactly cover their trail. An ape could have followed them."

Matthew said nothing for a moment, then decided to come clean. "I haven't seen anything."

Murray drew on his cigarette. "Come here."

Reluctantly, Matthew pushed away from his perch and walked over to Murray. His muscles, stiff from the few minutes relaxation, protested loudly. Murray crouched, scanning the ground carefully. He pointed to something a yard or two ahead.

Matthew followed the pointing finger, his eyes nar-

104

rowed in concentration. "What? I don't see . . ." And then he saw what Murray was pointing at. Nestled in the tall grass near the base of a tree was a single .30-.30 cartridge. His eyes widened, and he swore softly.

"And there," Murray said, pointing elsewhere. "And there. And there."

Matthew followed the directions, and picked out two more spent cartridges and a crushed beer can.

"These boys are joyriding," Murray said under his breath, almost distastefully. "Shooting at anything, just for the hell of it."

Again, Murray pointed, this time away from the trail. The bark of a thick oak, perhaps twenty yards away, was peppered with bullet holes.

Matthew shook his head, disgusted at his own lack of observation. Why hadn't he been looking for these signs?

Murray seemed to sense his thought train. "Takes years to get the hang of it, Matt."

Matthew laughed and felt a bit better.

"Ready to move on?"

He drew a deep breath. "Lead the way."

Murray grinned, and a shaft of sunlight, suddenly freed from cloudy encumbrance, lit the way ahead. He lifted the pack, shucked himself into it, and started walking. Matthew goaded his legs into obeying his brain, and followed.

They found Jack and Willy Burgess's camp half an hour later.

"This doesn't look promising." Murray removed the pack and dropped it to the ground.

The camp was a few yards north of the trail. A hastily constructed lean-to, now collapsed, and the remains of a small fire. Matthew followed Murray off the trail. When they were closer, he could see that the lean-to had collapsed backward, as if somebody inside it had suddenly risen and knocked it off its supports.

Matthew kneeled and began carefully picking through the personal belongings. A backpack, its contents spilled, lay on its side. A box of unspent .30-.30 shells littered what had been the floor of the camp. One rifle, a Winchester, unloaded, lay beneath a second pack. He picked up a near empty bottle of Wild Turkey. The dark liquid sloshed noisily.

"Where the hell did they go?" he asked softly.

Murray was inspecting the remains of the fire. "Looks like this fire was put out intentionally. This log is only half burned. Looks like water was poured on it. Except the ashes aren't dispersed. I don't know. Weird."

"Why wander off and leave a gun and two packs?" Murray stood slowly, knees creaking. "I don't know. Unless they were running from something." His features had assumed an unaccustomed, serious cast. Matthew did not like the expression. It didn't look good on Murray's country-boy face.

"What now?"

Murray removed his hat. Scratched his head. Checked his watch. He sighed and rubbed his belly. "Getting too late to keep looking. I don't like the look of this."

"Maybe, like you say, they got shit-faced and walked off."

Murray shook his head slowly. "We don't know when they camped here. Maybe yesterday, maybe five days ago. It gets cold at night, colder than you'd expect. Something is wrong."

"Wild animals maybe?"

"Not with the fire. Something else."

Matthew said nothing more. *Something else.* The silence of the surrounding woods was spooky enough already. Better the living shadows of a city alley any day.

Murray moved back to his pack and kneeled beside it. "Let's eat, then head home. We can come back tomorrow. Start early."

Matthew nodded eagerly, suddenly feeling hungry. Only the thought of returning tomorrow stopped him from enjoying Murray's expertly crafted sandwiches as

106

much as he would have liked.

They were approaching the clearing where the car was parked when Matthew noticed they were being followed.

The sky overhead had grown progressively darker during the return trip, until now night waited at stage side for an abrupt entrance. He heard the crashing sound to his left and stopped instantly.

"Murray!"

But Murray had already stopped and was staring in the direction of the sound. Matthew scanned the trees but saw nothing.

"I heard something, I swear it," Matthew said, feeling foolish.

"Something's been shadowing us for the past hour. Maybe even before that. I thought I heard something at the abandoned camp. Wasn't sure, though."

Matthew tried hard to control his anger, but failed. "Why didn't you say something, you son of a bitch? That thing could have killed us!"

"What thing?"

"That . . ." Matthew let his voice trail off, realizing how panicked he was sounding. "Damn it, Murray, you should have said something."

Murray shrugged. "You're right. Sorry."

"How far to the clearing?"

"Five minutes, maybe ten."

"Then let's move, for God's sake." Matthew had not felt this frightened in a long time. His eerie morning encounter with the mist, the memory of the dream, came back in full force.

They picked up their pace, breaking almost into a jog. Minutes later, the clearing appeared in a gap in the trees, the blue of Jack Burgess's half-ton, the black and white of Murray's car, and relief surged through him.

Murray slowed and came to a halt. Matthew almost ran into him. "Slow down partner, you'll kill yourself."

Matthew spun, listening intently. Sounds of crashing

came from south of the trail, drawing closer.

"Still coming," Murray said. He unslung his rifle and jacked the finger lever.

Matthew watched him incredulously. "What the hell are you doing?"

Murray only smiled. He raised the rifle to his shoulder, nestled it, and aimed in the direction of the sound.

"Let's just get the hell out of here."

"Shhh."

Matthew turned to follow Murray's aim. He saw the bushes moving. His muscles tensed. And then he saw the thing.

Beside him, Murray Carlyle's breath rushed out in an astonished hiss. "Jesus Christ, look."

Matthew *was* looking. He just couldn't believe it. He said nothing, his jaw locked tighter than a quarterback's ass.

"What a trophy," Murray said softly. "What a fucking trophy."

"What the hell is it?"

"It's a goddamned wolf, Matt. Bigger than anything I've seen. Will you look at that thing?"

The wolf had halted, perhaps a hundred yards away. It must have been standing on a slight ridge, Matthew thought, as most of its head and shoulders were visible above the low-lying brush. Its fur was pristine white, slightly gray around the throat and eyes. Its mouth hung open, the tongue lolling through jagged teeth. Even from this distance, the beast was monstrous. Its eyes seemed to glow red, pinning him. *I couldn't run if I wanted to,* Matthew realized in horror.

"Keep still," Murray whispered.

From the corner of his eye, Matthew watched as Murray slowly swung the barrel of the rifle, bringing the wolf into his sights.

"Hold it right there, you fucker. Don't move. Smile for Papa."

Later, Matthew would try to understand what had motivated him to do what he did. Perhaps it was the animal's eyes, he later reasoned, that seemed to focus directly on his, as if trying to communicate. Or maybe it was simply the understanding that he and Murray had been invading the wolf's territory, not the other way around. Or perhaps, it was the memory of the burning cat in the town circle, and Andrea's helpless pleading for him to do something. Likely a combination of all three.

At the time, he knew only one thing. The wolf did not deserve to die.

He raised his right hand and knocked the rifle barrel as Murray squeezed the trigger. The shot shattered the silence of the woods and smashed into a tree a few yards from the wolf. The animal started, then disappeared from sight.

"Goddamn it, Matt!"

"Sorry. I slipped."

"You ruined my shot. The biggest—"

"I said I was sorry."

Murray shook his head and slung the rifle back over his shoulder. "A fucking trophy wolf. Nobody will believe me now."

Matthew followed him to the clearing, saying nothing in response to Murray's whining. He felt guilty, even foolish. He knew that he had demeaned himself in Murray's eyes.

Somehow, though, he imagined that Andrea would approve.

There had been a number of bad days since coming to Marissa, Andrea thought, but this one had to rank near the top.

First, there had been the incident with Peter, which had left her depressed and longing for Minneapolis all afternoon, and now Matthew.

Since he had returned from his jaunt with Murray, he had been silent, uncommunicative, almost sullen. She understood that he was tired, bone weary in fact, but she could not understand the wall he seemed to have built around himself. He refused to answer any question about the missing hunters, and did not want to talk at all about his day in the woods.

Dinner was one of the most depressing meals she had ever eaten. She and Peter did not exchange a single word. In fact, the air between them seemed electric with animosity. Surely Matthew noticed. Apparently, however, he did not. He ate silently, nodding occasionally at either Peter or her, periodically offering curt replies to questions posed to him. She almost wished that he *would* notice, so that she would have an excuse to get the situation, quickly growing intolerable, out in the open.

After dinner, Matthew retired early to bed, and Peter spent the evening alone in his room. As she had all day, Andrea remained in the living room, alone and brooding.

What was happening to her family? Only a day ago, she and Matthew had made passionate love. She had felt such hope then. Only twenty-four hours ago!

She shook her head thinking about it, exasperated and confused.

Could she be blowing things out of proportion? Matthew had had a hard day, after all; perhaps he had a right to act this way.

She wanted to believe that, wanted desperately to find any explanation for what was happening to her family, but could not.

By midnight she was growing tired. She had just turned off the kitchen lights when her attention was drawn to the woods behind the house. Something flickered in the depths of the trees. A lamp of some sort.

She frowned and moved into the darkness of the kitchen, closer to the sliding doors. Again, she glimpsed the light. Then another, and another. Like fireflies. There seemed to be a string of them, as if a party of people were walking along the paths, swinging flashlights.

What would anybody be doing on those paths at this time of night?

Something moved upstairs. The floor creaked. It was Peter. He had emerged from bed. She followed his creaking step across the ceiling, forming a picture of him

110

in her mind as he pressed his face to the window.

Outside, the lights were growing fainter, until finally they disappeared amid the crowding tree trunks. Only darkness remained. And the beating of her heart.

Upstairs, the floor creaked. Peter was moving back to bed. *He knows what's going on outside. He knows all about those lights.*

In a few moments, silence returned. She remained at the sliding doors, staring out into the darkness of the woods. But the lights did not return.

Finally, confused and tired, she went upstairs to bed, where, staring at the back of Matthew's head, she fell into troubled sleep.

CHAPTER THIRTEEN

On Monday, Andrea spent an unfruitful day at the office. By five she was frustrated and growing angry. As the day wound down, she found herself loitering at the front desk. She had quickly grown friendly with the agent's most powerful ally in any realty office: the receptionist. Janice Ulcott, a young woman just entering her twenties, had the rare knack of being able to listen, sympathize, and empathize simultaneously. Within half an hour Andrea had spilled her guts.

Behind her desk, Janice nodded and tut-tutted. "It must be awful for you," she commiserated. "Moving from a big city like Minneapolis to a tiny village like Marissa. I don't think I could live in Marissa."

One of the other agents, a tall, fleshy man named John Gardner, who had twice asked Andrea out for drinks since Thursday, stopped on his way to the door. "What's wrong with Marissa? Scenic as all hell."

"Good night, John," Janice said.

Gardner ignored her. He sauntered over to Andrea. "You want a ride tonight?"

"No. Thanks, anyway."

Gardner paused. His thick-lidded eyes made an obvious tour of her upper body. "I'm going that way," he said.

"You're not going anywhere near there, John," Janice said with a laugh. "Leave her alone. Good night."

Gardner sighed and rose to his full height. "Well, I

didn't really want to drive near Marissa anyway. Spooky place. Damned woods pressing in from all sides."

Andrea surprised herself. "Oh, it's not that bad."

Gardner buttoned up his coat and moved to the door. "I'll tell you one strange thing. Hasn't been a property listed in Marissa in over fifty years."

Andrea blinked. "That's not possible."

"No? Did you buy your house? Who from?" Gardner grinned, pushing open the door. "The cost of buying into Marissa has nothing to do with money."

Then the door was closing, and he was gone. "Don't mind John," Janice said, "He's really quite harmless."

"No, it's not that," Andrea said. "It's what he said about Marissa. Is that true?" She was uncomfortably aware that she and Matthew had not purchased their house, that it had been part of a benefits package with Matthew's job.

"You'd have to check the records. I don't remember finalizing any deals for Marissa properties."

Andrea frowned, staring out the front door at passing cars. The 7-Eleven parking lot across the street was crowded. Fergus Falls, though small by Minneapolis standards, was at least recognizable as a town. She found herself wishing Matthew had found a job here, instead of in Marissa.

"Listen, I'll be finished in about twenty minutes. You want to go for a drink somewhere?"

Andrea turned to Janice and smiled thankfully. "No, I really shouldn't, Janice. I appreciate the thought. But I should get home. Haven't seen Matt or Pete since yesterday."

Janice nodded, not at all offended by Andrea's refusal. "Drive carefully."

By the time she reached the county road exit for Marissa, the sky was dark. She slowed the Pontiac to a halt and peered down the maw of the road. As it had the first time she had come this way, an impression of otherworldliness came upon her. The rising moon looked reluctant to leave

113

the treetops, and the trees themselves, like outstretched arms, seemed to strive to prevent this bitter parting. Stars swam at the edge of the sky. Somewhere in the distance, Marissa prepared for another dark time amid the woods.

I don't have to go back there. Nobody's twisting my arm. I could go back to Fergus Falls for the night, stay in a motel, or with Janice. Then drive to Minneapolis tomorrow.

She shook her head, shocked at her thoughts. Had she seriously been considering the option of not returning to Marissa? Running away from Matthew? From Peter?

The suspicion seemed much more than a possibility. She *had* been contemplating flight. *Admit it! Marissa has you beaten!* The presence of such thoughts, even as idle fantasies, was surely an indicator of a worm in the apple.

"Damn it, what were you thinking about?" In the compartment of the car, blanketed by the low idle of the engine, the question seemed to demand an answer.

Ahead of her, State 210 wound its way into the deepening twilight. Behind her, the lights of Fergus Falls cast a sickly pallor on the underbelly of an encroaching bank of dark clouds. Beyond Fergus, Interstate 94 promised new and more encouraging vistas. To her left, to the north, Marissa awaited her return.

The realization that returning home to Matthew, and Peter, to family, was not simply automatic, that events could conspire to turn her away from them, frightened her.

Lights glared in the rearview mirror. The approaching car swerved into the left lane and blared its horn as it sped by. She glimpsed the dashboard-illuminated face of a child peering out at her. The child's eyes glittered in dark hollows. Then the taillights arched around a curve ahead. Darkness closed in again, and silence.

But it hadn't been *events* that had conspired against her, she suddenly knew. It had been Marissa itself. Everything about it. She recalled an early impression, walking along the road with Matthew, that she had been here before. Preposterous as the idea was, she could not shake it. It

114

added to her unease.

She stared down the county road, now even darker than it had been a few minutes ago. She began to feel angry. *You can't have my family. I won't let you have them.* Shadows capered in the darkness to the north. She pursed her lips, nodding sharply. She hit the car's blinker, hesitated a moment, then turned toward town.

The house was lit up like a Christmas tree. Back in Minneapolis she would have admonished Peter to stop wasting energy, but tonight, seeing this colossal wastage, she felt an affinity with the boy she had not felt in a long time. The house was a beacon.

She paused in the foyer. Hushed voices came from the kitchen. She frowned. She had recognized Peter's voice, but not the other. She did not move. The voices continued to speak, and she caught glimmers of the conversation.

". . . I can't . . ." Peter's tone was almost a whine.

". . . but if she sees . . ." the other said.

". . . no, nothing, nothing . . ."

". . . and then what? My dear, you must . . ."

Recognition came in a flash, and she did not know whether to feel relief, or anger. She walked to the kitchen, careful to make as much noise as possible, not wanting to appear as if she had been quietly eavesdropping.

They were sitting at the kitchen table, facing each other. Peter's eyes widened as she appeared in the doorway. Clued in by his expression, Clarissa spun in her seat as if she'd been poked.

Andrea smiled a greeting, but it came out wrong. "Hello," she said. "What are you doing here, Clarissa?"

Clarissa blinked and turned to Peter. A conspiratorial silence settled on the pair of them. Smile locked in place, Andrea moved to the counter, picked up the kettle, and began to fill it with water.

"What were you talking about?" she asked without turning to face them.

For a moment she feared they would not answer at all,

but Clarissa finally coughed. "I just dropped in to say hello."

Andrea turned off the faucet and plugged in the kettle. She turned and leaned on the counter. A blush had crept into Clarissa's cheeks, and Peter would not look at her.

"What were you talking about?"

Again, Clarissa turned to Peter. Peter opened his mouth to speak, looked momentarily to Clarissa for support, then shrugged.

"Nothing," the boy said softly.

"I heard you talking," Andrea said. Her voice did not sound as casual as she wanted. For a moment she felt a stab of dizziness, almost déjà vu. She had acted out just such a confrontational scene with Peter only days ago.

Clarissa turned to Andrea again and opened her mouth to speak. "We were just . . ." she began, then faltered, silenced by the look on Andrea's face. The older woman looked nervously down at her hands.

The silence that settled in the kitchen was intense, like some lurking beast ready to pounce. Andrea drew a deep breath and stared steadily at Peter. What were they hiding? Why had her arrival precipitated this cloak of silence and tension? Her confusion turned quickly to anger.

"Peter, go to your room."

Peter blinked, shocked. She had never spoken to the boy like that before, and it surprised both of them.

"Go to your room."

He stood and stepped around the table toward her. Andrea held her breath. Again, she was reminded of Matthew. The coiled tension within him was frightening. But she did not back down. She glared at him, then took a step toward him. It was enough. He backed away, his eyes wide.

"Go to your room," she said, her voice modulated to a tone that refused to be questioned.

He looked like a boy caught reading a dirty magazine. A protest trembled on his lips, then died. He spun away from her and stormed out of the kitchen. His footsteps pounded on the stairs, shaking the ceiling. Upstairs, his bedroom

116

door slammed like a clap of thunder.

Andrea released the breath she had been holding, feeling not at all victorious. To the contrary, she felt as if she had lost something very valuable.

Clarissa stood rubbing her bony hands on her dress. She pulled her coat from the back of her chair and began to push into it. Her face was red with embarrassment, and she would not make eye contact.

"I really must be going, my dear. I'm sorry if you're upset."

"I'll drive you home."

"It's all right, my dear, I feel quite capable of walking."

"I'll drive you." She turned and unplugged the kettle. "We're going to talk."

Clarissa's throat moved, but no sound emerged. Her eyes looked desperate. In a moment she nodded.

In the car, neither woman spoke. Clarissa leaned into her door, her face pressed to the window, peering outside. As they passed through the town circle, Andrea craned her neck to peer at the pub. Matthew's car was parked at the curb.

At Clarissa's house, Andrea parked in the drive behind the green Dodge Dart. Clarissa moved to open her door, but Andrea placed a hand on her arm and stopped her.

"What were you and Peter talking about?" she said.

Clarissa sighed. "I was only trying to warn him, my dear."

"About what?"

Clarissa stared levelly at her. "There are dangers here," she said softly

Andrea felt her anger drain away. She shook her head and slumped in the seat. She felt tears coming but fought them back.

"What's happening in this damned town?" Her voice trembled. "Peter's changing. Matthew's changing." Now the tears did come, spilling off her cheeks.

"That's perfectly all right, my dear. Cry it out."

"I'm sorry, Clarissa. You must think I'm a fool."

Clarissa shook her head slowly. She patted Andrea's

back. "I did not realize how much you had seen."

Andrea blinked away her tears. "What do you mean?"

Clarissa gripped her hand fiercely. "My dear, you have seen, but you do not yet understand."

She pulled away, suddenly not at all sure she wanted to hear what Clarissa had to say.

Clarissa shook her head, as if weary of carrying an immense weight. "A dark circle is rising," she said. "Peter is involved. You had better come inside, my dear. There are things about Marissa you must know if you are to protect your family."

Clarissa stepped out of the car and moved toward the house. Andrea sighed. Then she turned off the ignition and followed.

CHAPTER FOURTEEN

Andrea settled herself in the sofa. King collapsed at her feet and rested his muzzle against her shin. She reached down to scratch his head. "What did you mean about a dark circle? About Peter?"

Clarissa, who had just returned from putting a kettle of water on in the kitchen, sat in the chair across from her. Her eyes were far away. "Peter is a unique boy," she said.

"Yes, he is," Andrea said. Her own feelings over the last weeks were that Peter was too unique for his own good. Unique was the wrong word for it. Stubborn, perhaps. Headstrong. Willful.

"Marissa, too, is unique," Clarissa said softly.

Andrea opened her mouth to say something, but decided against it. Clarissa was obviously trying to broach a subject she found difficult. In the kitchen, the kettle started to whistle. Clarissa ignored it.

"Marissa, my dear, is an ancient community. Her ties go back before recorded time. Her people are old beyond remembering. We are the children of the Craft. It is our treasure, and our bane."

Clarissa paused as if waiting for a response, but Andrea said nothing. What could she possibly say in reply to that?

"You have called us many things through time," Clarissa said, continuing almost reluctantly. "Pagans. Satan's children. Witches. Wherever we have gone, wherever we have lived, you have hunted us down, or chased us away. Until Marissa."

Now Andrea did respond. She could not help herself. She laughed. But it was a sound sharp with the ragged edges of uncertainty. "You mean that Marissa is full of witches?"

Clarissa said nothing. She stared uneasily down at King. The dog kept his eyes on Andrea.

"Up until now," Clarissa continued, oblivious to Andrea's disbelief, "we have lived peacefully. We are not a prosperous community, but we survive. When death is all you have known, even survival seems like riches. There are tales I could tell you . . ."

"I think you're already telling me one," Andrea said scornfully.

Clarissa ignored the remark. "But there are some of us who grow weary of living in fear, always wary that the outside world may one day break in and destroy what we have worked so hard to maintain. They ask us to turn away from our passive ways, to assert ourselves. In these dark days, those voices of unreason are becoming strident, are even gaining favor."

Clarissa's earlier words came back to Andrea, and found life on her lips. "A dark circle is rising," she said. "What does Peter have to do with this?"

"Peter is a male," Clarissa said simply. "The last in a line that extends back to the beginning of our people. Most males are powerless. The craft is a woman's gift. But sometimes, once in every few generations, a male is born who shares the power."

"But Peter's not from Marissa," Andrea said, caught up despite her disbelief.

"Matthew is one of us," Clarissa said. "He is my sister's son. We had thought, perhaps, that Matthew would be the one. He was not. But his son . . ."

"Oh my God, you're crazy."

"A male of the Craft is a rare thing. The horrible irony is that such males are its most powerful practitioners. A dark circle is rising in Marissa. Up to now they have been a local nuisance. If they can secure the powers of an active male,

120

however, they would rise beyond our capacity to control them."

"Peter," Andrea whispered.

Clarissa nodded. "It has been many centuries since your world has witnessed the rise of a dark circle."

"But Matthew never said anything about this," Andrea said plaintively.

"My sister took Matthew away when he was a boy. It is unlikely he would have learned much about Marissa. My sister was concerned for the boy. There were many families who fled Marissa, fearful of the rise of darkness." For a moment, Clarissa looked at her strangely.

Andrea shook her head. In the harsh light of the living room, with the darkness of the night an implacable wall just outside the window, Clarissa's story had achieved a veracity that would have eluded it during daylight. She tried to remind herself of this, tried not to get caught up in it. She was reaching for explanations of what she had seen and felt during the past week; the temptation was strong to latch on to Clarissa's story as truth. She fought it.

"Clarissa," she said, giving her voice a tone of calmness she did not feel, "I know there are pagan communities throughout the Midwest. I read about them years ago. Even some covens. It's a free country. But that doesn't mean—"

Clarissa laughed softly. "Marissa has nothing to do with them, my dear. We are a community unto ourselves. We do not offer an alternative to your modern world for those who wish to escape. We were never part of it."

Andrea drew a deep breath. The whistle of the kettle in the kitchen had turned hoarse, as if the water had boiled away.

"I don't know what strange ideas you've been putting into Peter's head, but I want you to stop it."

Clarissa's eyes widened. An expression of deep hurt settled on her features. "I would never do anything to harm Peter," she said. "Nor you, nor Matthew. You are my family."

Andrea said nothing. Her disbelief and anger had

formed a strong alloy of resistance.

"Peter has not yet joined their ranks," Clarissa said. "There is time to stop him, time to show him how to protect himself."

Andrea stood abruptly. "Clarissa, there's nothing wrong with Peter. He's a teenage boy going through a difficult phase." She allowed herself to be convinced by her own words. "You'll make it more difficult for him with your stories."

"But he may—" Clarissa began.

"Leave him alone. Stay away from him."

"I was only trying to help."

"You're interfering with my family. I won't stand for it."

Clarissa sighed. "My dear, you are making a terrible mistake."

"So you told me once before." She stood and moved to the door. Tail wagging, King waddled after her. Clarissa watched this desertion with a look of deep hurt

"You had better look after the kettle before it melts," Andrea said. She bent to pet King's head. "Stay here, boy," she said softly.

The dog sat. Andrea opened the door and stepped out into the night.

Behind her, King barked softly, once. She sat in the Pontiac a few minutes, calmed herself, then backed out onto the road and drove toward the town circle. The darkness had settled completely. The trees seemed to grow directly out of it.

By the time she reached the house, her mettle had softened and a helpless depression had settled upon her. She couldn't get Clarissa's story out of her head, couldn't quite latch on to her disbelief. She was relieved to find Matthew's car in the driveway.

She had just entered the warmth of the hallway when he appeared from the kitchen. His face brightened when he saw her.

"Hello, darling, have a good day?" he said.

She stepped toward him, gripped him fiercely, then

burst into tears.

It was a full hour later when her tears finally dried, and during that time she told Matthew everything. He held her close, stroked her hair, and kissed her cheeks and mouth as she divested herself of the weight of suspicion and fear that had grown to overwhelming proportions during the past weeks. Not once did he express doubt at her stories; not once did he in any way condescend to or patronize her. When she had finished, when the last detail had spilled out, it was this very facade of calm acceptance that brought her back to reality.

They were sitting in the living room, pressed into a corner of the sofa. Matthew's shirt was soaked with her tears. She pulled away, sniffled, and rubbed her eyes.

"It all sounds so crazy, doesn't it?"

Matthew said nothing for a moment. His narrow, angular face looked thoughtful. "You've been under a lot of stress lately," he said.

"No, Matthew, it's not just that."

"Clarissa is an old, crazy woman. Even as a kid I thought she was strange."

"You don't think there's anything to her story? About Marissa being an enclave of witches?"

He did not laugh. He shook his head. "Absolutely not. I'm sure Clarissa wishes it were true. Add a bit of romance to this place."

Andrea sniffled again and shook her head. She wanted desperately to believe him.

"But what about the burned cat, Matthew? That wasn't normal."

Matthew drew a deep breath. "We think we know who did it," he said.

"You do?"

He nodded. "Couple of kids from Battle Lake. And they've done this sort of thing before. Cruel bastards. But it's coming up on Halloween. Kids get crazy at this time of year. Even in Minneapolis it was a weird time."

123

Andrea shook her head, sensing the structure of paranoia losing its fragile foundation.

"What about the mist, then? I know I saw that mist outside Peter's room. I could have sworn I saw something in the mist. Something horrible."

This time Matthew said nothing for a moment. His shoulders tensed, and she felt the tension transfer itself to his hands, then to her shoulders.

"You saw a mist too, didn't you?"

He shrugged. "In the morning once. But it was just mist. Nothing else."

Something in his words didn't ring true, as if he were not telling her everything he had seen. He pulled her close and kissed her ear. "Darling, believe me, there's nothing going on here. And you're not going crazy. Marissa *is* a strange little town, there's no denying it, but it's nothing like Clarissa says."

Andrea drew a deep, shuddering breath. She felt exhausted and foolish. She pressed close to Matthew, seeking his warmth and strength. His strong arms enfolded her and held her close.

"Do you want to leave here?"

She started, pulled away from him again. "What?"

"We could leave Marissa," he said.

She knew that he was not joking. "Matthew . . ."

"I don't want to stay here if it's not what you want. You're my wife. You're far more important to me than this damned job."

She felt tears filling her eyes again, and hugged him tightly. "Maybe you're right," she said hoarsely. "Maybe I'm just tense. We can't leave now. Everything is going so well for you."

They remained silent a few moments, holding each other. Her tension seemed to slide from her body, as if Matthew were somehow draining it from her.

"You're right about one thing," he said.

She pulled slightly away and looked at him in astonishment.

"Peter," he said. "He's changing. I see it now, too."

124

She said nothing, just continued to stare.

"He spends far too much time by himself. I know he was rude to you. He was abrupt with me when I got home."

"It's just a phase," Andrea said hopefully.

Matthew shook his head. "No, it's not. And even if it is, it's gone too far. We have to live with him, and he has to live with us. It's that simple. I'm going to talk to him."

"Please, Matthew, not on my account."

"He's going to get civil, or there's going to be trouble."

She pressed back into his arms. "Let's go to bed," she said softly.

She felt him stiffen, and then relax. "Are you sure?"

She pressed her mouth to his and kissed him thoroughly. The talking, the release of tension, had brought her to life. Her mental exhaustion had been replaced with a well of energy.

"Guess so," he whispered hoarsely. In the bedroom, with the door locked, she gave herself to him completely, and took from him everything he had to give. When they had finished, her exhaustion returned. This time it calmed her, suffusing her with a feeling of satisfaction and calmness.

Matthew fell immediately asleep, and for this Andrea was grateful. She had no wish to expend energy on post-coital small talk. She lay in bed, staring at the ceiling, gathering her thoughts. Starting tomorrow, she would make a concerted effort to bring her family back together, to make the best of Marissa. It had not been easy the first time, back in Minneapolis, and it would not be easy now. The effort, she decided, was worth it.

This decision made, she closed her eyes. Sleep prodded at her consciousness with thick, clumsy fingers.

It was the creaking of floor boards that alerted her, and her eyes blinked open. She held her breath and listened. The creak came again. From Peter's room.

The boy was up and moving around. She formed a mental image of his room, and knew that he was standing at the window.

Quietly, she pushed aside the blankets and tiptoed to the

125

master bedroom window. Outside, darkness pressed down from above. The cloud bank that had edged the sky at dusk now blocked out all the stars. The trees seemed to touch the clouds.

Down below, emerging from the surrounding woods, a bluish mist coiled and billowed. Fingers of vapor felt blindly at the edge of the grass, but moved no closer. It was as if something were keeping the mist at bay.

Andrea moved back to bed. Matthew, oblivious, did not wake. She slid under the blankets, pulled them up to her chin, and closed her eyes.

Everything was fine. Nothing was wrong. Nothing at all. She squeezed her eyes tight to keep the mist from her dreams.

PART III

Circles

CHAPTER FIFTEEN

Voices woke Andrea just after 6 A.M. She opened her eyes and blinked against morning light. The voices became silent long enough to cause her to wonder if she had dreamed them, then they started again.

Matthew, harsh with anger: ". . . damn it! Now listen to me . . ."

And Peter, plaintive, rebellious: ". . . was her! She was the one . . ."

They merged into one angry note and then fell silent. She held her breath, feeling as if she had eavesdropped at a closed door, and remembered Matthew's promise to talk to Peter. He had not granted her request to leave well enough alone. It would be very difficult to face Peter now. He would rightly feel that she had gone above his head in complaining to Matthew. This might be the final straw to break the already straining back of their relationship. She felt suddenly angry at Matthew.

In the hallway, a door slammed. Footsteps pounded on the stairs. Silence returned, settled at the threshold of every room.

Fully awake now, she swung her legs out of bed and rose. She listened at the doorway before entering the hallway, assuring herself she would not run into Peter, then went to the bathroom and showered. When she went downstairs it was past six-thirty. Matthew was at the sink, wiping a dish.

"You're up early," he said.

She had managed to maintain an edge of anger with him, but now that anger dissipated quickly under his morning charm.

"I heard you and Peter arguing."

He raised his eyebrows and pursed his lips. Leaning forward, he kissed her chastely on the cheek, then took her firmly in his arms and kissed her thoroughly on the mouth.

"Watch the lipstick!"

"I know you didn't want me to, but he was becoming insufferable."

"Was he angry?"

She poured herself a mug of coffee and took it to the table.

Matthew sat across from her. "Confused, more like it. He'll be okay."

She sipped her coffee and said nothing.

Matthew reached across the table and squeezed her hand. "Don't worry. Everything will be fine. We'll work it out."

His words seemed to reach some hidden, previously inaccessible part of her, and she felt a calmness extending out of that place to infuse her. She drew a deep breath and smiled warmly.

"I should get going," she said.

Matthew shook his head. "Not yet. Wait for Peter to come down."

She raised her eyebrow, but did not argue. The thought of facing Peter had lost its menace. She nodded and went back to sipping her coffee.

Peter came clumping down the stairs a few minutes later, and she felt the tension return as if it had been lurking, waiting for her defenses to drop. When the boy appeared in the kitchen doorway, her heart pounded in her chest.

Oh God, he looks so much like Matthew.

Peter's dark hair, glistening from his shower, was combed straight back off his forehead. His narrow face would have looked predatory if not for his young age. He looked nervously between Matthew and her.

"Morning, son," Matthew said.

Peter nodded. His brow furrowed in concentration, or nervousness.

"Do you have something you want to say?" Matthew prodded.

Peter's brow became a ledge above his eyes. His hands, large and awkward, played with each other. "I . . ." He looked to Andrea, his expression one of pleading. "I guess I just want to say I'm sorry for the way I've been acting lately." His voice trembled.

She empathized deeply with his embarrassment and nervousness. "It's okay, Peter."

Peter turned to Matthew to find out if it was, in fact, okay. Behind her back, Matthew must have given his answer.

"I . . . I don't know why I've been acting so crazy," he said. Now his shoulders seemed to slump, as if the fight had gone out of him. "I guess it was the move and everything. I don't know. I didn't mean to be rude."

She could not take any more. She stood and stepped toward him. "This move has been difficult for all of us."

His eyes widened, and he stared at her as if he had never really seen her before. "I'm sorry, Andrea." His voice was hushed.

This is it, Andrea thought. *One more step and we can regain everything we lost.*

"Apology accepted," she said.

For a moment, they stood facing each other. The sincerity of Peter's apology was etched into his face. She thought he might be close to tears, and knew that if he did cry, she herself would break down. To forestall that possibility, she stepped toward him and opened her arms. He came into her embrace immediately.

When they parted, Peter smiled sheepishly at her, and she smiled back. She felt as if a great weight had been lifted from her shoulders, a shroud removed from her eyes. The morning actually seemed brighter.

"We better roll," Matthew said. "Come on, Peter, I'll give you a ride, or you'll miss your bus."

Peter nodded. He turned again to Andrea. "Bye," he said.

"Bye."

"Don't work too hard," Matthew said, rising and moving for the door. He grinned at her and winked. *See, I told you everything would be okay*, his smile seemed to say.

"You either."

Then they were gone, and she was alone. She sat at the table, sipping her coffee. She thought about Peter's apology, studying it from all angles. His words had carried a sincerity she could not doubt, had cast everything that had happened in an almost innocent light. *Nothing to it. Just the move.*

She felt as if it had all been put behind them. Skeleton back in the closet.

She frowned at this thought, not at all pleased with it. Skeletons in the closet she could do without. They had a nasty habit of popping out when you were least prepared to deal with them.

After dropping Peter in the town circle, Matthew drove directly to the station house. Murray Carlyle was nowhere to be found, and Matthew felt relieved. He enjoyed the first quiet hours alone at the station, enjoyed the time afforded him to get his thoughts in order.

Foremost on his mind was the situation at home. He had sensed that things were not quite right with Andrea and Peter, but he had not imagined they had gotten so far out of hand. What the hell was going on between the pair of them? Three months ago they had been as close, maybe closer than any natural mother and son. Now they were like strangers. Andrea was right. Peter was changing.

He did not like what was happening to his son. Not one bit.

And yet . . . Peter's apology really had seemed sincere.

Maybe that little talk had done the job. Maybe the scene with Andrea this morning had been more than a superficial show. Jesus, he hoped so.

Now all he had to worry about was Clarissa. He had always thought his aunt a little bit crazy, but up to now her craziness had been harmless. Almost funny. But Clarissa had frightened Andrea, and the last thing Andrea needed right now was to be frightened.

Settling into Marissa was difficult enough without stories about witchcraft and God knows what else.

He felt a sudden stirring of anger at Clarissa but managed to control it. He would talk to her. Make her see that she was causing trouble. The old lady might be crazy, but she was not malicious.

He shook his head, closed his eyes, and drew a deep breath. His family problems were the least of his worries.

Yesterday morning he and Murray had hiked back to the deserted camp. Nothing had changed. They had walked farther afield, and had found no trace of Jack or Willy Burgess. He remembered Murray's confusion.

"Son of a bitch. No tracks. Got to be some."

But after hours of searching, they still found nothing. Jack and Willy had disappeared.

It was Matthew who finally found the animal print. Murray had whistled, removed his cap, wiped his brow, and whistled again.

"That's our wolf. Look at the size of that paw." He was still upset about Matthew's intentional ruining of his shot.

"It *was* here," Matthew said softly. "You don't think—"

"Shit, no, Matt. There'd be signs of a struggle. Besides, wolves don't attack humans."

When he had suggested, for the second time, that they call in the State Police, Murray had vetoed the idea immediately.

"This is local work."

Now, Matthew found himself brooding on the problem. Why not call in the State Police? A well-organized search party would have more luck finding Jack and Willy than he and Murray had done. The more men, the better.

He was still brooding when Murray came through the front door.

"Don't you ever sleep in, Matt?"

Murray had obviously closed the Three-Horned Bull. His clothes looked slept in, his face unshaved. He disappeared into the back room. In a moment Matthew heard rushing water, then splashing and coughing.

"Asshole," Matthew muttered.

Murray emerged a few minutes later. His hair was slicked back, his face shaven. Spots of blood testified to the tremble in his hand. A cigarette dangled from his mouth. Matthew reeled at the cloying odor of after-shave and tobacco.

Murray regarded him a moment, then shook his head. Eyes narrowed, he drew on his cigarette and exhaled a cloud of smoke.

"What's eating you, Matt?"

Matthew frowned. "Nothing."

"You look like somebody stuck a magnum up your ass."

Matthew sighed. "Just trouble at home."

"Andrea still whining?"

Matthew held his breath and smothered the anger that glowed near flame. "Peter," he said at last. "And my Aunt Clarissa."

"Clarissa?"

He felt almost relieved to be bringing it out in the open. "She's been telling Andrea stories about witchcraft and voodoo and other crap. And Peter's been acting like a little bastard."

He had expected Murray to laugh, but Murray only frowned and turned back to his desk.

"What else has Clarissa been saying."

"I don't know. I'm going to talk to her. It really bothered Andrea."

"You do that," Murray said. "Old woman's crazy."

Matthew nodded and frowned. Although he recognized Clarissa's eccentricity, it bothered him to hear Murray say it.

"Listen, I've been thinking about Jack and Willy . . ."

"Have you?"

"I really think we should call in the State Police. We could be charged with negligence."

Murray chuckled. "Matthew, just calm down. I talked with Doreen Burgess last night. She couldn't remember how long Jack and Willy were going for."

"I still think . . ."

"We'll handle this," Murray said softly. "You and me. Not the fucking state troopers."

Matthew seethed. If he spoke, he would snap, and he'd regret it.

Murray regarded him curiously and finally smiled. "You like it here, Matt?"

Matthew blinked, taken aback by the question. "I like it," he admitted.

"You thinking of staying for a while?"

"I said I liked it."

"Then you better learn to do things our way," he said. "Marissa takes care of her own. Remember that."

Son of a bitch is threatening me! "You're the boss," he said under his breath.

Murray grinned. "That's right," he said.

CHAPTER SIXTEEN

By the time Andrea got to the offices of McQuage and Ronson, it was nearly nine-thirty. Janice Ulcott raised her eyebrows and tapped her watch.

"I know, I know," Andrea said breathlessly. "Would you believe I was even up early this morning?"

"Would you believe, no?"

"Well, I was." She walked quickly to the open office area at the back. There were no messages on her desk. She came back to the front reception area. "Where is everybody?"

"You really did forget, didn't you."

"Forget what?"

"Tuesday mornings. Sales meeting."

"Oh, boy."

"Mister McQuage was asking for you."

"Oh, boy, again."

Janice chuckled. "Don't worry. You're new. They'll forgive a couple of missed meetings."

That wasn't the point. As a newcomer, it was imperative that she attend the weekly sales meetings. Soon enough she would grow to hate them. The more established agents would think the worst, attributing to her a belief she was above such mundane matters. She shook her head, angry at her forgetfulness.

"Where is it?" she asked. "Mr. McQuage mentioned something about a dinner club."

"Other side of town. Don't worry about this one. Just make sure about the next."

Defeated, Andrea sighed and leaned on the edge of Janice's desk. "I'm making a wonderful first impression."

"Seriously, you are," Janice said. "Both McQuage and Ronson think they snared a good one."

"They said so?"

Janice nodded. "Funny thing is, even the other agents like you. They remind me of despicable children sometimes, the way they taunt each other and so on, but you've slipped under their defenses."

Andrea smiled, pleased to know this. "I guess it's back to the phones, then," she said. The prospect of another day of cold calling was not appealing, but for a new agent in a new area it was the only way.

Janice stroked her cheek. "I looked up something for you. Thought you might be interested. Actually, you and John Gardner got my interest piqued yesterday when you were talking." She opened her desk and pulled out a thick file folder.

Andrea picked it up and flipped it open. It was a set of computer sales listings. She scanned a few pages briefly, frowning. "What is this?"

"Sales listing over the past five years for the lake country. Marissa falls inside that area too. I haven't had a chance to look closely, but I couldn't see any listings for Marissa."

"In five years? That's unlikely."

"You're telling me?"

Andrea chuckled. "Sorry. I think I'll flip through these. Don't really feel like facing the phone."

Janice smiled. "I'll bring you coffee later."

Andrea walked back to her desk. She spent the next hour, and three cups of coffee, poring over the contents of the file. During the past five years, sales had been brisk in most of the lake district. If she'd had a map, had marked with a red pin every property sale, Marissa would have ended as an empty hole in a sea of blood. Not one single property transaction had occurred within Marissa.

She contemplated this naked fact as if it were a wound, or a complex scar, fascinated yet repulsed. Her curiosity shared equal time with a vague dread. What was so special about Marissa?

Do I really want to know?

When Janice came to the back and asked if she wanted another cup of coffee, she shook her head. Her hands were already shaking; whether from caffeine or from reading the file, she was not certain.

"Find anything?"

Andrea shook her head slowly. "Nothing. John Gardner was right."

"Isn't that strange," Janice said, shook her head.

"Do we have records that go farther back?"

"Not that I can dig out today."

"Shit."

Janice blinked. "You're really worried about this, aren't you?"

Andrea drew a deep breath and released it in a sigh. "Not worried, really," she said, and realized as she said it that it was a lie. The look on Janice's face showed that Janice knew it too. Andrea sighed again. "Well, I guess I am a little worried," she amended.

"Yesterday you made it sound like a pretty weird place."

"It seems that way to me, sometimes. This thing . . . no sales . . . it fits in. I mean, it makes sense in a way. I can't really imagine anybody buying property in Marissa."

Touching her cheek gently in a gesture of thoughtful contemplation, Janice said nothing for a moment. "If you really want to dig deeper, you could try the County Records, or the library."

Andrea stared down at the spread of computer paper on her desk. Five years of records had been enough to make her uneasy. What would the County Records do?

Again, the nagging doubt: *Do I really want to know?*

She looked up at Janice. "You know, I think I'll give it a try. If only to put my mind at rest."

Janice smiled and nodded. The corners of her mouth

138

tightened slightly. "That's a good idea" she said, but sounded as if she didn't mean it.

County Records was a two-story, glass-fronted monstrosity on First Street. Inside, Andrea talked with the clerk, a bent old man named Toby Wilkins. He confirmed what the office records had showed, and more. There hadn't been a property sale in Marissa as far back as the records went, probably farther, and he produced maps and bound volumes to prove it.

But Wilkins himself had a few memories of Marissa he was willing to share, and Andrea listened in rapt attention.

"Only spot of trouble I remember was back in '47." Wilkins scratched his head, reaching out a pale finger to tap the counter top. "County wanted to run a hydro'lectric line from Fergus up to Basswood, so they expropriated a strip of property through Marissa. Those good folks put up a fight, of course, but who can win against the county? The county paid them, pitiful small amount, a crime really, and made their plans. There were delays of course, couple of problems. Two of the county engineers died in a car crash. Young surveyor had his legs crushed when a preliminary excavation caved in. Lot of stuff like that. By '49 the hydro line was scrapped, routed along the highway. Folks in Marissa got to keep their money, n'after a few years the county gave the title to the land back. Never bothered 'em since then."

She thanked Wilkins for his time and left the building as quickly as she could. She walked the three blocks to the library, but paused on the front steps.

Did she really want to learn more about Marissa? The more she learned about the town, the deeper the mystery became.

She drew a deep breath. In the end, the truth was always better than a lie. Better to face it now than to wait. If nothing else, she could lay to rest the stories Clarissa had told her.

With firmed resolve, she climbed the steps and entered the building.

She found three books on witchcraft, none of which proved helpful.

Robbins's *The Encyclopedia of Witchcraft and Demonology* exercised a strange fascination over her, yet she found nothing in it that related even remotely to Marissa. The descriptions of the witch trials, the clinical depiction of extensive torture, held her captivated, as she had once been held, as a teenager, by accounts of Nazi war crimes. When, at last, she closed the heavy covers, however, she felt tainted, corrupt, and depressed.

They did those things to human beings, she thought. Innocent women. *Witches don't exist.*

Gerber's *Witchcraft in America* was worse. Written from the viewpoint of a sociologist studying an aberrant phenomenon, the book focused on child abductions and torture by so-called witch covens, devil worshipers, and Satanists. One chapter was devoted to a coven that vivisected animals in order to capture and tame their natural spirits. Again, she found herself morbidly interested in the details, and finally forced the book away.

She thought of the burned cat in Marissa, and shook her head. Not the same thing. She believed Matthew, that it had been a teenager's prank.

Finally, she spent an hour with Adler's *Drawing Down the Moon*, a sympathetic study of witches, druids, and paganism in America. This, too, she found fascinating, but for different reasons. These would-be pagans and witches were mild-mannered, almost naive. She found herself smiling as she read accounts of their masses, meetings, and orgies.

Children, she thought. *Playing a game.*

And again, she found nothing even remotely similar to Marissa. Could Matthew have been right all along? Was Clarissa simply a foolish old woman attempting to romanticize life in a rather dull, isolated town?

It was with a sense of relief that she returned the books to their shelves. The truth, she realized, had liberated her.

Nothing to fear in Marissa. Nothing at all.

She was approaching the exit when a temporary display of books caught her attention. Curious, she moved toward it. The display was situated in a small alcove. Somebody had taped a handmade sign above the shelf of books:

ESCAPE THE AUTUMN BLAHS

WITH A TRIP TO THE PAST!!!

The shelf, she saw, was loaded with history texts. The collection was eclectic and colorful. *The Fall of Rome. A History of Flight. The Taming of the West. First Men. Horses Through Time.*

One book froze her to the spot. Her hands trembled. Her heart hammered, and cold beads of sweat popped out on her forehead.

She reached for it and pulled it from the shelf. The cover was a photograph of a stone sculpture. A three-faced stone. Just like the one she had found in Peter's room. She stared at it, numb.

The title of the book was simply *The Celts.*

With shaking fingers she opened the book and flipped through it. She stopped at a page full of photographs of ancient broaches.

Charms.

She recognized the patterns. Similar, if not identical, to the charms she had seen in Marissa's Craft Shop. The hairs on the back of her neck rose on end.

She flipped the pages and stopped at another illustration. This showed a medieval Celtic village. A huge tree towered in the center of the etching. The villagers were crowded around it and were hanging small charms from the branches. She saw, with horror, that some of the charms were the severed heads of children and animals.

Nausea swept over her in a wave, and she slammed the book closed. The books on witchcraft had nothing to do with Marissa. Nothing at all.

But this . . . This *was* Marissa. She felt as if she had

opened a history of the town, and found that it had not changed in two thousand years.

Hands still trembling, she searched through the collection of books until she found two more titles. *The Druids*, subtitled *The Celtic Supernatural*. And, finally, *A History of the Celts*. She carried the books to the front counter and handed them to the clerk. She heard her own voice speaking but was hardly aware of what she said.

The filling out of library membership forms took five minutes, and she stood the whole time in a daze, signing when asked to sign, answering questions in a monotone voice.

She seemed to wake as she left Fergus Falls and embarked on the trip back to Marissa. She opened the driver's window and allowed the cool late-afternoon air to wash over her and refresh her.

Passages from *Drawing Down the Moon* came to mind as she drove, and she shook her head. Those people had seemed to be playing a game. Their paganism perhaps nothing more than a protest against the mechanization and depersonalization of contemporary life. Getting away from it all, she thought. Returning to nature. A shadow of the real thing. As close as a children's game could come.

Was Marissa the real thing?

She shook her head, not sure she wanted to know the answer.

CHAPTER SEVENTEEN

By the time Andrea got home, it was near dusk. Neither Matthew nor Peter were yet home, but even so, she kept the three library books hugged to her bosom as she entered the front door, as if fearful a secret observer might spot the titles.

As if Marissa itself might see. She shook her head angrily at the thought. She was making it worse.

She put on a kettle of water to boil, then stood at the rear sliding doors and stared at the inscrutable woods. Curtains of ochre leaves rippled and shimmered, given life by a light breeze. The longer she stared at the trees, the more confused her thoughts became. In her mind, Marissa had shed its Minnesota backwoods simplicity like a snake shedding skin, and had pulled close a dark mantle of history. The town seemed like a living thing. In the surrounding woods, she had read its personality. Constantly shifting, obscuring close inspection.

And why not? The people here, the homes, the roads, were a tiny scabby protrusion on the back of this larger creature of earth, and bark, and leaves. It was only natural that the larger entity should dominate, should exert its personality on the smaller. The same thing happened in the city, though there the human population was large enough to return the favor, exerting their own influence on the mass of concrete, steel, and glass around them, balancing the equation. Not here.

The whistle of the kettle pulled her from her reverie. She slumped and sighed, suddenly realizing how tense she had become. Jesus, what was happening to her? She poured the boiling water into the teapot and added a single bag. She resisted the urge to return to the window, but sat at the table and waited for the tea to brew. Then, with a steaming mugful before her, she spread the library books out on the table and began to read.

It was dark when she closed the books and pushed them away. The words on the page seemed to be speaking not of ancient history, but directly of Marissa. The feeling frightened her.

She checked her watch. It was nearly 7:30 P.M. Surely Peter should have come home from school by now, and Matthew had indicated he was growing tired of the constant overtime. An image came to her of Peter walking along the narrow paths behind the house, and she shook it off.

Well, to hell with them. They couldn't expect her to wait all night. It was about time they started making an effort to bring their schedule in line with hers.

Suffused with angry energy, she began to bustle around the kitchen, setting the table for supper. She opened the fridge, pulled out the carton of milk, and swore. Somebody, likely Matthew, had returned the carton to the fridge with less than a mouthful left.

"How many times have I told you . . ." She heard her own voice and cut herself off.

It seemed, at that moment, that she had done nothing but complain since she had arrived in Marissa. She wondered briefly if her trouble with Peter was a result of her own subconscious rebellion against the move here, rather than a change in the boy's personality. Which was more likely?

She closed the fridge softly, not liking the direction of her thoughts. Without thinking about it, she moved to the front cupboard and pulled on a light coat. She would walk to Robertson's Market and pick up another carton.

She opened the front door, then paused. The woods across the road were dark, forbidding, a press of shadows,

144

waiting for her. Above, although no stars had yet appeared, the sky was draining of color. The perpetual light breeze rushed through the trees. Leaves skittered.

The skin of Andrea's neck crawled, and she moved to close the door. To hell with milk, she thought. Then paused.

Here she was again, letting Marissa get the better of her, giving in to her fears and suspicions. It was early evening, damn it, in a place where she was likely safer than if she had been sitting in her Rosedale living room, and she was worried about walking to the store for milk.

Worried, hell. She was terrified.

The realization imposed a strange sort of calm upon her, a recognition of her own silliness, and she chuckled. The wind, again, sounded merely like wind—not a sigh, not an indication of life, simply wind.

"Marissa, you bitch, I'm going for milk."

She stepped outside, and closed the door gently behind her.

At Robertson's Market, Ewan and Barbara were both standing at the cash register, counting receipts. Ewan glanced up as she entered, a smile immediately curling his lips. His ruddy face beamed.

"Andrea!"

Barbara carefully laid down a small pile of bills and looked up, smiling. "How nice to see you, dear."

These two, she realized, were the only real friends she had made since coming to Marissa. She remembered how coldly she had treated their advances at first, and felt ashamed. She looked closely at Barbara's face and saw the lines of grief that had not been there only a scant week ago. The memory of Gray Eyes hung in the air of the store, thick as the smoke from burning fur.

Ewan regarded her worriedly. "You look like you've seen a ghost," he said.

"Just spooking myself," Andrea said.

"It's getting dark outside," Barbara said, as if that explained it.

145

"You shouldn't walk about in the dark," Ewan admonished.

Andrea smiled, pleased at their concern, and walked past them into the store. "Needed some milk," she said over her shoulder.

She took her time moving to the dairy cooler, enjoying the bright interior of the store. Marissa, she thought, may have seemed like a town magically transported from the past, but Robertson's Market, with its bright fluorescent lights, humming refrigerators, and gleaming butcher's fixtures, was a cool transfusion from the modern world. It made her feel at ease to be here. When she returned to the front counter a few moments later, she felt considerably more relaxed.

"Could I put this on account, Ewan?"

Ewan smiled, unable to hide his pleasure, and reached for the black notebook beneath the counter. As he scribbled on the page marked with her name, Andrea reached out and squeezed Barbara's hand.

"Still thinking about Gray Eyes?"

Barbara nodded slightly, her eyes narrowed, then offered a tremulous smile. "A little."

"Matthew says they think they know who did it."

"Oh?" She did not seem very interested.

"Sometimes it's easier to get over a thing like this when you've got something else to give your attention to," Andrea said.

Barbara frowned, not understanding.

"There's a pet store I pass every day on the way to the office. They had the cutest litter of kittens in the window the other day."

Barbara smiled warmly, but shook her head. "Thank you for offering, my dear. But Gray Eyes was my special friend."

Andrea paused, fearing she had made a great blunder. "Well, if you change your mind . . ."

Barbara nodded, but her eyes were the final answer. There would be no other cat.

"Just wait a minute," Ewan said. "I'll give you a ride back to your house."

"You'll do no such thing."

"But it's dark."

"Ewan, please, I'm a big girl."

Ewan frowned, glancing at Barbara for support. But Barbara was looking at Andrea. "Be careful, dear," the older woman said softly.

She nodded. "See you later." As she left the store, she seemed to sense their stares on her back, and again felt warmed by their concern.

The cool evening air braced her, and she shivered momentarily. It seemed darker now than it had a few minutes ago. She glanced to her right. Matthew's car was parked outside the pub. The sound of voices and music reached her, and she debated dropping by.

No, that was not a good idea. Twice in less than a week. Matthew would think she was checking up on him. Another night she could go with him, make an evening of it. She nodded at the thought. A much better idea.

She had begun to turn around when something gripped her arm.

"Did I startle you, dear?"

A shadowy shape coalesced into the form of an old woman, and she recognized the wrinkled face of Deirdre Farrell. Black eyes twinkled in the pale light from Robertson's Market. The gaunt hand, bones stuffed into skin, squeezed her forearm.

"Yes, you did!" She was surprised at the anger in her voice.

Deirdre Farrell smiled. "It's dark, my dear," she said, her voice almost a croak. "Even in Marissa, the night is not the safest of times."

Andrea said nothing for a moment, then carefully disengaged her arm. "Safe enough to walk to the store," she said.

Deirdre Farrell shrugged, and Andrea felt a chill grip her neck. For some reason, she was reacting to this woman as any normal person might react to the touch of a snake, or something vile. She tried to control her voice, but could not quite keep her feelings hidden.

"I should be getting back. Good night." She moved to

step past, but Deirdre Farrell blocked her way.

"You don't like me," Deirdre Farrell said. There was no surprise in her voice, no disappointment. She had been stating a fact.

Andrea smiled, but the effect was a grimace. "I don't even know you," she said.

"Many people don't like me."

I don't doubt it! "Well, I'm not yet one of them," Andrea said, and knew it was a lie.

Deirdre Farrell smiled. "Oh, I think you are," she said. "I think you more than dislike me."

Andrea stiffened. This conversation was so far out of her normal experience of social intercourse that she was at a loss, a raft floundering on a violent sea.

"I . . ."

"You and I, my dear, are bound by lines far stronger than like or dislike, of even love or hatred."

Above, a branch of the central oak began to shake. Andrea jerked her eyes toward it, and in a moment saw the group of birds. Their dark shapes fluttered like leaves. Were they crows? The branch strained under their weight. Again, she felt a chill. When she turned back to Deirdre Farrell, the other woman was smiling.

She glanced inside Robertson's Market, hoping that Ewan or Barbara might come to her rescue, wishing now she had accepted the offered ride. But they had moved to the back of the store to do some work.

"Excuse me," Andrea said, this time making a determined effort to step past.

"Run home, my dear! Don't stop for anything! We'll meet again!"

The words chased after her like angry bees, but she did not turn. A feeling of panic had gripped her, and now it goaded her into flight. She reached the opening of Lake Drive before pausing and glancing back. The circle was empty, Deirdre Farrell gone. A screech sounded high above, and she glanced up to see a dark shape float by overhead, then another, and another.

She had moved perhaps twenty yards up the road when

she heard the noise to her right. A breeze sighed through the trees. Leaves rustled.

You're spooking yourself again! Stop it.

She moved again, imposing a sense of calm upon herself. She had walked another ten yards when the noise came again. She stopped in her tracks. In the trees to her right, a branch cracked. Another. Leaves rustled loudly, as if something huge walked upon them.

Oh, Jesus, something was following her. Panic returned. She concentrated her will, and made herself continue walking. Something crashed in the woods. She did not stop this time, but turned toward it as she picked up speed. In the darkness between the thick trunks of trees, a pale patch moved with stealthy grace. She caught a glimpse of two red sparks in the gloom.

"Oh God."

Suddenly she knew with horrible certainty that whatever now stalked her did so at the bequest of Deirdre Farrell. Everything that Aunt Clarissa had said, everything she had read in the library books, rushed back and seemed to make a horrible sort of sense. What unspeakable monstrosity had the witch Deirdre Farrell set on her heels?

Trees rushed by. Darkness opened to swallow her, a long tunnel leading to madness. She rushed headlong into it, while behind her the thing that followed crashed loudly through the trees.

Her terror sensitized her hearing to an unbearable pitch. She could hear the ragged breathing of the thing following her. For a second the crashing stopped, and she almost came to a halt.

Then she heard the click and scrabble of movement on the road. Whatever it was, it had left the cover of the trees.

She screamed then. The trees swallowed the sound, returning only silence.

She was suddenly tempted to give in, to stop, to turn and let the thing have her, and she almost succumbed. But some deeper strength, laid bare by her terror, drove her on. Her legs pushed her forward at a pace she had not reached since being a teenager. She gulped air and spat it out,

149

gulped and spat, pushing herself faster. Behind her, the thing drew closer. Its movement on the road sounded like a garden rake drawn across pavement. Only claws could make a sound like that.

The house appeared ahead, and she cried out. It seemed so far away! Pain blossomed in her chest. She was near collapse.

Each breath emerged as a small scream, tearing at her throat. She rushed headlong into the driveway, almost running into the back of her Pontiac. Somehow she managed to avoid it and continued up toward the house. Behind her, something thumped the fender of the car. The sound of breathing closed in on her, until she seemed to feel hot breath brushing the back of her neck.

In a single movement she opened the door, burst through, and slammed the door shut. The living room windows rattled ominously.

Outside, something sharp drew across the stone steps. A sound filtered through the door, low and throaty. She leaned against the wall, clutching the carton of milk to her heaving breast. In a moment, silence returned. Whatever had followed her had moved away.

She closed her eyes, moaned softly, and fought back the urge to start weeping. Sweat spilled down her back and between her breasts.

Upstairs, a door opened. Peter appeared at the top of the stairs, and stared down at her incredulously. "Holy smokes. Are you okay?"

She peered up at him, incapable of speaking.

Outside, a bird cawed noisily overhead. She imagined she could hear the flap of wings. She looked up at Peter again. When had he gotten home? It must have been soon after she had left. Had he been walking along the trail behind the house?

An image came to her of Peter in the town circle, being handed the stone by Deirdre Farrell. A chill passed up her spine, like a touch of dead fingers.

"I'm fine," she said, answering him at last. "Everything's fine."

CHAPTER EIGHTEEN

On Wednesday, Matthew spent most of the day alone at the station while Murray Carlyle ran errands. By 5 P.M. he was feeling cantankerous. He had begun to suspect that Marissa had no need for two full-time police officers. Even one would spend most of his time with a thumb stuck up his ass.

The only incident worth noting had been the disappearance of Jack and Willy Burgess last week, and now that bone was turning to mush. He was beginning to wonder if Jack and Willy really were missing, or if the whole thing might not be a wild scheme concocted by Murray to make life interesting.

He swung his booted feet onto his desk, leaned back in his chair, and considered the possibility more seriously than he had intended.

In a few moments he shook his head. If he wasn't careful, he'd start acting just like Andrea. That thought started an avalanche of additional thoughts, and he let his feet slam back to the floor under their weight.

He picked up a paper clip, straightened it, then mangled it and dropped the broken metal to the surface of the desk. Last night had certainly been a strange one with Andrea. He had arrived home to find her sitting in the kitchen, pale and frightened. Her look was one he recognized, but not one she had ever worn. He had seen it on the faces of people who had witnessed family members murdered, on the faces of cops who had come close to death, even on the faces of drivers who had killed accidentally. It was a battle between two compulsions: fear, and a will to forget.

Seeing the same look on Andrea had sent an icy spike of fear right into his guts. His first thought had been of Peter.

"What's wrong?"

"Nothing."

"You look like you've seen . . ."

"Seen what?"

He had never seen her so argumentative.

Peter, it turned out, was okay. Something else had pushed Andrea to this edge. It took a while to coax it out of her, to convince her that he wanted to know, that he did not think her crazy. Her words remained etched in his mind, and even now, almost a full day later, thinking of them caused a shiver to race up his spine.

"It was big, Matthew, really big. I didn't get a good look at it, but it was pale, and I swear its eyes were red. It came out of the trees. I don't know if it was really trying to catch me, but it came close. I heard its breathing, and I heard its claws . . ."

His face had drained of color, and she had stopped speaking, her eyes locked on his. "You know what I'm talking about, don't you?"

He had regained his poise quickly. "No, but you're spooking me, too."

This seemed to satisfy her, and she didn't press her point. But the image that had popped into his mind as she had described the chase was of the wolf he and Murray had spotted in the woods. Pale fur. Red eyes. Massive jaws.

It followed me back. Somehow, it followed me back.

The thought brought him close to panic and returned him to the narrow, nearly invisible trail, with the crashing sounds of pursuit close behind. Jesus, no wonder Andrea was terrified.

But it couldn't have been that wolf. The town circle was nearly ten miles away from where he and Murray had last seen the animal. Did wolves range that far? The possibility seemed remote. Over the next hour he calmed and consoled Andrea until the incident had assumed the fuzzy contours of a dream. By the time they went to bed she was relaxed, half convinced she had imagined the whole thing. She *had* been tense, she admitted. Her imagination may have been fraught, she said, but did not say why. It *was* possible she had seen nothing. It may have been the wind shaking the branches. Leaves skitting on pavement might sound like claws. May it, might it, let it have been so.

Now, thinking about it, Matthew shook his head sadly. Marissa had not quite matched his paradisal expectations. He was bored with the job; Andrea hated the town so much she was imagining horrors behind every shadow; only Peter seemed to have no complaints. Was the boy's happiness important enough to warrant giving Marissa an honest chance? He nodded to himself, convinced he was right.

He had started to clean his desk when the radio buzzed. He stood slowly, yawned, walked over to the counter near Murray's desk, and picked up the microphone.

"Go ahead, Murray."

"What's up, Matt?"

He shook his head. The most productive thing the radio had been used for in the past month was to place the daily lunch orders. He held the microphone close to his mouth.

"Just about to head home."

"Maybe come on down to the Emmerson place before you lock up. Know where that is?"

"I know where it is. Can this wait until tomorrow?"

"There's something here you should see."

He slammed the microphone back in its cradle. He swore, pulled on his jacket, and went out to the car. He drove slowly along the county road, turning on his headlights after a few hundred yards. Although dusk had not yet settled, the low sky and close trees produced a darkness of their own. Three minutes later he came upon the access road for the old Emmerson place. He would have found it without the boulder. Murray's car, hidden within the trees, flashed like a beacon.

He parked behind Murray's vehicle, expectancy tightening his stomach muscles. Why the flashing lights? The blue and red throbbed ominously among the trees, against the leaning walls of the cabin. He walked carefully around the cabin, stepping over assorted trash. Murray was leaning against a dead tree, smoking a cigarette.

"Thought you'd never get here." His wide face looked ghoulish in the flashing light, his eyes narrow and glinting.

"What is it?" He was not in the mood for banter.

Murray stuck the cigarette in his mouth and walked toward the corner of the cabin. He paused, allowing Matthew to catch up, and nodded toward a nearly leafless oak tree. Two dark shapes hung from a low branch, swinging silently in the breeze.

"What the hell?" A sudden shift in the wind offered a thick, cloying smell of rotten meat. He turned his face and gagged. "Christ!" The two bundles creaked on their ropes as the wind moved them about.

"I think we've found Jack and Willy Burgess," Murray said, breathing deeply the smoke of his cigarette.

Matthew stepped closer, studying the two shapes hanging from the tree. There was something horribly wrong with them, but he could not quite grasp what it was. The tall grass below them was littered with assorted lumps. Body parts.

"Somebody did a number on the poor bastards," Murray said hoarsely.

Matthew hardly heard the words. His mind was clamoring like a fire alarm. *This sort of thing doesn't happen in Marissa. Not in Marissa. NOT IN MARISSA.*

"I would have waited until tomorrow," Murray said. "But there was something else."

Icy fingers gripped the back of Matthew's neck. "What is it?"

Murray moved beyond the corner of the house, and again waited for Matthew to catch up. A tarpaulin covered something on the ground. Whatever it was, it moved. A small noise came from the bundle. Matthew frowned, half recognizing the sound. Murray flipped back a corner of the canvas with his toe. It took a moment for Matthew's eyes to recognize the shape behind the bloody sheen that covered it, and when he did he collapsed to his knees.

"Sweet Jesus, have mercy," he whispered.

Andrea left McQuage and Ronson at 6 P.M., after spending half an hour debating whether or not to work even later. *I don't want to return to Marissa*, she realized. In the end, she had smothered her desire to stay away from the town, had packed her briefcase, said good night to Janice Ulcott, who was also preparing to leave, and started driving. Her problems at home needed to be faced, not run from.

She saw the flashing lights long before she reached them, slowed the Pontiac as she approached, and peered out the passenger window into the trees. She glimpsed, illuminated by the eerie light of the police flashers, the leaning husk of one of the abandoned cabins that had upset her upon her initial arrival in Marissa.

Curious, she stopped the car. Shapes moved within the lights.

Some prod of instinct stopped her from driving away. *Something has happened to one of my own.*

Those lights signified something terrible, something to do with her family. The longer she thought it, the more convinced she became, until her hands began to tremble on the wheel.

She put the car in gear, backed up a few yards, and turned into the narrow rutted path that led to the cabin. Parking behind Matthew's car, she left the Pontiac running and the door open. Slowly, as if exploring a maze, she edged her way around the cabin. In the darkness ahead, she saw two standing shapes, and recognized the square of Matthew's shoulders. He was playing the beam of a flashlight over a bundle on the ground, then he swung it up to pin Murray Carlyle, who was prodding at something hanging from a tree.

"Goddamnit, Matthew, keep that flashlight steady!"

"Sorry," came Matthew's reply. The beam of the flash remained on Murray, and she saw he was trying to release the swinging object from the tree. Whatever it was, i glistened wetly in the harsh light.

She stepped closer and cleared her throat. Matthew spur at the sound and swung the flashlight wildly. The nimbu of light darted around the small clearing like a hungry animal, blinding her momentarily and finally coming to focus. She held up her hand to block the light.

"It's me!"

"Andrea?"

"I saw the lights."

"Get her out of here, Matthew!"

"Andrea, go back to the car, go home." His voice was shaky.

It did nothing to diminish the premonition that had gripped her. "What's going on?"

"I said, go back to the car!"

She did not budge. Behind Matthew, on the ground something stirred. Her eyes were drawn to the movement Matthew heard it and swung his flash. For a moment the light played across the bundle, then swung away and back to her. But it had been enough, and Matthew realized his mistake.

"Oh my God," she whispered.

"It's okay, it's nothing."

She rushed past him, avoiding his outstretched arms and kneeled by the bundle on the ground. It was Peter. The boy was conscious, moving his head slowly from side to side. Although his eyes passed across her, they did not see her.

"He's covered in blood!"

Matthew was at her side, trying to lift her. She struggled out of his grip.

"It's not his blood," he said.

Murray Carlyle stepped close and nudged Matthew out of the way. He gripped Andrea's arm and hauled her to her feet. She tried to free herself, but his grip was iron. His

156

yes, shrouded in darkness, seemed to calm her.

"It's okay, Andrea. He's fine. Not a scratch on him."

"What happened?"

"It's the two hunters I told you about," Matthew said, his voice still shaking. "Peter must have found their bodies. He must have been walking in the woods after school when he ran into them."

She glanced up at the thing hanging from the tree and recognized, barely, a human shape. Another bundle, glistening and silent, lay on the ground next to Peter, a stretch of rope still attached to what might have been a foot.

"Oh, God."

"Now, Andrea," Murray said softly, "I want you to get back in your car and go home."

She jerked away violently, escaping his grasp. She kneeled beside Peter again and stroked his hair. Her hand came away wet and dark. The boy groaned.

"Can he stand?"

"Just leave him," Matthew said. "I'll get him home."

She ignored him. "Help me get him up. I'm not leaving him here."

Matthew said nothing for a moment.

"Go ahead," Murray said. "Maybe it's for the best. Let us get on with our work."

With Matthew's help, she lifted Peter to his feet. The boy swayed, but managed to remain upright.

"How could he have been walking like this? Where are his clothes?"

Matthew had no answer. She did not press him. They walked the boy to her car, and managed to get him laid out in the rear seat.

"Christ, what a mess," Matthew muttered. "You'll have to clean the whole damned car now."

"Matthew."

The sound of his name seemed to hit a nerve. He slumped, as if the life had gone out of him. She saw that his face was very pale, that his eyes were blank. He was dangerously close to a state of shock, she realized. She

157

gripped his forearm firmly.

"Matthew, come home quickly."

"There's so much to do," he protested.

She gripped more fiercely. "Come home as soon as yo can."

He was silent a moment, then nodded and turned an walked back toward the rear of the cabin.

He looks lost, she thought. *Like a little boy.*

She got into the car, turned it, and without glancing the mess in the rear seat, drove home.

CHAPTER NINETEEN

Getting Peter out of the car was the hardest part. The boy was barely conscious, and would not respond to her words. Her hands found no grip on his blood-slippery skin. Once or twice she managed to raise his upper torso to a near sitting position, while his head lagged backward like a newborn's, mouth slackly open, only to have her fingers lose their grip in the dark bloody mucous that covered him from head to foot. Finally she grasped his feet, using her coat to better her grip, and managed to pull him from the rear of the car like a heavy sack.

His buttocks crashed to the ground. The impact sent his head sharply forward, and his teeth crunched.

"Come on, Peter. Help me. You're going to freeze out here. Just hold on to me. We'll get into the house, and everything will be fine."

The words were for herself more than for Peter. The sound of her voice was an anchor to reality. The bloody heap in her arms was something out of a nightmare. She could hardly bear to touch him.

At last, with her rump pressed into the Pontiac's rear fender for leverage, she raised him to his feet. He wobbled precariously like a battered and bleeding drunk. She lifted his left arm over her shoulder.

Once she got him inside, she found herself dealing with another, almost overpowering factor. The smell. In the car, with the front windows open, fresh air buffeting her face, it had been manageable. Inside the house it was intolerable. There was an undertone of rot to it. She swallowed hard to keep her stomach in order.

By the time she had maneuvered him upstairs, into the bathroom, and finally, painstakingly, into the tub, she was exhausted, trembling, and very close to tears. She sat on the edge of the bath and looked down at him. He looked like a baby. Really, truly, like a monstrous newborn, still coated in vernix and amniotic slime. His eyes hovered between closing and opening, glinting darkly, seeing nothing. His hair was a bloody slick, plastered close to his skull.

"Peter, what have you got yourself into?"

His head lolled to the left, as if he had heard her, and he burped. A blob of dark red mucous spilled from his mouth, down his chin, and hung in a string on his chest. It was the last straw. Andrea turned away, fell to her knees, and bent over the toilet. Her stomach contracted, jumped, and emptied itself, until she was wracked with dry heaves. When she turned around again, Peter was staring at her, almost alertly, a senile smile curling his lips.

Andrea shook her head. "Oh, Peter," she said softly.

He continued to smile.

The next two hours turned into a series of brilliant, sharp-edged fragments of memory.

—Standing in front of the bathroom mirror, regarding herself appraisingly, still dressed in the clothes she had worn to work, now stained with blood and other liquids. A perfect, bright red hand print decorating her left shoulder, just above the breast.

—Bent over the tub, holding Peter's head with her left hand, while her right scrubbed his neck and shoulders, the dark, streaky water sloshing against the white porcelain, red suds clinging to her hands.

—Staring, hypnotized, into the whirlpool of draining water as a patch of bright red suds danced along the edge of the vortex before finally drifting in, disappearing with a throaty choking sound.

It was far easier to remove him from the tub than it had

been to unload him from the car; he seemed willing to cooperate now. He leaned on her as she led him to his bedroom, waited patiently as she peeled back the sheets, and lay quietly on his back as she tucked him in. His skin was pink now, scrubbed to a healthy sheen. Only the slackness of his mouth and the blind gleam of his half-hooded eyes testified to his true condition. His eyes followed her as she left the room, and they remained open after she turned off the light.

She stood at the door and turned to face him. Reflecting the hallway light, his eyes were jewels. His breathing sounded deep and regular.

"Sleep well," she whispered. "You've got a lot of explaining to do tomorrow."

He did not answer. She closed the door.

She did not know how long she stood under the shower, but she came to herself shivering, the water running cold across her breasts and abdomen. She turned it off and stepped out of the tub. Her discarded clothes lay in a pile in the corner, looking as if they'd been used by a slaughterhouse laborer. She turned away and dried herself briskly.

Wearing only a nightgown she went downstairs, debated whether to make a pot of tea, and finally poured herself a tall glass of the brandy she kept hidden in the kitchen. The alcohol traced a warm path to her stomach. Within fifteen minutes she had finished two glasses. She lay out on the sofa, her hands curled beneath her cheek.

"Hurry home, Matthew," she whispered. In her mouth, the words felt like marbles crushed against her tongue. It was ten-thirty.

She drew a long, shuddering breath, closed her eyes, then fell asleep.

She felt, rather than heard, Matthew coming home. One moment she was sleeping, the next she was rolling her shoulders so that he could stroke her back. His hands were warm, gentle, soothing. She did not open her eyes, but

161

allowed her lips to curl in a smile.

"Thought you'd never get home," she said softly.

He did not answer. His lips brushed her cheek, her neck. His breath was warm, almost hot. Warmth rose between her legs, but receded immediately as she thought of the blood that had dripped from her breasts.

"Not now, Matt."

He continued to knead her back. Her eyes began to grow heavy again. She could not bear to open them.

Matthew mumbled something, but she could not understand.

His hands moved across her back and slipped under her nightgown. Was he trying to comfort her with sex? That was so unlike him. He squeezed her right breast, and the pain brought a gasp to her lips.

"Matt!"

She opened her eyes. For a moment she did not grasp what she was looking at. A veil of light danced before her, diaphanous as a silk negligee. Shadows danced on the walls, turning the room into a spinning kaleidoscope. She felt dizzy, blinked, and tried to sit up.

Where was Matthew? Surely the sensations that had stirred her body had not been a dream.

She climbed another step to full wakefulness and regarded the shimmering light curiously. She could see the other side of the room through it, the outline of the living room doorway, the dark line of the stairway bannister.

The green light rippled. For a moment she seemed to catch an outline within the glow, something large and lean, and her stomach tensed. She saw no details, but was struck by the impression of *maleness*, as if she'd watched a subliminally erotic television advertisement.

"This is crazy." Her words, spoken softly, startled her. She sat bolt upright.

This is not a dream. This is real!

The fear that had somehow, miraculously, kept its distance, came rushing in like a dark, furious tide. She pushed back against the cushions of the sofa, retreating from the light. It seemed to sense the change in her attitude toward it. Dark lines appeared in the greenish veil, like streaks of anger. Again, she caught the impression of a male figure. This time it was larger, sharper edged, more forceful.

She closed her eyes, attempting to calm herself. As she did so, she connected the light and the erotic dream that had wakened her. The two ideas clunked together like cars at an intersection.

The man-shape defined itself within the green light. The light spread out, as if it were a cloud of gas, to fill the room. She felt its touch on her skin. She attempted to recoil, but it was all around her. The sensation was one of warmth. It made her think of Matthew.

No, no, no. This isn't happening!

Heat rose between her legs, and she arched her back to meet it. When she opened her eyes again, the man-shape, a pillar of ghostly light, was bent over her. Gaseous hands moved the fabric of her nightgown, exposing her breasts. Her pale skin looked like veined marble beneath the glowing, spectral flesh. She held her breath, fighting panic. The hands touched her. Her breasts moved as if by magic, indented by the weight of ghostly fingers. Her nipples stiffened.

Before she could stop them, sensations of pleasure raced through her body. A groan slipped from her lips. Above her, the face of the glowing man-shape brightened. As if by her own volition, her thighs opened. The ghostly hands moved between her legs.

The first touch sent her into a convulsion of pleasure like she had never experienced before. Her legs sprang open, as if before now they had been locked with a chain. Points of brightness sparkled throughout the room. For the first time she seemed to hear a sound emanating from the light, low and soft, like waves lapping against a sandy shore, or the murmurs of a lover. Or laughter.

Laughter, she thought. The thing was laughing at her!

Anger suddenly cut through the pleasure.

"GET OFF ME, YOU SON OF A BITCH!"

It felt as if a blanket had been pulled off her.

The light drew away, the man-shape became less clear. A shiver of revulsion ran through her body. My God, she thought, I was *giving* myself to that thing!

The room became still. In the space of a heartbeat, the light brightened and flared, defining the man-shape perfectly. She gasped at the sight of it. Shimmering light played across ghostly, rippling muscles. A shaggy mane of brilliant hair cascaded off the outline of a head. The hands that had produced such sensations of pleasure defined themselves into taloned claws. She saw, eyes wide, the beastly bend of the spectral legs, as if the thing were ready to pounce. Again, a sound filled the room. This time, it was low, throaty, almost a growl. Dark shadows filled the corners of the room.

When it came at her, she could not avoid it.

She felt the pulling of her hair, and then a sensation of warmth across her face. She tried to draw a breath, but could not. Blinding light played before her eyes. She heaved violently, trying to pull away, but could not budge. The thing was smothering her!

She beat at the air with her fists, encountering a vague, fuzzy resistance. A seeming eternity later, the hands released her, and she sucked in a burning breath. Another.

"No, please!"

It let her take two more breaths, then moved toward her again. The green light engulfed her, lifted her, and spun her like a baton. For a moment she was free, flying. She hit the wall behind the sofa and fell to the ground. The force of the collision knocked all the breath from her. Her lungs heaved, sucking in air. Lights sparkled inside her head, the inviting luminescence of unconsciousness. She resisted, forcing her eyes to remain open.

The glowing man-shape stepped over the sofa as if it were a pavement crack. Andrea tried to draw away, but found herself pinned against the wall.

For a moment, the thing paused and bent over her, as if it were studying her curiously. Again, she sensed that it was angry.

Its seduction failed, she realized. *I resisted its charms.*

"I won't give myself to you," she said softly. "You'll have to rape me, you son of a bitch. I won't give myself."

It backed away a step, and she breathed more easily. Her thoughts were a malestrom, but one stood out clearly. Somebody in Marissa had sent this thing to attack her. And instinctively, she knew who it was. Deirdre Farrell.

The green man-shape seemed to sense her thoughts. It stepped toward her again and reached out a hazy arm to cover her face, her nose, her mouth. She could not breath. She tried to scream, but no sound emerged.

The thing was taking her at her word. If she would not give willingly, then it would take by force.

Mercifully, as it lifted her into its embrace, she fell into darkness.

CHAPTER TWENTY

Andrea woke suddenly, and realized three things very quickly. It was daylight, she was in her own bed, and she was alone.

She swung her legs out of bed and sat there a moment. Her body felt as if it had been thrown from a train. She yawned. Pain lanced across her face, as if nails had been driven into her jaw. A sensation of cold raced through her body. She clutched the bedspread, her fingers trembling. It all came back then, in a torrent, unstoppable.

"Oh, God, no, please . . ."

Her body began to reveal what had been done to it, and each revelation brought an attendant throb of pain, a memory of violation.

She could not help it. She collapsed back on the bed and began to sob, so intensely she felt as if she were having convulsions. The pillow quickly became soggy.

Where was Matthew? The question came with a hot flash of anger conveniently attached. Had he come home at all last night? The bed looked well slept in, but that meant nothing. She could have tossed and turned enough for two people. Maybe even three. Had Matthew been the one who had taken her upstairs and put her to bed?

That made her frown. If so, he must have seen the state she was in. He must have realized that something was wrong.

166

After satisfying herself that she was not faint, she stood and stepped to the dresser mirror. The face that peered out at her was the same one she saw every morning. The dark hair was, perhaps, a bit more tousled; the eyes, if you looked closely, more bloodshot; the lips, if you knew what to look for, slightly swollen; but there was no obvious sign of what had been done to her. She opened her nightgown and studied her breasts. Holding the tender flesh in her hands, she winced.

Angry, she wrapped herself up and turned away. Had it all been a dream?

No. No. No. *Don't even think that!*

Slowly, stiffly, like an old woman, she left the bedroom and went into the hallway. Peter's bedroom door was open. The bed was made, the room empty. Her breath caught in her throat.

Where was he? Last night he had been nearly catatonic, not in any shape to move about, by himself or even with help. She went quickly downstairs, holding on to the bannister with both hands for support.

In the kitchen, pinned to the fridge with a pear-shaped magnet, she found one of Matthew's notes. She held it with trembling fingers and read.

Sorry I got home so late.
You were sleeping,
didn't want to wake you.
Why not stay home today?
Peter wanted to go to school, so I
drove him to the bus.
Probably better if he forgets.
We'll talk about it later. I promise.
I'll be home early.
Love, M.

She read it quickly the first time, then carefully a second time, hardly able to contain her incredulity. Peter had not remembered a thing about last night? Matthew had sent

167

the boy to school as if everything were normal?

She felt a stab of fury, and frustration.

For the second time that morning she began to weep. She leaned against the fridge, her body wracked with sobs. Her fists clenched at her sides. Unclenched. Clenched.

Later, dry of all tears, she went back upstairs to get dressed.

The morning was full of low gray clouds, gusts of wind, and constant drizzle. The weather was a perfect match for Andrea's emotional state. She stood on the steps before the small cottage and knocked sharply on the door. When it opened, Clarissa's face could not conceal her shock.

"My goodness, dear, you look just awful!"

Andrea twisted her lips into a grim smile. "May I come in?"

"Of course, of course, how thoughtless of me!"

She stepped past Clarissa, into the close warmth, and blinked to accustom herself to the dim lighting. Clarissa closed the door behind her, shutting out the wind and rain. She felt Clarissa's strong grip at her elbow and allowed herself to be led through to the living room. Once she was seated, Clarissa bent over her, studying her face closely.

"Would you like some tea?"

"That would be nice."

"I'll be right back."

The sound of water running came from the kitchen, the clinking of utensils, cups. She turned her head and looked out the living room window. Leaves drifted past the view, twirling on their final descent. She looked away, depressed, leaned her head back, and closed her eyes.

A warm touch at her hand made her open her eyes. King had laid his head in her lap and was staring up at her with wet brown eyes, his ears spread across her hands. His tail wagged slowly.

"Hello, boy, it sure is good to see you." She scratched behind his ears, and he pressed his head against her hand

168

for more. By the time Clarissa returned with the tea, Andrea was feeling better. The dog had provided a focus for her attention, and had made her forget, at least for the moment, the nightmare that had engulfed her.

Clarissa filled the two cups, handed one to Andrea, and guided King away. The dog went unwillingly, but finally lay down at his mistress's feet.

"Now, tell me, my dear, what troubles you?"

Andrea could not speak for a moment. She had needed so desperately to talk to somebody, but now the words would not come. She sipped her tea and looked out the window again.

"I can see," Clarissa said slowly, "that you have come to a better understanding of Marissa."

Andrea blinked, shocked at this perception. "That's one way of putting it," she said softly.

Clarissa leaned forward in her seat, cradling the teacup in her hands. "I know you find this hard to believe, Andrea. But I am not your enemy. Despite how clumsily I handled the situation with Peter, I only want to help. If you would only give me the chance."

Andrea drew a deep breath, honestly touched by Clarissa's words. She nodded. Then, in a voice that trembled with nearly every word, she said, "When you told me about Marissa, I didn't believe you. I didn't want to. It sounded so crazy."

"And now?"

"Some crazy things have happened."

Clarissa sipped her tea then lowered the cup carefully to her lap. Her eyes were sharp and unwavering, demanding attention and trust. Andrea found herself pinned.

"Tell me all about it, my dear."

Andrea nodded. She began to speak. She let everything out. For the first time since coming to Marissa, she had somebody to whom she could confide every suspicion. At every point, Clarissa nodded solemnly, or raised her eyebrows. When Andrea told of her visit to County Records, of the library books that had seemed to speak directly of the town, Clarissa smiled knowingly.

169

"I told you," she said.

You didn't tell me enough, Andrea thought.

When she got to the part about the thing following her from the town circle, and her suspicion that Deirdre Farrell had somehow set it on her trail, Clarissa blanched.

"Did you see what it was?"

"I was too frightened to turn and look."

Voice trembling, she told of coming across Matthew and Murray at the abandoned cabin, the discovery of the two mutilated hunters, and Peter at the site, covered in blood. Clarissa nodded sympathetically, yet this seemed not to faze her as much as the unseen presence that had followed Andrea home.

At this point, Andrea paused. She had finished her tea, and now placed the cup gently on the floor. King lifted his head to regard her, his liquid brown eyes as full of concern as Clarissa's, it seemed.

"There's something more, isn't there, dear?"

"There's more."

With her eyes locked on the living room window, unable to look squarely at Clarissa, she recounted what had happened last night. With every word that left her mouth, a weight seemed to lift from her shoulders, until, when she had finished, she felt giddy with relief.

Clarissa was silent a moment, then shook her head. "You poor, poor, dear," she said. "I had not realized things would get so bad, so quickly."

Andrea drew a shuddering breath. The act of confiding in Clarissa had brought her back to reality. She felt, for the first time in many days, as if her feet were on the ground.

"Now, it's your turn," she said, eyes locked on Clarissa's. "What's happening in Marissa?"

She paused, squeezing Andrea's hand reassuringly. "In the craft, as in most things, there is strength in numbers. A circle can achieve far more than any individual. But a circle, whether light or dark, must be complete to be effective. The weakest link in any circle, is the Woerloga. A male of power. Peter, my dear, is the most powerful male to enter our midst in twenty generations. The dark circle

170

has moved quickly to lure him into its grasp."

Andrea raised her head. "They need Peter?"

"Without him, they are simply a group of mischievous old women. Unfortunately, darkness has a way about it. A boy of Peter's age can be easily swayed. I fear they may be close to seducing him completely."

In her mind, Andrea ran through the changes she had noticed in Peter. It had all been real. He *had* been changing, drawing away. *Something* had been pulling him, altering him. She shook her head, suddenly angry.

"That he has not fully succumbed to their manipulations is a mystery I feel only now close to solving," Clarissa said carefully. She released Andrea's hand and drew slightly away.

"What do you mean?"

"Something, or somebody, has been thwarting their efforts."

"Somebody's helping Peter?"

"I had my suspicions even a week ago, but only now am I certain." She smiled nervously. "It is you, my dear."

"Me?"

"The first time you were here, I sensed it," Clarissa said. "I hardly believed it, of course, you being an outsider, and I convinced myself I had been mistaken."

"Me?"

"But when you visited a few days ago, and I saw how King was drawn to you, I knew I was right. You have a power stronger than many I have seen. My own special friend was drawn to you." She scratched King affectionately. "Somewhere, there is a familiar awaiting your call. You are a natural talent, my dear. Either by blood, or by temperament, you are closer to the craft than you know."

Andrea did not immediately respond. She looked down at King, and found herself getting lost in his eyes. *Somewhere there is a familiar awaiting your call.* A shiver ran down her spine. She shook her head, clearing her thoughts.

"I didn't know anything about any of this until I came

to Marissa," she protested.

"The craft cares nothing for place, or time," she said. "Whether you knew it or not, you nurtured a talent. How great, I did not suspect until today. Either by chance, or by design hidden even from you, you have been thwarting the efforts of the dark circle to draw Peter. That is why, my dear, they have begun to attack you. Like me, they did not suspect Peter would have an ally. You are a surprise to us all. But now you are in great, great danger."

Andrea swallowed hard. She wanted desperately to disbelieve what Clarissa was saying, but she did not dare. Not after last night.

"What can I do?" she asked softly.

Clarissa rubbed her hands together, and regarded Andrea speculatively.

"Do you love Matthew?"

"Yes," Andrea responded immediately.

"And Peter?"

Again, without pause, "Yes." And she nodded emphatically.

Clarissa smiled. "Then you must fight for them, my dear."

"But how? How can I fight back?" She remembered, suddenly, the groping, ghostly hands that had held her last night, and felt cold and frightened.

Clarissa reached out and touched her knee. "With my help," she said.

PART IV

Shadows

CHAPTER TWENTY-ONE

It was spitting rain when Andrea entered the town circle. In the dusklike darkness produced by the low clouds, the front of the Craft Shop glowed dimly. She clutched the sheet of paper Clarissa had stuffed into her coat pocket and crossed the circle.

There were no cars in the street, only a few pedestrians. A squall of rain blinded her momentarily, and she turned her face to blink her eyes clear. Above, the oak tree shook and trembled. Leaves, what remained of them, fell in droves, flying on the wind to gather in the gutters and on the pavement. The loose hem of her coat flapped like a ghoul's cape. This was not strolling weather.

Her fingers played obsessively with the paper in her pocket, folding it, unfolding it, as if by touch she might, somehow, fathom the mysteries written there. At the Craft Shop she paused and peered in the window. The dim interior lighting flickered, casting shadows across the walls. The shop appeared empty.

She suddenly felt ridiculous. There was nothing in this store that could help her. She squeezed the paper in her pocket and closed her eyes.

Even now, even after last night, I don't want to believe.

She straightened her shoulders, cleared her mind, and entered the shop. The bell above the door emitted a tinny rattle. She wiped rain from her forehead and cheeks, and unbuttoned her coat. The store was pleasantly warm, the air dry. The flickering effect was caused by single, low-wattage bulb, hidden behind a slowly spinning mobile made of what looked like bird's wings. She glanced furtively at the beaded curtain that blocked off the rear of the store, then moved to the counter and studied the charm display. In a moment, the beads rustled, and the proprietor appeared.

Andrea turned, smiled, and recognized the petite older woman who had served Clarissa on her earlier visit. "You're Mrs. Madden," she said.

"Please, call me Felicity, Mrs. Willson." She moved behind the counter and lifted one of the charms to show Andrea more clearly. "I knew, when I first saw you, that you would return to buy one of these. They are irresistible, aren't they?"

She was tempted to allow the woman to continue. That would be easy. Buy a charm, then run like hell. But she shook her head. "That's not what I'm looking for."

"There are some other nice things," Felicity Madden began, turning to a rack hanging with extravagantly patterned leather belts.

Andrea moved away from the counter, toward the beaded partition. She pushed through the curtain, closing her eyes as the beads brushed her face. She opened her eyes again in an area that was smaller and darker than the one she had just left. Two candles sitting on a pedestal near the back of the tiny room provided the only illumination. Shadows crowded in from all sides.

The walls were lined with narrow shelves, each shelf laden with small jars. There must be thousands of them, she thought. She stepped closer and found herself pressed against a waist-high counter, its surface scored and apparently burned. Still she could not see the contents of the jars clearly. Some were dark, some light. Some glinted as if they contained jewels. One shelf held a row of four or five books, large and tattered, their spines unreadable.

The curtains rustled behind her, and Felicity Madden pushed through.

"Mrs. Willson, there is nothing here to interest you." A tone of worry edged her voice. "Please, come to the front,

I'll show you some recent acquisitions."

"I know what I want," Andrea said firmly, surprised she had managed to sound so sure of herself.

Felicity Madden stepped closer and peered up at her face. Andrea found herself focusing on the glittering eyes. "What is it you want?" Felicity asked carefully.

"I have a list." She pulled the crumpled paper from her pocket and unfolded it. In the dim light, Clarissa's cramped handwriting looked indecipherable.

Felicity took the paper, moved closer to the candles, and began to read it. "My dear, what use could you have for these things?"

"I know their uses." She was beginning to feel angry.

Felicity did not respond, but returned to reading the list. She shook her head. "I'm not sure I even have all of it."

"You do. I can see that."

Felicity looked up, her eyes glittering. Finally, her voice subdued, she said, "It will take me time to prepare what you need. If you would care to return tomorrow afternoon, I can—"

"I need it now, Mrs. Madden. I'll wait."

She will attempt to dissuade you. Be firm! Clarissa's warning sounded clearly in her head.

But Felicity Madden said nothing more. She nodded resignedly, and moved behind the thick counter. Andrea watched, enthralled, as the little woman went to work. Although the light was dim, Felicity had no apparent difficulty seeing what she was doing. Her hands moved deftly, reaching into recesses of darkness and returning with jars and small sacks. Once, she pulled a single broad leaf from a sheaf hidden beneath the counter, wrapped it neatly in brown paper, and added it to the quickly growing pile. Another time, she carefully opened one of the jars, and a sharp, unpleasant odor immediately filled the room. Andrea wrinkled her nose, but did not turn away. Felicity reached into the jar with a pair of tongs and removed something small and wet. Andrea could not identify it, was not sure she wanted to. Felicity wrapped it and added it to the pile.

There were powders of various colors, patches of

something that looked like dried skin, two or three vials of liquids that might have been oil or might have been something else. There were leaves, and ground herbs, and to Andrea's horror, what looked like the severed limbs of a small animal. She swallowed hard as these were wrapped and added to her order.

It was nearly an hour later when Felicity stopped moving.

"That's it," she said.

Andrea studied the pile of small bags and neatly wrapped packages.

"I'll add it up," Felicity said, and moved to pick up a pencil.

"May I put it on account?"

Felicity looked up. Her eyes glittered. *She cannot refuse you.* In a moment she nodded, almost reluctantly. "Surely, you may," she said.

She began to pull the order together, wrapped it in a large piece of brown paper, then placed the whole thing in a bag. Andrea accepted the package, surprised at its lightness. "And may I have my list returned?"

Felicity paused. She fingered the list nervously, then handed it to Andrea. Her bony fingers were shaking.

"Thank you so much," Andrea said.

Outside, it was still raining. The wind seemed even stronger. It tugged her hair and flapped her coat. She hugged her parcel close as she walked.

She felt much better. The acquisition of the supplies was like a boost of energy. *You don't even know what you're getting into,* she thought. But she knew one thing. She had surprised Felicity Madden. And maybe some others. It had taken a moment to recognize the look in Felicity's eyes, but there had been no mistaking it.

Fear.

I've frightened them!

She smiled as she walked toward home.

Clarissa arrived within a quarter of an hour. She handed

178

Andrea a plastic bag as she shucked off her raincoat. "What's this?" Andrea hefted the bag. It was heavy. Something inside it clinked.

Clarissa brushed her hair with a hand, shedding water. "Our tools," she said.

The bag contained a mortar and pestle. Clarissa placed it on the kitchen table, and without delay began to unpack Andrea's parcel. She made soft clucking noises as her fleshy fingers opened each small package, inspecting the contents carefully.

"Good, good," she crooned.

The opened packages, spread across the table, looked like the remnants of a bizarre take-out dinner. Looking at it all now, in the bright light of the kitchen, Andrea felt her spirits sink. The powders were simply powders. Some might have been salt. Some might have been talc. It did not matter. Outside the confines of the Craft Shop, the supplies had lost their mystery. The glistening object she had glimpsed in the shop now revealed itself to be the pulpy eye of a small animal. Her stomach churned, half from nausea, half from disappointment.

"Oh, Clarissa, this is ridiculous." The feelings of triumph that had buoyed her only a short while ago had evaporated.

"My dear, you have mistaken all this"—she indicated the spread on the table—"for what it can bring about."

"It's all junk. Look at it. Toe of frog, eye of newt. This is just nuts."

"These sundries are for your own good, my dear. They have little to do with the thing itself."

"You mean we don't need them?"

Clarissa furrowed her brow. "Perhaps I could work without them. Many others could, I know. But you are a beginner."

Andrea continued to regard the small packets distastefully.

"We need these props. By themselves they are mere shadows, holding no power of their own. But our belief can bring the real power to life."

179

Andrea felt suddenly chilled. She shook it off. She drew a deep breath, forcing herself to regard the items on the table calmly.

"What do we do?"

Clarissa pushed the mortar bowl toward her. "I relax," she said, smiling. "You mix."

Clarissa did more than relax. She ordered, she guided, she conducted. Andrea listened, and did as she was told. She added two drops of this, a pinch of that. She applied her muscles to grinding powder into finer and finer dust, added drops of the oily liquids, mixed again, and again. An hour later, dripping sweat, having used at least a small portion of every package, she glanced at Clarissa questioningly.

"Next?"

Clarissa smiled. "We're finished."

Andrea looked down at the mortar bowl. Its white sides were coated in a thick, viscous fluid that looked like clotted blood. Flakes of torn leaves added a rough texture. She ran the pestle through the mixture, and it moved almost unwillingly, like a foot trapped in deep mud. A smell pervaded the kitchen, subtle, tenuous, unidentifiable.

"What do we do with it?"

"It's you who do something." She handed Andrea a small piece of paper. On it were two scrawled lines.

"This isn't English."

"No, it's not," Clarissa agreed. "Can you read it?"

She slowly mouthed the words.

"*Abhu nelkar reham ungoth . . . Telem lomet disanahr astol.*" She looked up at Clarissa.

Clarissa shrugged. "Close enough."

"What is it?"

"A spell of protection." She rose from the table and rubbed her hands. "Now, let's get to work."

They moved from window to window, from door to door. At each window Andrea stuck her finger in the mortar bowl, then ran the finger along the bottom of the sill. The blackish sludge left ugly marks on the white

180

paint. However, unless you were looking carefully, Andrea hoped, you wouldn't notice. At each window, after leaving the mark, she softly spoke the spell.

"Abhu nelkar reham ungoth, Telem lomet disanahr stol."

Soon, she stopped feeling ridiculous, and developed a facility for the words. They rolled off her tongue like her natural language, and she began to inflect some of the nonsense words with emotion. Clarissa, listening, regarded her strangely.

"Abhu nelkar reham ungoth, Telem lomet disanahr stol!"

It took a good hour to cover every window and door. In Peter's room, Clarissa directed her to draw a circle on the pane of glass with the black sludge. She uttered the spell twice. When she had finished, there remained only a drying scum on the inside of the mortar bowl.

Clarissa took the bowl from Andrea's hands and packed it away.

Andrea slumped into a kitchen chair, exhausted.

"Matthew and Peter will be home soon. You must clean up before they arrive. They must not know what you have done."

Andrea nodded numbly. In a moment she said, "Will it work, Clarissa?"

Clarissa moved from the kitchen, picked up her coat, and dressed slowly.

"You must believe it will work," she said solemnly. She opened the door. A gust of wind and rain hit her face. "One way or another, my dear, you'll find out tonight. You've played your cards. They know now that you are a real enemy. Tonight they will attack you in earnest. Have faith."

Then she was gone, and Andrea was alone. She moved back to the kitchen and began to clean up.

Her hands trembled.

CHAPTER TWENTY-TWO

Beneath the desk, Peter caressed the surface of the three-faced stone. His thumb found the indentations of eyes and mouth. When he did this without looking, he could almost imagine the faces were smiling. The stone was warm in his hands, and it seemed to throb as he handled it. Like a living heart. For a moment the comfortable warmth became almost unbearably hot. He loosened his grip.

His thoughts kept returning to last night. He had performed a valuable service for Longshadow. The Woerloga and Deirdre had feared that Matthew would soon contact outsiders in connection with the missing hunters. Such interference would be disastrous. So Peter had agreed to help. As one with Longshadow, he had hauled the decomposing corpses to the abandoned cabin, had strung them up in a tree. With his own son so obviously connected to the case, Matthew would be reluctant to turn to outsiders. But even Longshadow could not keep the horror of the task from him. It had been too much. Even now, he could hardly bear to think what he had done to help the Woerloga.

Only the stone, so warm and comforting in his hand, gave him the strength he needed, allowed him to go on.

I've been chosen! I can't be weak!

It would all end soon enough. None of this would matter then.

"Mr. Willson?"

The sound of his name cut through the fog surrounding him, and he looked up, blinking. Mrs. Reed's small blue eyes studied him as if he were some sort of microbe.

"I see you have finally decided to join us."

Peter fumbled with the stone beneath the desk, managing to push it into his jeans pocket. "I was . . ."

"Yes? You were?"

". . . just thinking."

"Next time, please think about coming to class awake."

A titter of laughter swept across the classroom, and Peter flushed hotly. Mrs. Reed turned to the blackboard and raised a piece of chalk. The final bell rang. Desks shook, voices rang out, and conversations sprang into life as the class rose en masse and moved for the door.

Myles Wheeler, grinning a yellow-toothed grin, bent low as he passed by and chuckled softly. "I hear you been licking that wrinkled old pussy, Willson."

Peter leaned away from the stale tobacco smell of the breath, reached for a deadly rejoinder, but found himself staring at empty space. Myles was gone. He waited until the classroom was nearly empty, then gathered his books. In the hallway, he found that Myles was waiting for him.

"So how does she taste?"

"Bug off, Wheeler."

He stepped beyond the apparition of black leather and acne-pitted skin, and moved into the flow of students. Myles cackled. His voice reached nimble fingers over the hum of hallway chatter.

"I think it's been long enough, Willson. I think today's the day I kick your faggot butt!"

Peter ignored the threat and continued on to his locker. In the past two months, Myles Wheeler's irrational hatred of him had become a daily routine. The worst part was that his own perceptions of himself were adjusting to fit Myles's warped view. He shook his head, angry. It was the price of being the new kid in a school that saw very few new kids.

He debated, for a full five seconds, about taking a text or two home to look at. But the feel of the stone in his pocket

183

dissuaded him. He had other things to think about, other things to do. He pulled on his light jacket, closed the locker, and moved back into the flow.

As a single body, a segmented worm, the students moved toward the main stairs, then down to the front entrance of the school. Peter followed for as long as he could, enjoying the jostle of elbows, the faceless anonymity that being part of the crowd provided. He freed himself from the main body at the emergency exit and pushed open the door. It closed behind him, blocking out the near deafening chatter. In the silence of the stairwell he drew a deep breath. How nice it would be, he thought, to continue on, to leave the school with everybody else. Living in Marissa had separated him completely. He began to descend the narrow stairs, down to the south parking lot where the school busses waited, ready to carry the outsiders back to wherever they had come from.

"Well, if it isn't the little faggot."

Myles stepped from the cluster of shadow in which he had been hiding, blocking Peter's way down the stairs.

"Get out of my way, Wheeler."

"Whassa matter, cock sucker? Your bum chums waiting on the bus?"

Peter moved to step past, but Myles brought his fist out of nowhere and smashed it into his stomach. Peter's eyes bulged. Nausea swept over him. He stumbled backward and hit the wall.

"How's that feel? Better get used to it. Here comes some more."

Myles lumbered toward him across the landing, his fist pulled back for another punch. Peter sidestepped the attack, and Myles thudded into the wall.

"Always heard you butt fuckers were good at dancing."

Peter spun around, freeing the stone from his pocket.

"Gonna show me that famous pecker of yours?"

Peter gulped breath and raised the stone. Its warmth reached into his hand.

"I'm going to show you something you've never seen before, Wheeler."

184

Myles, in the process of launching himself again, came to a halt and stared at Peter's hand. His eyes narrowed.

Peter smiled. As Longshadow and Deirdre had taught him, he focused on the stone, reaching for the power of the craft. He felt it, just beyond the edges of his normal perception, like some sort of beast ready to be tamed.

Behind Myles, the shadows cast by the single bulb on the wall seemed to congregate, flowing together as if they were liquid. The bully saw the motion from the corner of his eye and spun.

"What the fuck?"

"Say hello to your shadow. It's as nasty as you are."

As Myles spun, the living shadow spun with him, moving just beyond the edge of his vision.

"You'll never see it head-on, Myles," Peter said softly. "It'll always be behind you, getting closer, waiting for the moment when you're vulnerable. It's gonna drive you crazy."

Myles's eyes were now wide, a mixture of confusion and terror. A sound came from his throat, a strangled croak, as if he could not find the words to express himself. He twisted to peer over his shoulder. The shadow darted out of view.

"You crazy fuck! What have you done!"

Peter laughed softly. "Better get going, Myles. It's getting closer."

Myles jumped for the stairs, scrambled up them, and disappeared beyond the next landing. The shadow darted after him. As the door above swung open, a cry of terror descended, ricochetting down the stairs like a bullet. Then the door slammed, and silence filled the stairwell.

Peter squeezed the stone, shoved it back into his pocket, and began to descend.

In the parking lot, he zipped his jacket tightly. It was cold and raining. He moved toward the waiting bus.

In half an hour he'd be back in Marissa. The thought pleased him. He had so much he wanted to do. He needed to think more about last night, about the things he and Longshadow had done.

He climbed aboard the bus, moved to a seat near the back, pressed his face to the window, and closed his eyes. His hand moved to the stone in his pocket.

Matthew sat in the cruiser car, parked outside the Three-Horned Bull, and waited for Peter's school bus to arrive. It was just past 4:30 P.M., and the bus was due any minute. Normally he would not have cared; the distance from the town circle to the house was too short to worry about, and Peter would have been offended at such coddling. But today he didn't want the boy walking. Not on the trails behind the house. Not on the short stretch of Lake Drive that led home. Not anywhere. Not after last night.

Last night had been a nightmare, and it had not yet ended. There was still the matter of questioning Peter, of finding out exactly what he had been doing over at the Emmerson place. Hell, that was the least of it. Why was the boy buck naked? How did he get covered in blood? Did he know anything about the bodies of Jack and Willy Burgess? Could he, for Christ's sake please no, have had anything to do with the mess? Murray had not brought up the boy's name even once during the day, and for that Matthew was grateful. He had not felt up to dealing with the situation. He had felt, and the realization made him queasy, as emotionally fragile as when he had shot that kid in the alley six months ago. Were his foundations that weak, for Christ's sake?

You better believe it, sonny. You're living in a house built on sand.

"Shit," he muttered, and was surprised at the bitter sound of his voice.

He drew a deep, calming breath, and as he did so the yellow Fergus Falls District 2 school bus rolled into the town circle and blared its horn. It rolled to a stop near Robertson's Market. Matthew drove forward. As the bus moved away, the cluster of children dispersed from the pavement. He recognized a few of the grinning faces. Tommy Harborson. Sheila Bishop. Robert Cairns. Most

186

remained nothing more than grins and glittering eyes. He spotted Peter immediately. The boy, hands stuffed forlornly into his pockets, was walking with that peculiar scuff-footed gait he had developed recently, toward Lake Drive.

Matthew honked the horn as he approached. Peter stopped and turned his head. His face showed no emotion, no recognition. Matthew swallowed hard and rolled down the window.

"Just in time!" He grinned. "Get in."

Peter stared for a moment, frowned as if not sure what to do, and glanced up the road, then back at Matthew.

"Come on, get in."

"I was going to go for a walk."

Matthew said nothing for a moment. He breathed deeply. "Not tonight, Peter. Get in the car."

For a moment he feared the boy was going to argue. What would he do then? Chase him down and drag him, screaming, into the vehicle? Just the kind of scene to solidify his reputation. He held his lips tight, his teeth clenched.

Peter finally shrugged, stepped toward the car, and climbed in. The boy looked tired, Matthew thought. More than tired, he looked exhausted, run down. He began to drive slowly up the road.

"How was school?"

"Okay," Peter said. He kept his eyes out the passenger window.

"Everything fine?"

"Sure."

Matthew said nothing more. He turned into the driveway and parked behind Andrea's Pontiac. He reached to open the door, then paused. Peter was staring up at the house. He had not moved. The boy's face was white.

"What's the matter?"

"Nothing."

"Come on, then. Andrea's probably got dinner waiting."

Drops of rain continued to fall as they walked up the

187

path. The front door opened when they were a few yards away, and Andrea stepped out. She smiled nervously.

"Hi, guys."

"Hi," Matthew said. There was something different about her, but he could not put his finger on it.

Peter said nothing. The boy had stopped in his tracks. He was staring at Andrea as if she were a ghost. Then he looked up at the roof of the house. Matthew followed his gaze. Rain fell in Matthew's eyes, and he blinked.

"What wrong, son?" The boy was even whiter than before.

Oh, Christ, Matthew thought. *He's remembering everything. It's all coming back.*

He reached out a hand to support the boy, but Peter pulled away.

"Is he okay?" Andrea asked.

Matthew shrugged. He gripped Peter's arm again, and would not let the boy pull away. He led him toward the house. Peter's resistance increased with every step. When they reached the steps, a small noise began to emit from Peter's lips. Half moan, half choking sound.

"Help me get him in," Matthew said to Andrea.

Together, they pulled Peter up the steps. He was like a sack of meal, a dead weight. At the threshold of the door, he began to struggle.

"Hold him tight!" Matthew cried. "I don't know what's gotten into him. He was fine up until a minute ago."

Andrea did not respond, and Matthew found himself thinking: *She knows what's wrong with him. She's not surprised. She was expecting this.* He shook the thoughts away, recognizing them as ridiculous.

Peter's wildly kicking feet scored a hit on his shin. The pain was a knife stab that made him gasp. He stumbled forward, Peter still in his grasp, and fell through the doorway. His momentum carried Peter forward, and the boy crashed to the floor moaning.

Matthew jumped to his feet immediately and held Andrea back as she tried to kneel by the boy.

"Leave him be. He'll hurt you."

"We have to get him upstairs." Her voice was calm.

Matthew felt caught up in a situation quickly getting crazy. On the floor, Peter writhed as if he were being electrocuted. His lips pulled back from his teeth in a beastly rictus. *He looks insane,* Matthew thought. *Stark fucking raving mad.*

"It's the shock of last night," Andrea said. "This is to be expected."

She sounded, Matthew thought, as if she didn't believe it. But that had to be it, didn't it?

"I'll get him upstairs. You wait here."

"Okay,"

Matthew frowned. Her placidity was frightening. *Maybe she's crazy too. Maybe we're all going crazy.* The thought was too close to an honest suspicion, and he pushed it away, terrified he might consider it more seriously. He watched Andrea's back as she moved through to the living room, and thought to himself: *That's not the woman I left sleeping here this morning. Something has happened.*

Kneeling by Peter, he forced his mind away from the problem. The boy was now still, his face as calm as a country pond. The transition had been so sudden that Matthew had missed it. He stared at his son's face incredulously. Peter's eyelids trembled, as if already he was in deep sleep. Matthew shuddered, braced himself, and picked the boy up. He climbed slowly and carefully up the stairs, toward Peter's bedroom.

This is all a nightmare. I'm going to wake up soon. But that, he knew, was wishful thinking.

CHAPTER TWENTY-THREE

It was past eleven o'clock when the rain began to diminish, but gusts of wind continued to rattle the windowpanes. After a while, having grown accustomed to the periodic clatter, Andrea had stopped reacting.

She kept thinking of Peter. The boy had known she had protected the house. Somehow he had sensed it, had been unable to cross the threshold without help. She tried not to think about what that meant.

Matthew, exhausted, had retired shortly after settling Peter. They had not talked, and for that she felt relieved. Neither Peter nor Matthew had ventured downstairs since then.

When the noise came from the kitchen, she raised her head from her magazine, listened momentarily, then returned to reading. The wind again. When it repeated itself, this time slightly louder, she knew she had been wrong. This was something else.

She walked slowly from the living room and paused in the central hallway. Somebody, Peter or Matthew, had left a light on in the bathroom. A warm, inviting glow spread itself across the upper carpeted steps. The desire to climb those stairs, to slip into bed beside Matthew, to hold him tightly, was nearly irresistible.

I'm alone in this. It's up to me.

She moved into the kitchen. The room was nearly dark, illuminated only by stray light from the hallway. She reached for the light switch, then hesitated. Turning on the lights might be a mistake. With the large sliding doors, she would be like a fish in a bowl—perfectly visible to anyone, or anything, outside. She reluctantly drew her hand away from the switch and stepped into the darkness. The refrigerator hummed like a swarm of angry bees. For a moment, audible even above the refrigerator, she heard the faint wail of the wind. Nothing else.

She sighed, then laughed softly. "Fool," she muttered. Her hair would be gray by morning if she kept this up.

Something tapped the glass doors and she jumped.

That is definitely not the wind.

She closed her eyes and concentrated on breathing regularly, on staying calm. The tapping came again, insistent, sharp against the glass. Sweat popped on her forehead, and goosebumps rose in battalions along her arms.

Tap . . . tap . . . tap . . .

Because there was very little light in the kitchen, she could actually see through the sliding doors. She saw the dark wall of trees at the bottom of the yard, the fainter hue of the cloudy sky above. Nothing to justify the fear that had enveloped her.

Tap . . . tap . . . tap . . .

She moved slowly toward the doors, and stopped a yard away. Still, she could see nothing but the trees at the bottom of the yard, the sharp line where the deck met the grass.

Tap . . . tap . . . tap . . .

She glanced down, finally drawn to the exact source of the sound.

Tap . . . tap . . . tap . . .

The bird was barely visible above the lower frame of the door, a dark shape against the wood of the deck. Beady eyes, reflecting the stray kitchen light, glinted like marbles. Was it a crow? It did not look very large, but it certainly wasn't as small as the robins she was familiar with. The bird bobbed forward and pecked at the glass.

Tap . . . tap . . . tap . . .

191

Terror gave way to relief. She kneeled, and reached out a finger toward the bird.

Tap . . . tap . . . tap . . .

Its yellow beak glanced off the smooth glass, and its small head knocked the frame of the door. She winced at the sight.

"Shoo! Fly away!"

The bird cocked its head. Like a defiant child, its eyes glinting, the bird pecked again.

Tap . . . tap . . . tap . . .

Andrea flourished her hand at it. "Shoo, I said! Shoo!"

This time, the bird waddled backward. For a moment it seemed the glittering eyes were staring right at her, and she had the uncomfortable feeling she was being watched by someone she knew.

"Shoo!"

The bird remained immobile a moment longer. Then it released a single, grating *Caw!*, flapped its wings as if it were raising a cloak, and flew away. She followed the dark shape until it disappeared into the shadow of the trees. What had the silly thing been trying to do? To get inside? Why?

Her knees creaked painfully as she stood. "Stupid bird," she said softly.

Her eye detected the flicker of movement long before her mind offered an explanation. Dark wings coalesced out of darkness, flapping savagely. For a moment, as if captured in a camera's flash, the bird seemed suspended in midair. She caught a glimpse of yellow beak opened wide in a silent cry, marble eyes reflecting the kitchen light. And in that moment the bird smashed into the glass door.

It sounded like somebody had thrown a rock. She stumbled away from the glass. "Oh, Jesus!" Her heart hammered. She clutched a hand to her mouth.

She saw, horrified, a bloody spatter where the bird had hit—a smear of red and something else. She tried not to think what the something else might be. The bird lay on the deck, its wings extended but somehow crooked. It looked like it was craning its neck to clean under one wing. Blood leaked from its smashed beak to stain the wooden deck.

She fell to her knees by the door, still clutching her mouth. *Poor thing*, she thought. Had it been attracted by the soft kitchen light? Or by the gleaming floor tiles?

She touched a finger to the glass near where the bird lay. "Poor thing," she whispered. She thought about disposing of the body, but rejected the idea. Not tonight. She was not going to open this door for anything. She would ask Matthew to do it tomorrow morning. She nodded to herself, prepared to stand, and froze.

The scuff-board by the door had suddenly started to glow. She blinked against the thin line of light, so bright it cast her shadow across the rest of the kitchen. It came to her suddenly, exactly what she was looking at, and she stiffened. She had drawn the same line at every window, at every door, earlier in the day, using the dark sludge Clarissa had directed her to concoct. If it was glowing, that meant . . .

She raised her eyes and peered out the glass doors. Mist was pouring out of the trees at the bottom of the yard. Tendrils of blue vapor snaked their way across the grass, groping for the house. The blanket of mist writhed, as if hundreds of creatures scuttered beneath its cover. Her eyes were drawn to movement within the trees, now illuminated faintly by the glow of the mist, and she saw a large shape flash between the thick trunks.

"Oh, God." She scrambled to her feet.

Smaller shapes flashed across her field of vision, and she glanced upward to see three or four birds darting skyward. The sound of their calls dwindled, rushed off by the wind. She stared, entranced, as the mist spilled over the top of the deck and poured toward the door. It gathered there like rain water. The moment it touched the glass, the line of light glowed more brightly. She held up a hand to shield her eyes.

Suddenly the mist rose like a curtain to cover the door, and she could see nothing but faintly glowing blue. As if by magic, the shape of a hand, billowing and ghostly, materialized in the mist. It pressed itself against the glass, felt around like a blind man seeking a lock. Andrea stepped back, her heart pounding, remembering the attack of the other night.

But the door remained shut. The line of light at its base reached a blinding brilliancy, and she could no longer even glance at it.

It's working, she thought. *It's working!* She heard herself laughing, recognized the note of madness in the sound, and made herself be quiet.

Outside, the mist swirled. She heard a sound, like snow being driven against a window. As she watched, a network of fine cracks, like a giant spider web, spread across the glass, clouding it. She stepped backward, terror mounting.

"Oh, please, no . . ."

But the glass held. The line at its base continued to glow. And in a few moments, the mist began to withdraw. She watched it pull away, spilling off the deck to the grass. There, as if teased by the wind, it swirled and rose like a storm-tossed sea.

"You're not getting in tonight," she whispered.

As if it had heard her, the mist swirled violently. Shapes appeared on its surface, darted here and there, and sank into the glowing blue. She felt as if she were watching a child throwing a temper tantrum. She laughed softly, turned away from the glass, and left the kitchen.

They know now that you are a real enemy.

In the hallway, she turned to the door. A line of light glowed brilliantly at its base. She could see billows of blue through the window.

"Keep on knocking but you can't come in," she whispered.

In the living room, the glowing lines at each window filled the room with clean, white light. Almost like daylight. Outside, she watched the mist swirling around the cars, almost frantic. Two birds flitted by the window, emitting caws of futile anger.

"Fuck you too," she whispered.

194

She began to move about the main floor, checking all the windows. Everywhere she had spread the concoction, protective light glowed fiercely. Finally, she returned to the living room and dropped into the sofa.

I've beaten you!

She reached to pick up her magazine, then paused. Something thumped, somewhere in the house. She stiffened, listening carefully.

The sound came again, and this time she placed it.

The basement.

The feeling of triumph disappeared, as if it had never existed. Her heart hammered in her chest.

At Clarissa's direction she had spread the concoction and muttered her spell at every window on the main floor and upstairs.

But they had forgotten about the basement.

Trembling, she rose slowly and moved into the hallway, down to the basement door. She breathed deeply.

Calm down. You're safe.

She shook her head, unwilling to believe, then reached for the handle. It felt cold to her touch. She closed her eyes, then slowly turned it, opening the door a crack. Another crack. Another. Until she could see the base of the stairs.

Blue mist swirled across the floor, filling the darkness with eerie light. Tendrils of blue vapor slowly climbed the stairs, writhing and twisting. She caught a glimpse of one of the basement windows hanging open, and she gasped. She slammed the door and pressed her back to it.

"God, help me."

Idiot, idiot, idiot!

What was she going to do now? Clarissa had taken the mortar bowl with her. Besides, it had been empty. They had needed everything in the bowl just to do the work they had done.

Panic began to grip her, and her mind emptied. At her feet, mist began to leak through the base of the door. She closed her eyes, prepared to accept defeat, and the horror that accompanied it. And in that silent moment of despair, she seemed to hear Clarissa's voice in her head.

The mixture had been a prop. A crutch, to help her perform the spell. Clarissa had said as much. It was the spell itself that held the power, not the stinking sludge she had mixed in the mortar bowl.

Icy cold stabbed her feet, and she glanced down to see mist swirling about her ankles. She dropped to her knees, fighting terror. *Don't think about it, just do it, let it come naturally.*

Mist caressed her knees, her shins, her thighs, bringing numbness. The cold sent fingers reaching through her body. She closed her eyes and tried to ignore it.

"Abhu nelkar reham ungoth, Telem lomet disanahr astol."

The words slipped from her mouth as if they were her natural language. She reached her hand into the mist and drew a line at the base of the door.

"Abhu nelkar reham ungoth, Telem lomet disanahr astol!"

At first, she thought nothing had happened. Mist continued to pour through the space between the door and the carpet and spread out through the hallway. Blue light rose to encompass her. But as she repeated the spell, as the words came from her mouth with greater feeling, she noticed a change. The cold that had seeped into her began to leach away, and her arms and legs throbbed with a power that felt almost electric.

"Abhu nelkar reham ungoth, Telem lomet disanahr astol."

She rose to her feet, pressed her hands against the door, and spoke the spell. Again. Again. Until she was mumbling continuously, her eyes closed tightly, her body pressed into the door as if it were a lover.

"Abhu nelkar reham ungoth, Telem lomet disanahr astol!"

She opened her eyes, then slammed them shut again. The whole basement door was glowing so brightly she feared even that single glimpse had blinded her. Pain shot to the back of her head. She turned away, rubbed her eyes, and blinked. Sight returned slowly. The hallway was empty, the mist gone. Her shadow, cast by the glowing door, climbed the walls like a giantess.

From the basement, a clatter of sounds rose. Things fell. Glass broke. Once, she was convinced she heard a voice, plaintive and angry.

She moved away, down the hallway and to the kitchen. She watched, through the glass doors, as the mist receded. It flowed across the grass, a flood of blue, and disappeared into the trees. The forest filled with light. Shadows capered and danced as the mist swirled among the trees. She thought she heard noises, shouts, and screams, but she was not sure. Within minutes, darkness returned, and the trees melted into the returning night.

I did it. I really did beat them.

The light at every door and window diminished to a faint glow, and finally disappeared completely, returning the house to darkness.

CHAPTER TWENTY-FOUR

Matthew woke, as usual, before dawn. Andrea lay quietly on her side. He watched the blanket rise slowly with each breath. She looked like a child, innocent and oblivious. He swung his legs out of bed and sat there a moment, gathering his wits. The house felt strange around him. As if overnight, somebody had changed details all over the place. Nothing large, or obvious. Just small things. Invisible things.

Downstairs, with a cup of coffee, he sat at the kitchen table and stared into the backyard. It took him a few moments to realize that what he was looking at was not an effect of fatigue, and frowning, he rose and walked to the sliding doors. From top to bottom, the glass was fogged with fine cracks.

"Jesus Christ," he muttered.

On the deck by the door lay the smashed body of a bird. Blood leaked from its beak. There was a bloody smear on the window, about eye level. The bird must have dive-bombed the place last night. Christ, it must have been moving like a bullet. Dead instantly.

Andrea must have jumped out of her skin. He chuckled at the thought. Ghosts, she would say. Or she'd blame it on Clarissa. He remembered how she'd come to him with that story, nearly in tears. *Witches, Druids, Spooks* . . . Jesus. Funny as all hell. Ha ha.

He finished his first cup of coffee, poured himself another, tasted it, and dumped it, disgusted, into the sink. He went back upstairs. In the bedroom, he crouched at Andrea's side of the bed. He reached out to touch her face, then stopped himself. What if she screamed? That would be too much. He couldn't handle that. Not this morning. He pulled away a few inches and cleared his throat loudly.

Her eyes blinked open immediately and came to focus on him. He felt idiotic relief at the spark of recognition in her eye.

"Sorry, didn't want to wake you."

"'S okay. Time to get up anyway." She struggled to rise.

"No, stay in bed. Why don't you take the day off work. You're tired. We're all tired."

She smiled sleepily. "Maybe you're right," she mumbled.

"Of course I'm right. And keep an eye on Peter."

Her eyes widened, became more alert. "He's not going to school?"

"Thought I'd tell him to stay home."

After a moment, she nodded. "I'll watch him."

Matthew rose to leave. Andrea held out a hand. "Kiss," she said.

He bent down and kissed her, and by the time he stood straight again, she was sleeping. He left the bedroom and moved to Peter's room. The boy woke when Matthew poked his shoulder. He groaned softly.

"How you feeling this morning?"

"Terrible," Peter said.

"I don't wonder. You remember about last night?"

"No." Too quick.

"The night before?"

"A little, not much."

"We'll talk later. I want you to take the day off school."

Peter's eyes widened.

"Do you understand?"

Peter nodded.

"Stay around the house. Or there'll be hell to pay."

He nodded again.

Matthew reached out and ruffled his hair. "Back to sleep."

Peter closed his eyes.

Outside, sweat popped on Matthew's arms and back. Morning mist clung to the grass, seeping along the edge of the driveway. He felt a stab of fear so sharp, so strong, that he almost turned around and went back inside.

Like in my dreams.

His night, as usual, had been filled with nightmares. He remembered, vaguely, dreaming about blue mist. Something hiding in the mist, coming for him. And for Peter. Something he could not see, and did not want to see.

"Calm down, boy," he muttered softly.

He walked quickly to the car, climbed in, started it, and left the driveway in a spray of gravel. *Keep this up and you'll be jumping at shadows. Just like Andrea.*

The prospect did not please him.

The day went from bad to worse. Matthew spent the morning, and most of the afternoon, preparing paperwork for the Jack and William Burgess case. Yesterday, Murray had transported the carcasses to the county morgue in Fergus Falls, where Ted Cocoran, occasional pathologist, would perform autopsies. Three Glad Bags full of assorted body parts picked out of the grass near the Emmerson place had also been sent along for the ride. Matthew was not sure he wanted to know what had happened to the two hunters. His first instinct, like Andrea's, had been to call the State Police, but as expected, Murray had vetoed the idea. This time, however, Matthew had not put up much of an argument.

"We call in the State Police, there will be trouble. Matt. Trust me. They'll find out about Peter, even if we say nothing. I know your boy ain't involved, and you know it. But those State fellas don't use common sense. They'll hang Peter out to dry. You'll be letting yourself in for big trouble. We can handle this ourselves. Hell, I think it was animal attack anyway."

"They were strung up and mutilated, for Christ's sake!"

"Now calm down, Matt, just calm down. Draw a deep breath, boy, hold your shorts. Just 'cause they were strung up, doesn't mean they were murdered. I think they got ripped up by some animal, died near their camp. Maybe even by that wolf we saw."

"You said wolves don't attack people."

"Always a first time. I think that's what happened. I think some asshole punks from Fergus, tramping through the woods, found the bodies, thought they'd have a little fun with us."

"That's sick."

"Matt, Halloween is less than two weeks away. Brings out the morbid side of everybody. I think that's what happened. I'm sure of it."

"You believe that?"

"Sure I do. So should you."

Matthew hadn't believed it. Not completely. Who are you protecting, Murray? What aren't you telling me? But he had let it ride. For Peter's sake. For Andrea's sake. And now, slowly, inexorably, the daily boring routine of Marissa's police work, or lack of it, was falling back into place.

Today, Murray had been in one of his needling moods, and for the first time had managed to get under Matthew's skin. By 3 P.M., Matthew was tired, bored, and quickly sinking into the sourest mood of recent memory.

From his desk by the gunrack, Murray drew on his cigarette, guided a plume of smoke into the air, and grinned.

"Look at you, Matt. You're run-down, boy. You don't look good."

Matthew ignored him, and continued to add finishing touches to his report. In Marissa, there was time enough to make every routine report a masterpiece of literature.

"I've seen it before," Murray said.

Matthew, though he knew it was a mistake, put down his pen, looked up, and took the bait. "Seen what before?"

"Seen a man screw his chances for a woman."

"If you're talking about Andrea, you've got it wrong. told you she's okay."

Murray pursed his lips and narrowed his eyes. Matthew did not like the look.

"If you've got something to say, Murray, then say i You're driving me batty with your dipshit chatter."

Murray grinned. "See what I mean? She's got you o edge. You're jumping at shadows."

Matthew said nothing for a moment, disturbed at th echo of his earlier thoughts. "Andrea's okay," he repeate at last.

Murray shrugged. "That's not what I hear."

"What have you heard?"

"Oh, just little things. People talk. Most of the time, it just dirt somebody made up to hurt somebody els Sometimes, it's the truth. There's a lot of talk abou Andrea."

Matthew felt himself go cold, felt his anger turn into tight ball in his guts. "Like what?"

"She's been talking about ghosts and witches, con spiracies."

Matthew felt himself go cold. "To who?"

"I don't know. Nobody in particular. It's just talk."

Matthew opened his mouth to say something, the snapped it shut. How could he argue with that? She ha said the same things to him. He hadn't thought for moment she might take it outside the family. *Jesus Chris Andrea, what are you trying to do to me?*

"Somebody saw her the other day running into th loony store."

"The what?"

"The Craft Shop. You know, little place run by th cookie old broad, Felicity Madden."

"So what?"

"So, they sell charms, stuff like that. Loony stuff."

Matthew drew a deep breath. His shoulders slumped. didn't know that."

Murray crushed out his cigarette, tapped another fro his pack, stuck it in his mouth, and lit it. He exhaled oiling smoke animal. "I'm not one to butt into other people's business. But I like you, Matt."

Matthew turned up his lips in a humorless smile. *And I like you too, Murray, you prick.*

"You got a future here. You may not know it, but you do. Marissa takes care of her own. Wouldn't like to see it ruined by your wife."

"Andrea . . ."

"I know. She's okay." Murray drew on his cigarette. "You'd know better than me. You're a good man, Matt. You're carving yourself a niche here. People like you. They like you a lot. Like I said, you got a future. Don't let your woman ruin that for you."

"What are you getting at, Murray?"

Murray grinned. "Be a man. Show her who's boss. Flex your muscles a bit. Hell, she'll probably love you for it. Women love that kind of stuff."

Not the women I know, Matthew thought. *Not Andrea.*

An uncomfortable, palpable silence settled in the room. Matthew could not bring himself to look at Murray. He turned his attention to the report in front of him, but did not even see it. The ringing of the phone saved them.

He answered it before Murray had time to blink.

"Matthew?"

"Hello, Andrea."

Across the room, Murray winked. *"Checking up on you,"* he mouthed silently.

Frowning, Matthew shook his head.

"Sorry to bother you," Andrea said. "I just got a call from work. Somebody wants to see a property I've got listed in Battle Lake. They want me to run over there."

"But you said you were going to stay home. Where's Peter?"

"He's sitting outside reading," she said. "I don't have much choice, Matt. It's my listing. Besides, we could use the money. This looks good. If you could come home . . ."

"I can't come home now."

Murray grinned, winked, and laughed silently.

"Well, I can't take him with me."

"Then leave him there. He'll be fine."

"Are you sure?"

"Don't worry about it. I'll be home early. Go sell you're damned property."

She did not immediately respond. Across the room Murray was making mock pouts.

"Don't be angry, Matthew. It's not my fault."

"I'm not angry," he said, far too curtly.

She paused again. "I'll see you later, then."

"Okay."

"I love you."

"Okay," he said again.

Another pause, and this time the silence was heavy with meaning just out of Matthew's reach. He heard Andrea's voice, soft, almost tremulous. "Bye." And then the soft click of the phone.

He dropped the receiver back in the cradle. "Shit."

"Trouble on the home front?"

"Fuck off."

Murray laughed, but there was no humor in it. "Don't take it out on me, buddy. She's *your* wife."

Matthew sighed. "Sorry."

Murray crushed out his cigarette, swung his feet off his desk, stood slowly, and yawned. "Listen, there's nothing doing here. Let's hit the Bull."

Matthew sighed again, feeling weary and confused. "I don't drink, Murray."

"Always a first time," Murray said. "Come on." He put on his jacket, moved to the door, turned, and waited. "I got someone I want you to meet."

Matthew drew a deep breath, and released it slowly. *Don't screw me around, Andrea. You're twisting me up. I don't know what to think anymore.*

"You coming?"

Matthew stood, opened his desk drawer, and dropped in the report. "I'm coming," he said.

CHAPTER TWENTY-FIVE

Andrea spent nearly two hours showing the cabin, and by the time the prospective buyer was gone, it was getting dark. She stood on the empty porch, staring out across the water.

Battle Lake was gray and sombre. On the east shore, visible as a white smear, she could just make out the town. *Not at all like Marissa,* she thought. The atmosphere here was different. It felt open and friendly. She tried to imagine the pressing tress, the almost claustrophobic atmosphere of Marissa, and succeeded all too well. She shuddered, locked up the porch, and walked back to the Pontiac.

She climbed into the car, cranked the ignition, and began the drive to the highway. As she drove west on 210, she glanced periodically at the sky. It grew darker with every mile, and with every mile her tension mounted. Damnit, how had she allowed herself to be called away from Marissa so late in the day?

By the time she reached the Marissa turnoff, dusk was past and night was settling. She peered down the county road and blinked in astonishment. The darkness was unfathomable. The trees melted smoothly into the road, and the sky melted smoothly into the trees. An unblemished, impenetrable backdrop of utter darkness. She turned onto the road, drove a few seconds, then stopped the car. Her knuckles were white around the wheel.

Just calm down, sister, you're spooking yourself.

She drew a deep breath, held it, let it out, and drew another. Soon her grip on the wheel relaxed, and the tension in her shoulders drained.

She muttered under her breath, and froze at the sound of her voice: *"Abhu nelkar reham ungoth, Telem lomet disanahr astol!"*

The spell had turned into a sort of oral pacifier for her, the words coming naturally to her mouth, as she had once muttered the Lord's Prayer as a child. She shook her head at her own foolishness. Yes, the spell had worked at home. How could she deny that? She had seen its effects with her own eyes. But what good would it do, miles from home, in the car? And what was it supposed to protect her from out here?

She flicked on her brights. The trees on either side of the road seemed to swallow the light, but now the road was clearly visible ahead. She pressed her foot on the gas pedal, and began to drive.

Ten minutes later, as she neared the spot where the two hunters had been found, she found herself slowing involuntarily, peering into the darkness of the trees, as if she might, again, see something. This time, the darkness remained solid. No police lights. No hanging bodies. And yet, a strange feeling of cold seemed to grip her as she passed the spot, and she shivered violently.

"Jesus . . ."

Then she saw the light. Not from the side of the road, but in her rearview mirror. She squinted her eyes. Behind her, the road was dark. Frowning, she continued to stare. She could have sworn she had seen reflected headlights. For a moment she turned her attention back to the road, and as she did so, green light filled the car.

"Damn!"

She glanced in the mirror. The green face, a swirling pattern of misty light, seemed to lunge out at her. Andrea screamed. Her hands twisted the steering wheel, an involuntary reflex of terror, and the car swerved wildly. For one frozen, hanging moment, she thought she had things under control. The headlights showed the road curving ahead. The wheel in her hand felt firm and solid. One more twist, and she would be back on course.

But the moment passed. The trunks of trees rushed by in a blur, illuminated briefly by the passing headlights then swallowed quickly by the darkness. Then the car was sailing, flying, lifting from the road. She saw the branches of trees reaching for her, and realized they were far too close to the window. The car lurched sickeningly, slamming her into the door. She screamed again. The engine roared. She smelled smoke. Her chest hit the steering wheel as the car came to a shuddering, sudden stop.

She acted then on instinct. Her hands fumbled with the seatbelt and opened it. She jerked the door handle. It would not budge. The sharp tang of gasoline filled the compartment. Her head swam. *Oh, God, help me, it's going to burn, it's going to BURN.* . . . She slammed her shoulder into the door, and this time it opened with a sound of metal groaning. She threw herself out, onto the grass. Behind her, the wreck of the car groaned, clicked, and settled. The front left tire continued to spin, wobbled, then came to a stop.

Only the headlights, arching crazily into the trees, remained alive. Andrea scrambled away, pushing herself up the side of the ditch, until she hit the road. There was no sign of the ghostly horror that had precipitated the crash. *You imagined it. There was nothing there.* As she watched, the headlights faded, then cut out, and darkness came rushing in.

For a few minutes she sat there at the side of the road, surrounded in darkness, her mind a blank. Slowly, as if she were waking from deep sleep, the reality of her situation came drifting back in pieces.

She had crashed the car. She was a mile from home. She would have to walk.

She fought down panic. Not now, damn it. No time for panic, or for fear. Her body ached. She did not think she had broken any bones, but she was not certain. Right now, there was no time to check. She had to start walking. Had to get home. Time enough for the rest later. When she was safe.

She pushed to her knees, her body throbbing like one huge bruise, gritted her teeth, and stood. She wobbled there a moment, blinked, and gained her balance. Her night vision had slowly cut in, and now she saw the road curving ahead toward town, a ribbon of shadow against the darkness of the trees. She drew a deep breath, let it out in a painful hiss, and began to walk.

She had walked perhaps a hundred yards when the shape solidified in the darkness ahead. She squinted her eyes, trying to see better. Was it a person? Standing in the middle of the road? She kept walking until she was within a few yards of the apparition, until she began to recognize something in the posture of the person ahead. Relief flooded her like a drug, then left as quickly as it had come.

"You!"

"What a nice surprise, meeting you on the road at this time of night," Deirdre Farrell said. In the darkness, her features were mottled shadows.

She began to shake. "My car . . . I had an accident . . ."

"Yes, I know."

Andrea opened her mouth to say something, then closed it. She heard a noise behind her and spun around. Somewhere back along the road, a greenish light glowed. The trees looked dead, silvered with decay.

She turned her attention back to Deirdre Farrell. *Don't show her you're afraid. That's what she wants.*

Deirdre Farrell smiled. "Did you think that last night would be the end of it?"

"Please, get out of my way."

"You have entered waters far too deep for you, my dear."

She shivered, repulsed by the intimacy of the other woman's voice. She closed her eyes, trying to ignore the throbbing pain that seemed to be robbing her of clear thought. She drew a deep breath, and tried to calm herself. When she opened her eyes, Deirdre Farrell was regarding her speculatively.

"Such a little thing."

"Get out of my way."

Deirdre Farrell laughed.

The words came to Andrea's lips then, slipping out before she could hold them back. *"Abhu nelkar reham un—"*

"It's too late for that, you little fool."

Andrea froze, the words jamming in her mouth. *Say it! Say it, for God's sake!* But she could not speak.

"Now it's my turn," Deirdre Farrell said.

Andrea shook her head. "No!" Panic exploded within her, pushing her forward. She lashed out with her right arm, and connected with something. She heard Deirdre Farrell's cry of pain and dismay, and then she pushed past and began to run. The darkness seemed endless ahead of her, and she could barely make out the line of the road. Her legs churned beneath her and pushed her forward, sending jolts of pain spearing through her already pain-wracked body. Tears streamed down her face, and her breath came in gasping sobs. Behind her, as she ran, she heard Deirdre Farrell's high, cackling laugh.

Mercifully, her body became quickly numb to the pain of movement. Only her mind, hanging on to sanity by a quickly unraveling thread, suffered. She did not need Deirdre Farrell to conjure demons. Already they pursued her, brought to life by her imagination. The darkness writhed around her.

It was the crashing noises from the trees to her right that finally brought her to a halt. She knew, immediately, that she could run no farther. It must still be half a mile to the town circle. Deirdre Farrell's laughter sounded faintly behind her, wavering, insane. She stumbled to a halt, bent over, and supported her arms on her knees, gulping air in agonizing breaths.

Again, the crashing came from her right. She peered into the darkness of the trees, but saw nothing. Strangely, she felt no fear. *Whatever it is, it's got me. I can't run anymore. I can't.*

The crashing grew louder. For a moment, she thought

she saw something pale flash in the darkness.

Just like the other night. She held her breath and listened. Something moved in the trees. She heard branches crack. In a moment, a faint growling sound.

She had escaped the thing once before, but not this time. There was nowhere left to run. Fear, resurrected, prodded her. But she could not move. From down the road, Deirdre Farrell's laugh drifted like a scream on the wind. Andrea winced. Oh God, how could she ever have hoped to fight these people on their own terms? She was not one of them. She never would be.

Despair wrapped dark arms around her, and she began to weep. *Damn you, Clarissa, what have you done to me?*

She wept for an interminable time, blocking out the world completely. It was only the soft growling at her side that finally brought her back. She opened her eyes, wiped away tears, and raised her head.

The wolf stood less than an arm's length from her right side. Its head, she saw with horror, was nearly as high as her shoulders. She caught glimpses of smooth fur, silver in the darkness. Red eyes gleamed at her from a diamond-shaped head that might as well have been a lion's. She had never seen an animal like this in her life. Not in books, not on television. The growl that emitted from its throat seemed to reach to the very core of her being. The air itself seemed to shudder. Some instinct within her, long hidden, jumped to life. Human beings were not meant to stand before animals like this. They were meant to run.

She stepped backward. The wolf stepped toward her. Its jaws were open, and saliva dribbled down to splatter on the road. Its growl deepened, and she shuddered involuntarily.

"Please . . ."

The animal cocked its head at the sound of her voice, and stopped in its tracks. Again, its growl changed timbre. The hairs on the back of Andrea's neck rose. Soon, she knew, she would begin to shake. She would shake to pieces.

She heard another sound then, louder than it had been

before. Deirdre Farrell's voice. "I'm coming, my dear! You can't run from me! Tonight, you are mine!"

The wolf heard it too. In a movement so quick, so violent, that Andrea nearly fainted, the animal spun around. Its claws scraped on the road. To this point, its growl had been almost subliminal. Now, it erupted in full. The sound was like an idling chainsaw. Saliva spilled unchecked to the road. Over the animal's shoulder, Andrea saw the brightening of green light.

"I'm coming for you! You can't run!"

In a moment, Deirdre Farrell, and whatever lurked within that green haze, would come around the bend in the road. And then it would be over. Andrea felt the tears coming. Her knees wobbled.

Just give in. Let them have you. What's the point in dragging this out?

The prospect was so appealing, she almost collapsed. But even as she thought it, even as she prepared to fall to the road, the wolf spun on her. Its teeth flashed, and it lunged. She saw a red eye, a gate to hell. Smelled the foulness of its breath. The teeth slashed past her face, inches away. She stumbled backward.

The instinct she had felt earlier now raised its head in triumph. She reacted then like any animal faced with death. She turned, unthinking, and ran. Where the strength came from she did not know. She was a mindless mass of instinct. Her body knew only one thing. *Run! Survive!*

Deirdre Farrell paused in the middle of the road and listened. Ahead, she sensed that Andrea Willson had started to run again. Deirdre smiled. The damned meddling bitch was going to pay for what she had done. The memory of the thwarted attack still made her livid.

"Run, my dear, run! Distance won't protect you!"

She started walking again. Behind her, the glowing green form of the incubus followed quietly. Deirdre turned to it.

"I want to be there when you take her this time," she said to the thing.

The green shape glowed brightly. For a moment, she glimpsed the man-shape within the haze, and she turned away, shuddering. Even she was susceptible to the incubus's power.

She continued to walk. She had just rounded the bend where Andrea had disappeared, when she saw the shape standing in the road ahead. From here, it looked like some sort of dog. A large dog, granted, but . . .

She stopped in her tracks.

The dog, or whatever it was, now stood to its full height. Deirdre sucked in a harsh breath.

"Gods, that's a wolf!"

At the sound of her voice, the creature ahead lifted its muzzle and released a howl. The sound was like the screams of the damned, and goosebumps erupted along her arms and shoulders.

Could Andrea Willson have raised this demon? Was it protecting her somehow?

She took another step toward the creature. In turn, it moved toward her. In the darkness, its eyes seemed to glow like coals, pinning her with their malevolent gaze.

The wolf continued to trot toward her, and she marveled at the size of it. Muscles rippled beneath its white coat. It was the largest wolf she had ever seen.

Biting back a surge of fear, she raised her hand and waved it at the beast.

"Begone, demon!"

The wolf paused, and listened intently. But the minor spell seemed to have no effect. It trotted toward her again.

Deirdre stumbled backward as the thing approached, fear now gripping her firmly. The wolf stopped two yards from her. It emitted a low growl, its teeth bared. She tried to step past it, but it swung its head to stop her.

It was blocking her passage!

She raised her hand again and pointed at the wolf. "Who called you, creature? I demand to know!"

The wolf howled again, ignoring her spell. Whatever it

was, it was powerful. She turned to the incubus, seeking support, but saw that it had gone. She shuddered in anger. Vengeance had been snatched from her grasp! She sensed that Andrea Willson would now be within the safety of her home, protected from attack by the charms she had learned. And now this thing, this wolf, this demon, was adding insult to injury, refusing to let her pass.

She lunged toward it, waving her hand.

But the wolf did not retreat. Instead, it snapped at her arm, tearing a chunk of fabric from her coat.

Deirdre yelled in dismay, stumbling backward. The wolf growled menacingly. It turned its head and looked back along the road where Andrea had run, as if listening for her. In a moment, as if satisfied that she had escaped, it again turned its gaze upon Deirdre. She held her breath.

The wolf growled, raised its voice until it sounded almost like a whine, then turned and darted into the woods at the side of the road. In a moment it was lost from sight among the trees.

Deirdre drew a deep breath, and let it out.

"Andrea Willson, you have some surprises up your sleeve." She smiled grimly. "But not enough, my dear. Not nearly enough."

Fighting back her anger, she walked toward the town circle.

PART V

Woerloga

CHAPTER TWENTY-SIX

It was beginning to seem like a dream.

Matthew closed his eyes as tendrils of pleasure coiled through his body. He groaned, hardly recognizing the sound of his own voice. He opened his eyes again, looked down at the blonde head bobbing rhythmically in his lap, and looked away and up, into the dark recesses of the unfamiliar room. He placed his hands on the head, needing something to grip.

"Oh God," he said. He could not hold on much longer. He tried to lift her away, but she resisted, opened her mouth, and sucked him deeper. "Please," he groaned. "I'm going to explode."

She stopped her motions for a moment, lifted her face, and looked up at him. Even in the dim light she looked beautiful. Her eyes gleamed playfully. Her lips smiled. "I want you to explode," she said softly, then turned her face away and took him into her mouth again.

Matthew leaned away, pressed his back into the arm of the uncomfortable sofa, and let her continue her work. Her name was Rowena, and he had met her not even an hour ago.

I'm dreaming, he thought for the umpteenth time. *This isn't happening*.

The feeling of unreality was exacerbated by the alcohol in his system. Murray had plied him expertly, and Matthew, his emotions in turmoil, had succumbed. The smoky haze of the Three-Horned Bull had lulled him. The noises had turned into the rhythmic chanting of some ancient, obscene, tribal ritual. He had felt his senses diminishing, had felt the alcoholic haze sliding in, assuming that old familiar position behind his eyes. God, it was good. It had been so long.

He remembered, only vaguely through a blanket of pleasure and drunkenness, somebody coming up to him at the bar, saying something about Andrea.

"What?" he had blurted.

"We just saw her running through the circle. Looked to be in rough shape. Crying and all."

"Andrea?" For a moment, his concern had cut through the gauze of drunkenness. He remembered she had gone into Battle Lake to show a property, and he had assumed she would have returned hours ago.

But Murray had clapped him on the shoulders and grinned into his face. "Don't even think about her, Matthew."

"Is she okay?"

"Matt, it's the same old game."

"But . . ."

Then another drink had been shoved into his hand, and he had lifted it to his mouth, sucked back the burning liquid, and slowly grinned. *Yeah, I know what she's like,* he had thought.

Later—he did not know how much later—Murray had disappeared into the smoke and the milling crowd, and had returned in seconds with a beautiful woman in tow. Matthew had sat to attention, leering drunkenly. The woman, a girl really, had regarded him through dark, narrow eyes. Her face was a sculpture of light and shadow, accented with makeup. She wore clothes, he saw, better suited to a Minneapolis prostitute. A spandex top squeezed ample breasts into fleshy mounds. Matthew's eyes were drawn into the hollow between the mounds of pale flesh. Her perfume, applied liberally, reached out to surround him.

"Matthew," Murray said, and grinned. "I'd like you to meet Rowena Farrell."

Matthew could hardly speak. "Farrell?" he got out at last.

"Deirdre's niece," Murray said. "Rowena, meet Matthew."

"Hi, Matthew."

And then, somehow, they were alone. There had been little talk, just looks, and touches. He remembered sucking back a few more drinks, remembered the gauze in his mind thickening and solidifying. The milling crowd had turned into walls, surrounding him. The noise and music a blanket that blocked out everything but him and Rowena. He focused on her lips, her teeth, her tongue. His mind had followed paths he was not accustomed to, and he had been too drunk to be shocked.

She seemed to have read his thoughts. She leered back at him. Finally, she had bent close. "Let's go. I want to play."

There had been no conscious decision. Not really. She had led, he had followed. He remembered the bracing darkness as they stepped outside, the tug of wind. He remembered walking, holding her hand, groaning as her lips found his neck, his ear; quivering as her free hand slid into his pants to pull and caress. He remembered walking in darkness, being pulled toward the decrepit cabin along East Road. *Clarissa lives along here.* But the thought was lost before he could follow it.

Rowena pulled him along, and soon they were inside again. He remembered the smell of herbs, of stale cooking, a single candle burning.

A dream.

But it was no dream. It was real. He groaned, shivering as his climax gripped him. He coiled his hands in Rowena's hair. She pushed her mouth around him, gulping as he exploded into her. When it was over, she lifted her face and smiled at him.

"Oh God, I'm dead."

"No, you're not," she whispered hoarsely.

She pulled herself up and pressed her face to his neck. Her tongue burrowed into the hollow of his throat, a hot wet worm. He groaned at the sensation, and tried to pull away.

"You've wasted me," he said. "I'm too drunk."

She kissed his lips, pushing her tongue into his mouth. Her lips turned up in a smile. "No, you've got lots left. Let me show you."

Her hand found his softening penis, and stroked it. He had never felt anything like it. He hardened, and throbbed.

"My God, how did you do that?"

"A woman has her ways," Rowena whispered.

She pulled away from him, and peeled off her top. Pale breasts spilled out. Matthew's eyes widened. Her flesh looked translucent. It seemed to glow in the semidarkness of the room. She picked up his hands and placed them on her breasts. Her nipples hardened instantly, poking into his palms. Her mouth opened, and a groan slipped out. The sound of it sent a shudder through him.

"Now, it's my turn," she whispered.

She hitched up her skirt, freed one of Matthew's hands from its breast perch, and lowered it to her crotch.

"I can't do this," Matthew muttered. "For God's sake, I'm married."

"I need you," Rowena whispered.

She entwined her arms around his neck, raised herself, and sank onto his lap. Her aim was perfect. Matthew gasped as she drew him in. Her muscle control was perfect, exquisite. Arching her back and pushing her pelvis against him, she began to move. Then, holding his head gently, she lowered his face to her breasts.

Glow in the dark, Matthew thought incredulously. *Her flesh is glowing in the dark!*

He took one of her nipples into his mouth and began to tongue it. Within seconds she began to quiver, and the noises that came from her mouth were almost screams. Matthew felt himself rising to climax again, a sympathetic reaction to Rowena's sudden orgasm. It was over in moments, and she settled onto him, nestling her face in his neck.

"You're killing me," Matthew groaned softly.

Her eyes glittered in the candlelight. She kissed his lips, slowly and sensuously. Matthew felt himself respond. His eyes widened in astonishment as he felt himself harden again. Rowena grinned, kissed him, and began to writhe slowly in his lap.

"The night is young," she whispered.

"I can't," Matthew protested. "It's impossible."

"You can," Rowena whispered, and kissed him. "I need you."

Oh God, Andrea, forgive me.

He cupped her pale, glowing breasts in his hands, kissed them, and began, again, to move.

Andrea woke abruptly. There was no soft transition between dreamtime and reality. She blinked her eyes, once, twice, then sat upright in bed fully awake.

She heard Peter's voice. Matthew's. She glanced to the other side of the bed and saw with a sinking feeling that it remained unruffled. Where had Matthew slept last night?

She rose and moved to the dresser. The reflection that greeted her was gaunt and haggard. Lines of strain etched the pale face. A bruise marred her right cheek. Her eyes looked lost and frightened. She turned away in the grip of a terrible calm. She dressed slowly, cringing in pain as she worked to pull on jeans, a sweater. Her body felt as if it had been run through a meat grinder.

Okay, Marissa. Game over. You win.

With painful slowness she descended the stairs, gripping the bannister for support. Matthew and Peter were in the kitchen, sitting at the table. Both looked up when she appeared in the door.

Peter, his mouth half full of cereal, grinned. "Hi, Andrea."

She nodded. Peter, at least, seemed more normal these last few days then he had in a long time.

"Morning," she said.

Matthew did not look up from his plate. His uniform, she saw immediately, was badly wrinkled, his hair unkempt.

"Matthew, we need to talk." She moved to the table, carefully pulled out a chair, and lowered herself into it.

"I know," Matthew said. He did not look up from his

plate. "Maybe later."

"This morning," she insisted. This had gone on long enough. Last night had been the final straw—she had no more cards to play.

Now Matthew looked up from his cereal, and she forced herself not to react. There was something different about him, and it took her only a moment to place it. His face was pale and puffy. He looked, she thought, like he used to, in the bad old days. His eyes were hooded with the guilt she had not seen in a long, long time. He had been drinking. A lot. She wanted to turn away, wanted not to see him like this.

"I said we'll talk later," he said softly.

"Why didn't you sleep here last night?"

Something happened to his face that she had not been expecting. He looked, for a moment, like a child caught stealing. And she knew, with utter certainty, that he had been doing more than simply drinking. He looked at her a long time, and his eyes told her everything. The hurt that blossomed within her was like nothing she had known in her life. It was worse than any physical pain she had ever endured. It shook her to her foundations. She felt betrayed, abandoned, alone. With her family about her, she felt as if she were among strangers.

"Oh, Matthew."

"It was just a few drinks," he said, trying to salvage the situation. But he must have seen something in her eyes, for he abandoned that line immediately. "It was nothing," he said.

Peter, who had listened with great interest, now began to fidget restlessly. "I think I'm going upstairs," he said.

After the boy had gone upstairs, Andrea turned back to Matthew. He had regained some of his composure. He was looking at her almost sadly.

Leave it be, she thought. *It's not his fault. It's this damned town.*

"I had an accident last night," she said.

"An accident?"

"I crashed the car. About a mile out of town."

Again, that look of horror on his face. *Where were you,*

Matthew? What were you doing? Did you know about my accident?

His eyes confirmed all her suspicions, and she shook her head.

"You said your family was more important to you than this job."

He nodded, almost reluctantly.

"Well, I want to leave."

"But things are just—"

"It's tearing us apart. It's destroying our family."

"It! It! What the hell is *it?*"

"Marissa. The damned town. And I want out."

Matthew stared at her. His jaw quivered. A battle raged in his eyes. "You women," he said.

"What?"

"A guy gets a chance to get ahead, and you fuck it up."

"Matthew."

"I've got a good job here, Andrea. They like me. I'm set."

"There's *nothing* here."

He laughed. "You're just like Murray said you were."

"What did he say?"

"He said you'd find a way to screw this up for me."

"I don't want to screw anything up for you. But I'm frightened."

"We're not going anywhere," he said firmly.

"I want to leave."

"Then leave. I can't stop you. Take the VW. I don't care. But I'm not going with you."

"Matt, you don't know what you're saying."

"I've got to get to work."

He pushed away from the table, looked down at her a moment, shook his head, and walked to the front door. She followed, stunned to silence.

"If you're staying, make sure Peter doesn't wander too far." He pulled on his coat, opened the door, held it with his hand, and turned to her again. "If you're here later, I'll see you for supper." Then he stepped out, closing the door behind him.

CHAPTER TWENTY-SEVEN

Andrea's mood, a mirror of the weather, remained bleak most of Saturday morning. Matthew's words stung her every time she thought of them. She had not deserved what he had said, and yet she could not be angry at him. Somehow, as it had with Peter, Marissa was changing Matthew. She wanted to leave, but not without her family.

I won't let you have them, Marissa. Not that easily.

She tried to do some housework but found, after dusting the same coffee table three times, that her mind was not on it. Toward noon the cloud cover broke, and sunshine slanted down through the trees. Peter, who had spent a quiet morning in his room, came tramping down the stairs, entered the kitchen, and sat down at the table across from her.

"Getting hungry?" she asked the boy.

"I can wait."

"I'll make something for both of us."

"I'm going to sit in the backyard. Read my book."

"Don't wander away."

"I won't." He smiled at her again.

Outside, he set up a deck chair, lowered himself into it, and opened his book. Andrea sipped her coffee and watched him. He looked so small and lonely out there. These past few days, he had seemed almost like his old self. Quiet, polite. She wondered briefly if it was possible that she had imagined the changes in his personality. Or had the spell of protection she had laid helped him.

So far, the boy had not talked about the incident with the two dead hunters. It was as if he did not remember it at all. Matthew seemed to think that was fine. He had not questioned the boy at all, and that, she knew, was unusual. Peter had been found at the scene of what might be a double murder—surely he would be expected to explain his presence there. Matthew, and presumably Murray too, seemed content to leave well enough alone. The boy, obviously, was not a suspect.

Why isn't he a suspect? I suspect him.

She shook her head, ashamed at her thoughts. Yet she could not rid herself of the feeling that Matthew and Murray were sweeping the incident under the rug.

Outside, as if he had read her thoughts, Peter craned his neck and peered through the doors at her. He smiled. She smiled back. He turned back to his book, and she allowed her face to relax.

She studied the boy's back and felt, for a moment, a surge of protective love for him. Whatever he had become, whatever he was becoming, it was not his fault. He was being used.

She rose and began to prepare lunch. She put some bacon on to fry, and boiled some water for soup. It had been a long time since she'd played mother. Perhaps that was part of the problem. Perhaps if she was here for her family, there would be less trouble. Clarissa's early admonition came to her suddenly and she blushed, thinking how she had rejected the advice.

Marissa looks after her own, but you must look after your family.

She poured herself another cup of coffee, turned to look out the glass doors, and froze.

Peter was gone.

Andrea stood at the foot of the yard and stared into the trees. The breeze tugged her hair and ruffled her windbreaker. The opening of the path before her was as wide as the pavement of the town circle, a golden trail of fallen leaves. Roots coiled like snakes across its width. Fifteen yards into the trees it curved to the right, out of sight. She shuffled her feet and kneaded her fingers, unwilling to set foot on the trail.

"Peter!"

The woods swallowed her voice and returned it to her as a rustle of leaves. Above, wind sighed through the nearly naked branches. Why had Peter done this? He had promised, damnit, that he wouldn't!

"Peter!"

Again, the only response was a sigh of wind. How far could he have gone? She had turned away for only a moment, and he had disappeared. Surely if she went after him, she would catch him in a few minutes. She nodded, convincing herself, and stepped onto the trail.

The path opened up before her and drew her in. She lifted her feet high off the ground as she ran, careful not to trip on exposed roots or fallen branches. She followed the path as it curved to the right, watchful for any sign of Peter. Fifteen, perhaps twenty yards on, she halted. The path forked, a narrow trail to the left, a slightly wider one to the right.

"Oh Jesus."

The right fork was undisturbed, the leaves smooth and moist. The left, however, had been recently used. Footprints marred the surface. Torn leaves, broken branches, and churned mud marked the way. She grinned triumphantly.

"Thank you, Peter."

She lifted her foot to continue onward, then paused. How far should she take this pursuit? What if she got lost? She peered back toward the house. Sunlight glinted off the second-floor windows, and she could follow the square, utilitarian outline of the roof through the crippled branches. No problem. The house should be visible for quite a way, especially now that most of the leaves had fallen.

Relieved, she continued onward. She kept her eyes

down, following the damage Peter's scuffing feet had caused. It was an easy trail to follow, and soon she began to feel confident. One way or another, she was going to catch up to him, and when she did . . . She smiled grimly. There would be a confrontation. Oh boy, would there ever be a confrontation.

She kept her pace steady, slightly faster than a walk, slightly slower than a jog, for about five minutes, then she halted when the path diverged again. This time, it wasn't so easy. Footprints, torn leaves, and broken twigs marked both forks.

He did this intentionally.

She shook her head and fought back a smile. It was all a game to the boy. She added another point to the list she was going to bring up when she caught him.

"Fifty-fifty chance," she muttered to herself, closed her eyes a moment, and took the right-hand fork.

Three forks and ten minutes later she was utterly lost.

Peter paused, leaned against the trunk of a young oak tree, and caught his breath. The forest was silent around him. He listened for Andrea's voice, but she had fallen back. He had doubled his tracks at every junction of paths. If she was not hopelessly lost now, she soon would be. He laughed softly at the thought.

"Have a nice afternoon, Andrea."

He pushed off the tree and started running again. Within minutes he came to the clearing. Breathing hard and sweating profusely, he collapsed against the fallen tree trunk. Cool air brushed across his face. He closed his eyes, and let himself relax.

When he opened them again, a small dark shape was circling overhead. He waved his arm at it. The bird responded with a caw, a small sound swallowed by the distance. It began to descend, swooping low on invisible streams of air, until it swung into the clearing in a tight circle and fluttered to a halt a few yards away. Its black eyes gleamed mischievously.

"Hello, Deirdre, wherever you are," he said to the bird.

The bird cocked its head at his voice. It cawed noisily.

"So what are we doing today?"

The bird waddled toward him. Peter froze at a sudden touch of icy cold at his feet. He glanced down to see blue mist spilling around the ends of the log, pouring into the grass toward the bird. The bird waddled away nervously, not at all sure of itself. Peter laughed gleefully.

"Longshadow!"

The mist rose into a pillar, and the shape of Longshadow seemed to materialize within it. Peter found himself struggling with a mix of emotions. There was the joy he felt at seeing the being who had become his mentor, but also a feeling of dread. The sight of the Woerloga, draped in the skin of corpses, was unsettling. The other night, when he and the Woerloga had walked as one, the feeling of the dead arms hanging over his shoulders had been almost too much.

The mist swirled as an invisible hand reached out to him. Two red sparks focused on him.

"My young friend, why have you come here today?"

Peter stood, stepping toward the misty figure. "I had to tell you something."

"Something so important it could not wait until I came to you?"

The note of anger in the voice was disconcerting. He had never heard it before, and he did not like it.

"It's my stepmother," he said quickly. "She wants to leave Marissa."

The bird cawed. A shimmer of green light passed through the mist.

"She told my dad this morning. He said forget it, but I'm pretty sure he'll do what she wants if she pushes it."

A sigh came from the mist. "You did the right thing to come here," the Woerloga said.

Peter grinned.

"But there is no need to fear. Soon, nothing will be able to keep us apart."

"When?"

The mist swirled. "I will come for you," the Woerloga

228

said. "Perhaps tonight. We will bring about a new age."

The bird cawed. The Woerloga turned toward the small animal and reached out a hand.

"I must go now. I must reserve my strength. Stay with the boy. Protect him."

The bird cawed. As quickly as it had arrived, the mist seemed to flow through the grass, back into the trees. In a moment, Peter and the bird were alone.

"Did you hear him? Did you hear what he said? Maybe tonight!"

The bird waddled closer and made a soft cooing sound.

Peter ignored it. Tonight!

And after that, Andrea wouldn't matter. Nobody would matter. He would be able to do anything he wanted. Anything at all. Just like Deirdre and Longshadow had promised him.

He reached out a hand to the bird and motioned it toward him.

"Come on, come here," he whispered. "Teach me some new tricks."

Murray Carlyle stood on the step outside Clarissa Halloway's cottage and drew nervously on his cigarette. He dropped the butt on the step, crushed it out, and rapped on the door. He felt as nervous as a horny teenager calling on a date.

Damn it, boy, you shouldn't be doing this.

For a moment, he wished he had minded his own business. If Clarissa wanted to get herself in trouble, then let her. She had been warned many times. She knew the dangers.

Still, he couldn't let it slide. He had known the old woman all his life, knew where she was coming from. Thick-skulled she might be, but she was not a bad old thing. When it came right down to it, it took guts to cross Deirdre Farrell. Guts, or stupidity. Maybe a combination of both.

He drew a sharp breath as the door opened. Clarissa peered suspiciously through the narrow space.

"Murray Carlyle?"

"Clarissa, I need to talk to you. Let me in." He glanced nervously about. Nobody had seen him.

"It's been a long time since we've had anything worth talking about."

"Damn it, Clarissa, this is important. I could get in trouble coming here. Let me in."

She shook her head sadly and opened the door. "I never thought I'd see the day when you'd be running scared, Murray." She stepped aside to let him through, then closed the door after he was inside.

He heaved a sigh of relief, glad to be out of sight.

"Would you like something to drink? To eat?"

He shook his head abruptly. "This isn't a social call, Clarissa. I've come to warn you. Now just listen to me."

She put her hands on her hips, regarding him as if he were a small boy.

"You've got to stop interfering. You've been putting ideas into Andrea Willson's head. You've been talking to Peter. You're going against the wishes of the council."

Clarissa laughed bitterly. "Can I help it if the council is full of dunderheads and fools?"

"That makes no difference, and you know it. There was a vote. It was decided." He shook his head, exasperated. "Damn it, Clarissa, we need this dark circle."

She said nothing. Her eyes narrowed.

"Look at this town," he continued. "Marissa's fading away. Nobody comes here anymore. Give us ten more years and we'll be gone."

"Maybe that'd be for the better."

"You don't mean that. Now Deirdre says she can give us a lot. She's not asking for much. Just a little cooperation."

"The price is too high, Murray. Look what they're doing to Peter Willson."

"They're not hurting him. They just need him as part of the circle. You know that."

"How do you know what kind of hurt they're doing to him? Dark circles are *not* harmless, Murray." She poked him in the chest. "Look what happened to Barbara

230

Robertson's cat."

Murray shrugged. "She was warned. She was like you. She kept interfering."

"And that makes it right?"

"Damn it, you can't go against the wishes of the council."

"And what about Jack and Willy Burgess? Did they interfere? Does Deirdre have an explanation for that? What kind of dark circle is she raising?"

The question caught him off guard. He drew a deep breath. "Nobody said there wouldn't be sacrifices. Deirdre said it was necessary. Hell, Jack Burgess isn't exactly a loss."

"Willy was just a boy."

He had no answer for that. Neither had Deirdre. It wasn't supposed to have happened like that. He shrugged again.

"I don't have all the answers, Clarissa. I just want to warn you. You keep this up, you're going to get into trouble."

Now she laughed, and this time it was full of humor. "What can they do to me, Murray? I'm old. My King is old. We're ready to pass over any day now. I've got nothing to lose. And nothing gives me more pleasure than standing in Deirdre Farrell's way. If you're too blind to see that she's simply using you, that's your problem."

"Well, I warned you."

"That you did, dear. Now run off before Deirdre finds out."

"You won't—"

"I won't say anything." She laughed again.

He turned to leave, then paused. He faced her sadly. "Are you sure you have nothing to lose, Clarissa? There are worse things than death, you know."

She blanched, and he knew he had hit a nerve.

"You had better leave, Murray," she said softly.

He nodded and went outside. The door closed behind him. He lit a cigarette and walked back to his car.

CHAPTER TWENTY-EIGHT

Andrea was getting more lost by the minute.

Minneapolis, with its concrete, glass, and steel landscape, seemed a figment of her imagination, the daydream of a silly girl. Even Marissa, its civilization only a shadow of the larger city, seemed unreal. She lost track of the number of forks she passed through, half convinced they might be the same one every time, but not certain. Tears blinded her, but fear drove her on.

She stopped only when she realized that she was no longer following Peter's tracks. She stood on the narrow trail, breathing loudly, and leaned over with her hands on her thighs. The trail ahead of her was unmarked by recent passage. Now, the direness of her predicament suddenly apparent, her knees wobbled precariously beneath her. She leaned against a nearby oak for support, wrapping her arms around the thick trunk and pressing her stinging cheek to the rough bark. She leaned there, exhausted and sobbing. Between sobs, her neck craned back, she shouted her stepson's name.

"Peter! . . . Peter! . . . Peter! . . ."

There was no response. She hadn't really expected one. Her voice was an invader in the forest, as sharp and sudden as a gunshot. At each call the hidden life around her responded in some way. A flutter of wings. A scamper of feet. She glimpsed a squirrel, frozen in a moment of terror, gripping the branch of a tree across the trail from her. A grouse, or some similar bird, made threatening noises to her right. But Peter did not answer.

Time passed, though how quickly or slowly she did not know. Finally, there were no more tears to cry, and her panic turned into a feeling of resignation. The pain of her exertion was a numbing blanket draped across her shoulders, a weight she could not shuck. She pushed away from the oak, turned to face the way she had come, and began walking.

There was no pattern in her movement, no attempt to choose a specific path. She walked, and she walked, almost a mindless shuffle, allowing the forest to lead her. She imagined, at times, the trail shifting around her, curving ahead of her when she wasn't looking. She would go where the forest led her. It didn't matter. She kept walking.

It began to dawn on her that she might have fallen into some sort of shock state, and the realization came, like a bolt of lightning: *I'm going to die out here.*

She stumbled to a halt, suddenly sober and frightened. *I'm going to die out here, alone, in the forest.*

She shook her head, unwilling to believe or accept such a possibility.

"No, damn it, no."

And that's when she saw the stones.

At first, she thought there was only one. From this distance, about fifty yards, it appeared as a solid mass of gray through a space in the trees. Its shape, tall and square, reminded her of a building. She might have been looking at one of Minneapolis's downtown office towers from a distance. Hope blossomed and died within the same moment. There were no buildings out here.

She moved along the trail, careful of the roots that seemed to be coiling in greater numbers at her feet, her eyes locked on the stone. It was too smooth, too geometrically proportioned, to be a natural formation. A sudden wide space in the trees afforded her a clearer view, and she again stumbled to a halt. From this position she could see a

233

second stone. A third. How many were there? She took another step, another. The gap in the trees widened, and sudden comprehension dawned on Andrea.

"That's not possible." Her voice, whispering and fearful, did not sound like her own.

She saw, from this perspective, that there were many of the stones. Most seemed as tall as the first she had seen. Some were smaller and squarer. They formed a rough circle that extended to the other side of a small clearing. Within the circle of larger stones was a ring of smaller stones, and within the smaller ring, another.

Stonehenge.

She had seen many photographs of the stone circles found throughout Britain and Europe. Massive, impressive, mysterious . . . yet abandoned. She had looked at the photographs, had tried to imagine the ancient people performing their ceremonies within the towering, brooding stones. She remembered reading that the Druids had not constructed Stonehenge; they had simply found it, and used it as their own. Some earlier culture, forever lost, had been responsible. What had it looked like then? What purpose had the stones served, other than superficial astronomical observations?

Yet what she was looking at now was different from any of the photographs she had seen. This was what she imagined they might have looked like at the beginning of time. There were no fallen or missing stones here. Mounds of earth throughout the circle looked well maintained. A narrow ditch running around the perimeter appeared to be in good repair, well shored against collapse. Vines, currently leafless, roped from one stone to another, looking like a gigantic spider web. Pathways through the circle, between the stones, were well trodden. This was what Stonehenge might have been like when it was active.

She shuddered, goosebumps rising on her neck and arms. Who had built this place? The answer came immediately: Marissa.

And then she heard the voice. Peter. Laughing. Talking, as if to somebody. She raised her head and blinked in astonishment. Then she moved away from the standing stones, toward the voices.

She came upon the small clearing suddenly. Peter was sitting on a fallen tree, leaning into the stump of what must have once been a thick branch, his legs extended languorously into the grass. Scattered about him were empty pop bottles and candy wrappers.

So this is where you come to.

Andrea moved behind the cover of a large oak, pressed herself against the rough bark, and watched. A large black bird hopped about near Peter's feet, cawing intermittently. Peter said something to it, but she could not understand the words. He laughed again.

At the other side of the clearing, a large gray squirrel pushed its head out of a patch of tall grass and sniffed the air. Peter's head jerked at the sound, and he pinned the animal with his gaze. He said something. As if attached to a leash, the squirrel stumbled farther into the clearing. Its legs stiffened, as if trying to resist the pull, its small eyes wide with terror. High squeals emitted from its mouth.

Peter laughed. He held out his hand toward the animal, made a fist, and said something.

The squirrel squealed, twisted onto its back, and began to thrash madly as if it were in agony. Peter laughed softly. He opened his fist and squeezed it tight again. Muttered words came from his mouth.

The squirrel's squealing rose in pitch, becoming almost like the crying of a baby. Andrea closed her eyes, trying to block out the sounds. When she opened them again, the squirrel's legs were kicking and jerking spasmodically. Peter was staring at it, frowning. He opened his fist and squeezed it again. The squirrel stopped moving, for a moment. Suddenly, a stream of frothy blood erupted from its mouth in a geyser. It kicked again, once, and was still.

The black bird hopped over to the dead animal. Its eyes glittered malevolently. It reached down and deftly pecked out one of the squirrel's eyes, then carried it back toward

Peter. The boy held out his hand. The bird reached its head forward and dropped the bloody eye into Peter's palm. He raised it to his face, studied it as if it were a marble, made a small sound of disgust, and threw it away.

Wings fluttered above, and Andrea craned her neck to see two more birds circling the clearing. The sight sent a chill through her, and she thought of Deirdre Farrell. *Bitch.*

Peter stood and stretched. He walked over to the dead squirrel. He looked down at it curiously, then extended his hand toward it. He squeezed his fist, then made a waving motion. Andrea watched, horrified, as the body of the squirrel raised itself on wobbling legs. Mewing piteously, walking as if drunk, it wobbled off into the trees. Peter laughed.

"Oh, Peter, what have they done to you." She spoke the words before she could stop herself.

Peter spun, his face a mask of shock. His eyes pinned the tree where she was hiding.

Don't be intimidated. Face him.

She stepped out into the clearing, and moved toward him.

"Andrea!"

"Peter, you shouldn't have left the house. I told you. Your father told you."

He blinked. "How did you find—"

"Oh, you weren't hard to follow," she said, offering a smile she did not feel.

"But . . ."

Andrea made shooing motions toward the bird. Its black eyes would not leave her face. Its yellow beak opened, and released an angry caw.

"Get out of here!" She stepped toward it, kicking out her feet violently.

The bird fluttered its wings, rose into the air with another caw, and flew. High above, the three birds now circled the clearing. Peter stared upward, frowned, then looked back to Andrea. He was obviously flustered and confused, not sure how to deal with her intrusion. She decided to take the offensive.

"Come on, let's get back," she said.

For a moment, his eyes locked onto hers, and she saw something in them that frightened her badly. He did not look like himself. She had seen the same expression somewhere else, and in a moment it came to her. Deirdre Farrell. She tightened her lips, holding her anger in check.

"I said, come on. Let's get back."

He stepped toward her, his features softening. "I only wanted to be by myself for a while."

"So I saw," she said.

He glanced toward the bloodstains on the grass, then blushed. He sighed.

"You lead the way," Andrea said.

Peter nodded, then shuffled out of the clearing. She fell in behind him, almost stepping on his heels the whole way. The trip back took only fifteen minutes, and Andrea was astonished. She did not recognize any of the trails. Had she been this close to home all the time?

When she saw the top of the house through the trees, she almost yelped with relief. Two minutes later, still dogging Peter's heels, she stepped from the pathway into the backyard. Sky opened up overhead.

"Oh God." Relief surged through her, intoxicating.

Peter turned to stare at her, frowning in confusion.

She stared at him, breathing deeply and slowly. "Go upstairs. Get cleaned up. Then go to your room."

He looked as if he might argue, but something in her face stopped him. He nodded once, then walked up to the house. She followed, waiting in the kitchen as he climbed the stairs. In a few minutes she heard the shower running, and she allowed herself to collapse into a seat at the kitchen table. Her hands were trembling. She stared at them and shook her head.

An image of the stone circle came to her, and she shuddered. It all seemed so much like a dream. Unreal. She shook her head, and made a fist of her hand. No dream.

In a few minutes she rose. The kitchen clock read three twenty-five. She had been walking in the woods nearly three hours. Her legs throbbed painfully.

She moved to the phone, picked it up, and paused. Was this the right thing to do? She thought of the attack on the road last night, the monstrous wolf following her. She thought of Peter, changed into something she hardly recognized, killing a squirrel and laughing. She thought of Deirdre Farrell, her threats.

Yes, yes, there was no other choice.

Clarissa had told her to protect her family, but obviously she was going about it the wrong way. Spells of protection were helpful, but they were not enough. It was time to strike back. Strike first, and strike hard.

CHAPTER TWENTY-NINE

The cabin looked like a derelict, Andrea thought. She could not imagine anybody living in it. It was hard to believe the contrast between Clarissa's cabin, dollhouse perfect, only half a mile along the road, and this leaning pile of boards and dirty glass. Perhaps the approaching dusk was making it look worse than it really was, she thought. Perhaps in daylight it would look better, less menacing.

"Are you sure this is the right place?" Andrea asked.

Clarissa, walking beside her, nodded. "Deirdre Farrell and I have been neighbors for longer than you have been alive. I'm sure I know where she lives by now."

"And she lives alone?"

"Yes, my dear, alone."

At the foot of the unkempt gravel drive leading up to the cabin, they paused. Andrea scanned the grounds with watchful eyes. Fallen boards, empty cans, and automobile parts littered the spaces between the trees. The grass at the front was nearly knee high. The thought of walking through it gave her the shivers.

"How do we find out if she's home?"

"She's not home," Clarissa said softly.

"How do you know?"

"I can tell."

Andrea did not push the matter. She stepped onto the

driveway, then paused and turned around. "Aren't you coming?"

Clarissa was staring up at the cabin, her expression thoughtful. She drew a deep breath and sighed. "A little farther," she agreed.

They walked, side by side, up to the cabin. The closer they drew, the worse it looked. The wooden steps leading to the front door were rotten and falling apart. Rusty nails protruded from soggy wood, like bones from flesh. At the foot of the steps Clarissa stopped and put a hand on Andrea's arm.

"This is as far as I shall accompany you."

Andrea pulled her attention away from the house. The decay of the place, the almost deathlike shroud hanging over it, fascinated her and repulsed her at the same time. She held out her hand and squeezed Clarissa's.

"Thanks for all your help, Clarissa."

Clarissa nodded. She did not look happy. Andrea turned, but found herself still firmly within Clarissa's grasp.

"My dear, are you sure you want to continue on this course? There is still time to change your mind."

The look of concern on Clarissa's face, almost of sorrow, nearly broke her. *No, I don't want to go through with this,* she thought. *I don't want to be anywhere near this place, or this town.* But she said nothing.

"I would much rather have you lay stronger spells of protection," Clarissa continued after a moment of silence. "At least remain within the domain of the benign, my dear. To explore the realm of darkness is far more dangerous than you know. I can't stop you, of course, but—"

Andrea held up her hand to stop the other woman talking. Anger tightened her guts. "Clarissa, you didn't see Peter this afternoon. He's changed, changed horribly. He looked evil. He looked . . ." She closed her eyes and drew a shuddering breath. "Anyway, *she* did it to him. Or she had a hand in it. You didn't see her on the road last night. She attacked me. She made my car crash. She sent something chasing after me. She . . ." Words failed her. "The bitch."

Her vehemence surprised Clarissa. "My dear, I couldn't agree more with your appraisal of her character, but—"

"Please, don't try to dissuade me. Sitting back and waiting for her to come to me, waiting for her to destroy my family, won't cut it. I can't do it. Not anymore. Clarissa, please understand. I have to show her that it's not going to be easy for her. That I'm going to fight for what's mine. You know what they say. The best defense is a good offense."

Clarissa tried to smile, but her lips only trembled. Andrea looked away, disturbed by the other woman's reticence. Couldn't Clarissa understand that attacking was the only way to get Deirdre Farrell to back off? Defensive posturing just wasn't enough.

"I do understand, my dear," Clarissa said softly. "I understand very well. Do you think I haven't been in the same position myself?"

"Then help me, don't stand in my way," Andrea said abruptly.

"I won't stop you, my dear. I couldn't if I wanted to. But you must understand that the road you choose, whatever it may be, will demand its own toll."

Andrea considered that a moment, then shook her head. "I don't have time for metaphysical gobbledegook, Clarissa. I'm fighting to protect my family. I'll worry about costs later."

Again, Clarissa seemed taken aback by her vehemence. She nodded curtly, then handed Andrea a small paper bag. Andrea opened the bag and looked inside at the powder she and Clarissa had hastily crushed less than an hour ago. She removed a crumpled sheet of paper and read the words Clarissa had scrawled.

"Will I be able to do this?"

Now Clarissa smiled, but there was no humor in her expression. "Darkness gives itself willingly to those who seek it," she said solemnly. "It's the other road that is hard to follow."

241

Andrea ignored the comment, determined to carry through with her plan. "It won't hurt her seriously, will it?"

"Enough to frighten her," Clarissa said. "The very fact she is being attacked will be enough." She sighed. "Marissa hasn't seen anything like this in a long, long time."

"Then perhaps it's long overdue," Andrea said softly. She looked up at Clarissa, trying to ease the tension between them with a smile. "Don't worry, Clarissa, Everything will be fine. Will you wait for me?"

Clarissa paused, then shook her head. "No, my dear, I must return. I have no wish to be part of this."

Andrea nodded, saddened at what she perceived as Clarissa's disappointment with her. She tightened her lips, determined not to be dissuaded. "Thanks for your help," she said.

Clarissa shook her head. "I don't wish to be thanked for this." She turned and began walking back to the road. She had gone ten steps when she paused and turned around, expression serious. "Be careful, my dear. Deirdre Farrell is no fool, and she is powerful. You are making a dangerous enemy."

"So is she," Andrea said.

Clarissa nodded. "Beware her spies."

"Her spies?"

"Her birds."

"Oh."

Clarissa regarded her thoughtfully a few more moments, then turned and walked to the road. Andrea stood on the steps and watched the older woman as she walked back to her cabin. When Clarissa disappeared beyond a curve in the road, Andrea shuddered. She felt alone. Vulnerable.

Just do it. Get it over with.

She drew a deep breath, then climbed the shaky steps and entered her enemy's home.

She sensed it the moment she crossed the threshold. It

came at her so suddenly, with such force, that she stopped dead in her tracks and stared wide-eyed into the darkness of the living room.

Matthew has been here.

She did not question her intuition, did not probe the how or the why of it. She just knew it. A sixth sense, a tightening of every muscle in her body. Her skin crawled. *Matthew has been here.* His presence seemed to exude from the walls themselves, hanging like a shadow from the corners of the ceiling, fighting for room amid the lingering odors of cooking and neglect. At home, this same sense of his presence calmed her, comforted her. It belonged. But here . . .

She stepped slowly into the living room, almost reluctanct to move her legs. A blanket covered the window, hung by its tattered corners with two rusted nails, as if to seal out the sunlight. With dusk approaching, the room was oppressive. Shadows seemed to swirl in the corners, conglomerate at the edge of things, as if preparing for the night.

Why had Matthew come here? What business could he have with Deirdre Farrell?

And suddenly she knew. Last night he had not come home. This morning he had squirmed with guilt. His eyes had told her everything. Another woman.

But Deirdre Farrell? The thought shocked and repulsed her. No, it was not possible. Matthew may have been vulnerable, may have been ready for an adulterous fling, but surely not with an old hag like Deirdre Farrell! An image of Deirdre's pinched, wrinkled face came to her, the wiry bend of her body hidden behind layers of clothing.

"Not a chance," she muttered. The room swallowed the words.

But what if . . . What if it had been the same as her own attack? What if Matthew had been seduced by a creature . . . not human. She remembered that night, the ghostly hands caressing her breasts, the almost irresistible *maleness* of the creature. While asleep, her body had responded. Perhaps, with Matthew drunk, a similar creature, a female, might . . . He wouldn't have stood a chance.

She groaned, sure now that she was right.

"Oh, Matthew."

Her anger intensified so quickly that she began to tremble. Her fingers tore at the paper bag in her hands until it ripped. *Damn you, Deirdre Farrell*, she thought. *Damn you, damn you!*

Why go after Matthew? What was the point?

But she already knew the answer: divide and conquer. By breaking the family apart, it would be easier to pick the spoils. Peter.

She fumed, her heart hammering in her chest. *You can't have him. You can't have either of them.*

She closed her eyes and breathed deeply to calm herself. Then she reached into the paper bag, pulled out a handful of the coarse powder, and flung it in the air. She backed away as it spread and fell, drifting to the ground like snow, or ash.

As it fell, she concentrated on the crumpled sheet of paper Clarissa had given her. *"Omho thela yegoss nardum, a bendeh cor de fallium gorroth!"*

Her mouth formed around the words as if she had spoken them many times, as if she understood what she was saying. She said them again, reached into the paper bag, and flung more of the powder. A faint draft carried the new cloud to the corners of the rooms, and she watched in awe as it sank to cover furniture, the carpet.

"Omho thela yegoss nardum, a bendeh cor de fallium gorroth!"

She opened her arms wide, as if to encompass the room, held her head back, and repeated the spell. Again. Again.

You're going to pay for what you've done, Deirdre Farrell.

Moving from room to room, she threw more of the powder and uttered the spell wherever she went. After the first time, she no longer even looked at the paper Clarissa had given her. The spell had burned itself into her mind. Her anger intensified with every throw of the powder, until she feared she might scream, or start breaking things. As she uttered the spell, she seemed to sense a tension running through her, as if she had been connected to a hidden dynamo, as if a thousand volts thrummed through her body, ready to explode into whatever she touched.

"Omho thela yegoss nardum . . . Abalah, gerran yus-sagh fellak . . . Demah nodos rematar yohtton!"

Where had that come from? Those were not the words Clarissa had written. Fear lanced through her, sharp as a needle, cold as ice, but she quelled it. The words, strange and unfamiliar, spilled from her mouth like water from a spigot. She did not know where they'd come from, or what they meant; she knew only that they had to be spoken. Soon, the bag was empty, the powder depleted. But still she uttered the spells, uttered things she could not comprehend.

Later—she did not know how much later—she collapsed against the front door frame, gasping for breath. Sweat poured from her forehead, soaking her face and shoulders. Cold trails ran down her neck, between her breasts.

My God, what had happened? She felt as if she had just . . . *given* herself to some greater power, had become a doorway through which things unspeakable had passed. Fear gripped her; confusion muddled her thoughts.

Get out. Get out of here now.

Sobbing, she pushed open the front door and stumbled down the steps. The rotten wood creaked ominously beneath her feet. This had been a mistake. A big mistake. She ran along the gravel drive, stopping only when she came to the road. The cool evening air braced her and seemed to wake her as if from a nightmare. She looked down the road, toward the town circle, but saw nothing besides the shadows of trees. Above, the sky was turning dark. Clouds swirled, moving eastward with ponderous grace.

It's done. There's no going back.

She drew a deep breath, held it a few moments, then released it. She began to feel better. Within minutes, she felt invigorated.

Why should she run? What was there to run from? She had laid her trap—now she would wait and see it sprung.

Smiling, she stepped off the road, into the bushes beside Deirdre Farrell's drive. The darkness surrounded her, took her in, and concealed her.

Hurry home, Deirdre. Hurry home and see what the postman delivered.

She crouched and waited.

CHAPTER THIRTY

As Deirdre Farrell left the town circle, she found herself plagued with concerns. A decade of planning and work would culminate tonight. All the hours of research, the years of waiting for Peter Willson to reach a suitable age, were coming to an end. Tonight, Cardew Longshadow would walk in the world again, clothed in the body of a young man. The world would never be the same.

But instead of feeling joy at this imminent event, her mind was preoccupied with Andrea Willson.

As she walked up the road toward her house, she glanced into the sky. Her birds circled lazily above. For a moment she allowed herself to be drawn to them, to experience the bird's eye view of town. Vertigo gripped her, and she backed off instantly. She was too old for games like that. Perhaps, after tonight, it would be different. The Woerloga was certain to reward her for her efforts.

But Andrea Willson was a bother.

From the first time she had met the woman, she had known there was something different about her. She was an outsider, yes, and ignorant of craft ways. But unlike most outsiders, the boy's mother revealed an affinity for the craft. A closeness to it that was unusual in those outside the craft. How else had she managed to protect her home against attack? Granted, the spell itself was simple, almost childish, but it should have been impossible for an outsider.

And today . . . today was the most troubling of all. The stupid bitch had stumbled upon the earthworks. The birds, circling overhead, had reported everything they had seen. Granted, she had not entered the sacred circle, but she had seen it. Such an occurrence should have been impossible. The Nemeton was alive with spells of protection and deception. No outsider could ever hope to find the earthworks unless . . . Unless it drew them to itself.

Could that have happened? Could the sacred circle itself be acting on Andrea Willson's behalf?

Deirdre tensed and came to a standstill in the middle of the road.

No. No. It could not be. An outsider? Yet what other explanation could there be for an outsider who could practice, albeit rather clumsily, the ancient craft?

"Who are you, Andrea Willson? Why have you come here?"

Longshadow, it seemed, was not concerned. The mother, he said, was merely a nuisance. Tonight he would deal with her, once and for all.

Still, as she walked up the dark road, Deirdre could not rid herself of her concerns.

Andrea Willson was not what she seemed. And things that were not what they appeared to be, she knew, often turned out to be dangerous.

The shadow moved along the road toward her. Andrea pushed deeper into the cover of the bushes and held her breath. Surely this wasn't Deirdre coming now? No, this thing was slung low to the ground, like some sort of animal. Her mouth became instantly dry. The shadow moved closer, closer.

Oh God, it was coming this way. She heard a snuffling sound, the crunching of branches. It was coming right for her! A small sound emitted from her throat; her heart seemed ready to explode.

Then the dark nose poked through the grass toward her

knee, and she expelled her breath in an explosive cough of relief.

"King!"

The old springer spaniel wagged his tail and pushed his nose into her side. She reached down and scratched his ears.

"You silly thing! You almost scared me to death! What are you doing here?"

King wagged his tail, and she knew the answer immediately. Clarissa would not stay with her, but she had done the next best thing. She had sent her special friend.

"Thank you, Clarissa," she said softly. Then, scratching the spaniel behind his ears again, she said, "Thank you, King."

King pressed into her warmly.

A bird squawked in the air above them. Andrea held her breath and hugged King tightly. She pressed her face close to the dog's. "Shhh." As if he had understood, his expression turned almost solemn, his mouth shut tight.

Another caw from above. Another. Andrea peered up through the dark cover of branches. Three birds flew in lazy circles above the cabin and its front yard. As she watched, another joined the trio. It was almost as if they were scouting the yard, checking for intruders. She tried to push deeper into the bushes, tried to make herself invisible.

Along the road, she heard a voice. The shape of Deirdre Farrell materialized slowly as it moved toward the drive. The old woman walked slowly and carefully, hugging a large brown bag to her bosom. Her small eyes scanned the ground ahead of her, periodically lifting to study the woods on either side of her. At the foot of the drive, less than five yards from Andrea's hiding place, she paused and looked up at the sky. She muttered something.

The birds above cawed in reply.

One of them descended in a flutter of wings and came to a flapping stop on the gravel near Deirdre's feet. Andrea closed her eyes, terrified. The game was over. She was going to be found out. King, stiff as a mannequin, remained pressed into her side.

Deirdre crouched and said something to the bird. It cawed noisily and waddled away from her. She watched it a moment, then walked up the drive to the house. The bird waddled across the drive and onto the grass. For a moment, its beady eye seemed to focus on Andrea through the thick bushes and grass.

It can't see me. It can't see me. She willed herself to be invisible, squeezing her eyes tightly shut as if that might help.

In a moment, the bird waddled away, released another caw, and rose into the air to join the others. Deirdre Farrell, standing on the front steps of her cabin, craned her head to peer up at them.

Go inside, you bitch. Go inside.

Deirdre paused, peering into the yard. Again, Andrea felt as if she had been pinned by the gaze. She closed her eyes. Held her breath. When she looked again, Deirdre had turned around and was opening the door. At the threshold she paused, glanced over her shoulder, then stepped into the cabin and closed the door behind her.

Andrea released a sigh of relief. She had not been seen. She hugged King fiercely. The spaniel nuzzled her hand.

"Now we wait for the fireworks," she said softly.

As if he had understood, King raised his head to peer over the tall grass toward the house. As the seconds passed, Andrea's tension increased exponentially. Her hands balled into fists. Her teeth worried her lips. Her breathing became so rapid she neared the point of hyperventilation.

Still, nothing happened. She waited some more. A light came on in the living room, flickering softly. A candle. She calmed herself. And waited.

Nothing.

"Damn it, Clarissa, you said . . ."

She thought at first that a cloud had passed over the moon, as a shadow suddenly enveloped the cabin. But there was no moon tonight. The sky was dark.

She stood up. The shadow, like a pair of monstrous wings, seemed to pull close about the leaning structure. A moment ago she had been able to see the doorway, the steps, the glow of light from the living room. Now she saw nothing but shadow, a vague outline swathed in darkness.

"Oh boy," she said softly.

At her feet, King began to whine.

A new light flickered within the cabin, but this one, Andrea knew, did not spring from a natural source. It seemed to seep beneath the doors, around the edges of the window, as if the cabin had somehow been filled with a phosphorescent liquid. The ground beneath her feet began to tremble, as if a freight train were passing near by. The branches of the trees above began to rustle.

I've unleashed a terrible power, Andrea thought, and was suddenly afraid.

The cabin began to shake. Groaning noises slid into the night: the creaking of boards bent too far, the strain of nails twisted out of shape.

A scream, definitely human, pierced the night.

"Oh, Jesus." Andrea stepped from the cover of the bushes onto the drive, her eyes fixed on the spectacle of the cabin, no longer even remotely sure she had done the right thing.

A roar, like the passage of a jumbo jet overhead, erupted into the night. Andrea raised her hands to cover her ears, cringing in pain at the sound. The cabin shook. She watched, horrified, as one rear corner trembled and collapsed. The living room window exploded outward, sending shards of glass hissing through the air. The glittering particles embedded themselves in trees, or fell to the grass.

Another scream. Deirdre Farrell's voice. Light beamed from the windows, pale green and vile-looking. Andrea shuddered as she saw it.

The front door opened, and a figure stumbled out. It was Deirdre Farrell. Her clothes were torn and shredded. Traceries of light danced across her exposed flesh, writhed along her arms, and flew into the air like shafts of lightning. The older woman fell down the steps and collapsed to the gravel drive.

251

From the house, the light seemed to coalesce. It pushed its way through the front door. Andrea winced at the sound of wood splintering. And suddenly the thing was towering over the fallen woman, a monstrous apparition. It seemed, at one moment, to be a giant face, its fangs bared in anger. At another, streaked with shadow, a pair of wings, reaching.

Deirdre Farrell screamed again, and for the first time Andrea felt a pang of remorse. For a moment she was back in her own living room, struggling with the ghostly apparition reaching for her body. She swallowed her guilt. The woman before her now had been responsible for that. For much more than that.

The light seemed to draw darkness from around it, a shadowy cloak. Still formless, a pulsating amorphous giant, it reached tendrils for Deirdre Farrell.

Deirdre scrabbled away, her eyes wide in terror. She raised her hands toward the shape, as if to embrace it. She muttered something. Andrea cocked her head and tried to understand.

The light shuddered.

Deirdre waved her hands again. This time her motion was violent, almost a wave of dismissal.

As quickly as it had begun, it was over.

The ball of light began to shrink, becoming a pulsating pillar filled with streaks of darkness. Deirdre waved her hand again. The light dropped to the ground, as if it were liquid, and rushed out in all directions. Andrea gasped as one edge of the spreading stain passed across and through her. A sensation of icy cold gripped her. Sweat popped out on her arms and back. Then it was past. A faint moan seemed to dwindle into the night. The trees of the forest, in all directions, rustled at the passage of the thing.

Deirdre Farrell clambered to her feet, sobbing. She brushed bits of gravel and grass from her arms, her legs. She muttered something and continued to sob.

Andrea stepped toward her and the other woman looked up, her face a mask of fear. The fear disappeared instantly and was replaced by anger.

"You!"

Andrea nodded.

"*You!*"

She held her ground. She smiled. The look of horror, of shock, of anger, a plethora of emotions, each trying to control Deirdre Farrell's face, was a joy to see.

"Stay away from my family," Andrea said softly.

The look that now firmly took hold of Deirdre Farrell's face was fear. Unadulterated, pure. She regarded Andrea with an expression close to awe.

"You have begun something that—"

Andrea shook her head angrily. "No. I've just ended it. If you bother us again, you'll suffer for it."

The calm, almost calculated way in which she spoke was a shock to Andrea. She could hardly believe she was standing up to this woman.

Deirdre stumbled away, clutching a withered hand to her throat. She sobbed and climbed the steps to the door of the now almost ruined cabin. She turned to face Andrea again.

"I'll . . ."

But at that moment, lights lanced up the road, pinning Andrea. She held up her hand as the car approached and slowed. It was Matthew's cruiser. He rolled down his window, unsure whether to look toward the cabin or toward Andrea.

I know what you're looking for, but you won't find it tonight, Andrea thought bitterly. She swallowed her anger.

"What are you doing here?" Matthew asked.

Andrea turned toward Deirdre and waved once. She turned back to Matthew. "Just visiting," she said.

She kneeled and held out her hand to King, who had fallen silent as the fireworks began. He edged forward warily, sniffing her hand as if he was no longer sure of her.

"Good boy," she whispered. "Go home now. Tell your mistress that everything is fine."

King wagged his tail. He licked her hand once, then trotted off down the road.

"What the hell is going on here?" Matthew asked softly, now staring at the cabin.

She walked around the car and slid in the passenger side. She closed the door hard. "Nothing," she said. "Take me home, Matthew."

Matthew turned to her, his face unreadable. He said nothing for a moment, then shrugged. He put the car in gear and began to drive.

The feeling of accomplishment, of calmness, that had settled upon her slid away like a ghost. Behind them, rising into the night, she heard Deirdre Farrell's high, contemptuous laughter.

CHAPTER THIRTY-ONE

Clarissa was aware, through King, of what had transpired at Deirdre Farrell's home, and knew only that it should not have happened. The incantation she had shared with Andrea was low-level and simplistic. A harbinger of nuisance, nothing more. As children, they had used it often to frighten boys, or outsiders. She had thought that if Andrea revealed to Deirdre that she was capable of such a conjuring, then Deirdre would desist.

But Deirdre Farrell had come close to being destroyed. Somehow, Andrea had conjured a deadly power. It was only Deirdre's quick thinking that had saved her. She shuddered, trying not to think of what would have happened if Deirdre had failed. Would Andrea have been able to stop what she had started?

Maybe. Maybe not.

Only one thing was certain. Andrea was a mystery.

"Special friend, something bad is happening," Clarissa said softly.

The dog seemed to understand. His tail stopped wagging. She debated making a pot of tea, then decided against it. Instead, she retrieved a quarter-full bottle of brandy from the cupboard over the sink and poured herself three fingers.

She leaned on the sink, gazed into the amber liquid, and pressed the glass to her forehead. "Give me strength," she whispered, then gulped half her drink.

As the liquid burned its way into her stomach, she moved quickly through to the living room and sank into the accepting bulk of the easy chair by the door. She took another mouthful of brandy and swallowed. The alcohol was working. Tendrils of warmth coiled through her body, a fine net that seemed to be holding her together. In the semidarkness of the room, illuminated only by the kitchen lamp, she allowed her mind to sort itself out.

For the first time, the suspicion assailed her that a dark circle might be the least of Marissa's problems. Every circle, she knew, needed a male. She had assumed that Peter Willson, with his strong innate talent, was the chosen one. Yet, now that she thought of it clearly, the idea was preposterous. Deirdre Farrell was impatient, far too impatient to wait for Peter's powers to develop. With Peter as a cornerstone of a circle, it might be years before any useful work was accomplished. Deirdre might be dead by then. She could not imagine that old hag going to all this trouble for altruistic reasons. If there was no benefit to herself, she would not be interested.

Think . . . think . . .

Why the persistent, sometimes brutal attacks on Andrea Willson? Why the two dead hunters? Had their deaths been accidental, or had there been another, darker motive involved? Even Murray Carlyle was not sure.

Suddenly, she found herself remembering a conversation with Deirdre almost thirty years ago. Even then, there had been enmity between them. The topic of discussion was Matthew, at the time only a boy. Deirdre had accosted Clarissa in the town circle, demanding that Clarissa talk to Matthew's mother.

"She is your sister. Your words will convince her. Matthew must be brought into a circle."

Clarissa had laughed. "Deirdre, don't be foolish. The craft has missed the boy completely. He would be useless in a circle."

Deirdre had been unwilling to believe. "He is of the bloodline of Cardew Longshadow, the greatest Woerloga that ever lived. How can he be powerless?"

Even thirty years ago, the very mention of Longshadow had made her skin crawl. Furious, she had stabbed her finger at Deirdre. "That is a despicable part of our history. Longshadow was monstrous. He has been dead for two thousand years, and long may he remain dead."

"You may live to regret those words, my friend," Deirdre had said, smiling. Then, "Imagine, if we could bring him into a circle today. Imagine our power. No more hiding, Clarissa. The world would tremble in fear!"

"And so would we! Even to think such things is insanity."

But wrapped up in her fantasy, Deirdre had not heard. "Perhaps those ancient powers can be drawn through the boy. Perhaps he is not totally useless."

Stunned by Deirdre's impertinence, and by the very perversity of the idea, she had turned and walked away. She had related, somewhat reluctantly, the incident to her sister. Soon after, her sister had taken Matthew and departed Marissa. Three other families had fled at the same time, fearful their children, both male and female, might be ensnared. There were ways of accomplishing what Deirdre wished. Better not to take the chance, even if it meant joining the outside world. Such craftwork had not been attempted in centuries. But with Matthew gone, with no direct descendent of Longshadow to work with, Deirdre was effectively declawed.

Until now. Matthew Willson had returned to Marissa. He had brought with him his only son, also of the bloodline of Cardew Longshadow. The craft had not missed Peter. If anything, it had blessed him doubly. Deirdre could not have asked for a greater gift.

How could I have let you come here? How could I have forgotten the very reason for your departure!

Angry at herself, Clarissa went through to the kitchen to pour another drink. Already, unaccustomed to such excess, her thoughts were slowing. She returned to the living room and kneeled by the bookcase. Her fingers ran along the spines of the small library. In her life, she had not done much reading. Even the books here were mostly for reference. It had been a long time since she'd pulled one from the case.

Now she did so, her hands trembling as she slid the ancient tome from its place on the shelf. She lifted the heavy volume and laid it atop the bookcase. She sipped her brandy and stared at the cover. The faded and peeled gold-leaf lettering was unreadable. She put her drink down gently and lay her hand on the cover of the book. It was cool to the touch, and she shivered. It had been passed through five generations since its original printing.

She opened the cover, flipped to the title page, and squinted down at the old English lettering.

A HISTORY OF THE DARK CRAFT

Her fingers riffled the old, familiar pages until they fell open at a well-thumbed place. Now, holding her breath, she stared down at the page and felt a chill pass over her.

"Matthew, forgive me. I should never have allowed you to come here."

The page before her was a woodcut illustration of the greatest of the ancient dark Woerloga. The lettering beneath the picture was crisp and black. CARDEW LONG—SHADOW.

The illustration above was grotesque and perverse. She shuddered to look upon it. It showed a man standing before a hut comprised of human limbs. Severed arms and legs, piled atop one another, formed the walls. Severed heads on spikes decorated the arched doorway. Beside the hut, smiling, stood the beast who lived therein. In his hand he held a staff, inscribed with runes. His cloak was a patchwork of human skin. Entwined around his neck were two arms, bloody and ragged, obviously freshly procured, the dead hands resting on his breasts like those of a lover. To the side lay the limbless torsos of his victims. Judging by the expressions on their faces, they were still alive.

Clarissa allowed her eyes to focus on the face of the monster Cardew Longshadow. The woodcut eyes seemed to hold her, as if the soul of the beast were captured on the page. Matthew Willson might have posed for this. In the slight turn of the lips she also recognized Peter.

They are of the bloodline of the monster.

It was the sound of the front door opening that drew her attention from the book. King, who had been sleeping quietly at the entrance to the living room, raised his head and growled softly. Clarissa turned from the bookcase, more curious than frightened, and moved toward the hallway. The door swung completely open, and Deirdre Farrell stepped in. Behind her, misty rain filled the night. Her dark coat glistened.

"Get out of my house," Clarissa said. She stepped angrily toward the other woman and was satisfied to see a momentary reaction of fear.

Then Deirdre lifted her hand. "Don't be so rude, Clarissa," she said.

Clarissa stopped her forward movement and wobbled on her feet. Damn the alcohol. The room seemed to swirl around her. Deirdre noticed her instability and smiled. King began to whine. With his belly pressed to the floor, he slunk to the rear of the house. Confused, Clarissa watched his departure, then again turned her angry attention to Deirdre.

"What do you want, Deirdre? You are not welcome here."

Deirdre smiled and moved past her into the living room. Clarissa turned and followed. Deirdre glanced at the bookcase, saw the open book, turned, and smiled.

"I see you have deduced the truth of the matter," she said.

Again, Clarissa felt icy cold. "You fool," she muttered.

Deirdre laughed softly. "I have somebody for you to meet," she said. Her eyes reflected the hallway light.

"To meet?"

She felt the new intrusion as a wave of cold air across her feet, and glanced down to see blue mist spilling across the floor. She gasped and spun to face the door. Outside, a wall of blue mist had risen to obscure the yard, the trees, the road. As she watched, the mist spilled through the door swirled around the legs of furniture, and climbed the stairs. Somewhere at the back of the house, King's whining reached a fevered pitch.

She spun on Deirdre, suddenly very frightened. She tried to sound angry when she spoke. "I want you to leave. Right now. Just—"

Deirdre laughed softly. Mist rolled across her feet. Her eyes moved from Clarissa's face and focused on something behind her. Clarissa turned slowly and drew a sharp breath at what she saw. Even the front doorway was hidden now, lost somewhere behind this wall of swirling blue. She squinted her eyes, trying to focus on the motion that seemed to draw her attention from all directions. The mist swirled. And suddenly, as if she had been looking at it all the time but had not seen it, a shape seemed to materialize before her eyes. She saw the outline of broad shoulders, a high head. Two red sparks for eyes.

Clarissa took a frightened step backward, and the shape moved purposefully toward her. The mist followed it like a cloak, then seemed to spill away, as if finally agreeing to release its hold on the figure.

She raised her hand to her mouth to stop another gasp. The shape before her, manlike though it was, was invisible, clothed in bloody scraps of human skin. Four distinct arms were draped over the invisible shoulders, bloody hands clustered where a chest might have been. She recognized one of the hands, or rather the wedding ring on it.

Jack Burgess. Greenish light swirled within the outline as if a shape were struggling but failing to materialize. The red points of the eyes seemed to pin and freeze her. From behind her, she heard Deirdre Farrell's soft voice.

"Clarissa Halloway, I'd like you to meet our savior Cardew Longshadow. Do you recognize him? Or perhaps his clothes are familiar?" Deirdre chuckled.

"But . . . why do you need Peter," Clarissa managed to say. Her voice sounded feeble.

"Oh, we don't really need Peter," Deirdre said. "Just ha

body, my dear. A new home for the greatest of Woerloga. They look alike, don't you think?"

Clarissa wanted to scream, but could not get another sound to emerge from her throat. Terror as she had never known it blossomed within her like a poisonous flower.

"You see, Clarissa, you have made a powerful enemy."

Clarissa's mind scrambled to understand. "But how could the council countenance such a terrible plan?"

Deirdre laughed. "The council knows nothing. They believe I work to raise a dark circle, and in that they have assisted me willingly. They wish only to see Marissa turn to more prosperous times. My own goals are of a grander nature, I'm afraid."

Clarissa could not take her eyes away from the two red points drawing closer to her.

"I once hoped we could be allies, Clarissa. You of all people can understand how far we have fallen. We are losing our traditions. The craft is slowly leaving us."

"That's not true."

"But it is! Don't you know what tonight is, Clarissa?"

Clarissa blinked, taken aback by the question.

Deirdre laughed harshly. "Even you are forgetting. Twenty years ago, this would have been a night of celebration."

It came to her then, and a pang of loss stabbed to her core. Deirdre was right. She *had* forgotten. The old ways were slipping away. "The Eve of Samain," she said softly.

"Yes! Yes! The Eve of Samain."

A new and terrible understanding came upon Clarissa. The Eve of Samain, when the boundaries between all worlds were weakest. If Cardew Longshadow were ever to claim Peter, then it would be tonight.

Deirdre, seeing the understanding in her eyes, smiled.

"You don't yet understand how powerful Andrea Willson has become," Clarissa said slowly. "You will not succeed."

"I freely admit I do not understand her. But it is you who gave her the spells. You who turned her against me. By herself, she is nothing."

261

"You're wrong. I think the stones themselves are working through her. You know very well that she found the earthworks."

Deirdre smiled. "No matter. It is not I who shall deal with her."

Clarissa stepped slowly backward. A smell of rotten meat surrounded her. She wanted to gag, to drop to her knees and vomit, but could not even twitch. Her mind screamed. This wasn't happening. It couldn't be happening.

"If it were up to me," Deirdre said, "I'd simply banish you from Marissa, separate you from the people and the craft. You have worked against us. Worked against the craft."

"No," Clarissa said.

"But it's not up to me, I'm afraid. The Woerloga has other ideas."

Although she could not turn her head, she sensed Deirdre moving, saw, from the corner of her eye, as the black-clad figure walked past her, into the mist. She heard Deirdre's voice from where the door should be, shrouded in mist.

Don't leave me alone with this thing! Please!

"Good-bye, old friend," Deirdre said, her voice a whisper in the mist.

Then she was alone. And the two red points were moving toward her again. Mist swirled, assuming the outline of reaching hands. The cloying odor of decay, of soil, of uprooted weeds, surrounded her, as if she had stuck her head in a rabbit's hole. She felt herself gripped and held. And then her face was being drawn toward the rotting skins of Jack and Willy Burgess, toward the thing hidden behind that dead facade.

She managed to move her lips. But her mouth was filled with rotting flesh, and her screams strangled in her throat.

PART VI

Queen of Men and Shadows

CHAPTER THIRTY-TWO

Andrea was standing in the kitchen, pouring herself a glass of milk, when the shape appeared at the window. She gasped and almost dropped the glass of milk. Cold liquid splashed across her hand.

"Brother!"

She waited until her heart stopped racing, then carefully placed the glass on the counter by the stove. She moved to the doors and slid them open. King, standing a few feet away, whined at her.

"King, what are you doing here? Did Clarissa send you?"

The spaniel whined. His tail, she saw, was flat against his behind. She stepped out into the cool air, kneeled on the deck beside him, and held out a hand. His cold nose pressed into her palm. He whined. In the light from the kitchen, the dog looked old and frightened. His sagging eyes looked diseased.

"Come on inside, boy." She stood, then moved back into the kitchen. King watched her, stood, and followed reluctantly. Once inside, he would not move from the door, and she could not close it. He whined insistently.

"What are you trying to tell me, boy?" For a second, not even that long, his eyes locked onto hers. A small growl erupted from his throat, as if he were angry that she could not understand. And suddenly she knew.

A feeling of cold swept over her, and goosebumps

pebbled her arms. "It's Clarissa, isn't it?"

King whined, backed partway out the door, and paused as if waiting for her.

"You want me to come?"

The spaniel whined as if to confirm her deduction. Andrea drew a deep breath and whistled it out. The feeling of cold dread that had swept over her was now replaced with a tingle of anticipation. She kneeled by the dog again and scratched his ears. "Just wait here a second. I'll be right back."

She turned away from the dog, left the kitchen, and went quickly upstairs. At the master bedroom she paused and opened the door slowly, being careful not to make noise. The room was dark. Matthew was facing away from the door, on his side. He snored softly, already asleep.

"Matthew?"

He continued to snore.

"Damn." She closed the door, reluctant to wake him. What could she tell him? *King came to get me, I think we should go with him back to Clarissa's.* She imagined his reaction, his disbelief, and extinguished a sudden flare of anger.

She moved to Peter's room and opened the door. Again, darkness. Peter also was sleeping. His breathing was deep and regular. She watched the sheets rise and fall. She closed the door. She wouldn't be gone for long. Surely neither Peter nor Matthew could get into trouble while they slept. She tried to convince herself that was true as she went downstairs. She pulled her windbreaker from the hallway cupboard and returned to the kitchen.

King jumped to his feet when she appeared.

"Let's go," she said.

Although it seemed like hours later, it was only minutes after leaving the comfort of her own home that King led her to the door of Clarissa's cottage. Andrea paused, catching her breath. Somewhere inside, a light was shining. The living room glowed like a dying ember. King

266

paused at the open front door and looked back at her.

"Where's your mistress, boy?" she whispered.

The dog whined softly. Again, Andrea felt herself overcome by a feeling of cold dread. The front door hung open, but she could see nothing beyond it. A faint smell hung in the air, made worse by the pervasive drizzle. It seemed to surround her, like a smothering cloud.

She stepped past King and knocked on the door. "Clarissa?"

No answer. The house seemed far too silent, like a tomb. She shuddered, partly from the cold, partly from the fear mounting within her, and knocked again.

"Clarissa?"

She pushed the door open, then coughed as the cloying odor strengthened exponentially. She recognized the smell now. Burnt meat.

Reluctantly, fighting an urge to turn and flee, she stepped into the cottage, holding her hand over her mouth and nose.

"Clarissa?"

King followed her in. His whining had stopped. She found the light switch by the door and hit it with her hand. The hanging lamp above came on, sending spears of light throughout the house. Curtains of smoke hung everywhere, drifting slowly. She had entered a frat party once, years ago, and seen something like this. Then, the air had been redolent of tobacco and marijuana. Here, it was roast pork. Only it wasn't pork.

"Clarissa?"

At the doorway of the small living room she froze, her eyes drawn to a shape on the floor by the sofa. It looked as if somebody had dropped a long, twisted log on Clarissa's nice carpet. The log moved, emitting a high-pitched noise.

In a flash, as King brushed past her leg and moved toward the burnt shape on the floor, the scene snapped into focus. It felt like somebody had punched her on the forehead. Her head literally snapped backward, her mouth dropping open. She winced at the clack of her own teeth as

267

her mouth snapped closed again.

Beside the moving, squealing shape on the floor, King began to wag his tail. The thing, she now saw, was human. What once had been legs tapered off into blackened, cracking stumps. Clear liquid seeped to the carpet. Raw, wet redness glistened in the fissures. Where arms should have hung, there were only black branches, crooked and frail.

Andrea moaned and stepped backward, her hand clasped to her mouth. Panic clawed at her mind, threatening to shred her meager composure.

She leaned against the door frame, closed her eyes, and breathed deeply.

Calm down! Calm down!

King's whining drew her attention, and she opened her eyes to see the dog licking the blackened stumps of the burnt legs. Horrified, she lunged forward.

"King!"

Startled, the dog scurried away, then moved back quickly. He looked up at her, as if pleading, and whined. *This can't be Clarissa. It can't be. Not this . . . thing.*

The thing uttered another sound.

"Clarissa?"

The black crust of flesh trembled. Andrea closed her eyes and bent closer.

"Clarissa? Who did this to you?"

Amazingly, miraculously, the head seemed to move. Cracks appeared in the blackened skin and wept fluid. The lipless hole of the mouth opened wider and tried to close.

"Wawagah."

"I can't understand, Clarissa, I can't—"

"Wawagah."

Another squeal. Andrea closed her eyes and lifted her hands to her ears to block out the horrible sound. The charred body before her began to tremble. The mouth moved.

"Kuh."

"What?"

With superhuman effort, skin cracking and weeping with every move, the charred mouth carefully formed the word. "Boo-kuh."

Andrea blinked. "Book?"

She turned her head and scanned the room. A large book lay open on the bookcase. She rose, glad to move away. In the dim light, she could not see the page. She reached for the table lamp, clicked it on, and blinked her eyes against the light. This time, when she glanced down at the page, her heart pounded.

"Oh God." She turned to face the thing that had been Clarissa.

The charred mouth moved again, and this time there was no mistaking what it said. "Woerloga."

Andrea turned back to the book. The monster depicted there, draped in human skin and body parts, might as well have been Matthew. The face was the same. The eyes. The mouth. Frantically, she scanned the lettering at the bottom, seeking an explanation. Woerloga. A *male* practitioner of the craft. Sorcerer.

"Cardew Longshadow," she whispered. She turned to Clarissa again. "What does this mean?"

Clarissa groaned. Again, her charred lips struggled to move. Andrea edged closer to listen. Even warped by the mutilation of her features, Clarissa's words were understandable. Somewhere, she had found the strength to speak through her pain.

"Longshadow . . . related to Peter and Matthew by blood . . . called back . . . Deirdre . . . wants Peter . . . needs boy's body . . . reincarnation . . ."

Disjointed, barely audible, the gibberish made a horrible sort of sense.

". . . tricked us . . . tricked Peter . . . just want his body . . . that's all . . ."

"What can I do, Clarissa? What can I do?" She wanted desperately to reach out, to hold the dying woman. But such an act would only bring agony.

Clarissa groaned. "Tonight is the Eve of Samain. Boundaries weak. He can take Peter tonight. Don't let him. Stop him. He is not yet powerful. Once he has Peter, he will rule."

"But how? How?" Her voice trembled. The tears started to come. It was all too much.

"You are strong," Clarissa said. "Stronger than they know. He can be stopped. Bind him to Earth."

She began to cry. The tears slid down her cheeks and fell to Clarissa's blackened skin. The eyeless face turned to find her. The lips moved.

"I'm sorry I cannot help you, my dear. You must act alone. Save your family. Call your own special friend. It is time."

"Oh, Clarissa . . ."

"Protect King for me, my dear. He is a baby."

At the sound of his name, the dog wagged his tail. Clarissa groaned. Breath hissed from her open mouth. In a moment she was still.

"Clarissa?"

This time, there was no answer. King sensed her passing immediately. He backed away and seemed to shrink in on himself. As if drunk, he stumbled to the end of the sofa and lay down. With his head on his paws, he began to tremble.

"Oh, Clarissa, I'm sorry," Andrea whispered. Whatever had happened to Clarissa, it hadn't happened very long ago. Probably just before King had scratched at the door.

Crying freely now, she stood. King watched her, his eyes sleepy. She remembered what Barbara Robertson had been like at the death of her special friend. What must it be like for King? Did the bond go two ways?

She moved to the dog and kneeled by him.

"Come on, boy. Come with me. I'll look after you now."

She stood and moved to the door. In a moment, King wobbled to his feet and followed her. He paused in the hallway and looked back at the body of his mistress.

"Come on, boy," Andrea said.

Obediently, the old dog followed her outside.

Matthew woke with a start.

The noise came again, a loud thump. Definitely not a dream. Fully awake, he swung his legs out of bed. The digital clock read 10:30 P.M. He'd been asleep nearly an hour and a half. Andrea still hadn't come to bed. He smothered a pang of resentment, closed his eyes, and listened carefully.

Silence. Absolute silence. That was worse than a few noises.

He reached for the table light, clicked it on, and rose quickly from the bed. He pulled on his bathrobe, stood at the bedroom door a moment before opening it, and suddenly felt silly. Why was he acting so furtively in the comfort of his own home? Intruders were unlikely in Marissa.

He stepped out into the hallway. The downstairs lights were still on. Peter's bedroom door was wide open. Frowning now, he moved toward it. One glance was enough. Peter was not in bed.

He turned away and went slowly down the stairs. The main floor was silent. At the bottom of the stairs he paused, his hand resting on the bannister.

"Andrea?"

No response.

"Peter?"

Again, nothing.

"Jesus H. Christ. Where the hell is everybody?"

He glanced in the living room. Andrea's book lay closed on the coffee table. The reading lamp was still on. He moved to the kitchen. The stove light was on. No sign of Peter or Andrea.

"What the hell is going on here?"

This time his voice was hushed, fear beginning to temper his anger. He leaned against the kitchen door frame and scratched his chin. The house remained silent and unresponsive about him.

"What the hell," he said again.

And then he saw the lights through the sliding doors. Bluish and hazy. His heart suddenly pounded, and sweat broke out on his forehead. He moved across the kitchen. At the sliding doors he peered outside in disbelief. A blue mist stretched across the grass, billowing among the trees at the far end.

Just like the alley. Just like my fucking dreams! He fought back a surge of panic. Breathed deeply. Closed his eyes. Looked again.

It was worse.

The mist had receded into the trees, and seemed to be flowing away. But now he could see shapes, dark and shadowy, moving about between the trunks.

Then he saw Peter. The boy, dressed only in his windbreaker, was walking through the mist. It seemed to climb his legs, to tug at him with vaporous fingers, as if leading him. Again, panic surged through Matthew. His dream had come true.

He scrabbled at the door latch, and finally got it open. He stepped out onto the deck. He cupped his hands to his mouth, opened his mouth to yell, then froze. Some deep instinct, suddenly given life, warned against drawing attention to himself. That would be a big mistake.

He watched as Peter disappeared into the darkness of the trees. The mist had vaporized, as if it had never been.

It was all a dream. It had never happened.

He shook his head and went back inside. Upstairs, he dressed quickly. From the cupboard in the front hallway he retrieved his revolver, ensured that it was fully loaded, then went through the kitchen, out through the sliding doors, and into the backyard. The cool night air seemed to cling like a wet sheet.

At the foot of the yard, one foot poised to enter the darkened trail, he hesitated.

If you go in there, you'll be lost. Really lost. Forever.

He fought down his fear and swallowed hard.

"Jesus, it's my boy," he muttered softly, angry at his own cowardice.

Lips tight, one hand resting on the butt of his revolver, he stepped onto the trail. The woods swallowed him without a sound. Soon, he began to run.

CHAPTER THIRTY-THREE

Marissa was deserted. Andrea knew it the moment she and King came out of East Drive into the town circle. Every storefront was dark, even the Three-Horned Bull. She slowed as she crossed the road, eyeing the pub warily. Less than half an hour ago, light had beamed from its window. At Lake Drive she paused and turned to regard the circle. At her feet, King did the same.

"Where is everybody, boy?"

The dog whined softly. She looked down and saw that his hackles were up. He almost looked ferocious.

Once, as a child, she had visited a ghost town in Arizona with her parents. She had stood at one end of town, holding her father's hand, and listened to the town. Then, like now, it had been silent. The buildings, devoid of life, had seemed to rise from the desert like a monster's ungainly skeleton. In Marissa, the impression was stronger. Here, the world had grown around and through the town. Like some Mayan temple lost in the jungle. The desert purified its dead, making them into mummies. Here . . . Marissa was a rotting corpse.

Ghost town.

And right then, in a flash, she knew she was defeated.

I can't beat them. I don't even know what the game is. She nodded hard and drew a deep breath. "I'm sorry, Clarissa. I can't stay and fight. I can't." King whined softly at the sound of her voice. She reached down and scratched his ears.

Whether Matthew agreed or not, she was leaving Marissa. And she was taking Peter with her. That, at least, she could do. Get him out of Deirdre Farrell's clutches. Away from whatever monstrosity had been raised to possess him. What would their reaction be to that? Never mind winning or losing the game, she would simply end it.

She smiled at the thought.

"Let's go, boy."

With King at her heels, she began to jog up Lake Drive. Within minutes, the lights of the house glinted through the trees, and she released a sob of relief.

But as she drew nearer the house, she knew something was wrong.

She paused at the foot of the drive. Lights beamed from the main floor windows, as she had left them. Upstairs was darkness.

King began to whine.

"What is it, boy? Do you feel it too?"

He looked up at her and whined again.

Fighting panic, she ran up the drive to the front door. Inside, she paused and listened. Silence. She stepped farther into the hallway. In the living room, her book was where she had left it, undisturbed. She glanced through to the kitchen.

The sliding doors were open. The tiling glistened with rain that had blown in. At the base of the door, a thin line glowed feebly. She crossed the kitchen quickly and kneeled down by the door. Cold moisture soaked through her jeans. She ran a finger through the glowing line. The remnant of the mixture she and Clarissa had mixed. Her first spell. She lifted her finger close to her face and studied the glowing speckles. As she looked, their life fizzled, leaving a gritty residue on her skin. She wiped it off on her jeans.

If it was glowing, that meant . . .

She scrambled to her feet and ran for the stairs.

"Matthew! Peter!"

Her feet pounded the stairs. Glass rattled on the main floor. King, making small panicked noises, followed in a flurry of limbs.

Both Matthew and Peter were gone.

She had wanted to run, to flee Marissa. But now even that option had been taken away from her.

Feeling the weight of her body as if it were a two-hundred-pound sack of flour, she went back downstairs. King, pleased with the slower pace, followed quietly. In the living room, she slumped into a corner of the sofa and hugged her knees up to her chest.

"You won, Marissa, you bitch. You took the prize."

Her voice sounded hollow, lifeless, that of a stranger. King, lying on the floor by her feet, cocked his head and looked up at her quizzically.

"I don't know what to do, boy," she said to him softly.

His tail wagged once, then became still. She reached down to scratch his head. The she pressed her face to her knees and cried.

Matthew understood his predicament within minutes of entering the trails. At first the choice of forks was simple. Ahead of him, the blue light filled the forest with eerie shadows. He moved toward it, always choosing the path that took him in that direction. Four forks later, the light was a faint glow in the distance, and darkness was closing in around him.

The smart thing to do would be to go back to the house right now, call Murray, and mount a search. Surely, with such well-marked trails, it wouldn't be difficult to discover where Peter had gone.

He debated the idea a few moments, then rejected it. Somehow, the idea of confiding in Murray Carlyle was not appealing. Murray's disparagement of Andrea over the last week, though perhaps warranted, had struck a discordant note in Matthew. At first, Murray's comments had seemed right on the money. Andrea was definitely acting out of character. She was definitely on some sort of edge. But hell, she was right about a lot of things. Like about Peter.

He sucked in a deep breath, closed his eyes a moment, selected one of the trails, and began to jog along. In a moment the trail curved slightly to the right, toward where he had last seen the blue shadows. He swallowed hard with relief and began to pick up his pace.

As he ran, his thoughts returned to Murray, to Andrea. Murray was a co-worker. Andrea was his wife. To whom did he owe the greater loyalty?

He felt a sharp pang of guilt at the answer that came to him. *I should have been more supportive, Andrea.*

But Murray had only been trying to help, hadn't he? It wasn't as if the other man were intentionally trying to sow seeds of unrest in his relationship with Andrea. He chuckled softly at the idea, but as he continued to run, it didn't seem so funny.

He slowed to a halt at another intersection of trails. Now, the glow ahead was so faint it might simply have been his imagination. Any of the openings facing him might be the right one.

"Damn it, Peter, what the hell are you up to?"

Where could the boy be going at this time of night? What was the meaning of the blue mist? Even thinking about it sent a stab of fear through him, transporting him back to that dark alley. *Did I really see mist that night?* He recalled his dreams, and smothered the memories instantly. Those were dreams, this was reality. *And never the twain shall meet.*

Or shall they?

He shuddered, unable to keep the dream memories locked away. Had the mist in his dreams been blue, or was he simply colorizing in retrospect? What about the mist in the alley in Minneapolis? The blue light there had simply been from the cars, hadn't it? He couldn't remember clearly. Certainly, there could be no connection between that nightmare incident, his dreams, and the present. Surely not. He had not seen enough mist in his lifetime to form an opinion as to what it should look like. Maybe all mist had a bluish tinge to it.

He shook his head at the idiocy of the notion.

Again, he chose one of the trails facing him and began to move along it. Soon, it curved away to the left, almost doubling back on itself.

"Son of a bitch."

He began to retrace his steps, moving back toward the junction. In the darkness, he could hardly see two paces in front of him. The trees were thick shadows, towering above. A stray branch slashed across his face. He raised a hand, covering his eyes until the pain subsided. He would be blind by morning if this kept up. When he opened his eyes again, he saw the light.

A yellow glow, dancing in the trees less than twenty yards away. One, two, perhaps three distinct lights.

Flashlights!

He dropped to his knees and held his breath. Voices emerged from the shadows of the trees.

". . . we won't miss anything . . ."

"Don't worry, we'll be in time." He recognized this voice. It was Fiona Campbell.

"I still don't like it." He could not place this one.

"What's not to like? Nobody's going to get hurt." Fiona again.

The voices drew closer, and within moments he could hear the crunch of footsteps on the trail. Jesus, they were coming this way. Somehow, he understood that he did not want to be discovered. Not like this. That would be a mistake.

He moved as quietly as possible from the trail, into the brush at its edges. The lights drew closer.

Over to his right, he suddenly glimpsed another cluster of lights. And then another beyond that. It was as if the entire town were out walking in the woods. Where were they going?

Fiona Campbell spoke again, this time as close as arm's length. "What about your partner? He won't be any trouble?"

"None," came Murray Carlyle's reply. "Got him just

277

where I want him. Doesn't suspect a thing. Thinks his wife is crazy."

"That's cruel," Fiona said with a small laugh.

"Ain't it, though?" Murray said, and laughed also.

Then they were past. Their lights flashed by and began to recede down the trail, casting long shadows.

Matthew scrambled from cover. His heart pounded a crazy rhythm inside his chest. His hand reached for the butt of his revolver, stroked it, and squeezed it.

He had not understood all that had been said, but had grasped enough to know that something was up. Something involving him. His family.

Again, guilt stabbed through him.

You were right all along, Andrea.

His lips compressed, his anger tightly checked, he began to follow.

The change was like a tide coming in.

Andrea was not sure how long she sat, curled into the sofa, crying. She knew only that finally, without warning, there were no more tears. The reservoir was empty. Her emotional barometer had somehow managed to stop the wild swinging of its needle. It was time to act.

She sat up straight, rubbed her nose, and wiped her eyes. King, lying at her feet, raised his head to regard her.

You took everything from me, Marissa. Everything I value. Everything I love.

It was this realization that banished the last of her confusion, the tiny remnants of fear and self-pity that had immobilized her.

I have nothing to lose.

She drew a deep breath and stood. King scrambled to his feet and watched her warily.

"I know where they've gone, boy," she said to him.

He cocked his head and wagged his tail.

She moved to the rear sliding doors. King followed her in a mad dash. At the door she turned, kneeled, and reached out to stroke his neck.

"No, my friend. You must stay here. I'll be back soon. Don't worry. I won't leave you."

The dog lowered slowly to his rump, his head sagging. She petted him again. Then she stood, opened the door, and went out onto the deck. After she had closed it again, King moved close and pressed his face to the glass. She touched the glass next to his nose. She watched him a moment, then turned and walked to the end of the yard.

At the opening of the trail she paused. The forest was dark and silent. The thought of entering it frightened her. She closed her eyes, and held her breath until the trembling in her limbs subsided. *There's nothing more you can do to me.*

She released her breath, drew another, and stepped onto the trail. She walked for perhaps five minutes, then stopped and kneeled. Moisture seeped through her jeans.

She lowered her head to the ground and pressed her cheek to the moist earth. The odor of rotten vegetation, living things, wet soil, surrounded her face. She breathed it deeply and slowly. She knew her lips were moving, knew also that it was not entirely of her own volition. As had happened earlier, she felt herself at the mercy of some greater power.

"Special friend," she whispered. "Special friend."

The call radiated from her, more than simple words. She felt it, a flexing of hidden muscles she had not even been aware of. The ground itself seemed to become part of her. The trees. The sky. Radiating her message, her need.

An incredible, exhilarating feeling of peace encompassed her. *This is my natural state.* As she thought it, she accepted it. Her whole life up to this point suddenly seemed to her as nothing more than a process of metamorphosis, an interminable time spent inside a cocoon.

"Special friend . . ."

She was not sure how much time passed. Her mind seemed to drift away, and when it returned, she discovered that she was shivering, cold, and still on her knees. Her cheek was numb, covered in muck.

279

A noise to her left startled her. She rose to her feet and stared into the trees.

It came again. A crashing of branches. Again, closer.

In the darkness, she could see nothing. She stared, wide-eyed, alert and waiting.

The noise came again, now to her left. She spun, caught a flicker of something pale moving between the branches, and suddenly she was terrified. *Oh God, what have I done?*

The crashing grew louder, drawing closer. Now, it was accompanied by a sound that was obviously breathing. Heavy and hoarse.

She began to back away, retreating along the path. And then she froze.

Why are you running? Whatever it is, you called it.

Ahead of her, the bushes trembled. A pale shape stepped onto the trail and moved toward her. Her heart began to hammer.

It was the wolf.

Now, its eyes blazing red and angry, it approached her. She swallowed hard, forcing herself to remain still. The animal was huge, nearly as high as her shoulders, something out of legend. Wolves didn't grow this big. She knew that. This thing might have been a lion.

It stopped in front of her, a foot away. Its face was immense. She felt the hot breath rushing from its mouth, redolent of blood and torn meat. A low growl slid from its throat.

She sensed immediately that it was not threatening her.

It stepped toward her again. Her throat constricted, ready to scream. Her muscles would not take her away. The wolf's muzzle pressed into her throat. She felt the gentle nip of huge teeth. Then it backed away, its red eyes regarding her curiously.

Andrea drew a deep, shuddering breath. She stared at the animal, drinking it in with her eyes.

Again, the feeling of power consumed her, buoyed her. *We were meant for each other.*

Slowly, tentatively, still not entirely sure of the animal, she reached out and ran her hands along the animal's long snout. The fur was coarse. She pushed her fingers into its thick, bristling mane. As she did so, its look seemed to soften. Its growl receded, becoming almost a purr of pleasure.

And suddenly she understood, Those other times, when she had been chased on the road near home, when she had encountered Deirdre Farrell on the road, the wolf had not been attacking her. He had been helping her. Urging her to run. Standing between her and danger. Protecting her.

"You need a name," she whispered.

The wolf rubbed its head against her palm. Its red eyes transfixed her. She searched her mind, looking for names that might fit. She could not imagine this beast answering to any of them.

"What do you want to be called?"

And then, as if her mind had somehow become connected to that of the wolf, she found her lips forming around a word. It seemed to materialize in the air between the two of them, and she knew, immediately, that it was right.

"Sentena," she said softly. "I name you Sentena."

The wolf raised its head, opened its jaw, and howled. The sound cut through the night, and the forest seemed to tremble. Even Andrea felt herself shudder at the terror of it.

Then, with a deep breath, she leaned forward and again stroked the beast's head. Her fingers dug deep, scratching the skin beneath the coarse fur. Sentena growled with pleasure.

"Special friend," she whispered, "we have work to do."

CHAPTER THIRTY-FOUR

Sentena loped ahead. His huge paws tossed moist divots of the trail into the air. Andrea was forced to run to keep up. In the darkness, she could hardly see where she was going. Branches slashed at her face and tore at her clothes.

"Don't move so quickly!" she gasped.

She followed as well as she could. Each step brought a painful tightening of her muscles, a tightening that grew worse with every passing minute. Each breath burned in her throat, seeming to bring not quite enough oxygen. Her arms ached. Her head pounded. And still, Sentena ran, and ran.

She knew she was approaching the point of exhaustion when the dizziness came. The darkness swirled about her. The trail ahead seemed a bottomless pit, ready to suck her down. Around her, the trees were an army of shadows raised against her.

Then, mercifully, when she could not take another step, the trail came to an end. The huge leaning stones materialized out of the darkness ahead. She stumbled up behind Sentena, came to a halt, and gripped his neck. Together, pressed low to the ground, they crawled toward the edge of the stone circle. She heard low, murmuring voices, and as she pushed around the edge of one of the stones, she saw the crowd that had gathered.

The group stood in the center of the circle, forming a crescent around a small fire. Logs and peat were piled near the fire. Beyond the flames, cast in flickering light, was a small cluster of stones. Peter lay atop one of these, his hands clasped across his belly. He was naked and shivering. Behind him, with arms raised, stood another figure. She thought, for a moment, that it was an animal. Jagged antlers rose from its head, and yet its body seemed human. But in the flickering light of the fire, something glittered on one of the upraised hands. A ring.

Andrea blinked.

Deirdre Farrell.

The antlers rose from the skin of a buck draped over her head and shoulders. Now, she could see the wrinkled, pendulous breasts within the folds of the animal skin. The old woman bent over Peter and ran her hand over his naked stomach.

Andrea felt her guts tighten. "Leave him alone," she muttered.

A figure stepped away from the small crescent surrounding the fire. She recognized the slump of the shoulder, the unkemptness of the hair. Murray Carlyle. He said something, but his words were unclear. Deirdre moved beyond the fire and came toward him, her arms now at her sides.

Do it now. Get out there. Stop them.

Andrea drew a deep breath and closed her eyes a moment. She gripped Sentena fiercely.

"Let's get them, special friend," she whispered.

Something grabbed her from behind and covered her mouth. She could not even scream.

Matthew clamped his hand over Andrea's mouth and pulled her backward, away from the circle of stones. She screamed against his palm, but the sound was muffled. The group in the dell did not hear a thing.

She was much more difficult to subdue than he had anticipated. Her arms windmilled. Her heels kicked back violently. Twice she caught him with her elbow, pushing the air out of his lungs in sharp coughs. When he spun her around, supporting her with one arm, her eyes were wild above his smothering palm.

"For God's sake, keep quiet!"

The terror left her eyes slowly, replaced by the shock of recognition. When he was sure that she would not scream, he lowered his hand.

"Matthew, what—"

He held up a hand to silence her, frightened their words would carry into the stone circle. He leaned closer to her, keeping his voice a whisper. "They took Peter from the house. I followed. Got lost. When I saw you, I tagged close behind." He glanced wildly around. "And keep your eyes open. I saw that damned wolf again."

The bushes rustled to their left, and Matthew spun, reaching for his revolver. Something stepped out. Matthew's heart nearly exploded. He stumbled backward, away from the monstrous head. The wolf leapt.

"Sentena! No!" Andrea's voice was a harsh whisper.

The animal checked its leap and came to a halt beside Andrea. Oh Christ, it would kill her. The size of the thing! He fumbled for his revolver and pulled it out of the holster. Andrea stepped between him and the animal.

"Don't make any sudden moves. I don't know how much control I have over him."

He could hardly believe what he was hearing. "Control?"

She stepped toward him, blocking his shot completely. "Don't shoot. You'd waste your bullet. And then I probably wouldn't be able to stop him from tearing you apart. Just put the gun away."

Stunned, he let his hand drop. From behind Andrea, the huge beast moved closer, poking its head past her shoulders.

"For God's sake, what is it?"

Andrea reached down and helped him to his feet. "He's my special friend," she said softly.

"Special friend?" The words had connotations he could not comprehend.

"Sentena, this is Matthew." She curled her arm around the wolf's huge neck and hugged it close. "Matthew, this is

284

Sentena. I don't want you to kill each other."

Matthew brushed himself off. He regarded, in turn, Andrea, and the wolf. "I'm going crazy," he muttered softly.

"You're not crazy. And neither am I. They're going to hurt Peter. We have to stop them."

She tugged his arm, pulling him back toward the stone circle. They crouched down, then crawled past the outer circle of stones on their bellies. The wolf, also crouched, remained concealed behind a small ridge of boulders. Matthew's eyes kept darting over to the creature, terrified it would attack without warning.

In the center of the circle, Marissa's population was gathered around the fire. In the flickering light, he could see Peter, prone on a stone altar. Above him, the hag Deirdre Farrell waved her arms and muttered gibberish.

"Is the whole place nuts?"

"They've resurrected a creature almost two thousand years old. One of your ancestors. He needs Peter."

Matthew was too far gone to question her. He felt the words come to his lips, could not stop them. "The thing in the mist," he said softly.

She nodded. In the circle, Deirdre Farrell had raised her voice. Her arms hovered over Peter, as if she were ready to pounce on him.

In response, the crowd backed away from the altar. A murmur of voices reached them. Deirdre Farrell stepped away from Peter. Blue mist began to pour in from the base of the altar. It swirled, hissing, through the fire. It poured like water around the feet of the now agitated crowd.

Deirdre Farrell said something else.

The mist rose in a pillar before her, defining itself into a manlike shape.

"Oh boy," Matthew said.

"Here we go," Andrea said.

Peter pressed his palms flat against the edges of the altar and squeezed the rough stone. Beneath his fingers it felt warm and alive. He shifted his weight, lifted his buttocks, and lowered himself. The stone seemed to adjust itself to whatever position he assumed, like some sort of high-tech armchair. *Dad would love it.*

The thought of his father made him smile, but he forced his lips back into a neutral expression as quickly as he could. Deirdre wouldn't like to see a smile on him. Not yet.

He rolled his head to see what was happening inside the sacred circle. The townsfolk, ignorant of what was about to transpire, had shuffled away from the altar, frightened by the appearance of the mist. Deirdre had been right. None of them knew what was happening. They had wanted so badly to believe her story of a dark circle that they had refused to look beyond it.

He closed his eyes and drew a deep breath. The night air was cool against his skin, but not uncomfortable. When the mist finally engulfed him, he knew, there would be time enough for cold. He could see the flickering of the fire beyond his closed eyelids, could feel the warmth against his skin. For the moment, he savored it.

He opened his eyes at a touch on his shoulder. Deirdre was bent over him. The old hag's face was twisted into an expression that might have been sexual ecstasy.

"Are you ready, Peter Willson?" Her breath was sour.

He squeezed the altar tightly. "I'm ready."

As ready as I'll ever be. He closed his eyes.

He felt Deirdre's cold touch on his belly and opened his eyes again. She was staring down at him with a vague sort of smile on her dry lips. Behind her, the blue mist swirled and rose. He felt a prickling along the entire length of his body, as if he had received a mild static charge. The hair on his head crawled.

Deirdre bent over him so that her face was close to his. Her eyes glittered with eagerness. She stroked his face with a cold hand, and Peter shuddered. Deirdre smiled.

"You will never know the great service you have done," she said softly, almost sorrowfully.

Her words put a firm dent in the joy of his expectation. He looked directly into her eyes and did not like what he saw there.

"It is time to meet your destiny," she said.

Peter opened his mouth to respond, but snapped it shut again without saying a word.

My destiny.

He nodded slowly. This was not time to be entertaining doubts about what was happening. He was far beyond the stage of doubting. He moved his eyes away from Deirdre, to the mist behind her. The swirling vapors had coalesced into a roughly manlike shape. Within the ethereal blue cocoon he glimpsed something solid. The first glimpse of Longshadow was always a bit disconcerting. The first time, he had almost turned and run. The hanging strips of skin, the smell of rot . . .

Now, there was no horror as he waited for Longshadow to appear. The closest experience he could remember was Christmas morning, waiting in bed, the silence of the house surrounding him, knowing that soon, soon, he would rise and open his gifts. Tonight, the gifts were coming to him.

The mist swirled. Deirdre, still smiling, stepped aside. Peter drew a deep breath and held it.

Like a veil, the mist parted. He heard a gasp of surprise before he even knew it was his own. He had known, of course, that tonight, the Eve of Samain, Cardew Longshadow would be at his strongest. He had sensed, during every visit, a greater degree of power in the Woerloga, like a battery slowly charging. But he had not expected this!

Until now, the Woerloga had been visible only by the outline of dead flesh hanging from him. There had been times when he had glimpsed the points of red eyes, and once he had seen a footprint appear in soft mud as the Woerloga crossed it. Now, however, within the strips of dead skin, stood the outline of a body, murky and incomplete, as if viewed through the depths of a muddy pond.

Peter pushed himself up on his elbows for a better look, unable to hide his astonishment.

The boundaries are weak. He can cross over.

He swallowed hard. In another minute, he and the Woerloga would be as one, sharing the same body.

My body.

He drew a deep breath, suddenly frightened.

Behind him, he heard a murmur run through the townspeople. They had not been expecting this. But it was too late now for them to do anything. They could only watch, whisper, and soon . . . kneel in subjugation to the Dark King.

The Woerloga stepped closer to the altar. Blue mist swirled around the half-visible feet. An odor, thick and corrupt, wafted over Peter. He cringed, lifting a hand to cover his mouth. As the Woerloga stepped closer to the altar, Peter saw in horror the maggots writhing in the dead arms about his neck. The flesh of the dead fingers was purple and puffy. Fluid weeped from beneath blackened nails.

Peter turned away, unable to look any longer. The thought of the dead skin hanging from his own shoulders filled him with revulsion.

Don't fight it. It'll be over soon.

He opened his eyes again. The Woerloga was close, within touching distance.

Deirdre Farrell took a step toward him, her eyes wide. "Yes," she hissed. "Yesssss."

The Woerloga lifted an arm and reached out toward him. Peter closed his eyes and waited.

Nothing happened.

He opened his eyes again.

For a moment, the fire blinded him. He squinted his eyes. At the other side of the clearing, shrouded in darkness, three shapes had entered the circle.

"Nooooo!" Deirdre Farrell's wail was like a nail dragged across a blackboard.

One of the figures stepped closer and became momentarily illuminated by firelight. Peter gasped, hardly believing his eyes.

"Andrea!"

CHAPTER THIRTY-FIVE

The moment Andrea stepped into the circle, the dizziness hit her. Her head swam with a hiss of voices. It felt, for a moment, as if a warm breeze had swept into the clearing and was caressing her with gentle fingers. Her skin tingled. She swayed on her feet.

The sudden trembling of the ground was like a slap in the face. She blinked hard and held out her arms for balance. The gathered crowd wobbled on their feet and hung on to each other for support. Around the circle, the standing stones trembled. Dust fell from them, drifting to the ground. Outside the circle, the forest was silent.

This place was expecting me!

The moment she thought it, she knew it was true. Here was the source of the power she had used these past weeks. She felt it now, the very ground itself, reaching out for her, as if trying to swallow her.

"Andrea!"

She glanced toward the altar. Peter had slid from the stone and was standing on his feet, wobbling precariously as the ground shook. His face, in the firelight, was pale, his eyes bright. For a moment, their eyes locked, and she found herself looking into the frightened face of a thirteen-year-old boy who had become inextricably entwined in something beyond his comprehension.

She held out her arms to him. "Peter, come to me."

As she spoke, the shaking of the ground subsided. A

terrible calmness settled on the circle. In a moment, the murmur of voices grew, becoming a hiss of fear and confusion. From the corner of her eye she identified Murray Carlyle, Fiona Campbell, Ewan and Barbara Robertson.

The confused expression on Peter's face intensified, but he took a step toward her. Behind him, Deirdre Farrell lunged past the altar and blocked his way. Silhouetted against the flickering flames, her antlers quivered. Her eyes glittered in a mask of shadow.

She raised a shaking arm and pointed a finger at Andrea. "You! Leave the circle!"

Andrea remained where she was. To her left, Matthew shuffled closer.

"How the hell are we going to get out of here?" His voice was flat, emotionless, beyond shock.

She did not avert her gaze from Deirdre as she answered him. "Just draw your weapon, Matthew. Be ready. Move away from me."

For a moment he did not respond. Then she heard the shuffle of his leather holster, the scuff of his shoes as he stepped away. Beyond Matthew, Sentena began to growl. The noise seemed to fill the circle. Some of the crowd gathered around the altar began to shift restlessly on their feet.

"I want my son," Andrea said carefully.

Deirdre Farrell laughed. "You are too late, little one. He is no longer yours."

Andrea stepped forward. The blue mist was swirling around Peter's feet. The boy had not noticed. Behind him, the nightmare shape of rotting skin drew closer.

"Peter!"

Peter blinked. He began to take another step away from the altar. Mist billowed in front of him, blocking his path. He paused, waving his hand to clear it. Behind him, Longshadow drew closer.

The union happened quickly. Andrea raised her voice to shout a warning, but by then it was too late. The cloak of rotting human skin and limbs embraced Peter, falling across his shoulder. One moment, she was looking into the face of her son, his eyes wide in shock. The next, his skin was clouding, becoming mottled, as if superimposed over another, not quite matching image. His eyes blinked. Blinked. Blinked again. She found herself staring into the two red pinpoints of Cardew Longshadow's eyes.

Deirdre Farrell raised her arms and released a peal of triumphant laughter that might have been a scream. She fell to her knees before Peter, lowering her face to the ground.

Even from the edge of the clearing, Andrea heard her voice, and she trembled.

"Master!" Deirdre whispered. "Master!"

Peter raised one of his hands and held it before his face, as if studying his own fingers. His lips curled in an unfamiliar smile.

"Peter!"

Peter lifted his head to regard her. For an instant, less than a second, it seemed a small war waged across his features. It was over quickly. His eyes glowed red. His lips curled maliciously.

He raised a hand and pointed directly at her. She stumbled backward, as if she had been physically punched. A wave of cold air passed across her, and she felt her skin tighten.

"Bitch," Longshadow said, the word hardly intelligible, as if he was unsure how to use lips and a tongue. "I have waited for this moment a long, long time."

He stepped toward her.

Matthew reeled as the blast of cold air passed by him. To his right, Andrea stumbled as if she'd been shot. Her arms flailed to keep her balance. He tried to make eye contact, needing to know she was all right, but her face was pinched in effort as she leaned into whatever Peter was throwing at her.

My world is falling apart.

He could see it happening, right before his eyes. The

rules he had lived by all his life, the building blocks of reason, expectation, normal order, were crumbling and falling.

The thing that had been Peter, its eyes glowing embers plucked from a fire, took another step toward Andrea. The air between the pair of them rippled and shimmered like a heat mirage. Leaves on the ground rose in columns, swirled, and capered. Whatever Peter . . . no, not Peter, *Longshadow* . . . was doing, she was resisting. She raised her arms, looking for a moment like a Bible illustration of Moses parting the Red Sea, and faced the monster.

If I step between them, I'll turn into a smoking crisp of flesh.

As the battle progressed, the crowd of onlookers backed away. Matthew watched, astonished, as one by one they drifted out of the circle, moving between the standing stones, merging with the shadows and darkness of the forest. Within minutes, the circle was nearly empty. Only Deirdre Farrell remained, standing close to the fire, her eyes glittering in the light from the flames.

Andrea was losing the battle. She was buckling under the attack. Whatever powers they played with, Peter was the master. He raised his arm, squeezed a fist, and punched toward Andrea. Leaves exploded from the ground. She raised her arms to protect herself, then collapsed under the force of the invisible blow.

Peter raised his face and laughed triumphantly.

Peter, sensing his advantage, stepped closer. He swung his arms, as if throwing a net, toward her. Andrea raised her arms and formed a shield before her. For a moment, leaves rose to obscure the pair. When they cleared, Andrea was again standing.

A look of shock passed across Peter's face. He stepped backward.

She can beat him! She's surprised him!

Matthew squeezed the butt of his revolver and raised it slowly. He watched the black barrel, as if he were watching a movie, rise and aim toward Peter. His finger tightened on the trigger.

This is my son. My baby boy.

"Peter!"

The boy did not turn. His attention was riveted to Andrea. It was Deirdre Farrell who responded. She stepped beyond the fire, toward Matthew.

"No!"

Matthew spun, swinging the revolver to cover her. She paused in her tracks. The antlers on her head quivered.

"Do not interfere," she said softly.

Matthew kept the gun aimed on her. "Stop them," he said. "Make them stop. Or I'll shoot him."

Deirdre said nothing. Her eyes narrowed.

"Make them stop," Matthew repeated. "I mean it. I'll—"

The sudden screech from above alerted him. He averted his face as a black shadow darted out of the darkness above. A wing tip brushed his eyes as the bird swooped by. He twisted to watch it rise and circle above. He turned back to Deirdre.

She was looking up at the sky, waving her arms. Her lips moved silently. In a moment, a chorus of screeches sounded above. The sound of fluttering wings descended to the circle.

He turned back to the battle waging beside him. Both Peter and Andrea seemed to be locked in a stalemate, staring each other down. The air between them rippled and shimmered, an earthbound Aurora. The ground at their feet writhed as if alive, with fissures opening up between them. Peter's eyes glowed brightly. Andrea's face was a mask of effort. Sweat spilled from her brow.

Something smashed into the side of Matthew's face, and he fell to the ground in agony. The bird fluttered in its death throes and became still in the dirt beside him. Its beak was covered in blood. He raised his hand to his face and felt the deep gouge in his cheek. He turned to Deirdre. She waved her arms at him. Above, the birds began to descend.

Matthew scrambled to his feet. Another bird swooped

toward him, its eyes glittering black, its beak open to tear. Matthew ducked his head and raised his arm. The bird smashed into his bicep, tearing a chunk of coat and shirt. Blood welled through the gash. He gasped at the impact, the sudden pain. Squawking piteously, the bird fell to the ground, its neck broken.

He stumbled away, avoiding another of the suicide attacks. The bird whizzed by and lifted into the sky for another approach. Matthew raised his gun and pointed it at Deirdre.

"Call them off. Or I'll blow your fucking head off."

She froze in her tracks, her eyes locked onto him. And suddenly he knew what she had been doing. She had been diverting his attention from Andrea and Peter. And she had succeeded. Her eyes gleamed triumphantly. He heard the titanic struggle behind him, yet dared not turn to observe it. If he gave Deirdre the chance . . .

His eyes registered the pale shape flitting between the standing stones, and he turned to see the wolf bound into the clearing. Its eyes gleamed as brightly as Peter's. Its jaws were open, its teeth bared. Matthew backed away. But it passed him by and loped purposefully toward Deirdre. The old woman's eyes widened in terror and she stumbled backward, raising her hand to protect herself.

But the wolf did not attack. It stood before her, its teeth bared and snapping. Strings of drool fell to the ground at Deirdre's feet. The growl coming from the animal's throat sounded as if it could shred flesh without the help of teeth.

Deirdre tried to move, but the wolf sprang easily on its powerful haunches and blocked her path. Her triumph turned to a mask of hatred. She glared angrily at Matthew. Above, the birds circled but did not descend.

Matthew felt a laugh break from his mouth. The wolf was helping him! Somehow, Andrea had commanded it!

He freed himself from Deirdre's glare and turned to face the raging battle. Andrea was on her knees. Her eyes were closed, her teeth clenched with the effort of resisting Peter's attack.

Matthew stepped toward the pair.

"Peter!"

The boy did not respond.

Matthew raised his gun. "Peter!"

Behind him, Deirdre squealed in anger and frustration.

"Peter!"

Nothing.

Matthew raised his revolver and aimed.

CHAPTER THIRTY-SIX

Andrea could not breathe.

She felt as if she were being squeezed within a giant fist, crushed into bloody shreds of flesh and shards of bone. She had naively allowed herself to believe what Clarissa had said, that she was a *natural*, that the power of the craft was her servant. What was now painfully obvious was that Peter, or this thing he had become, had far more control of craft power than she herself.

With each wave of his arm she felt herself battered, like driftwood flung against a rocky prominence. With each squeeze of his fist, she felt the foundations of her control slipping and crumbling. It was all she could do to defend herself.

But Clarissa had been right about one thing. The power did exist. It was no figment of imagination. In Marissa she had muttered spells that twisted and warped the power to her own end. Such was its nature, to be used by those who understood it. The uttering of spells, she now realized, was a simple external expression of the talent needed to work the craft. A tool, a crutch. The utterances themselves meant nothing. Here in the sacred circle, where the power was more clearly manifested, such crutches were unnecessary. She felt it as part of herself, an extra arm. She need only utilize it.

Peter took another step toward her. His face was twisted out of its natural expression, as if new bones had been slipped beneath the skin. Coarser bones, sharper edged. The eyes that locked onto her and would not let her go were filled with hatred.

For a moment, the crushing fist loosened its grip. Andrea stumbled backward, and almost fell. She caught her balance, then prepared herself for a new attack. But Peter was grinning. The rotting flesh hanging from his shoulders had left smears of black and red on his pink skin.

"I know what you are," he hissed. "You cannot stand in my way."

What am I? Andrea thought. *What am I?*

"All I want is my son back," she said, fighting for breath between words.

Peter regarded her a moment. *It's not Peter*, she corrected herself. *This is a monster. Don't think of him as Peter.*

"He gave himself to me willingly," Longshadow said thoughtfully. It was Peter's voice that spoke. He raised one of Peter's fine-boned hands to finger his chin.

"He didn't know what he was doing," Andrea said, disconcerted. "You tricked him. He's only a boy."

He continued to regard her, his expression caught somewhere between thoughtfulness and anger. He looked as if he was not quite comfortable with the weight of flesh.

"Why do you fight me?" His words were softly spoken, almost pleading. "I will bring your son greatness."

Andrea did not respond. The monster was attempting to lower her guard. How easy it would be, she thought, to give in to him. She drew a deep breath and released it in a weary sigh.

"Andrea! Don't listen to him!"

She spun at the sound of Matthew's voice. He was standing less than ten yards to the left, his revolver aimed steadily at Peter. He did not look at her as he spoke.

"Don't listen to him. He's trying to trick you. This isn't Peter. Peter is dead."

Beyond Matthew, she could see Sentena crouched before Deirdre Farrell. The old hag was trembling, her arms raised from the slavering jaws of the wolf.

Keep her there, Sentena, she thought. *Don't let her interfere.*

As if the wolf had received the message, his bushy tail whipped from side to side then was still.

"What will happen if I shoot him?" Matthew said carefully.

Andrea opened her mouth to respond, then shut it. She did not know what would happen. Longshadow slowly turned Peter's head to regard Matthew.

"This body will succumb to death," he said. "You would kill your son."

"And you'd die too," Matthew said through gritted teeth.

Andrea felt a pang of sympathy for him. He'd come here to Marissa to rebuild his life, only to have it pulled out from under him once again.

Longshadow laughed, a dry sound that Peter would never have emitted. "Tonight is the Eve of Samain. In this body or another, I am reborn this night."

He turned his head slowly back to Andrea. "I grow weary of this game." He extended a finger toward her, his eyes gleaming. "I will crush any who stand in my way. Even you, pretty little one."

Andrea suddenly felt very afraid. *He's been playing with me up to now. Gauging my abilities.*

Longshadow smiled. "Given time, you would have been powerful," he said. "Even now, you are closer to the craft than any I have ever met. You have gained a meager measure of control over the spirit of the world. But not enough. It is a great pity that you cast your lot against me."

His smile turned cold. The finger extended toward her suddenly retracted. The hand squeezed into a fist.

"Good-bye," he said.

Andrea stumbled backward, raising her arms to protect herself. She had sensed, upon entering the circle, a monstrous entity coiled beneath the network of standing stones. *This is the power of the craft*, she had thought.

Now, in terror, she sensed the coils of that monster

unwinding, reaching for her. At Longshadow's command, it poised to strike at her, to wipe her out. A blast of icy air washed over her. The ground trembled beneath her feet. *It's over*, she thought. *It's all said and done.*

She fell to her knees, lowered her head, and squeezed her eyes tightly shut. Sentena's howl suddenly erupted, full of anger and loss.

Good-bye, special friend, she thought.

She heard Deirdre Farrell's voice raised in a high laugh. Then a single word shouted by Matthew. Almost a scream: "No!"

A gunshot split the air.

At the sound of the gunshot, Andrea opened her eyes. The pressure of whatever forces Longshadow had amassed against her suddenly abated. She sucked in a harsh breath. Another.

Peter stumbled forward, his arms held out before him for support. Blood spurted from a ragged wound in his left shoulder and splashed down his chest in glistening rivulets. His face was contorted, the muscles tensed beneath the skin. One moment she recognized the boyishness of her stepson, the next those same features were transformed into the depraved mask of Cardew Longshadow.

Behind Peter's stumbling figure, she saw Matthew silhouetted against the flames of the fire, and behind him Sentena, still crouched before the cowering figure of Deirdre Farrell. Matthew took a quick step toward her, his gun still raised.

"Stay away from her!" His yell was sharp and commanding.

And suddenly she knew what was going to happen, understood clearly the drama being enacted before her. Matthew could not see Peter's face, could not know of the damage his first shot had inflicted. Even now, the Woerloga was preparing to abandon Peter's body. After a two-thousand-year hiatus, the pains of flesh were a heavy burden. The added trauma of a gunshot wound made them unbearable, even for the Woerloga. He was abandoning ship.

Yet Matthew did not know this. He saw only the stooped figure, with arms outstretched, moving toward her.

"Stop! I'll shoot!"

"Matthew! No!"

And suddenly she saw it on Peter's face. Longshadow knew it too. He was deliberately stumbling toward her, perfectly aware of what Matthew was about to do. Peter's lips twisted into a knowing smile, his eyes gleaming.

If I can't have him, then nobody can.

She raised her arms and tried to wave at Matthew. But he was concentrating on Peter's back, his eyes narrowed. *He knows it's his son, his own flesh and blood, but he's doing this for me.*

She saw the sudden tension in his arm, the flash of the muzzle. Saw the sudden thrusting out of Peter's chest as if his back had been punched. Saw the explosion of blood from the center of his rib cage, the dark wet hole that appeared there, the triumphant smile that twisted his features like a death mask.

"No!"

The boy fell heavily to the ground, his arms stretched out before him.

And where he had stood, shimmering like a mirage, stood the remnant of the Woerloga. She glimpsed the man-shape as if from the corner of her eye. When she tried to focus on a specific part—a hand, the face—her eyes lost it. Here was a creature meant to exist on the periphery of the real world, forever relegated to a life of glances. As she watched, he began to drift across the clearing, toward the fire.

She turned her attention to the figure on the ground, and despair flooded through her. Its force was tidal. She could not deny it, could not stand up to it. Peter was dead.

She collapsed to the ground beside him.

She allowed the despair to take her, allowed the sobs to slip from her body. Whatever happened now, she no

300

longer cared. The Woerloga had won. He had destroyed her family.

She watched through her tears as the green apparition moved across the clearing toward Matthew.

But she no longer cared. Nothing mattered anymore.

And as she succumbed to hopelessness, as the last vestiges of her will slipped away, she sensed it.

The power she and Longshadow had commanded, the power they had used against each other, began to uncoil below her. For the first time she sensed the awesome nature of the thing. Its incomprehensible extent.

At one point she had felt herself a rider on the back of some incredible beast, attempting to control it. She saw now how silly that impression had been. This power, this spirit, was not for the controlling, not for the using. Sometimes it let itself be used, but that was not its true nature.

She closed her eyes. But that was worse. What was invisible in the real world was apparent here in her inner darkness.

Clarissa's words seemed to rise from her memory, clamoring for attention. *The road you choose will demand its own toll.* At the time, she had not been concerned about costs. She had used the power to frighten Deirdre. She had used it to protect herself against Longshadow.

But now it was time to pay. Five minutes ago she would have struggled. Five minutes ago, her son had still been alive.

Now, she had absolutely nothing to lose, absolutely nothing to gain. She was lost, however you looked at it. For a moment fear surged through her, and she tried to exert control over the thing that was taking her. The effort was futile. The game was finished. The time of control was over.

She shuddered, suddenly aware of her smallness, her worthlessness in the face of this thing, this spirit, this magic. *I have nothing that it wants*, she realized. *I have nothing to offer it.*

But suddenly she knew that wasn't quite true. She had one thing to offer it. The only thing she had left.

From somewhere in the recesses of her memory, the words came to her lips. *"Dark horsey, you've come for me."*

She did not hesitate. She gave what was asked.

Absolute, unconditional surrender.

CHAPTER THIRTY-SEVEN

When Peter dropped to the ground, Matthew felt a piece of himself die. It felt as if he had just woken from a dream. A moment ago, the thing walking away from him had been monstrous; now it was simply Peter.

I shot my own son.

Six months ago, in that dark alley, he had shot an innocent boy. Then, too, he had been sure he'd been facing some kind of monster. Now, those same feelings of despair, terror, loss . . . flooded back to take him.

Nothing has changed. I didn't get away from any of it.

He allowed the weight of the gun to drag his hand down to his side. Where Peter had stood, there now hung a green veil, swirling with darker streaks, like a pond clouded with blood. So this was the thing that had possessed Peter, the thing Andrea had been trying to tell him about for so long, the thing that had *changed* the boy. He watched as it moved away from his son's crumpled body, slowly angling across the clearing toward him. Behind it, Andrea collapsed to the ground with a sob. In a moment she was silent, still as death.

Matthew heard a cry echo through the clearing, and realized in a moment that it had been his own voice.

I've lost everything.

Numb, he stepped backward as the glowing shape came closer. When he looked directly at the thing, it seemed to fracture into a hundred different facets. An eye here, a foot there, a hand somewhere else. Only when he looked away, when he saw the thing from the corner of his eye, did he get a comprehensive image. Definitely a man-shape, stooped and reaching. He stumbled away from it, suddenly sure of its intentions.

If it couldn't have Peter, then Peter's father would do nicely. Cold fear gripped him.

Christ, no . . .

He glanced toward Andrea. She had not moved. Both she and Peter looked dead. Behind him, Deirdre Farrell hissed. He did not turn to look at her, but her voice was clear.

"Yesss, yesss! You are powerful enough now. Take him. He is of your blood!"

Sentena growled softly, but even that sound had lost some of its menace. It was as if the wolf knew that Andrea had succumbed, that he had lost her.

The green apparition moved closer. He saw arms rising, searching for him.

No, damn you, no, I won't let you.

He raised the revolver and placed the barrel in his mouth. The metal was warm against his tongue, the taste acrid. He closed his lips over it, turned to watch the shimmering green.

Around the barrel, he whispered, "Come on, take me. Find out what it feels like to get your head blown off."

And suddenly, with absolute certainty, he knew he would do it. Just one squeeze on the trigger. End it all. Wipe it all out. The green shape faltered and stopped moving. It hovered less than a yard from him. He averted his eyes to see it more clearly.

Was there a rictus of anger on that appalling face? Confusion? He could not tell for certain.

"He wouldn't dare!" Deirdre said softly.

He did not turn at her voice. Instead he squeezed more firmly on the trigger. The shimmering green curtain backed away. From the corner of his eye he watched one of the arms raised in a placating gesture.

"Do not kill yourself." The voice crackled like a badly tuned radio heard from a distance. "That is a pleasure I wish to save for myself."

The shape began to move again. It made a wide circle around Matthew and headed toward the fire. Toward Deirdre Farrell. The old woman stepped nervously backward as the shimmering green pillar approached her. She held out an arm to ward it off.

"No! I am not of your line."

"For a short while, you will suffice." Again, Matthew got the impression of a radio heard from a distance. He slowly pulled the revolver from his mouth, letting it hang again at his side.

Somehow, the thought of the green monster possessing the withered body of Deirdre Farrell was not so frightening. The two were akin, if not by blood then by spirit.

Deirdre became encompassed by the swirling green. Her mouth opened to scream, but before a sound had emerged, it closed again. Her dry lips turned up in a smile. For a moment, the two shapes seemed to be superimposed over one another, Deirdre's stooped body seen through the green haze. And then the shell of light shrank on itself, as if being absorbed into her body.

Sentena, his belly pressed to the ground, slithered away with a small whine, then turned to watch from a distance, his eyes glowing red in the light of the fire.

With a mixture of horror and wonder Matthew watched the transformation take place. The deep wrinkles etched into Deirdre's gaunt face seemed to disappear, as if smoothed out from within. The dull black eyes assumed a healthy glow. The prune lips became full and inviting. Where once her body had stooped, like a crippled tree, it now straightened. Withered limbs gained flesh and filled out.

"Oh, my God," Matthew said softly, not daring to believe what he was seeing.

The new Deirdre took a step toward him. With a flourish of her hand, she loosened the constrictions of her clothing. The dowdy rags fell from her body like old skin, forming a pile at her feet.

In the light of the fire she was revealed. Matthew held his breath, tried to quiet the pounding of his heart.

The woman before him could not be more than twenty-five years old. Her breasts were firm, her flesh taut and smooth. Blond hair curled around her shoulders and neck like spun gold. Her face was a sculpture of shadow and light, in which green eyes glowed like jewels.

And worst of all, worst of all by far, he recognized her.

"Rowena." His own voice was a hushed whisper. She smiled. The same smile she had offered him so many nights ago, when she had used his body like an expert, conducting a performance from him he had thought impossible. His mind became a kaleidoscope of tangled limbs, open mouths, grunts and groans.

He stumbled backward, his eyes squeezed shut, under the onslaught of memory.

No, no, please no. It was Deirdre all along.

When he opened his eyes again, she was standing less than two yards away, still smiling, her eyes still gleaming. She held out a hand to him.

"Come to me, Matthew. Be with me."

Against his will, he felt his body respond. He stepped toward her.

It's an illusion! She's using you!

As if she had read his mind, the woman shook her head. "I satisfied you once before, Matthew. I can satisfy you again."

And as she spoke, he seemed to see the old Deirdre below this glossy veneer, her sagging breasts and folded skin.

"You bitch," he said softly. "You tricked me."

He raised the revolver so that it aimed directly at her belly. Even though her face was hidden in shadow, he sensed the change that came over her, the sudden shock and fear that twisted her features.

"You're not going to trick me again," he said. With his thumb, he cocked the gun.

"No," Rowena whispered.

Matthew grinned, suddenly exhilarated. "Yes," he said.

But she was not looking at him, or at the gun. Her eyes were focused on something beyond him. With his gun raised, Matthew spun, and froze at what he saw.

Andrea was standing. Except this was not the same Andrea. She seemed larger somehow, a statue rather than a woman, as if she had sprung directly from the earth and were not simply standing upon it.

"Matthew," she said. "Put down your gun."

He shuddered at the sound of her voice. The earth beneath his feet trembled. Outside the standing stones, the trees rustled as if they had suddenly come to life. Above, clouds swirled and parted to reveal stars. A sudden wind whistled through the stones. Sentena raised his head and howled into the night. The sound sent shivers through Matthew. He stepped aside as the wolf bounded past him toward Andrea. At her feet, the animal lay on its side. She looked down at it and whispered something. Sentena rolled to his feet, then stood with his flank pressed to her leg.

Matthew lowered his gun. Behind him, the thing that had been Deirdre Farrell began to scream.

Andrea knew herself to be changed.

The metamorphosis that had begun the moment she set foot in Marissa was complete. Or had it begun before that? Vague memories of strange stirrings she had felt years ago, even as a child, came to her. Why had the name "Marissa" seemed so familiar when she had seen it in that classified ad?

Missa, Missa, Missa, Mommy, will we ever go back to Missa?

Vaguely, she remembered her childhood. The admonishings of her mother. *Never think of it, ever, ever.*

Understanding came in a bolt that left her numb, breathless.

The dark horsey had once come to claim her. Now she had returned to it. The horsey had been the craft itself, seeking her out. Not a faceless power, but a living thing, an entity. A spirit. She was the one it had always waited for, the one through which it could act, through which it could become incarnate. Her whole life, she saw, had been manipulated. Meeting and marrying Matthew. The shooting of the boy in the alley. Everything. Her parents' flight from Marissa had been futile. The craft was patient. It had awaited her return, certain that one day she would do so.

It wasn't Peter who had been called. It was herself.

Longshadow himself, she now understood, had been manipulated. The catalyst to carry her into the craft. He was a nuisance, nothing more. The craft had used them all, orchestrating the human drama toward this moment. She, Andrea . . . Gillian . . . was the main attraction.

She drew a deep breath, held it, and released it slowly.

None of that mattered anymore. What she once had been was merely an intangible memory. What she had become was the reality she needed to deal with.

She had surrendered to the craft, and it had taken her. The moment she had let loose the meager reins of her control, it had enveloped her. It was as if her very consciousness had been drawn into the earth. She sensed the forest, the sky, the running streams, the animals skittering here and there. And in return, the consciousness of the earth had been drawn into her. Through her own eyes, she saw the world anew.

Two worlds, not one.

Her eyes saw the physical world before her . . . saw Matthew, and Sentena, and the trees, and the scattered townsfolk now hiding in the outskirts of the stone circle, and the standing stones. Yet another part of her saw the other world, the world that coexisted with the one she knew. Shadowy figures skulked among the stones, small creatures scurried between the trunks of the trees, huge winged beasts flapped overhead, their eyes glittering malevolently.

We live in our own worlds, ignorant of what walks beside us.

But now, to her, the boundaries no longer existed. She

saw the world as it was meant to be, as one. And the creatures in both worlds, one and all, were aware of her. As Matthew turned to her, his face shocked, a large lumbering shadow parted from one of the stones and approached her. Its shape was roughly human, but its features were blurred. Shadow atop shadow. In time, she knew, she would see it more clearly. As she became accustomed to the world of shadow, the darkness would open up for her. But even now it saw her, as Matthew saw her, and yet neither Matthew nor the thing saw each other.

I, and I alone, am of both worlds.

At her feet, she saw Peter. The boy was not yet dead—she sensed that immediately. He was close, but he was fighting for life. She allowed herself to be drawn to him, into him, allowed the feel of his muscles to surround her. The damage to his body was profound, but she used her new power to perform a perfunctory repair, to heal the destructive path of the bullet. There was not enough time to heal him completely, but the danger of death receded.

She left him, feeling an immediate pang of guilt and remorse. Such use of the craft demeaned it. For such chores it did not exist. If the boy were to die, then so be it. He would simply pass from one world to another . . . a world she had not yet glimpsed. To intrude on this process was foolhardy.

Again, she drew a deep breath.

Matthew moved toward her, his expression a mixture of shock and hope. Though he did not know it, could not possibly know it, he passed within a hair's breadth of the shadow creature who stood near him in the other world. She watched as Matthew's step faltered, as a shiver ran up his spine. It was all he would ever know of the other world. How often had she felt the same thing herself, not realizing what it was? The shadow creature twirled, looking over its shoulder as if something had passed close by, but it, too, perceived nothing. Two worlds, she thought, split asunder.

And I have been called to join them again, to heal the wound.

"Andrea?"

"Matthew, please don't come closer."

He stopped where he was, staring at her. She regarded him with eyes that saw too far, too deep. He was neither a fully good man, nor a fully bad man, she knew, but like nearly all men, an uneven mix of the two. But one thing she saw, and did not need her new power to perceive . . . he loved her, and loved her deeply.

And in that moment, she understood the full extent of the price she had paid. For as she looked upon him, as she remembered that once she had returned his love fully, she knew her emptiness. For she felt nothing for him in return. She reached for the despair she knew she should feel at such a realization, but that, too, was denied her.

Everything that made me the person I was, every emotion that made me human, has been taken from me.

She looked directly at Matthew. "Matthew, please step aside."

He did not hesitate. The expression of hope he had worn now disappeared, and was replaced by outright fear. *He may not see what I have become, but somehow he understands it, and he is frightened.*

In the other world, the creature of shadow also moved aside. She found herself with a clear view of Deirdre Farrell and Cardew Longshadow.

In this world, he was a ghostly apparition. She saw his tenuous form draped over the body of Deirdre like a cloak, transforming her. Yet like herself, he had an extension into the shadow world. There, he was shapeless, a shadow darker than any other. Around him there, like demons tormenting a damned soul, capered and gibbered his retinue of servants. Like those he snared in the world Andrea knew, like Deirdre Farrell, these were the weak, the ineffectual, the easily swayed. She perceived the network of spells he had laid to trap them, to bind them to him, and felt, mingled with her revulsion, a wave of pity. Weaker than his, but still apparent, were the spells laid by Deirdre herself. They flowed behind her like a cloak of glowing thread. Spells meant to manipulate, to use, to pervert. But

310

compared to Longshadow, she was nothing.

His presence in both worlds was like a cancer, a suppurating wound. He was part of neither world. By rights, he should have passed on to another place, the world of the dead. Somehow, with perverse magic, he had held himself here, awaiting a chance to cross back to the world whence he'd come. If he had succeeded . . . if, somehow, he had managed to bind himself to Peter in this world . . . the stability of a body would have increased his power exponentially. Now he was weak, a mere nuisance. Given time, he would have become a terror.

In Deirdre's body he raised an arm, released a scream, and threw a spell at her. She saw it coming, but did not flinch. It passed across her, ineffectual, like a light breeze. Ten minutes ago, it would have destroyed her.

She shook her head and raised her hand to stop him.

As she looked upon him, the one emotion remaining to her began to flood her, to fill her. Anger. Righteous and pure.

It was this Thing that had changed Peter, this Thing that had killed Clarissa. It was because of this Thing that she had been called here, transformed. He was an abomination, the enemy of all worlds. And she, willing or not, had become the Champion of all worlds.

Her fury burned within her. It blinded her.

"Abomination, your time has ended."

She raised her arms, and called on the craft. A week ago she had needed spells to manipulate the fabric of the world. Now, she was the world Itself. She needed only to flex her own muscles.

With a wave of her hand she did the deed.

Cardew Longshadow's spirit separated from Deirdre Farrell's body and rose into the air like a small hurricane. She saw, too late, that Longshadow continued to cling to Deirdre's spirit. They were as one.

So be it. It's what she always wanted.

She felt Longshadow's straining as he attempted to escape, felt his desperation. But there was no escape. He was as much a part of the world as the trees, as the stones, as she herself had once been. Thus, he was under her control.

Clarissa's words rose in her memory. *Bind him to earth. It is the only way.*

The poor old soul. She had understood little, but in that she had been right.

Her eyes fell upon the small pile of peat next to the fire. She did not hesitate. As if she were throwing a ball, she flung the discorporate spirits at the pile. In that final second, she experienced the icy cold of Longshadow's anger, and Deirdre Farrell's terror.

And then it was over.

For a moment, Deirdre Farrell's body, now restored to its true form, stood naked in the clearing. Her eyes were open and blank. For one disconcerting instant, Andrea thought the spiritless body was staring at her, accusing her. Then it toppled, arms wide, to embrace the ground.

CHAPTER THIRTY-EIGHT

Matthew's world was falling apart, and there was nothing he could do about it.

It had started earlier in the night, when Peter had left the house. From then on, it had gotten worse. It felt as if the world were going insane. Things were happening that just couldn't happen. And he knew that the world just didn't go insane. Which meant that it was him.

He was losing it, and losing it fast.

"Matthew."

He spun at the sound of his name, and found himself face to face with Andrea. Except this wasn't Andrea. Not the Andrea he had married, not the Andrea he had made love with. This was something else. Something cold and distant. Something beyond his comprehension.

His first instinct was to drop to his knees before her, to bow his head in supplication. He closed his eyes and suppressed the shudder that ran through his body. He felt the touch on his shoulder and opened his eyes to see that Andrea had stepped closer to him.

"It's over, Matthew."

He swallowed hard. The body of Deirdre Farrell lay still on the ground. The thing that had possessed her, the thing that had possessed Peter, was gone. He studied the wrinkled sack of skin on the ground, and felt revulsion rise within him.

I made love to that thing.

He turned his head away.

"It's okay, Matthew. None of that matters anymore."

He stepped away from her, out of her reach. "Don't touch me."

She lowered her hand, and suddenly he felt guilty. "Jesus, I'm sorry, Andrea."

"Take Peter. Go back to the house."

The sound of Peter's name startled him. He turned to stare at the body on the ground. The rotting flesh of Jack and Willy Burgess was still draped over his shoulders. Blood welled from two wounds in the boy's back and trickled down the pale skin to pool on the ground.

God help me, I've killed my only son.

"He'll be okay, Matthew. Just take him back to the house."

He ignored her and moved over to Peter. He kneeled by the boy and pressed his fingers to the narrow throat. Although faint, he felt the pulse.

"He's still alive."

Andrea said nothing.

With his shoe, he pushed the cloak of dead limbs from Peter's back, then worked his arms under the boy's body and lifted him carefully. Peter's eyes remained closed. Blood bubbled on his lips. Matthew turned to Andrea.

"Are you coming?"

She did not turn to face him. She was staring at something in the middle of the clearing. Matthew followed her gaze. There was nothing there. In a moment, she turned to him. Her eyes were wide and mad. She seemed to be looking at things over his shoulders, as if she could see something that he could not. Years ago, he'd arrested a schizophrenic child-killer during a stakeout. The guy's eyes had flittered like moths, just like Andrea's. Within hours, Matthew had felt some of that insanity rub off on him. The feeling was the same now, looking at Andrea.

She's nuts. Over the edge.

"I'll be there soon," she said in answer to his question.

"I don't like the idea of walking in those woods," he

314

said. "All those fucking loonies are still hanging around."

"Don't worry, they won't harm you."

"It's not me I'm worried about. It's you. Come with me now. We'll go back together."

She shook her head. "I have something to do. You go. The paths will lead you."

Matthew sighed. *The paths will lead you.* Fucking nuts.

He nodded, then turned and walked to the edge of the stone circle. The trail was apparent, although he could not remember having seen it before. Peter's body was a heavy weight in his arms, but he ignored the pain and held the boy tightly. He paused before stepping onto the trail, and turned to regard Andrea.

She had moved to the fire and was kneeling by the small pile of peat. He watched her as she reached into the pile and pulled out a single square. In the flickering firelight she looked less than human. Far, far less than human.

A shudder ran through him.

My God, Andrea, what's happened to us?

Her shoulders stiffened, and she began to turn. Before her eyes could find him, he stepped onto the trail and began to walk.

Andrea held the square of peat in her hands. It writhed as if it were alive. The rough fibers scraped her skin. She squeezed it tightly.

"Be still, you two," she said softly.

The squirming stopped.

She looked down upon the brown square. Inside it, she sensed the two imprisoned souls. She felt their hatred, their fear.

She shook her head.

"You were foolish," she said.

The moss remained still.

"You have caused much misery, Cardew Longshadow. And you, Deirdre Farrell, have been an accomplice to that evil."

Now, she felt the moss shudder. She squeezed it again.

"Cardew Longshadow, you belong in the place of the dead. You should have gone there long, long ago. They

315

have been waiting for you. And you, Deirdre, it is where you belong too. Your time in this world has ended. It is my privilege to be the bearer of your punishment.''

This time, the moss began to quiver, and would not stop even when she squeezed it tightly.

She held the small square in one hand and passed her other hand through the slowly diminishing fire. The flames suddenly licked higher and began to burn more brightly. Although no heat touched her face, she knew the flames were the hottest she had ever seen. Their touch was purifying.

She held the peat moss toward the fire.

It began to squirm in her hand.

"For Jack and Willy Burgess," she said softly. "For Clarissa. For Peter. For Matthew. And for what you have done to me."

She tossed the small square into the flames.

As it began to burn, she turned her face away. For an instant, before averting her eyes, she glimpsed the face of Deirdre Farrell in the flames, twisted into an expression of agony beyond comprehension. And with her another face, its pain mingled with confusion and shock.

As the two souls burned, their agonized screams rising smokeless into the night, she stood and walked away from the fire. Shadows flickered before her eyes. Shapes moved in the trees and turned to watch her, awestruck. Sentena. who had watched the proceedings silently, now padded after her. She bent down to scratch his head.

As she reached the trail, she sensed the followers behind her, a mixture of the folks of Marissa and these others, shadows, ignorant of each other, following only her.

The trail opened before her. She walked quickly back to the house.

EPILOGUE

When he heard the noises outside, Matthew rose from his seat at the kitchen table and moved to the rear sliding doors. King followed closely, rubbing his shins. Light from the kitchen cast ghostly illumination across the deck, toward the trees. Vague shapes moved in the woods. He opened the door and stepped out onto the deck. The cool night air caressed him, and he shivered.

Noises of crashing, vague murmurs, voices conversing, emerged from the woods. He stood quietly, watching and listening. In a moment, a shape defined itself at the mouth of the path and stepped into the yard.

It was Andrea. Close behind her came the wolf.

King whined, and his tail began to wag.

She stopped at the bottom of the yard and stared at Matthew for a full five seconds. He did not move. Did not blink. Finally, she turned to Sentena, kneeled, and whispered something to the animal. It raised its head, released a small howl, turned, and loped off into the trees. Andrea stood, turned, and walked toward Matthew.

It looks like Andrea. It walks like Andrea. But it's not Andrea.

Matthew closed his eyes as she approached, and when he opened them again, she was standing before him. Her face, illuminated in light from the kitchen, was pale and tired. Sweat beaded her forehead. There were scratches on her cheeks where branches had whipped her.

Somehow, these all too human details seemed extraneous on Andrea, as if they'd been applied by an artist very careful not to have his work identified for what it really was. The thought made his stomach muscles tighten.

When she lifted a hand to touch him he flinched, and then felt immediate guilt. A look of astonishingly deep hurt passed across her features. In a moment it was gone, replaced by something equally identifiable. Loss. He reached for her.

"Andrea, I'm sorry."

But she was past him, into the kitchen. She kneeled by King and touched his muzzle. "I told you I'd be back." The dog pressed joyously into her. "Where's Peter?" she asked.

"In the living room," Matthew said without turning. He listened as her footsteps crossed the linoleum. He kept his eyes on the trees at the foot of the yard. Shapes continued to move within them, through them, around them. He watched for a few more seconds, chilled, then turned and went inside.

Andrea was in the living room, kneeling by Peter. Matthew had laid the boy out on the sofa, resting his head on one of the cushions. He had tried to clean the muck and congealed blood from Peter's body, but had not gotten far with the chore. It was obvious that the bullet wounds in the boy's shoulder and chest were healed, the skin puckered like mouths ready to be kissed, and the very touch of his son's skin after that had repelled him.

Andrea was stroking the boy's hair, staring into his face. "It's going to be all right, Peter. Everything is going to be fine. It's all been a bad dream. Everything is better now."

The words might have been spoken by any concerned mother. Coming from Andrea, there was something missing. There was no feeling behind them. They were spoken entirely by rote.

She turned and looked up at him. "He'll be okay."

Matthew nodded. *But he should be dead.*

She stood, and again stepped past him. This time, he spun and caught her arm, twisting her to face him. The words started to spill from his mouth like water from a

318

burst dam.

"Listen. I've been a jerk lately. A total asshole. I should have listened to you. You were right all along. Marissa is weird, very, very weird. I can't explain half of what happened tonight. Hell, not even a tenth. But I know . . ." He drew a deep breath. "We'll pack up tonight. I don't care about the job anymore. It's not worth it. We'll drive out tomorrow morning. No, tonight. We'll take Peter to the hospital in Fergus Falls, get him looked at. Stay in a motel. After that, we'll move. We'll just get out of here. Far away."

Finally, he stemmed the flow. Andrea was staring at him, but the expression on her face was all wrong. A terrible sadness seemed to have settled on her features, a sadness so deep there might be no end to it. She reached out and touched his face.

"Oh, Matthew. I've been running from Marissa all my life. I can't run any longer."

He wanted to speak, wanted to tell her that everything would turn back to normal if only they could leave this place, if only they could leave right now . . . but again, a chill gripped him as he looked upon her, and he could not move his lips.

Outside, something made a noise in the backyard. Andrea looked away from him and walked through to the kitchen. He shuddered, shaking off the hold she had on him, and followed.

The yard was full of people. They stretched from one side to the other, from the trees at the back all the way to the deck. He recognized many faces in the group. Murray Carlyle was near the front. He cast one troubled glance at Matthew then, like all the rest, focused on Andrea.

She raised her arms to encompass them. "Fear no more. I have come to set matters right."

A murmur ran through the crowd. *She's insane,* Matthew thought. *They're all insane. The whole fucking bunch of them.*

Andrea turned and walked into the kitchen. Matthew stared at the silent crowd a moment longer, then stepped

319

inside and closed the door. Outside, the people of Marissa began to scatter.

When he turned, Andrea was moving through to the living room. Silently, he followed her. Her eyes seemed to dart from one corner of the room to the other, as if seeing things that only she could see. Once, she turned to look at something next to Matthew. Her lips moved, whispering. Then she stepped past him.

At the stairs she paused, then raised her head as if watching something that climbed.

It was too much. He couldn't bear to watch it. He took the bottle of bourbon from the liquor cabinet, carried it through to the kitchen, sat down at the table, and began to drink. Andrea did not bother him.

It must have been an hour later when he heard the scratching at the front door. By then he was drunk beyond reclamation. He stumbled from the kitchen into the hallway. Andrea was nowhere to be seen. Peter lay still on the sofa, breathing quietly. The scratch came again.

Matthew moved slowly to the door, his hands held out for balance. He gripped the handle, then twisted and opened it. Through the haze of alcohol he saw vague shapes moving about the yard. Some turned faces toward him. He shook his head to clear it.

Some sixth sense, brought to life by the drink, made him glance down, and his breath caught in his throat. A rabbit, neatly slaughtered, lay on a bed of woven corn husks. Blood matted its fur and dripped to the stone step.

He kneeled down, picked it up, carried it back inside, and placed it on the chair by the door.

A sacrifice. For Andrea.

She was standing at the top of the stairs, staring down at him, a small smile curling her lips. He turned away from her gaze. Numb beyond terror, beyond fear, he closed the door and went back to the kitchen.